CRUISE SHIP HEIST
OCEAN ATLANTIC

By
Stuart St Paul

There will be more than a few thousand guests and crew on the huge ship, who have no idea of the even bigger dramas going on behind the scenes. Sometimes it is a fight to ensure they don't know.

'Cruise Ship Crime Investigators are crime novels set around the cruise industry.

Stuart St Paul is an award winning director and screenwriter having directed movies for Universal and Icon, and worked for all the majors from HBO to the BBC who trained him back in 1973. (see biog in rear pages). He is often found on ships talking about his films and books series.

Stuart lives near Watford with his wife Jean Heard who he met in the theatre in 1978. His daughter actress Laura Aikman has assisted with these books. She and son-in-law Matt Kennard, as well as his entrepreneur son Luke Aikman, his wife Dawn and granddaughter Heidi all live nearby.

This is the first book in the series CRUISE SHIP CRIME INVESTIGATORS. C.S.C.I.

Also see

CRUISE SHIP SERIAL KILLER:
OCEAN PACIFIC

CRUISE SHIP LAUNDRY WARS

CRUISE SHIP HEIST
OCEAN ATLANTIC

First Edition

Copyright © 2018 Stuart St Paul
All rights reserved.

ISBN: 9781798236024

DEDICATION

This book is dedicated to a great man, Simon Ricketts. He was a long time friend and sounding board, and our chats about news, politics, football (Watford), work and characters often sent me away to rethink. But me dragging Simon to the Cannes Film Festival to go behind the so-called 'art' of film and into the real nitty-gritty industrial 'bull', sent him away to think.

Without him, I and so many would have not had the encouragement he could always give in a way that made us all feel that our work was meaningful. Yet he was the master, finishing his time at the newspaper he loved, The Guardian, who treated him well through the years of illness.

He checked out right at the end of 2018 and is missed, but remembered in every time I write. I'm sure I am not the only one he has had that effect on. I have never seen a memorial attended by so many people. Hundreds and hundreds. He touched so many.

Why a dedication? He sadly left us all too late, and I wish to ensure he is still remembered.

Chapter 1 - Problem   1

Chapter 2 - Baggage   6

Chapter 3 - Not So Fast   11

Chapter 4 - Uniform   15

Chapter 5 - In Plain Sight   17

Chapter 6 – Hull Limpets   21

Chapter 7 - Cabin   25

Chapter 8 – Cross and double cross 30

Chapter 9 – Port Cristobal, Panama 35

Chapter 10 – Found us.   41

Chapter 11 – Shore leave cancelled 47

Chapter 12 – Turn and strike   50

Chapter 13 – Bag of Chicken   54

Chapter 14 – Big case   58

Chapter 15 – Not the trunk   62

Chapter 16 – Panama Bus   65

Chapter 17 – On ship   68

Chapter 18 – Four Cases   70

Chapter 19 – I am sailing   75

Chapter 20 – and quiver   77

Chapter 21- Crows Nest meet   81

Chapter 22 – Chagres River, Panama 85

Chapter 23 – Supply boat   87

Chapter 24 - Reward   91

Chapter 25 – Blue lights   96

Chapter 26 - Commentary   99

Chapter 27 – Stowaways   103

Chapter 28 – Hot spice   106

Chapter 29 – Doris Visits   108

Chapter 30 – Under Clay   112

Chapter 31 - Outlawed   114

Chapter 32 – More news than the news   116

Chapter 33 - Big glasses   119

Chapter 34 - Cartagena   121

Chapter 35 – In plain sight   123

Chapter 36 – Cash laundry   125

Chapter 37 – Let's have dinner   128

Chapter 38 – The trickster   131

Chapter 39 – The King   134

Chapter 40 – The atrium   136

Chapter 41 - Nightclub   140

Chapter 42 – G&T   143

Chapter 43 – Red shoes, red seats   145

Chapter 44 – Looking out   149

Chapter 45 – My share   152

Chapter 46 – Embarrassing silence   154

Chapter 47 - Audit   157

Chapter 48 – Chess game   161

Chapter 49 – Something's wrong   164

Chapter 50 – Wrapping tape   167

Chapter 51- The bed   171

Chapter 52 – Serious concern   175

Chapter 53 – Time for bed   180

Chapter 54 – St Vincent & Bequia   183

Chapter 55 – Time to play   186

Chapter 56 - Bequia   190

Chapter 57 – God's work is free   194

Chapter 58 – House of cash   199

Chapter 59 – Wet money   205

Chapter 60 – Chinese whispers   209

Chapter 61 – Hot air   212

Chapter 62 – Ship has sailed   216

Chapter 63 – Where's it gone?   221

Chapter 64 – Jill?   223

Chapter 65 – The scam begins   227

Chapter 66 – Where's she gone?   230

Chapter 67 – Late night Loopy   233

Chapter 68 – What is next?   236

Chapter 69 – On parade   238

Chapter 70 – Let's play   242

Chapter 71 - Discharge   245

Chapter 72 – The story   247

Chapter 73 – Lunch everybody?   251

Chapter 74 – The stash   255

Chapter 75 – The setup   260

Chapter 76 - Dad   264

Chapter 77 – Dressed to kill   266

Chapter 78 – The quiet ones are the worst   269

Chapter 79 – No cover   275

Chapter 80 – No payout   279

Chapter 81 - Missing   281

Chapter 82 – Seconds from death   286

Chapter 83 – Joint Mission   292

Chapter 84 – Proof of life   294

Chapter 85 – Deadly game-on   299

Chapter 86 – Families living in war   301

Chapter 87 – The plan   306

Chapter 88 – Team of three   310

Chapter 89 – In Town   314

Chapter 90 - Fireworks   317

Chapter 91 - Honey   320

Chapter 92 – Winged and down   324

Chapter 93 – New day   326

Chapter 94 – Never look back   328

Chapter 1 - Problem

You learn to sense when something's very wrong, but the advanced class is to figure what it is before it hits you hard. Maybe I'm over thinking things again, suffering from no longer being in military service, maybe I need more therapy. But, maybe I'm right. I used to be paid to feel this right.

The hairs on the back of my neck and the sensitive skin under my ears and on my cheeks sense the change; the pressure, the texture and the temperature. The air in this small plane has been less fresh than on my long-haul flight, but the doors must be open. People reaching overhead for their bags, hurrying to queue, to leave, feel nothing. Their impatience is like so many young soldiers I watched rush in under fire when a cool head might have saved them. Not that these people will die, well they will, but not today. At least I hope not today. They could be rushing to work or to meet loved ones, but the struggle with heavy bags from overhead lockers suggests re-location. A mass exodus from Colombia to Costa Rica? Maybe not, but what is wrong?

I look around without being obvious. An awkward lift then twist has a passenger avoid a swinging case and it repeats down the plane. Passengers moving in harmony suggest this happens regularly. Perhaps they're hawkers, off to sell to tourists on the beaches and this excess hand luggage is their stock. That explains the impatience, every minute lost is a missed sale. 'Stand up and join the queue', I demand of myself, but I remain fixed in the penultimate row at the rear of the plane, part of me not ready to stop profiling others and join civilians. I never asked to be a real civilian.

I'm not in a rush, I changed planes for the second time at Cartagena after a long flight across the Atlantic so I'll have to wait for my checked-in case, if it managed to follow me. My hand luggage is two uniforms; 'parade' for a casual event, and 'ceremonial' for formal evenings, plus black boots. None of that ever leaves my side, especially now I can no longer replace them. Everything else I own is replaceable and stowed below, hopefully. I'm wearing civvie hiking boots just in case I can get to see Braulio Carillo National Park before we sail out. I'm ready to dump bags and run, but I suspect that's a long shot. A travel-day more often than not vanishes, and so far this has been two days, three planes.

I feel the heat now, but I'm used to that. I convince myself that the queue is the reason I remain seated, foreseeing another queue at immigration, only to then wait again at baggage reclaim, which will put me behind the semi-locals with the excess hand luggage at customs. But that's not the real reason.

It kicks off. An argument has started, but it's not my issue. No one has a gun on my back; well they shouldn't have, even though this is South America. They all went through security, albeit the same airline joke security as most places in the world; 'Did you pack your own bag? Are you carrying anything sharp?' I only have a sharpened wooden pencil, which I could only use to slay a vampire. The problem is, vampires don't exist but pencils do kill. There are soldiers being laid off from the forces who've been trained to spot and deal with terrorists, and they can't get jobs back in the UK. No country ever wants their military back; they train them to kill then don't know what to do with them. Many ex-soldiers would be better off getting refugee status rather than adding to the urban homeless on bended knee. I can't think of a more fitting description for them, 'a displaced person who has been forced to cross national boundaries and who cannot return home safely'.

The plane is emptying, no one has died. Time to stand and join in. At a little over six feet tall I've no problem sliding my bag out of the overhead compartment, but I'm not the last. There's a tall woman behind me biding her time, waiting and watching. We've noted each other's presence, neither of us being South American. I wait for her to pass she is not going to allow that to happen. She stops to let me out. I don't like to have anyone on my six. I prefer a clear field of vision; no surprises. It seems neither of us feels comfortable with someone behind us.

"Thanks."

I smile and move out noticing she is built like an athlete, wide shoulders, toned arms. Smart short sleeve shirt, easy skirt below the knee and flat shoes. Moving into the aisle from between the seats, I listen intensely because anyone is a potential danger that close behind. At the middle bulkhead of the plane's toilets, I walk through the vacated seats to the other aisle. It may be daft, but not a bad thing to have those instincts even if it's now more a game rather than a real threat. She's no longer behind me, but she's noticed my action. My actions have her eyeing me again. She's trained, military? She has a solid stance and the same caution. She travels light but I'm not sensing danger. We exchange a knowing nod before I'm blocked by an older couple struggling to reach their case in the overhead locker. They're both small like I expect many descendants of the indigenous people in this part of the world to be. The Toltec, Aztec and Mayans were all short. I'm sure these two have some stories to tell.

I slide their case out and lower it for them. They look like they've been together forever and I bet he used to do this for her. She's so comfortable with him, even though he can't do what he once could. I wish I had someone like that now. A partner in my line of work would have been a risk; someone who could have been used to get to me, a weakness, or is that just a feeble excuse for me to avoid real life? I've got no excuse now. I'm Mr Joe Public off to join a cruise ship.

Cruise Ship Crime Investigators

"Preocupes, amigo," I say, giving them their case.

They move off quickly, passing a tall lady about my age, early fifties, maybe younger. It's hard to assess age with that beautiful clear Spanish skin, vivid dark hair and clear eyes. She laughs at me politely.

"What did you want to say to them?" she asks.

"I said 'no worries'."

"No, you said, 'worry my friend', like you were going to kill them!" She laughs. "'No te preocupes amigo', is what you should have said."

"Excuse me! No te preocupes amigo," I shout after them with a better attempt at accuracy.

The old couple laugh and nod, now relaxed.

"Gracias," the old man says.

"Hombre agradable! Hombre guapo! Guapo," the older lady says and her husband moves her off looking worried. He catches my eye, then looks at a man still asleep in the window seat, then back at me.

"What was that?" I ask my translator.

"He said thank you," she offers.

"I got that bit, I mean the other."

"Nothing," she says smirking.

She's holding back, my look demands an answer.

"She said you were handsome, very handsome. She's old… must be going blind!"

Her look tells me to lift her bag down, a returned favour. I've become a baggage handler! Actually, I was for a while at Beirut International Airport when working undercover, before the attacks, before the name was changed to Beirut–Rafic Hariri International Airport. Is that her husband asleep? Why doesn't he lift her bag? Why hasn't she woken him? I lift it anyway, it's very heavy, no wonder she left it for me. Maybe she is a beach seller, what's in here? Watches might be this heavy. Expensive watches. That seems more her style than sunglasses or handbags. However, her clothes are far more expensive than the sleeping guy, and there is no way those heels would work on the beach. She takes her case from me, smiling. No wedding ring, but the skin on her hands shows that my first assessment of age was right. She has a few age spots beginning to appear. Hands give a lot away. She moves off ignoring the sleeping man, he obviously isn't her husband.

If I was with the squad, one of the lads would've made an encouraging remark by now. I say nothing. She looks down to her bags as if she'd like me to carry one, but I avoid her engagement. Maybe it's my training; don't linger long enough to be recognised, don't take anything that's not yours. Why would she have three hand luggage bags? Why does everyone have so much junk? Relax, I think, I'm looking for trouble that isn't here. Perhaps she'll be on my ship, I ponder, but then again why would guests be joining a ship here mid cruise?

She's gone. Maybe I should've carried that case. It's not the foreign weapon left in a jeep as an attractive 'keepsake' cabled to trigger pounds of nasty explosive. I should've taken the time to be nice, should've tried harder. Maybe that's why I'm still single, no social skills unless I'm with a pack, and those days are over. I've been honourably discharged; kind of.

Being sociable, I lean over to wake the guy by the window but he doesn't move. I touch his skin and it's cold. He's dead. I've felt bodies like his before so maybe it was good I found him and not the Latino woman sitting next to him. He's not young but he looks too young to die. The last time I touched a dead body it was a child, spread-eagled in the street and I was helpless. That child was one too many and I knew I had to get out. I reach above him and press the button to call an attendant. There is nothing I can do to help him. There was a lot I could do to help the children living in the streets of Syria, but that was not why I was deployed there. The attendant arrives against the flow of people and breaks my wandering thoughts.

"I gave him a nudge, but he seems in a deep sleep. I hope he's OK."

I know he's not asleep, but I just want to go. The attendant reaches over and comes to the same conclusion I did, but he doesn't want to engage any kind of hysteria either.

"You can go, Sir, I've got this," the young man says.

It seems he is used to dead bodies as well.

Chapter 2 - Baggage

The baggage collection area is chaotic with people fighting to get to the front, clogging access to the rotating belt with their empty trolleys long before they can see any bags. I give them all a wide berth and walk around the outside, to where cases first drop on the carousel. The bags begin to arrive quickly so I might get to see the rain forest today after all. Over thirty years in the army and I was never deployed to a jungle. Unless you can call Northern Ireland a jungle.

"Thanks again." I hear whispered from behind me in her slight Spanish accent, very sexy, and I acknowledge her with a smile.

What am I supposed to do? What should I say? The only place I've ever met women is in bars, and 'do you want a drink?' won't work here. Well, it could, we could go to a bar. But a good looking woman like her, so smartly dressed, surely can't be single. I see a case rise up through a veil of industrial plastic curtain and I step forward automatically. It matches the style of the hand luggage I just lifted down for this beauty from the plane. I turn for confirmation and she nods. My arm takes it and again it's much heavier than I expected. I notice the 'heavy' label attached to the handle, as I place it on a nearby free trolley and wheel it to her. I lift her other three bags from beside her feet and her shoes must be worth a fortune alone. I place the bags on the trolley preparing her to leave.

"Thanks again." She smiles as she rips the heavy label off and drops it. Even that act of littering was quite sexy.

"My pleasure. Enjoy your holiday."

I turn away to disengage, scolding myself. If I'm going to survive in this outside world I need to open doors, not close them. 'On holiday?' would have been better, an invitation to converse, far more socially engaging. Or is it just prying? I'm not equipped for this game though I could do it so easily as an agent. I accept defeat as I snatch my case from escaping away around the rotating carousel and into the crowd. A minor distraction nearly caught me off guard, a page one mistake.

I deliberately take a different queue to the one she stands in at customs, I don't want to look like a stalker, but she's noticed and strangely, doesn't seem to have given up on me. I raise my eyebrows in surprise, just enough to suggest I didn't notice her there. Obviously, I did.

"Peoples, please take the other queue, this line is clos-ed," a large customs officer shouts in a rhythmic Latin accent. He is guiding all of that queue into ours.

It's hot and the officers are wearing jackets and carbon fibre protection vests, but I guess they get used to it. I wore heavy kit in the Middle East and I'm not sure I would want to do it again. The Latin beauty is coming my way, I'm now trapped again, or is it a second chance?

The customs officer turns back to the other two officials at the heavy fixed inspection tables at the front of the queue. They're searching a Spanish looking woman, I would guess local, and the tall fit woman who got off the plane behind me. She looks like she's scanning the area to assess the strength of the force. She is sensing danger. The situation bites as the lady being searched is pushed roughly towards the table and told to put her hands flat down. The tone in the room has changed.

The military looking woman is now grabbed and pushed down. This could turn very nasty. Slowly she complies but I can see she has her eye on the gun clipped in the officer's belt. She digs her elbow into his leaving him gasping for air. Her hands go up immediately like a premiership footballer acting innocence. She didn't like the way he searched her body but didn't take his gun, which she could have easily. She is way too cool to be a civvie, or even rank and file military, not least because this is South America which can be one of the most dangerous places in the world. I have worked out the nearest guard and his weapons before reminding myself it's not my fight.

A small dog leaps up onto the table and sniffs the local woman's case as a large officer scans her passport and papers. A third official unzips her case with the panache of a magician ending his act. Whatever they were expecting to find in her inexpensive luggage isn't there and their expression is both the disappointment of their failure and anger. The officers turn their backs on those two and follow the dog to our large queue. We are next. They are obviously looking for something or someone.

Behind them, the released women both stride out but very separately. The local woman angrily passes through the exit, whereas the British looking military woman stops and glances back. She was confident of her release. I wish I was, especially here in South America where power is money and those with guns are officials. She is looking back at me. Does she suspect it's me they're after? I feel vulnerable and exposed. Why on Earth fly me into Costa Rica? Why am I even on this cruise? Why am I getting on the ship here for a job in Panama? My mind is racing because the police here don't need an excuse to arrest you. Nothing can be taken for granted, least of all freedom. The officers inspect the line in front of me and I have flashbacks of being tortured.

"I'm not on holiday."

My beautiful translator is back in my ear, waking me from my momentary nightmare, picking up on the earlier conversation when I helped her. I hesitate. There's still a side of me that doesn't want to open up, even though there's no reason to withhold anything now. I'm a normal human being, well trying.

"Me neither," I whisper without moving my lips, leaving her eyes boring into me for more information. What does she want? We can only have minutes before our lives will separate. I know, if I tell her I was a soldier she'll ask all the usual boring questions. 'Have I ever been shot?' 'Been in Iraq?' Then the deal breaker that everyone wants to know but then can't cope with the answer; 'have you ever killed anyone?' My smile's not coming out to play, not now. But that's not stopping her full-scale intrusion into my personal life. The crowd in front are being pushed through slowly.

"I'm here to see my daughter," I say, without turning back towards her. My admission was probably a deal breaker, undoubtedly the worst thing I could've said if I was searching for romance, and I should be. I should find love and settle down, that's what my daughter keeps telling me but maybe she just wants a mother figure. Despite being sent out to defend Queen and country with accuracy, this is where I misfire, with women. Eyes front, I tell myself.

"No wife?" she demands in a sexy tone.

Am I imagining it? I twist just enough to sense she's looking past me, not at me.

"No," I say, hoping it's enough. But her smile is a question, and I feel she'll make all Port Limón customs officials wait until she's got my story. Maybe she is a customs official and this is a honey trap. A very expensively dressed honey trap. That makes no sense.

"Single dad? I like that." She's not giving up the interrogation. If we were in a bar she should be buying me a drink; this is her third approach to me; I've become the entertainment.

"Yes, and no," I say, watching the officers advancing with their dog, pulling at its short lead, in and out of the people just in front of us.

"So this lady, she still around but not your wife?" She tilts her head edging a little closer.

Her tone has changed, is that impatience?

"There's no she, or wife," I add.

"Gay dad?" she enthuses.

Why has that excited her? Gay? Is that how I come over? I turn away and edge my weight to the old couple in front of me whose case I also lifted down.

"Are you all right?" I ask the short old couple who are looking very worried. They edge away as the dog and officers pass us, then jump as the dog starts barking excitedly drawing everyone's attention behind and giving me permission to turn. The officers manhandle the Latina, dragging her and her cases away from the queue. I wait for hands to grab my shoulder and pull me away too, but nothing. I dodged a bullet by a second. My sixth sense still works. The officers forcefully present her to a table, hands down. The tall woman I thought was looking out for me earlier is still by the exit, silhouetted by the bright sunlight from outside, she acknowledges me and leaves as if content now she knows I'm safe. How strange; was she waiting to help me if it kicked off in the same way my adrenalin built as she was questioned? A good police or customs guard may have detained all three of us for the interactions, but not these guards. These are rough and ready security, sometimes the most dangerous and trigger-happy.

The Spanish beauty is at the table. The dog jumps up to her three red cases, barking. She had four cases before, what game is being played? I look back to the trolley, the floor... no fourth case. I look to the exit but the tall woman has gone. I don't remember her having a red case.

I try to understand the rushed Spanish of the interrogation officers, but I can't. The dog leaps up on the table as her cases are lifted and forcefully opened. Barking loud the black mutt is the star of this show.

I never got to know her name, but her body language has changed. Her bag is unzipped, a thin top layer of clothing removed, and a false base, way too high, is ripped up with a sharp flick knife, revealing blocks of money tightly packed. She must be a courier. The crowd gasp like an audience and rather than curtsey to them, the woman stays focused on the guards. She knows she's in trouble. The dead body she was sitting next to on the plane now seems suspicious. Too much here does not make sense.

Chapter 3 - Not So Fast

The queue moves rapidly now past a female customs officer. The old couple in front of me is dismissed through with a wave but I'm stopped. I present my passport and lift my case ready to be searched, hoping I too will be waved through.

"Purpose of visit?"

"I've come to see my daughter," I blurt out then wonder why I said it.

"She live here? You planning to live here, Sir?"

This could still all go wrong.

"I'm joining a cruise ship. She's a dancer there." I'm being precise, trying not to engage further interest.

"Nice. Nice father. You have nice day with your daughter." She waves me through.

What an ordeal! Feeling free I check my watch to assess the time lost from my plan to get to the rain forest. You can release the soldier from service, but not military precision from the man.

I accelerate out of the terminal into a wall of heat and see a small man holding up a sign with three names on it, mine, Kieron Philips is at the top above a Ron and a George. Damn, I have to wait for two others. I slow down in defeat and offer a false smile.

"I'm Philips."

"Captain Philips!" He laughs in a way that shows he's been saving this joke for ages. But it goes over my head. "Tom Hanks," he adds as if I should now applaud, "You... Tom Hanks... Captain Philips."

I have no idea what he is on about. I scan the area where there are few taxi drivers left hustling for trade. My mystery military wing woman from the plane strides in from the flank. She taps a name on the card,

"That's me. 'Miss', Ronni Cohen." She smiles and turns to me. Ron is a woman.

"So, you're not a gay dad, and there's no wife or partner? Nice timing, avoiding the ambush. I thought she had you."

"You can either lip read or you have very sharp ears! I adopted! Had she not been arrested I could have enlightened her with the rest of my boring story. But I guessed she wasn't interested in me. My daughter Auli'i is a dancer on the ship, you missed that bit, I told that to the customs officer. If they all get together later, they'll have the full story. I'm guessing we're all going to the same ship." I offer my hand, we shake.

"Ronni. Navy, marine biologist," she offers knowing I'll return similar information.

"Kieron Philips, Royal Tank Regiment."

"Cavalryman?" She grins, it's not really a question. She's showing she knows my regiment.

Historically 'tanks' descend from the horseback Cavalry Regiments and she'll have assessed that I'm too tall to have ever been inside a tank. She probably thinks I'm from the Household Cavalry. I match her grin and we both turn back and look towards the terminal, waiting for the last person. I'm thinking Ronni's no biologist, and hoping she's not thinking I'm all 'ceremonial duties'.

"Do you get the feeling…" I start.

"That she's not going to make it?" Ronni finishes. "Our girl will, the Latino woman is not who we're waiting for."

"I thought she was with you. I was waiting to see if you'd step in when she was arrested."

"No. And I'm not with anyone… Wherever I lay my hat," she offers, meaning she has no real home, she's military.

"I don't even have a hat."

We both know we are orphans of the world. The taxi drivers have all drifted away from the front of the airport, indicating all the passengers are through and the day's industry has finished. I sense our driver's impatience.

"So, do you normally do the commentary through the Panama Canal?" I ask her.

"No, why?"

"Sounds like your field; Navy. And I'm hoping that I don't have to do it."

"I'm the eco officer on board, I deal with compliance at sea. I do rules and regulations; I don't do shows," she says smiling.

"Me neither, but someone seems to think I might have a few interesting stories," I say, staring at the airport which is now like a ghost town.

"Best ones are always the ones you can't talk about."

"Or don't want to," I add.

"Why do it if you don't want to, you must be on a hansom army pension?"

"I wish. They stripped me of that. This is a new career."

"You'll do fine, the canal was built by an army of men and big trucks, you know all about them. The rest must be on the internet. 'Tank' commander."

"We go," our driver suggests turning impatiently.

We both stand firm. It must be a military thing not wishing to leave a man behind, that if given just a few minutes more they might make it. The driver relents and stands dwarfed between us with a grunt.

"Ship doesn't sail for hours," Ronni says.

A small local man carrying a pegboard displaying local lottery tickets walks our way and stops. If he is leaving, the day is over. I've no idea why he thinks a tourist would buy a ticket he can't collect on, as much as I would love to win a fortune. But, I'm about to get on a cruise ship and get paid for it. Life's not all bad. Our driver shoos the old man away.

We all focus on a new woman rushing from the building, heading for us. She pulls a case on wheels and has a large bag trapped under her arm like a rugby ball. She powers into us and beyond, not wanting to stop.

"That's me!" she says nodding at the driver's sign, "Thanks for waiting! Let's keep it moving, the shortest distance between toilets please!" She is off walking fast.

She turns to me.

"Kieron, right?"

I nod.

"You don't look six foot three, though I'll give you the dark, slim, handsome and charismatic bit in your biography."

"My agent must have written that."

"In the agent box it said direct, so I'm guessing you wrote it," she says striding faster.

I watch her strange long double bag on wheels in an ill-fitting cover wobble, held only by her squeezing the two handles together. What can be the hurry after being so late?

She pushes her carried bag into the arms of the taxi driver, a diva on a mission. She has to be an entertainer.

"Thanks for waiting, Ronni," she shouts back.

"Always welcome, Georgie," Ronni says.

Of course, these two know each other, they're fellow crew.

The driver lifts the tailgate and dips down for her bag but she gets there first. The ill-fitting cover is hiding a hard red case on top of a cheaper one. A red case like the one I'd lifted from the overhead locker for the Latino woman who was arrested. The cover is a disguise. I don't double take, show surprise, or even skip a breath. Neither does Ronni, though she may not have noticed if she's a marine biologist. Georgie turns for my case, she's in a hurry and the driver is confused.

"I'm not well. For the sake of your vehicle, I suggest the fastest route to the ship."

I'm not sure I believe that story.

Chapter 4 - Uniform

"Did you bring your uniform?" I'm asked by Georgie, as the driver powers through the traffic. She leans over to him clutching her hand luggage tight to her chest as she shakes his shoulder.

"You'll never be a racing driver!" she teases to hurry him.

Georgie turns to Ronni who I can see is quietly amused by her. "How is it I never see you on board?"

"Ship's a big place?" shrugs Ronni.

"Eco-warrior. We won't say where we met, eh?" She delivers with enough punch and intrigue to have a drummer wrap out a two-bang sting before she looks at me. I need to learn from her.

"I did," I offer before she can speak.

"Did what?" she asks.

"Bring my uniform."

"You'll do fine then. Even though I bet you know nothing about the Canal, right?" She laughs.

"I didn't say that," I correct her, but it does seem ridiculous that I'll be posturing as an expert to a few thousand guests after having done a little homework on Google.

"We never sent the British army to Panama?" She mocks surprise.

"No, but, Britain was part of the plan in 1843, though it was never carried through. Had it been-"

"-you'd have been on it," she cuts in.

"No, but it might have been called The Atlantic and Pacific Canal. They may have even tried to fit British in the title."

"Just testing, I don't need to hear the whole act," she says. "None of the Panama lecturers were ever at the build, they all studied it, don't worry."

"But, I am an expert on tracked vehicles, big diggers, building bridges, people movement and operations. Maybe I'll be different."

"I can see you're different." She smiles.

In the backseat, it's easy for me to look behind and check on her bag hidden under the cover. I'm in no doubt it's the same trim and style as the Latina's from the plane. It has to be the missing fourth bag. Her other bag was full of money in one hundred dollar notes. If it's heavy, I would guess this one's full of money too, and someone may well have died for it. So what's Georgie up to? Ronni notices me eyeing the luggage in the rear of the bus. She's far too wise for a navy biologist, she's not just worked in the field, she worked in someone else's field. I suspect, like me, she's done duties she will never speak of, so that'll be a conversation we don't have. We're now both interested in Georgie. Too interested, which she may suspect, as her verbal cover-up has ceased fire. Maybe she's consumed with guilt because she's smuggling money. Worse, maybe Georgie's bag is full of drugs and it was an exchange. That could be a serious haul of cocaine, the size of which sees you locked up for life anywhere. Is this girl a major drug smuggler? Are the cruise ships part of the drug route around the world? I'm now assessing her in a different way.

"I'm your manager and also your daughter's boss."

"I have two uniforms; I'll look the part." I hold her guilty gaze.

"Save them for your stage lecture. They won't see you do Panama commentary, they'll be looking at the canal. You'll be on a microphone on the bridge. And I suggest you don't try and out-uniform the Captain."

"Well I am Captain Philips," I say repeating what was supposed to be a joke.

"That's not funny," she says, and I have to agree, no idea why.

I glance behind me and she knows I'm looking at the case. I look to the port gates, the armed guards, security and customs control to get to the ship.

"More customs?" I ask Ronni, but I know the routine. Off the plane, into the country, out of the country on the ship.

Ronni looks at the security, then Georgie. Georgie is now uneasy, fearful of this next stage of our journey. The guards stop us. One at the front of the car, another with a mirror on a pole looks underneath. A third guard opens the back door, looks at the cases then straight at me. He takes a probe with cloth on the end and rubs the cases, one then the other. The swab goes into a detector which is triggered, we wait for the lights to settle. It looks like I won't be going to the rainforest.

Chapter 5 - In Plain Sight

The tension has still not lifted, although we're through port security easily and looking at two huge ships.

I turn from the port gates to what's ahead. Beyond a line of palms along the edge of the dock are two huge cruise ships. Ships had often carried my old units; the trucks, tanks, and sometimes horses. I thought ours were large vessels until now. Two colossal ships are docked next to each other, one each side of the long pier that extends out to sea, and passengers walk back and forth as a small brass band play at the entrance. This group of tourists can easily be dismissed as innocent. There many senior passengers, some struggling to walk, there are wheelchairs and scooters. These are not smugglers but do these vessels sit in plain sight, sailing smuggling routes that few suspect?

The shape and style of these floating hotels are different to the military ships I'm used to. I'm excited to see everything inside that has been explained to me with such enthusiasm by my daughter. It makes me so proud that she's happy. I know I can't see her until the evening, so perhaps I could still make the rainforest after all. I'd looked at a few options for tours in Costa Rica and my instinct was to hike by myself or hire a private guide. Auli'i suggested the Monster Bus, but that looks like it's just leaving and is already noisier than I would like. She enthused about the charms of Caribbean rum, reggae buses and how I'd love them. It goes to show how little we know of each other's deep background and how precious this working holiday is.

I'm not sold on a reggae bus, but it certainly would mean I'd see some small towns and get down to the Banano River. It would be just the sort of step my therapist insists I should take to reintegrate with civilian life. My daughter's on my therapist's side and gave me a full rundown of options, anything to dissuade me going off alone. Apparently, there's a guide who takes you into the forest and points out the poison dart frogs and other jungle creatures. She laughed when she mentioned that all the tours add in a banana plantation like she has seen too many now. I've never seen bananas growing, but I'm watching that noisy monster bus pull out of the port gates as our bus stops near the ship. Party over.

The driver opens our door, walks to the trunk and reaches in for the first bag, but Georgie beats him to it, grabbing hers. The driver lifts out Ronni's and my bag, slams the door, rounding back to his driver's side in one motion and with a rushed 'adios' he leaves. He knows we're staff, so doesn't expect a tip plus we have already made him late for his next job.

We walk down the long pier between the ships, to the bottom of the gangway and are acknowledged by a junior officer inspecting cruise cards of guests. We don't have cards, so he checks our names and asks us to wait. He radios to announce us and ask for our cruise cards to be brought down, then continues the re-boarding of passengers who already have the magic plastic. Another holdup. I hear a second reggae bus draw to the end of the pier long before I turn and see it. I'm warming to the idea, I just need that cruise card and to dump my bags and hang my suits. I can unpack the rest and inspect the ship later.

I look up the gangway and focus on where it enters the ship via a security X-ray arch.

"Nice suitcase Georgie," Ronni says cutting the air.

"Very nice," I add.

"I'm sure I've seen that style before," Ronni whispers testing her.

I realise Ronni's not involved in Georgie's plan, not until now, but that sounded like an offer. Good job she didn't see the dead body on the plane because she might not have wanted to get involved.

"Someone else had those bags searched at the airport. The army may never have sent me to Panama but they did train me to notice things," I offer. "Do you mind if I just rush on first when the cards come?"

Ronni straightens, looks up the ramp, then pins me with a look and turns to Georgie.

"I noticed you behind me approaching the queue and when you saw me being searched, you turned around and went back," Ronni starts but Georgie stops her, raising her hand,

"- I panicked. I found this bag and I was trying to find the owner but figured if it was full of drugs, no one would believe that. So I ran to the toilet to dump it."

I smile knowing my canal lecture is no longer in danger of her criticism. I figure Ronni knew Georgie had the bag and that she'd eventually make it out of the terminal, which is why she stopped the taxi from leaving. She was eyeing me as an unknown potential problem.

"Money?" Ronni asks.

Georgie nods. "I would have been happy if it was full of her shoes, she looks exactly my size. But no, money."

"Such a disappointment," I add sarcastically.

"Maybe you can buy all the shoes you want, if only," Ronni adds.

"I put some in this bag," she gestures at the hand luggage she still holds tightly.

"Before you gave the case back to its owner?" I suggest, knowing the report from my new boss on my lectures is improving by the minute.

"No. I thought I'd just dump her case," she admits.

"How you going to get any of this past the X-ray machine and onto the ship?" Ronni asks.

Georgie's previous bravado has vanished, she seems sure the bag won't make it past ship security.

"Three-way split," Ronni says. "None of us ever talks about it."

I'm stunned to silence; I'm about to go on a reggae bus, there's no three-way anything. I want no part in anything that killed the man on the airline. But, the money would be a convenient answer to my position, having blown any hope of an army pension by my perceived poor conduct in Syria. More interesting, there is something about solving a problem that people like me and Ronni just can't resist.

Georgie looks relieved. Ronni studies the bow of the ship where two men are painting an area of the ship's hull. She drops her bag to the floor next to the water cart at the bottom of the gangway,

"Both of you, follow me!"

And Georgie does instantly as ordered, clutching her bag and towing her own case with the stolen red case on top in the cover.

"Let's go," Ronni barks.

There's no way this woman is just a marine biologist. I drop my bag by the gangway and follow loosely behind. I have agreed to nothing.

Chapter 6 – Hull Limpets

"I hope neither of you two hull-limpets is dropping paint in this beautiful Costa Rican sea?" Ronni shouts to the workers painting the hull as she sorts through the dust sheets and goods left in their adjacent wheeled work cage with its side off.

"No, Miss Ronni," one says.

"Sea will be as crystal when we sail out, Mam," the other shouts as they continue to work.

CRUISE SHIP HEIST – OCEAN ATLANTIC

Ronni pulls out a large white dust blanket and shakes it open, folds it in half dangling over Georgie's case. She lifts the fold in the sheet, her foot against the side of the lower case to hold the cover on it as she lifts the blanket with the upper case inside. I see her play, feel myself being dragged deeper into this… I turn away and point to the hull.

"You've missed a chunk," I joke, a well-timed misdirection.

A distant police siren is getting louder, closer. Ronni is laying the sheet in the wheeled cage and calmly taking a second sheet. But Georgie is in a panic, clutching her bag and noticing the police car with flashing lights stop momentarily at the port gate. I don't need to turn, I can tell the sirens are stationary. Then police car is let through and accelerates the siren having the horrifying nearing Doppler effect, a crescendo with speed as they come straight for us.

"We should be getting on our international haven!" I urge, turning back to the ship wanting to distance myself from the other two.

"We're going to be arrested," Georgie worries.

"Not sure they can do that now we are dockside," Ronni says calmly.

"We're in South America, they are police, assume they can do what they like," I add without turning.

"Help me fold this sheet Georgie, handbag in hand, and now it's gone," I hear Ronni firmly instruct.

I hear various other noises which I assume relate to the cage, then Ronni joins me quayside. She looks at me, then at the hull.

"Are you questioning the crews work?" she jokes loudly.

We need to get out of here, but I point at the hull staying as cool as I can,

"Are they painting it or washing it?" I jest.

The police car stops at the end of the ship, maybe fifty meters away and three officers get out and rush from the end of the pedestrian jetty towards us.

"It was a short-lived fantasy," I suggest.

"They can't be for us," Ronni says privately to me.

I take another step forward, there is nowhere else to go or I'll be in the water but I want as much distance as possible and as much connection with the workers as I can get.

"We're filling all the holes, Sir," one of the painters laughs without stopping work.

I glance over my left shoulder to see Georgie with just her cheap case. I feel cheated that she doesn't wave her arms and take a bow at Ronni's magic trick like the lovely Debbie McGee, but she is frozen with fear. I look right and see the two policemen and a policewoman rush up the gangway and onto the ship. I turn back to the workers,

"Good job guys."

Heading back to the gangway, Georgie overtakes me, pulling her personal, much smaller case with the cover still twisted but looking like it belongs.

"Slow down. We're clean, nothing can be found on us," I suggest to calm her.

"Georgie!" a female officer in whites shouts from the gangway we left minutes earlier. She has such a beautiful smile it makes me instantly consider my need to improve my social skills. She has a clipboard and waves our cruise cards. My two 'partners' just have cards, mine is inside a concertinaed ship's map with my cabin number on. A dangerous reveal if the anonymous card were lost with it, a bit like putting 'home' in your car sat nav.

"At three o'clock, please come to reception for a lifeboat drill and to register your credit card so you can purchase items on board," the officer says.

I collect my case and look around for the police presence, pausing to let Georgie go first but she insists I do. Ronni keenly jumps in front.

"Excuse me, but I should make sure those clowns painting the hull deal with all their rubbish and paint properly. Eco-considerations here in Costa Rica are huge," she offers, now blocking the gangway.

"That's bigging your part up."

I am speaking to be noticed by the very pretty officer, who smiles at me in a way that makes me melt. I'm guessing she's Malaysian, though I've no idea why I think that. What a day! A collection of stunning women and I've not even jumped on the rum bus. This officer does not trigger any alert buttons as the Latina did and I find myself looking down to see if she's wearing a wedding ring, I am human after all, and I'm urged to engage rather than retreat as I did before. Her ring hand keeps moving, hidden, under the clipboard then damn! A ring. Damn, defeat.

"Costa Rica is one of the greatest biological diversities in the world, and very safe, it abolished all its armed services," Ronni throws back as she climbs up. I'd forgotten she was still there, I was in a trance.

"Oh yeah? And how is that working out for them?" I shout up.

I notice Ronni isn't wearing a wedding ring, but she's on a mission and doesn't turn until she's at the top of the gangway.

"They now spend that money on social, medical and educational needs."

"Sounds like something a politician would say," I tease.

"It won them a Nobel Peace Prize."

I grin, but Ronni has left, she's going to meet her painters. I couldn't have predicted today, and I've no idea what tomorrow will bring. Georgie smiles at me waiting for me to climb the gangway. I walk up, entering a new phase in my life.

At the top is a security desk where I hand over my card and it's scanned.

"Please stand there, Sir. I need a picture," the officer at the entrance says. He holds a mini internet type camera on a cable attached to his computer and adjusts until I must be in the frame. I offer the smallest of smiles, more than you would for a passport. My picture is taken and he nods, allowing me aboard. I place my case on the x-ray machine belt and Georgie, who is now relaxed and smiling does the same with her own case. The beautiful Malaysian officer wafts past us, still melting me with her smile and it hits me that she told me something. I turn to Georgie.

"Did she say to be at reception for three o'clock?"

"Lifeboat drill," Georgie explains. "I have to do it too. It only takes a few minutes."

"I was hoping to grab a reggae bus and go out for the day," I say, walking through the body scanner.

"Not today." Georgie smiles. "But, there's always another reggae bus. See you at the drill." She leaves.

I feel suddenly alone. I collect my case off the belt and wonder what to do next. I look at my ship map and cruise card folder... time to find my cabin.

Chapter 7 - Cabin

Through my cabin porthole, I see lifeboats. They hang outside my window, obscuring the view. I read the few official envelopes left on my bed. One is from Ricardo, the production manager asking me to attend a stage safety briefing and rehearsal. The note I want to read is the one from my daughter.

CRUISE SHIP HEIST – OCEAN ATLANTIC

Hey, Dad! I'm rehearsing all afternoon, then two shows tonight. Please come and watch the last one, see you after! Love you. Auli'i.

Lifeboat duty is the three of us being shown how to put a lifejacket on. The other two must've done it more times than the young officer demonstrating but neither object, there's not even a hint of a joke. On completion, the officer has us sign a sheet of paper then he leaves.

"Let's get changed and meet for a drink in three hours, mid-ships, Westward. It's the top bar," Ronni suggests firmly.

She's led troops before, clear concise orders. I check my watch, that will be 1820 hours. I nod, but Georgie has gone quiet. She wanders away.

-

The ship has three stairwells. Mid-ships is the middle, the top lift button seems logical for a top bar. Not rocket science but ship science. Tonight the dress code is casual so I'm wearing chinos, a collared shirt and jacket. Everyone is dressed for the evening even though it seems early. It is past six o'clock which is the witching hour for dress code rules, but no one else is wearing a jacket and I feel self-conscious. I look out of the window at the white water washing past us in the red evening glow. I go into the bar I think is Westward, but have to check with the barman as neither of my two comrades are here. I order a beer and relax on a bar stool, pulling out the note I've read a dozen times.

.... please come and watch the last one, see you after! Love you. Auli'i.

I'll see both shows, I tell myself. My proud smile is broken by Georgie's arrival next to me.

C.S.C.I.

"You counted it?" she throws as a side remark whilst handing her cruise card to the barman and ordering a drink.

"Let me…" I offer my card but she shakes her head.

"We don't do rounds, we're all in the same ship. Even if you can afford it. How much did you get?"

"I've got nothing, wasn't expecting anything. I was smiling at 'Dad'; it's such a great word." I show her the note.

"Take a load off," I suggest, moving away from the bar to a table and pulling a chair out for her.

"This is not a bar where I'm supposed to sit down with passengers. I can stand," she says, handing the note back to me. I stand with her.

"You can sit, you're guest staff. Best of both worlds. So, Auli'i's actually your daughter?"

"She calls me Dad, that's more than enough for me. It's complicated." The tale needs more time than she might wish to spare.

Ronni places a beautifully wrapped parcel in front of me.

"You shouldn't have gone to so much trouble."

I turn the sizeable brown paper block that gives nothing away.

"I didn't, I had them do it in the gift shop," Ronni jokes. "It's your new pension."

She orders a beer at the bar. I look to Georgie.

"Mine was delivered, along with my empty handbag," she says, weighed down by the whole thing.

"Didn't know your cabin, Philips. Trust me, they're equal," Ronni says, taking her glass from the bar and raising it as she joins us. "The small pleasures in life, let's hope they never end."

I raise my glass to toast. "Agreed."

Georgie's not keen to toast anyone just yet. "Is it as much as the young engineer got?" She asks.

I fight to hide my confusion; my army poker face is getting tested today… who is this fourth person? Did one of the painters get in on the deal? Has the money been cut into four? Not that the money matters, I never wanted it, and none of us has a clue how much was even there but is it now four people that know about the heist even before the sun has fully dropped? I place Auli'i's note on the money-brick. She had nothing a few years ago, I had some savings and an asset until I put my house up to pay for her safety and sanity. But, many of her friends still have nothing. Maybe I can help more of them to justify taking this. This money could be put to very good use. That's a reason to be interested, now I want to gauge the weight.

"I never counted it in detail, I did it in stack size and assumed they are all the same notes. It is enough not to ask or argue," Ronni answers.

The engineer must have just won some other financial prize.

"A lottery win?" I offer thinking that might have been the engineer's luck.

Georgie looks sombre, the guilt is laying heavy on her. She needs to shake herself out of the dark mood. She was saved from a huge error in her judgement unless she knew Ronni was on her flight and that she'd solve the problem.

"Hey, you got lucky. Like the engineer, you got the winning ticket," I say, trying to lighten the load.

"He didn't win the lottery; he was a whistleblower," Ronni corrects me her eyes threatening me just enough.

Now I'm even more intrigued, my frown requests her to expand. Maybe that's what Georgie's worried about, us being turned in.

"A trainee on another ship saw a discharge of illegal sludge and couldn't live with it. He turned whistleblower and the shipping company was fined forty million dollars. He got the first million," Ronni explains.

"Wow. That took some balls."

Now Ronni toasts me. "He did the right thing."

"And what's the right thing for us to do?" Georgie fires curtly. "Who will turn us in?"

"Don't either of you consider it." Ronni says sternly.

"I've got plans for mine," I add philosophically because I'm now certain where this windfall will go. I turn over the brown paper parcel.

"You don't even know how much it is," Georgie charges.

I look at Ronni for a number, but I get no response. It is over a million and given the size it could be more. There isn't much you can do with cash. Large sums of it can be useless, if not threatening. You can't bank huge sums without questions. Georgie may have moved on to the new problem, where to put it, how to use it?

"What if someone wants it back, what if they saw me take it?" she blurts out.

I handled large sums of government money in the forces, took them to foreign leaders as bribes for their support. That cash was often marked so it could be traced, I wonder for a moment if this is marked. I turn to Ronni, she predicts my question.

"I checked for simple markings," she says.

I want to open the package and find a razor blade to scratch across the surface and see if any dust comes off. If microchips had been added to the print, they come off by shaving them, if you know how. I only once lightened a payment keeping a portion back, only once, carefully shaving every note. I felt I'd earned every last pound by the time I'd finished. Once was enough, and worth it. The money was needed to get orphaned children out of Syria to Turkey. Auli'i was one of them, the only one I really saved. The only one that calls me Dad, and she's about to perform on stage and expects me to be watching.

"What happened to the officer who released the sludge into the sea?" I ask Ronni, my mind jumping back to reality.

"Rumour is he's on permanent gardening leave, he won't work again," Ronni answers.

"Did the company ask him to dump the waste?" I probe.

"No, never." But, Ronni's holding back.

"Then why do it?"

"Must've felt he needed to hit targets he couldn't meet any other way. It was stupid. This isn't stupid Kieron, it's not marked, it's no ones' money," Ronni says.

"Do you think it's drug money?" Georgie asks quietly.

"Drugs leave South America, hundreds of tonnes each month. Money goes the other way; in. So maybe, but maybe not," Ronni muses.

"Was she stealing it, trying to escape with it?" I speculate.

"If she was, they'll make an example of her," Ronni says.

"God rest her," I find myself toasting Ronni as if we'd lost a soldier. I neck my drink like a squaddie. Ronni slides the package at me.

"It's just the right size for your room safe." Ronni smiles.

It seems she has thought of everything, but I bet she hasn't shaved every note.

"My daughter's on stage soon so I'd like to find the theatre." I excuse myself.

Georgie stands, and I realise that she did break the rules and sit down after all. Today's a day of breaking rules.

"I have to introduce them," she says leading the way.

I touch knuckles with Ronni, fist to fist. We've bonded and it feels good to know I have a friend on board. I don't know about Georgie, who I catch up in a few strides.

"Do you think she's dead?" Georgie asks me as we walk.

"The Latino woman? If she crossed a drug cartel, she probably is."

"Isn't that what we've just done? Cross them?"

"No," I say, end of.

Chapter 8 – Cross and double cross

I'm not sure what I was expecting. A theatre's a theatre and this is a theatre, except it's a real theatre, it's huge. Two tiers and boxes. I squeeze past passengers and arrive at a vacant seat in the middle of the row. Sitting, I wonder why no one is sitting in the middle. The pattern is the same both sides, people hogging the ends of rows. Are they expecting an emergency evacuation?

I'm only slightly less uncomfortable with people behind me, but tonight is not about me. I scan the room counting the rows, then the seats and multiply, there must be over eight hundred seats. The middles of the rows are awkwardly filling now as they're the only seats left. I ponder the irony of those arriving early so they can leave fast if that's why they've done it, they will spend the same time in here as those arriving late. Maybe they've chosen the edge in case they don't like the show.

A voice offstage announces 'Please welcome, Georgie, your entertainment manager!' Georgie waltzes on to applause, knees cutting through a slit in a long black dress, heels and a smile I've not noticed before. She walks like a dancer, maybe she was one once... so this is where older dancers end up, in management. Life's the same everywhere. Auli'i's dream was to dance on a stage. It seems so simple and might be many a girl's dream, however, few come as far as Auli'i to realise it. If you're born in Syria, where your village is destroyed and your parents are killed, dreams don't come true.

CRUISE SHIP HEIST – OCEAN ATLANTIC

I'm so proud to see her singing, dancing in step, as sharp as anyone up there. I can see the extra hours spent to ensure she will stand out. My message has always been that you need to work and work to be the best because if you're not the best, you're just one of the rest. Auli'i will never be ordinary in anything. Her name means neat, perfect, and she is. I hope that isn't me being a proud Dad, but she's the best. Not that I know the first thing about dancing, but I've watched troops, I've seen talent and those who go that extra mile. I guess there was something in her that made me help her more than the other orphans who begged at the sides of dusty destroyed streets, kids we always shared our rations with. I've moved over fifty children out of war zones now and found them families in neighbouring countries, but she's the only one who I smuggled into the UK. It nearly bankrupted me. She's the only one who got her dream; a new name, a new future. She's the only one for whom I acquired papers and it was the hardest thing I've ever done. It finished my career and emptied my savings.

I'm not sure my ageing mother approved of or enjoyed the short inconvenience of Auli'i living in her house in north-west London. With a determination and a survival instinct that only death and destruction breeds, Auli'i made it into performing arts college. The private theatre school made few demands in academia, and thankfully held on to her even when I couldn't make the fees.

This brown paper parcel might help me forge a proper answer to save some other war victims, and now I'm no longer serving with the military, this could be the next part of life's rich tapestry.

The show ends to tumultuous applause and I stay rooted to my seat in awe still thinking of the strange twists and turns life takes. The stage goes dark, the auditorium is lit and I wonder if the array of leaving passengers will remember the show in a

STUART ST PAUL

week? It hits me that this is the stage I'll have to stand on, alone to do my talks. Congestion leaves people backed up in the isles as the first ones wait for elevators outside, I'm more interested in the doors either side of the stage marked emergency exit. They must also be stage doors and I wonder which one Auli'i will appear from. Is she happy here? Has she made friends? Is she still haunted by the past like I am? She must be. I start to count the number of times I've actually had face to face father-daughter talks rather than just on the phone; it isn't enough. We did have a ritual of watching Moana on the sofa with a bowl of popcorn, on the pretence it was improving her English. How can you worry about someone so much? Is that the true meaning of the word parent; worrier? If it is, then Georgie would make a great mum.

The right-hand door gives way to a wave of young energy bursting out and Auli'i is right in the middle of it. On seeing me she runs. I rush to the end of the row, we hug as she kisses my cheek, then introduces me to all her friends. Relieved, I remember the parcel and turn back to my seat where I left it on the floor by my feet. I can't see it. I check under the seats but it's not there. My blood chemistry changes, hit by panic, forcing me into the dark place that grows inside when something is wrong. Just one moment of weakness, one lapse of judgement explains why people who do my job don't have families. Auli'i runs down the row behind the one I'm searching and she bends and bounces, leans over into the next one.

"Is this what you've lost?" she says retrieving the wrapped parcel.

I must've moved forward two rows when I greeted her. An unacceptable drift in orientation. I don't like making mistakes like that.

"For me?" she asks.

Should I have brought her a present?

"For once, it's not," I admit and she hands it to me without a fuss.

"I need to dump my things in my cabin then we'll make a plan," she enthuses.

"Plan? We're on a ship, who needs a plan?"

Her eyes are open wide, her friends joined at the hip and I know she has found a place in a world where she so easily could've continued to be a victim.

"There's a sports bar, along to the middle and up one deck. Meet you there?" she asks but it's not really a question. She's about to vanish when a thought hits me and I stop her.

"Auli'i! Have you got a safe in your room?"

"Yes." She frowns. "Why?"

I offer her the brown parcel which she takes and holds.

"I don't want to accidentally leave it somewhere else. Would you mind locking it away very safely? Especially if we're drinking."

"We can't drink." She says noticing my shock. "You can, you're 'guest staff', you don't have lifeboat duties. We're on call 24/7 and we can be drink or drug tested any time." Auli'i shrugs, kisses my cheek and is gone.

I stress about giving her too much responsibility. However, her not knowing what's in the tightly wrapped parcel means she won't feel the pressure. Just as not drinking shouldn't be a problem for a Middle-Eastern girl of strict religious upbringing.

Walking through a corridor of expensive paintings posing as an art gallery I puzzle the finance and exposure to theft, but see cameras in the ceiling. Where could a thief go with the pictures? No one can leave a ship with stolen goods, but then, no one can get a case of money on board without being seen, right? This huge floating city could be locked down and searched. I pass a cinema with 'film in progress' on the closed doors. I turn into the central area where there's a shopping arcade. The sparkling diamonds in the Jeweller's window stop me, and I stare, not because I have any need to buy gems but this seems an absurd place for them to be on sale.

Re-focus, concentrate. I climb the ornate staircase and find the sports bar opposite an open plan casino. I order a drink, life on board is relaxing. I could get settled in front of one of many TV screens showing a British Premiere League match from earlier today, but the casino has my attention. We could all run our money through the casino, a week of sitting like James Bond? Auli'i snatches me from my gaze.

"Can't use the casino, not even guest staff," she says standing next to me, her native accent totally gone. "Let me show you the ship. Where first?"

"You're world. The stage."

"Bring your beer."

"Guest staff can walk around with drinks?" I ask letting her lead me away.

I have just walked this route, but now I see far more. It's a modern Roman city, where at each gap in the colonnade, vendors have space to sell. She shows me backstage, her new world; where she manufactures her act in a tight little team. Flat pack theatrical set sections are strapped into pens, curtains hang, ropes are looped, engineering both modern and ancient and then, the big open space facing the seats where she is on-show. She follows me as I walk downstage looking at the huge empty modern-day amphitheatre from my new vantage point.

"You'll be great, Dad."

I'll be alone and I'm not the superman she thinks I am. This will be a whole new experience.

"I'll wear my uniform, that'll be my protection," I offer.

"That won't stop someone taking a shot at you." She smiles.

Chapter 9 – Port Cristobal, Panama

I'm woken by the sound of engines changing gear and revving. It's different from the constant drone of the propellers forcing us through the sea, we must be entering a port. This will be interesting because I've read the tourist blurb about it being the biggest free trade area in the western world, 'the next Dubai', and the contrasting press reports on its failure, poverty, poor food, hotels and lack of fruit.

Sunlight powers round my closed curtains and I check my watch. I've slept well. It's late by my standards. I dress for the gym and leave the cabin.

Gyms are the same everywhere but this one looks out to sea or the dock as we're now stationary. Captain Feldman comes on the public address, which I'd miss if I were in my cabin, I've not yet worked out how to hear his messages on my TV. He announces that there's been a secure zone built around the ship and we can leave via deck four, mid-ships, showing our cruise card. That magic card replaces the need for any papers or a passport, amazing. Auli'i is not allowed off the ship today as she has rehearsals, so I'm on my own and in no rush. Colón a hundred years ago would've been something to see, awash with wealth during the construction of the railroad and canal works. The gold rush. Immigrant workers from everywhere, bars, theatres, music and madness have all been left to go to ruin from the videos I've seen online.

I go from the gym to the buffet for breakfast. The choice is extensive, though I imagine it might get monotonous. I choose kippers because it's a rare treat; who keeps kippers at home? Cooking them leaves a smell that spreads. I take a mug of coffee and sit by the window with a great view of passengers scurrying away from the ship to various coaches. It looks like all the coaches to the left are the excursions, and to the right, there's a free shuttle bus, which most people are directed to. I'm not sure there will be much to see in this transit town, but I'll go and inspect for myself.

Guests queuing to get off flood the mid-ships area of my deck, but turning into my corridor it becomes quiet, just a couple squeezing past the house-keeping trolleys. My cabin door is open; the steward must be cleaning. I walk in cautiously, looking in the bathroom and open closet area as I pass. The empty room is not as I left it.

I look under the bed and behind me. The room has been turned over, this is no cleaning duty. I had left everything neatly folded and stacked. The safe is open, my case has been undone, the drawers and cupboards have all been searched and the contents tossed. Yet nothing has been taken, my wallet is lying in the open safe; cards and money are still inside. It hits me. They're after the big money, my brown paper brick. I grab the phone on my desk, pulling the 'Guest Entertainers Welcome Pack' open, which has every number I need. I call Auli'i.

"Sorry Ee, were you asleep?"

"No worries, Dad. You going out?"

"D'you still have that parcel I gave you?"

"I guess so, why?"

"Please check."

I hear her opening the safe, they all make the same monotone beeps as the code is entered.

"Yes."

"It's complicated, but please keep the safe locked, keep your door locked and tell no one else we're connected. It's a vast donation to help more children. I think someone's after it, my room's been turned over. If they think I've given it to you they might break into your room. If they do, let them take it," I add hastily.

"Dad! They'll have to kill me to take Syrian children's money!" she insists.

"Do not be a hero!" But I know she means it, which is worrying, she has seen how cheap life can be.

"Dad, you can find out who went into your room, they have cameras."

"Stay safe. Love you," I say hanging up and ringing Georgie's office next.

"Hello," she answers.

"Georgie, it's Kieron, your speaker and partner in... whatever."

"Yes I remember, the tall good looking one with far too much cheek."

"My room has been turned over, safe opened. They're after the money. Nothing else has gone."

"They got your money?" she panics.

"No. I don't know Ronni's number; can you warn her?"

"Meet me at my cabin now, in case they're there. G109!" She hangs up.

I rush out of my room, slamming the door. Up and along G-deck where I see Georgie running towards me from the other end. The door to 109 is open. I burst in.

A cabin steward turns from cleaning her room, most confused at seeing me.

"Can I help you, sir?"

Georgie enters at speed using me as her brake. She looks to the safe, punches in the numbers, checks it, then closes it and re-enters the numbers. I got the quickest of glimpses of the bundles of perfectly packed bank notes in her safe, and I look down to see the brown paper wrapping in her waste bin. The cabin steward looks at both of us.

"Do you need the room, Georgie?" He grins cheekily.

Georgie pecks me on the cheek with an affectionate kiss.

"Come on, let's have breakfast." She pulls me to the door. "Manesh, don't let any other men into my room."

"You, Georgie? Men chasing you? I think they'll be in for a surprise," the cabin steward jokes as Georgie pulls me along the corridor.

"I woke Ronni and her cabin is untouched so it's just you. Why you?" she asks.

"Because I was with the woman on the plane? I lifted the bag down from the locker, I stood with her in the customs line. If someone was watching they've connected me to her and traced me here." I can think of no other answer.

"Good, I'm not connected, we should stay apart so I don't get drawn in."

"You are drawn in, you're my boss, I have to be seen with you!" I say.

She is treating me like toxic waste she wants to cast aside.

"If they've got on this ship already, they'll be connecting the dots. Before they do, can you access the cameras outside my room?" I ask. "We need to stop this now. Whoever it is, they're on this ship for a reason!"

Georgie changes direction, pulling me out of the public area and into a staff lift that goes down a lot further than the passenger ones. We walk together along an undecorated, wide corridor.

"Where is this?"

"Affectionately known as i95, crew deck. You're not allowed down here," she says, walking at speed.

I follow her as she turns into what is obviously the security area. There's a wall of screens flicking between cameras on every part of the ship. A fit, upright male officer slowly cranes up with a look that suggests he knew we were coming. I guess no one walks into this office without a problem that needs solving.

"Hunter, do me a favour, look at who was on F Deck down by 521 between…?" Georgie looks at me.

"I went to the gym just after we docked and rang you about half an hour ago."

I notice the name sign on his desk, 'Hunter Witowski, Head of Security.' Slow and controlled he punches into a control panel and my corridor comes up. A few passengers walk back and forth in fast forward. He rewinds to a maintenance man in green overalls entering my cabin. Forward, back, zoom in, freeze frame, and he prints a picture of his face. Then he lets the video run to see him enter my room. Minutes later he re-appears checks the corridor is clear and moves swiftly out. Hunter changes camera and follows him down through crew stairs to a cargo area where he's seen talking to a forklift truck driver on another camera.

"What was stolen?" Hunter asks slowly in a very deep relaxed American accent as he turns to Georgie and me.

"Nothing. Wallet and phone untouched," I say, realising how daft that sounds. "Has he got me confused with whoever was there last week?" I add to play innocent.

"Why d'you think you've been robbed if nothing's gone?" Hunter asks ignoring what I have said.

"All my drawers were turned out and the safe was opened, so he was looking for something. He obviously found I'd nothing worth stealing, or I was the wrong guy. But that's still a problem."

Hunter picks up a radio and slowly growls in a low octave voice. "Control to 56, go to F521 and photograph the room? Keep the steward out until we have dusted for prints. There's been a break-in."

"Roger that." Is the squawked reply.

"Control to 21 and 24, come back to base," Hunter asks.

"Roger that. Travelling, Sir."

Hunter then freeze-frames another image of the man and hits the print button. He rises to collect the sheets from the printer and looks me up and down. We are the same size and stature.

"Guest speaker, right? British infantry?" he asks.

"Tank Commander, then Horse Guards, ceremonial, retired," I say, now paying attention to his every move. He is opening a cupboard behind him and taking out a fingerprint case.

"I looked you up."

"Bet you didn't find that much, not an interesting career."

"I wasn't looking on Google," he says with quiet confidence. He steps out from behind his desk. "Beats confronting guests who steal silverware from the dining table."

"Seriously?" I say in surprise. "Silverware?"

Hunter nods slowly, digging deep into my eyes.

"Leave it with me, I'll find what's going on. I always do."

Georgie pulls me away before I can explore more of what goes on in his world, or he can of mine.

"Thanks, Hunter," she says.

"I'd like to ask the thief some questions," I say turning back to him.

"Why? Sure you've no idea why he'd go in your room?"

Georgie insistently pulls me away with her arm linked in mine. She's certainly more assertive and confident today, she must have decided to keep the money, and she wants nothing to go wrong.

The problem is, it has gone wrong. They've found us.

Chapter 10 – Found us.

CRUISE SHIP HEIST – OCEAN ATLANTIC

I sit opposite Georgie in the officers' mess, my second breakfast in less than an hour. There's a sparkle in her eyes that I'd missed in all the drama of last night. Maybe it's the money; I've not counted mine and no one has really mentioned a figure, but however much it is, she looks great on it. Ronni never even confirmed what currency it's in, though I guess US dollars. She said she measured it by stack height, every denomination the same size, and weighs about a gram. My parcel weighed about 10 kilograms so at worst, it's ten grand and I suspect it's a lot more. Who would save one dollar bills? Ronni would have glanced quickly to see they were the same. I'm more puzzled as to why her cabin steward, who clearly knows Georgie well, was so amused. His name was Manesh and he called her 'Miss Georgie'. He said the men chasing her were in for a surprise. Does she have some special form of defence? What did he mean, how can I frame that question?

"Why did she leave a case behind at the airport?" Georgie asks me.

"Squirrelling."

"Squirrelling?" she has no idea what I meant.

"You did it, subconsciously. You moved some money out of one bag into your hand luggage in case you lost the main bag. It's like leaving nuts here there and everywhere. She had three bags, if she lost them she could go back and try and retrieve your one from the airport when it was quiet and law officials had left," I suggest. "Not a great plan. It was more being prepared to lose one, than expect to walk through customs and passport control with three."

Her pager goes, she checks it instantly then excuses herself.

"We'll talk later," Georgie says, before powering away, leaving me in an area my contract specifically says I shouldn't be in.

I try to follow her, without drawing attention, but she's vanished. Not up the metal stairs, nor down. I'm lost on a ship in South America, where money means drugs, and drug cartels kill police and government without blinking. How am I going to resolve this? I can't turn the clock back. Extricating myself now is going to be impossible, even if I was to return the money, so there is no point thinking along those lines. The money will clear the debts I acquired getting Auli'i this far, I just have to hold on to it. Then maybe I can help other children who are one step away from being left sprawled dead across a road. Some visions never leave you, some never should.

I walk back along the crew deck, sure it's the way Georgie led me, and re-find security. I stop and linger outside. I see Hunter with his back to me at the door. Beyond him are two security officers holding the man in green overalls seen leaving my room. It didn't take him long and he seems to have no need for the fingerprint case in his hand. The prisoner sees me and gives my presence away with a huge grin. Hunter turns towards me.

"Where is she?" the man in green demands with a thick Spanish accent.

"Who?" I say genuinely puzzled.

"At least you've got him talking," Hunter says, holding the door open for me to enter, then closing it behind me.

The man reaches into a pocket and both guards tighten their retention of him. He raises his hands showing he has no weapon to put them at ease. This is not the first time he has been arrested.

"You already got my guns, gringos," he snarls.

Slowly he produces a folded piece of paper, which Hunter takes from him, unfolds and studies. I look at the semi-automatic lying on the desk with magazine out, chamber cleared and realise this is deathly serious. Hunter passes the paper to me. It's a printout, time-stamped and from a high angle security camera at the airport.

"That's me." I feign surprise.

"Where is she?" the man in green growls.

"Her?"

I take the printout that connects me to the money. I can't deny meeting the stunning Latina but I can protest.

"She asked me to help her, wanted a heavy case lifted on the plane."

"That's not on the plane." Hunter points out, wanting more information.

"No, she followed me to baggage collection and I had to lift her other case off the carousel. She would've had me carry all her bags for the rest of the day!"

"So you don't know her?" Hunter questions.

"Never met her before yesterday. No idea. I thought she was giving me a look because she fancied me."

"Don't you have any mirrors in your room?" Hunter teases. Military banter.

"She just wanted a slave. But she was arrested. The police took her." I protest.

"She had money! Enough to pay the police more than we were paying them to keep her," the man snaps.

"But they arrested her, they took all her money."

"They're dead!" he threatens.

I try to ignore that remark, but he has no reason to state it unless it's true. She has a price on her head.

"I bet she uses people all the time." I want answers, not questions. "She must be used to having people do things for her?"

"Yes." The man moves in closer to me, he's sure that I have something to do with this woman. His breath smells, his teeth are bad. This is a hired hand desperate for money, working to orders and threats. "So where is she, dead man?"

It's time to go on the offensive, to get information rather than have him threaten me, but I need to stay innocent.

"You searched my room. Did you think she was hiding in my safe? You're not looking for a woman; you're a thief!"

"I look for her passports, you get her new papers." He leans into me again.

The guards pull him back but he shakes them off violently.

"If I wanted to kill you, you'd all be dead. You want that on your pretty ship? No, so you help me get her!" he spits.

I may be getting tamed into civilian life but I am not sure he would have killed me. But this is not a contest and the room has fallen silent. As good as Hunter is, and as curious, I can see that his job is not to police the world but keep the name of the ship clean. All he wants to do is get this man off it, and maybe me. Hunter picks up the phone.

"Billy, ask the harbourmaster to send a detail on-board to escort a local illegal off my ship."

The phone goes down and the clock's ticking; deportation is inevitable for him.

"Local? I don't live in this shit hole! They won't keep me. I be in Cartagena tonight," he says with the confidence of a gangster who's always right until he's dead.

I'm new to being posted in South America but extremists with guns are the same the world over, there's never any reasoning with them; their gang is their tribe. Hunter nods to the guards.

"Lock him up until they come for him."

Hunter takes the gun and locks it in a cubicle behind his desk, then drops the ammunition clips in his desk drawer.

"I'm not the only gunman on this ship," the prisoner shouts back at the door.

"I worked that out myself, anyone as bad at their job as you would never be trusted to work alone," Hunter retorts, "you're just an expendable grunt, sent to do a job, and you failed!"

"It's not over. We get her back before you sail," he barks back.

The guards slam him into the wall to stop his struggle. I look to check their belts again, they're not armed so he can't pull their weapon. No one in the room is armed, the game is over for him. Hunter is baiting him hard for information, he's worked in interrogation. I can see why many of my ex-colleagues must end up working in security, an eco-compliance officer makes sense, but guest entertainer? Hunter approaches him again with the picture.

"Is this woman as stupid as you?" Hunter gets right into his face.

I know he's enjoying this hiatus from what must be a very tedious routine of petty theft by passengers.

"Very clever woman, strong woman, killer. But, she can never leave 'El Rey'," the man defends.

"They sent you to take her back to Cartagena?" Hunter acts amazed.

The man smiles, proud of his assignment.

"D'you know where this ship's going?" Hunter laughs.

The man looks hate back at Hunter, refuses to see he's outclassed. The men are eye to eye, and he studies Hunter's face like he's in a cheap card game, but he's already played his hand. I know the cards Hunter is about to reveal.

"I'm guessing you don't. I'm guessing you got on this ship because our entertainer here, the man who stands on stage and sings for his supper, got on this ship."

"Frank Sinatra, gangster," he snarls.

Hunter does not even turn to me. He wants to win this. I admire his composure. "And, I'm guessing that if she, whoever she is, has even a little more intelligence than you, just a tiny bit more, she'll have got on the other ship docked alongside us at the pier in Port Limón. That ship sailed away from South America and will now be in George Town, Grand Cayman, whereas this ship is going to Cartagena! The clever lady will have escaped on the other ship, idiot."

The guards manhandle him away and his anger grows.

"She was with your mariachi!" he shouts back.

"I guess that was part of her plan, idiot, you got suckered." Hunter insults him before the door is closed behind the gunman then looks at me.

"A bullet has your name on, 'mariachi'," the villain shouts through the closed door.

"I thought I dodged my last a while ago," I admit.

Hunter walks back behind his desk, but he does not sit.

"You have absolutely nothing to do with whatever that was?"

"Nothing," I say in a way that would beat a lie detector because I can.

"Good, but just in case he's not the only gunman on the ship, call me before you make a mess."

Hunter hands me his card, then points at the screen. He starts to playback a recording. It is an external security camera from yesterday's long pier in Port Limon which shows Ronni magic the case from Georgie into the work cage that the painters were using.

"Nothing to do with that?" he asks.

The screen shows I'm just an innocent bystander with my back turned so I can play Judas.

"Amazing what happens behind one's back. I seem to have had quite an introduction to my first cruise."

Hunter turns the recording off as the police car skids to a stop. We have both seen enough.

"I'm sure it's just a piece of cabaret, totally unrelated. But, I'll take that up with Georgie and Ronni. Whatever's going on, I'll find out. I'll find out who you are and why you're here."

"Holiday. Cruise ship speaker. They were after whoever had the cabin before me."

I make no connection to my daughter that could put her at risk and make me vulnerable. I turn to the door, thoughts rushing through my head. One problem might be solved, but another's just begun. The purse may have got smaller if Hunter is to be included, but as head of security, he could be a good addition to the group. All this because the company probably saved a few pounds flying us three into Cartagena and then up to Costa Rica.

"Philips," he says softly.

It would be rude not to stop and turn for his Colombo-like epilogue.

"The guy in the cabin before you; Pastor Mike. Regular on the ship. He does Easter, Christmas and joins us when he can, just for a 'holiday'. He was here for Christmas." he pauses. "No one's ever shot him or turned his room over."

Chapter 11 – Shore leave cancelled

Today in Cristóbal, I was planning to go ashore, but Panama can be a nasty place and as my face may appear on a local watchlist, maybe I should stay on-board. I've finished dodging bullets for a living, or for fun. I'm glad Auli'i's rehearsing, we will both stay safely on the ship and perhaps we could have lunch together, eating seems a popular pass-time here.

I look over the lido deck-rail at the distant skyline. Colon's just a few miles beyond the port of Cristóbal, at the Caribbean entrance to the Panama Canal. I should be looking at my notes on the nearby Gatún Locks and the Gatún Dam built years ago 'with limited technology and scant concern for life in a rush for gold'. A fight over money I remind myself.

This area was once in control of the Spanish mainland and I wanted to visit Fort San Lorenzo here, which is supposedly a well-preserved reminder of times when Europeans came to buy and sell slaves in order to get rich. A theme that has repeated throughout history; even now someone sells the drug smugglers arms and ammunition so they can feed America's epidemic-scale thirst for drugs. White powder addicts support political lobbyists of those who profit directly or indirectly from the illegal trade. No US government will ever be allowed to get strong enough to legislate against weapons, build borders or curb the drug trade. I've carried cash for governments to pay middle-eastern clans to keep access to black oil, same shit, different country. White powder is the new oil.

I'm going to have to open that parcel very soon now we have a new team member to cut in. I suspect there'll be a fifth before the day's out, then a sixth, that's life. My cut's becoming smaller before I've had the chance to get excited by knowing what it's worth. I could get off the ship, grab a train to Los Angeles and disappear. The Panama Railroad was built as a fast route to California during the gold rush. I envisage the old Wild West, run by bullies, controlled by guns, fuelled by gold all wasted on booze and sex.

I shake it off. There's no point lingering on death and destruction, I look down and watch our holidaymakers being sent to their tour coaches or wandering towards the town to adventure alone. I see Ronni strides down the gangway, she too turns to walk into town. She is wearing a plain short sleeved shirt, her long trousers and boots but somehow still looks sexier than most of the scantily-clad guests. Hunter obviously didn't get to question her this morning.

Two local men fold in and follow, shadowing her at the same pace on the other side of the dock, hidden close to the pallets of supplies. I can see that from my bird's eye view, but she can't and it looks like she's in trouble. Two police cars speed towards our ship with sirens blaring. Two men shadowing Ronni don't even turn to look at the cars that pass them. She is being tailed. Instinctively I rush along the deck towards mid-ships, keeping them in sight. The police car below stops, two uniformed officers get out and march up towards ship security, they'll be for the gunman. Ronni is in trouble.

I dash inside, no time to wait for a lift, and I run down the stairs two by two, turning and jumping. As I reach the exit, the area is cordoned off by security to allow police visit. I can't wait with the other passengers until they have left, I slip past to the officer at the computer who checks guests out.

"Sorry Sir, you will have to wait," he says to me lifting his hands to point me back behind the barrier.

"You can either scan my card and let me get to my tour, which is about to leave, or I stand here and make a scene, encouraging the others to join me."

"If you wish to shout sir, please do it in the queue," he says standing his ground politely.

"Call Hunter, head of security and tell him you are preventing Kieron Philips from leaving the ship." That caught him off guard just enough. I push my card under the infrared reader so it beeps. Then I'm running down the gangway, technically I'm now checked out, my face is on his computer and I've already passed him. Hunter may know within seconds, but that could be a good thing.

Striding at a pace I fall in behind the two men fast on Ronni's 'six'. I lengthen my stride heading right to flank a four o'clock position checking left and right for any other followers. The police sirens start up again and the cars pass me. I spot the man in green sitting between two uniformed officers on their way out of the port. Everyone is preoccupied with the police car, everyone except Hunter, who is standing on the gangway, watching me. I hold his gaze for just a second, point to my eyes and then to Ronni, then make a wide berth to exaggerate that I'm following two men. He will understand my signals and that they're following Ronni. Now we'll see if he wants in on the money. I focus on Ronni, carefully gaining on the two men.

Leaving the dock, they mix with cruise passengers, funnelling through security at a port gate into Panama's second largest city. Outside the port gate is a transport centre, where boats meet taxis and trains, and hawkers sell tours. Almost all the guests are walking purposefully left, but Ronni turns right, like she knows where she's going, but she definitely doesn't know she's being followed.

A few blocks further ahead, Ronni turns down a side street, the two men look before following. We're heading downtown, and it feels dangerous, she is exposed. Sensing she could be taken in seconds, I break into a jog. I hear footfall behind me, heavy and accelerating. Trouble in front, trouble behind. Without looking back, I dart sideways into a derelict shop doorway, ready to turn and strike.

Chapter 12 – Turn and strike

Hunter tucks in with me and passes me a handgun.

"That's my pistol. Don't use it."

"Why would I do that?"

He is close enough for me to notice he's wearing a bulletproof vest under his white uniform jacket. That was fast dressing.

"You take the opposite side, you have a more likely angle to shoot from," I suggest, seeing he has the gunman's other gun, the large semi-automatic. His look shows he is not used to taking orders, but he is better equipped so he does it, without the need for further explanation. Like me, he has been in a street situation like this before.

I'm nervous. In Helmand Province, I had a full kit; helmet, vest, boots, ammunition, medical pack, comms and a gun I could use. I haven't even counted the rounds in my clip, because however many it is, it's all I've got. Exposing myself more than I'd like, I forward cross the junction, festooned with cables hanging from corner to corner. City development has not stretched to these zero value back streets, where the once brightly painted verandas are faded and torn. Hunter and I dig into opposite doorways; unless Ronni is in danger, we've no need to escalate the situation. The two bandits appear to have lost her, backtracking slowly towards us, kicking in every door, hoping to expose their prey. Now frustrated, they will be at their most trigger-happy. I look across at Hunter and it strikes me he is also wearing gloves in this heat. Using the gunman's semi-auto is no accident. Can he be doing this for his split of the money? But then he doesn't know about the money, or does he? What's his motive for helping us? Putting himself in danger? And he knows he's in danger. Or is this just instinct; 'never leave a man behind'. Maybe Hunter did speak to Ronni this morning and there's more to this than I know.

The two gangsters are exchanging fast chat. I see them each side of a shop front, egging each other on to enter first, panicking that their moment of hesitation, of indecision, could lead to their last breath. One is by the first door, the other by the second. This could be the time for us to move but it would mean a gunfight in the street, which could cause the neighbours to join in, and they will all have guns. That could lead to random fire from anywhere; we both wait.

A window breaks, the nearest man is unexpectedly ripped from the sidewalk and snatched inside. His partner calls out.

"Manuel?"

Two flashes from inside with the dull double bang of a pistol, then a tense silence. Both Hunter and I have the remaining combatant in our crosshairs. The shots sounded controlled like they might be Ronni. If we start shooting, the sound of shots outside could invite unnecessary risk. If they weren't her shots, we're too late.

Another crash and a body bounces on the sidewalk in a shower of broken glass and as it settles it is soon obvious that it's not Ronni in her white officer's uniform. Hunter and I continue to hold positions. A car screams around the corner and slides sideways, mounting the sidewalk in front of the remaining gunman who rushes into the building. That was uncontrolled driving, and the vehicle looks a wreck.

Four armed men get out of the car advancing aggressively, guns aimed at the house. Ronni doesn't stand a chance against five of them. We have no choice. Hunter and I move forward in sync.

"Hey!" I shout.

Why did I do that? I've a raised gun that I can't shoot, and no vest on! Hunter rains bullets taking out each of the four before they could shoot me. Before I can feel like the expendable diversion I move to the doorway, check it's clear, then stand guard flanking it. Hunter is by the car looking into the shop. I hear gunfire behind me and a body fall. I don't turn.

"Clear inside!" It's Ronni shouting.

"Clear outside Ronni, what's that in the wall?" Hunter shouts back, inching forward, him looking in inquisitively, me looking out for any movement anywhere.

I hear banging and ripping and falling rubble, Hunter is peering in, trying to see what's there.

"Ronni?" he shouts.

"You got transport?" Ronni shouts back from inside.

"Four door saloon, doors open, engine running," I inform her.

"Open the trunk," she demands.

"Stay put," Hunter says to me, rounding the car, swinging the doors open without leaving prints and moving the four bodies clear of the wheels.

I scan every door and window in the street.

"Clear. Good job as I don't have a gun I can use."

I hear thuds down by my feet, something heavy is being thrown around but I can't take my eyes off the street. We're vulnerable and this is taking way too long.

"Clocks ticking," I urge.

Ronni moves up to my shoulder.

"Nice, we have loads of transport. Hold your position," she says and vanishes again.

My eyes flick back and forth, up and down the street, knowing we will be attacked by either fellow gang members or police. More thuds drop around my feet.

"Ronni, we need to go. I'm on holiday!"

"OK," she says calmly joining me and handing me a pistol from one of the dead, "I'll get you a bucket and spade."

Ronni ducks down and underarm throws parcels to Hunter who throws them into the car's rear footwell.

"Bullseye Ronni, keep it coming," Hunter shouts.

I stand with two guns held pointing out, but that's daft. Not only does it look like a cheap movie but I would not know which gun to use and which one not to shoot if it kicked off. I belt Hunter's private pistol and check the remaining pistol. At last, I am armed and I look down and see what they are playing catch with.

"Is that what I think it is?"

"Walls here are made of hundred dollar bills," Ronni says still throwing.

"Shit. Should we be doing this?" I ask, still not taking my eyes off the street.

"It might be a bad decision, but can we think about it later?" Ronni says dragging a body to the rear of the car, where she and Hunter bundle it in. Ronni moves round to the driver's seat and gets in, reversing it ready to escape.

Hunter breaks open a bundle of money and scatters notes over the street.

"So thoughtful Hunter. This place looks like it could do with some financial help."

Then he's done and gets in the car.

"Let's go!" Ronni shouts.

Uncertain whether we should have taken the money or indeed a dead body, but needing to leave, I leap into the car and close the door. Ronni pulls the car away quietly and slowly, although it might be struggling with the weight. Hunter throws the last notes into the wind. Ronni indicates before turning left.

"Did she just indicate?" Hunter jokes.

"I think she did, Hunter. Think she was sending up a flare saying foreign driver in town."

"Well I was turning left," Ronni argues.

"She was turning left, Hunter," I repeat.

"She's a compliance officer, they like to do everything properly," Hunter mocks.

"OK fine, no more signals." She puts her foot down.

"Wouldn't want you to get arrested Ronni, you do whatever's in the Panamanian highway code."

Hunter reaches over and fist bumps her.

"Now keep your hand on the wheel." He smiles and fist bumps me.

"How are we ever going to get back on that ship with all this... or are we?" I ask.

Chapter 13 – Bag of Chicken

A street of shops reveals a lot about a place; its wealth, diet and its ability to produce and consumer goods. Most of the world sells cheap goods mass-produced in Asia and this area is no exception. An argument between two shop owners is not about the amount of sidewalk they occupy, it's over a sofa. Well, not a sofa it is makeshift cardboard. One is selling a cheap garden bench with cushions on, and his commercial neighbour is offering three plastic chairs together with folded cardboard stretched across a blanket thrown over with cushions and at half the price; it's not quite the battle to sell sofas we're used to in the west. I need to pass by quickly as it is getting nasty and drawing a crowd, which might be the purpose if they are super clever.

I left Ronni in the car a few blocks back and I can see the nose of the vehicle just revealed down a side street. I'm being watched by Hunter, on the other side of the road, who is buying a coffee he'll probably never drink. I'm trying to act every bit the 'cruise tourist', even though there do not appear any others that have strayed this far downtown and I need to hurry. He stands out, a tall fit naval officer in his white uniform, which helps me to be invisible. I begin to fear I might not find what I need here, a tourist area would be better, but the car we have is a huge risk and travelling in it has to be limited. Hunter certainly could not sit in it unnoticed.

Feeling increasingly conspicuous, I buy a dull and forgettable hat. A man with a hat can be two people, hat on, hat off.

I also buy a doll of a Panamanian man with a donkey, I need to blend in a bit now I only have one twenty-dollar bill and a few small notes, the rest are big ones. It was all the small money we had between us.

A small kid approaches me with his hand out. I'm hit with a flashback of a homeless, parentless kid on the streets of Syria. One of many, starving, injured and displaced children whose images will never leave me, you just have to learn how to live with the memories, and the PTSD. I reach out just touch the boy's cheek, I need just to feel he is alive.

"What d'you need, buddy?" I ask him with an American accent.

"Eat?"

I want to feed him rather than give him money, which will go to a pimp. I'm subtly looking for his handler who'd no doubt see more value in me than the kid does.

"Food mister," he says, his tone changed to desperation.

If he's acting it is worthy of an award. A few shops up is a street café that has rotisserie chickens, but I really don't have time for this. This kid could easily pickpocket me if I was off guard, but he's not tried any of those moves. He looks thin and feeble. I drag him to the cafe then look across to Hunter who is shaking his head at me. He hasn't found the answer though, what we want might not be here.

"US dollars?" I ask at the cafe.

The owner nods, but I see no prices and he knows I'm not local so I guess he's imagining how much he can overcharge me, so I don't give him the opportunity.

"Chicken, a whole one, in a bag, and ten of those." I point at the flatbread wraps. As he serves me, I grab a plastic bag and fill it with four sodas from the fridge and some chocolate bars. He watches everything I take but I'm careful, and I offer him the only twenty I have.

"Keep the change," I say, and I see him trying to build the courage to tell me it's not enough, but I know it's more than enough and my look dictates the same. I invite the kid to help himself to food from inside my bag. As long as I have the food, I have the kid.

"I need your help," I tell him softly.

The kid looks up at me, fearing he might lose the food. Desperate to eat, he overfills his mouth.

"You can eat, it's OK, but take me to a shop to buy a bag. A big bag for all my clothes. For travel. And I need to buy make up, for my wife, nails, eyeliner." I mime, still being as American as I can, donkey doll under my arm.

The boy's hand dives into the bag again and grabs a handful of chicken then he pulls me over the road. This investment will save me time and achieve a goal that might have been tough. It's an old trick I used back when moving through the Middle-east.

There's an art in walking fast and eating at the same time, and this kid has mastered it. He finishes his fist full and wipes his hands and face on his shirt before dragging me into a shop I'd never have found alone. I look around for his handler, for any kind of trap but see nothing then I check Hunter is still across the road, keeping his distance.

The street kid introduces me to the owner in broken Spanish and some English. The Spanish part is no doubt claiming a finder's fee, I can interpret that without language skills. He deserves a commission. It's a shop with travel cases and unsurprisingly the owner starts at the top of the range. While I appreciate his salesmanship, bright white does not work for me.

"Dark, black?" I ask. "Man's case. Must have wheels - heavy."

The boy translates and the man almost moves to slap him with annoyance but controls himself. The kid backs away and I pass him the food bag. If he runs now, the job is done. Then it hits me that he could report back that he's found a rich American, but he has not run, he is looking at the little school bags near the front of the shop. The owner looks from the boy to me as he points to a huge case, discarded at the back of other stock.

"Expensive," he offers.

Cost's not an issue, so I nod. As the owner digs it out, I notice the kid has taken a liking to a pink rucksack with a cartoon on it.

"You want a rucksack, kid?" I ask him.

"My sister. School."

He sneaks a crafty handful from the chicken bag and hides his chewing in a smile. I give him the chicken bag and he turns to the pink bag. He is boldly asking the man for the pink bag as his commission, I'm amused and impressed by his confidence. The shopkeeper would rather shoo him out, but he wants my sale. I can see the kid is thinking of running now he has the food and I don't want the kid to go. Hunter might not take too kindly to a kid running, who knows what or who he is running to or why.

"I'll pay for the kid's bag at the end," I offer and look to the boy and give a thumbs up. If Hunter thinks he's a leak, it could be the kid's last day's work, ship uniform or not. He must stay in here until I can walk him out.

Chapter 14 – Big case

"Big case." The owner spins the large case at me.

It might hold a lot but we will never lift it.

"One hundred litres," is his hard sell pulling out the telescopic handle, as if I needed to have suitcase explained to me. He straightens his shirt and tries to look smart.

I bend down and flip it open, knowing the Russian doll effect will reveal another case. The owner thinks it hugely funny. We can't do this inside the car. I guess the maximum size, eighty to a hundred pounds each is absolute maximum.

"Four wheels, this big. Four cases." I sign as I speak.

The footwell and rear seat are piled high with tightly vacuum-packed stacks of one hundred dollar bills. Every moment they are on show, we're at risk. Every moment I stay here many things are at risk. At a guess, the money fills these two large cases but we would not be mobile.

"Forty litres." He smiles. "And inside, thirty litres."

I pull the descriptive bag tag from the set and torment myself with the maths and memory of what is stacked poorly in the car and moving money for the government in the Middle East.

I've lost the attention of the shop-keeper who has pushed me further into the back of the shop. He walks to the front to meet two local men who have just walked in with their own youngster. I can see they are both packing guns in their belts so I hide amongst the stock at the back. I can see Hunter outside has got closer and is watching. If they have come looking for me then the two kids could both be collateral damage in a shootout.

The kid with them looks at my boy eating, snatches the bag and pushes him into the wall. He is the son of bullies, and I can't volunteer to get involved. The kid looks to me for help and I wave him away. My simple action tries to convey so much so fast; ignore me, don't worry.

The shopkeeper opens his till and shows it is empty, but they hustle his pockets for the notes he has and I relax because it is a local protection racket. As much as I would like to do something about it, I can't and they leave.

I see the perfect case, solid, four wheels and claiming another inside. Two sets of two would be perfect. One hundred thousand dollars is just over four inches, ten of those is a million. We have a shit load of money.

Re-focussing, I figure the bricks were standard four-and-a-half-inch stacks. All American bills are the same size, six inches by two and a half, they could be ones, they could be hundreds which is why Stevie Wonder used to demand to be paid in single dollars. I'm betting without looking that ours are all one hundred dollar bills and I've a couple in my pocket. Not great in a local market but the guy needs the cash if he is being hustled.

The small case will fit three stacks deep by two stacks wide, and four across and fill the depth. There must be millions there, and it will weigh hundreds of pounds.

"This size, four." I mime four fingers and point at the slightly larger one. I also see a plain square canvas backpack, almost military. I pull a flatted one from the flat stack piled high.

The owner shows me the case but I don't need to see it. They are both dark red, dark enough to be neutral. I nod to hurry him.

"Expensive. Strong," he says but I am already sold.

I take my canvas bags to the till to make it look like he might lose the sale and he begins to speed up and wheels both cases forward.

"Plus these six bags, I'm done," I say closing the case flat backpacks.

I wheel both cases towards my young assistant and see that from where the pink back satchel came there is one in blue. I offer it to him.

"Both?" I offer.

His eyes widen and I turn with it.

"How much?" I ask.

"All?" the man questions in surprise, again trying to compute a price he can get from me.

"Mister?" The kid pulls at me.

I turn and smile at him hoping a price will materialise soon.

"Your wife!" the boy says.

I am confused, but, he doesn't give up and he moves towards the door and points out eye make-up and lipstick. Now I remember. I focus on the nail varnish and look to the owner, miming taking off the nail varnish. He smiles, and between us, in this game of Charades he's understood and offers me nail polish remover. Two I signal. The shop owner has seen all the makeup we have taken, so I stuff it in the pink bag to complete the ruse.

"One hundred thirty-five dollars." He announces as confidently as he can.

What a payday for him. I only have two hundred and I know he has no change. I slide two notes out of my pocket.

"This is all I have, just been to the bank," I declare.

The owner is in shock but he won't let a Benjamin or two slip away.

"No have change," he says offering me a small number of small notes he had hidden away from the till.

I pull a couple of tee-shirts from his shelf and take the cash with a gesture asking if we are square and he agrees superfast. What I want to give him now is the pistol I have in my belt, the one Ronni gave me in the house. It must have my prints on, it is just the worst move I could make.

"Kid, take the cases and wait for me outside."

The kid wheels them out super fast. I pull the gun from my belt. The shopkeeper throws the two hundred dollars back at me and puts his hands up.

"No, pick them up. You ever used one of these?"

He shakes his head as I clean it with a tee shirt and the nail polish liquid.

"Keep it under the till. I was never here, right? Never."

The shopkeeper takes the money and the gun. It could be the worst move I ever made but he needs help. I give him two more notes and leave the shop.

My young assistant wheels one of the luggage pairs, feeling very proud of himself. But I have taken the other one and am setting the pace. I hand him his sister's new bag as he walks, then his.

"Thanks, mister." He says hugging my arm. There are some things in life money can't buy.

As we arrive at the main street, I give him most of the local money as my ride drives up and stops.

Hunter, who has been tailing me, takes a case and the excited over-helpful child runs to the trunk and flips it open. I'm too late, I can't stop him.

Chapter 15 – Not the trunk

If the world was ever in any doubt about how fast decisions are made, how quickly a trigger might be pulled, how easily a child can die, then the speed Hunter moves to slam the trunk shut is a frightening reminder. I saw a glimpse of the body, thankfully the child never did. He never had the chance. Had he seen the body there might have been four of us in the car driving away, but he was lucky.

"Trunk's full. We'll manage." I high-five him and ease him away from the car.

"Clocks ticking," Ronni says.

"For your girlfriend!" I tease the kid, pushing all the make-up except the nail polish remover into his new school bag.

"I'll buy more at the airport this afternoon. You have a great day."

It's a story planted as misdirection in case the child is interrogated about us. I watch him run across the street dancing with the traffic.

"Can't adopt them all." Hunter hurries me.

Hunter knows about my daughter. He rounds the car with one case, opens the back door and slides in. I get in the front with the other case.

"Comfortable in the front you two?" Hunter asks.

"Yep," we both answer in unison.

"How exactly am I supposed to get this case open here in the back?" Hunter moans.

"You should've seen the bigger one."

I open mine and pull the small one out. One between my legs in the footwell and I hold the other ready. I adjust the rearview mirror to watch him and he has opened his.

"I wasn't using that," Ronni digs.

"It's a bit small." Hunter moans, finding the inner case.

"I guessed the small one will hold just under four million, the larger one maybe six million," I offer.

"Maybe," Hunter says filling it with money bricks.

"The woman on the plane had four smaller cases, because of the weight. We'll manage."

I reach back, but it is awkward in the small car.

"Let's fill them, get them back to the ship and see if we have time for a second trip then," Hunter suggests.

"No," both Ronni and I say in unison.

Not having access to blocks of money while Hunter is packing the first case I watch until he closes it with almost exactly what I had computed. Hunter passes it forward to me. I slide it onto Ronni's lap.

"So, I'll be off, nice knowing you guys," Ronni jokes struggling to drive over the case.

"Don't sell yourself short."

I pass my larger empty case back and lift my smaller empty case to the side window on my thigh as Hunter passes me the second and larger filled case.

"That is heavy!"

I am twisting awkwardly with what must be a hundred pounds in weight.

"It would be heavier if it held six mil', but it doesn't," Hunter says.

I push my seat back on the runners to get it down between my legs, ease the empty one back then take Ronni's and hold it on my lap. I must be holding around ten million dollars.

Hunter has filled the two rear cases now lying on the back seat and is now filling one canvas bag with what we could call loose change. Four canvas bags are tucked on top and Hunter folds the blanket used as camouflage.

"We've enough bags to go back," Hunter suggests.

"No. The locals will have found the money blowing about at that safe house by now. It will be mayhem."

"Hopefully," Hunter adds because that was his plan.

"You think they'll be ripping the rest of the walls down in a cash frenzy, or too frightened?" Ronni asks.

"Who can resist used bank notes blowing in the wind?" Hunter says philosophically.

"Obviously not us," I add.

"If it looks like the locals took it, we're away clean." Hunter smiles.

"How much more was in there?"

"It seemed endless!" Ronni says, "But I stopped at around twenty-one million, seven each. No point in being too greedy."

"You were counting?"

"We could probably buy a small island," Hunter says.

I awkwardly reach in my pocket for the nail varnish remover then rip a tee-shirt into rag sections.

"Let's clean the guns."

"Then torch the car," Hunter adds.

"I feel like a bank robber," Ronni says.

Is this a dream? Do I wake up tomorrow with seven million dollars? There is a saying, that when something seems too good to be true, then it probably isn't true. Or is there a saying, or my guilt? I look round, out of the windows, pinch myself, and realise it's a nightmare.

"Suggested plan; Kieron, we drop you at the bus station. Sit and wait with the four cases. We take the car a few blocks away, put the body in the driver's seat, scatter money all around, leave the pistols and burn it. When you see us come back, hail a taxi to the train station. We'll hail another cab and follow you," Hunter finishes.

"Train? Are you running with this?" I ask thinking of Auli'i.

"Where could we go in the USA with this amount of cash? It's useless, which is why they cement it in walls; the ship is our only way out," Hunter suggests.

"I got a better idea," Ronni offers. "Leave me at the bus stop with twenty-mil. Then you two can go wherever you like."

"Don't you think friends are worth more than money?" I throw in, lost in this tale.

"We'll see won't we," Hunter says in a testing moment of truth. "I'll take my pistol."

"It's all I have to protect this."

"Where's the gun Ronni gave you?"

"I dumped that in the shop."

The car stops at the bus stop before I can be interrogated further. Hunter holds the look then confirms his orders.

"Let's start with looping out to the train, if we're not followed, back to the ship," he says.

Hunter opens his door and passes out the two cases but keeps the canvas bag with about a hundred thousand dollars in.

I get out with a struggle, the cases do weigh around over forty kilos each, quite a workout. I stand with four matching heavy dark red cases and watch the car pull away and I'm alone, with what feels like a target on my back, front and forehead.

I've carried money over the border to tribe leaders and never taken a dollar. Never this much. I'm at a bus stop with twenty mil', give or take, determined that not one dollar's going back to the drug cartel. Ever.

How did this happen? How did I get here, and will I ever get out of Panama alive?

Chapter 16 – Panama Bus

Cristóbal is a busy, over-crowded place. There's a wealth of expensive cars, top hotels, offices with workers supporting what might be an affluent future, and streets full of poorer people. The buildings that are well-kept are painted in vibrant pastel colours, the amenities and street furniture hangs in tatters.

I sit watching buses come and go, those queuing around me get replaced with each bus, leaving me here conspicuously alone until the next crowd forms waiting for a bus that I don't catch. The cab drivers have noticed and I keep having to wave them away, so others will have noticed too. If I could manage the weight I'm guarding I might walk around a little, the smaller cases are not too bad, the larger cases are hard to manage, over a hundred pounds. With four cases, I have two hundred pounds on each arm. That can never look pretty; I have to sit tight.

An explosion cracks above the din of traffic. Most bystanders don't flinch, but I've been waiting for it. A thick black plume of smoke rises up, ten or more blocks away. Progress is being made. I'm alone again as another bus leaves but a policeman has taken interest in me now, just as the finish line is in sight. Where are they?

Ronni is a welcome sight on the other corner, towering above the local Panamanians. I hail a cab. It may not legally be allowed to stop here at the bus terminus, but I'm a tourist and they'll want the premium. The driver looks at the policeman advancing in the distance as he flips the trunk from the comfort of his driver's seat. I play the superhero, lifting the two heavier cases into the trunk first, knowing I can't show effort. The policeman has me in his sights and is striding fast.

"Prisa!" the driver shouts.

The third case is harder to fit in, there is no way his boot will hold four. The trunk full, I slam the lid. I look up knowing I'm going to struggle with manipulating forty kilos onto the back seat through the small back door, but I fill with relief as I see Hunter catch the policeman with a question to divert his attention. By the time he is free to look back, I'm in the cab and it is moving.

"Train station," I say.

I see Ronni hailing her own cab.

"You could walk to Atlantic terminal," he says too late as he has started to take me however few blocks it may be.

"Bags are heavy and I'm tired. Getting old," I excuse.

"Tell me, brother," he sympathises.

I suspect this man is younger than me but looks like he's had a hard life. Not that mine has been easy, it started in Northern Ireland when I was a squaddie and got worse, putting a Q on the end of IRA; nothing much changed apart from the sunshine.

The short drive is unexciting. The cruise ship is occasionally visible and so close I could just leave the cash and walk back, but somehow that doesn't seem like an option now. This is not a route any tourist would walk. When we stop, I'm confused. It looks like a shed, a platform with a roof, not a famous station. Is this the right one?

I pay the taxi driver with half the few small local notes and coins that were hidden away from the till in the shop, leaving him counting for a beat so I can quickly retrieve my own cases. I lean the two smaller cases on the slightly larger ones, back to back to self-standing on their four wheels. The cab driver gets out,

"Not enough," he says holding out the money, and indicating back towards his meter which I know wasn't working. Now that the fare's in contention my ability to pay might be. I offer him more local money from all I have, he takes it all and curses walking away. My worst thought is that if this is the wrong station all I've got are Benjamin's, mucho de Benjamin's, and those big notes will cause a bigger problem.

To my great relief, Ronni arrives by cab, jumps out and looks around before walking up to me.

"We weren't followed, let's go," she manages between mouthfuls.

She has only half eaten the wrap in the white plastic bag but tosses it into an old oil can. Two children run for it quicker than a flock of London pigeons. We have enough money to feed all the kids in Panama in these cases, but we probably wouldn't get out of the country alive. Ronni takes two cases and I pull the other two easily.

"I'm out of local money," I tell her.

"I have small notes, should we wait for Hunter?" she asks.

"He didn't say to."

"This is not a drill, right?" she asks reflecting back on the madness.

A taxi circles in and stops. It drops an elderly couple off who pay.

"Is this the Great Panamanian railroad?" they ask the driver.

I had the same thought, it's not exactly a tourist attraction but we would like their taxi before they change their minds. The taxi driver nods to them and as they walk away Ronni steps forward to snatch the cab.

"Cruise terminal?" Ronni asks and the driver nods, too lazy to get out.

Ronni joins me at the trunk, lifting the cases.

"I guess the load will feel lighter when it's spread between the four of us," I offer.

"Four?" Ronni asks.

"Me, you, Hunter, and Georgie?"

"Georgie wasn't running around the streets with a gun today," Ronni whispers meaningfully heading for a car door.

As our car swings around and accelerates away. I ponder Georgie's exclusion despite us being included in her find. Then glance back to see the local children chasing a few hundred-dollar bills that are blowing in the wind.

Chapter 17 – On ship

Neither Ronni or I rush at the dock gates. Our cruise cards are checked with just a glance, as the only required form of identity to enter the secure dock area. Technically we have left the country, but we are still very much at risk even in this secure perimeter. I let Ronni go off ahead. This morning she was definitely a target. I stop, turn, then look through my pockets scanning all around. I leave my cases, walk a few steps back and pick up an imaginary dropped item as the idiot tourist abroad and pocket it. Hunter strides past me swinging the empty canvas bags I bought.

"Let's go. Take the gangway to security," he says ignoring me.

At the bottom of the gangway, Ronni waits for me, but she's looking past me scanning the dock.

"It looks clear," she says.

"All we have to do is walk on board."

I join the long queue of returning passengers from their half-day visit. At the top, we can see every bag, handbag, camera, water bottle or souvenir being placed on the conveyor belt for the x-ray machine. This is where it all goes wrong.

Hunter re-appears from inside and looks at the queue. He's not in uniform so talks to the officer next to him, who then addresses everyone.

"OK lovely guests, we are going to speed this up so you can all get upstairs for tea," he delivers with an expensive smile.

A cheer rises from the crowd.

"Those with the bigger bags and cases, like you two, follow Senior Officer Hunter Witowski, head of security, round to the large x-ray machine at the forward staircase," he explains pointing at us.

My cruise card is taken, scanned and I follow Hunter with what seems like a good plan, but with other guests who may not have been expected. I let them overtake. By the time we arrive at the x-ray machine, their bags are going through. Hunter stops them.

"Can I look inside?"

He finds two bottles of vodka. That is what they were trying to smuggle on board and must have felt this would give them a better chance.

"I'm afraid you're not allowed to take these on board from a port, so I will need to take them and stow them until you leave the ship, then they'll be returned," Hunter says to them.

The machine has now stopped and switched off. Hunter produces a pad and offers it to the guests to fill in, taking the two bottles, placing them in a box and adding the tear slip from the form they are filling. They are not pleased they have been caught but while they are writing Ronni manually pushes our cases through. As they appear the other side Hunter manually pulls them out and I lift them down. Four cases. Hunter waves us on.

Four cases of money and a gun still tucked in my belt, we turn back into the guest area of the ship, Ronni looks at me. I feel exhausted.

"I share a room, you'll have to take them," she says.

"I could do with a little help."

"You'll manage."

She vanishes and once again I am left with all four cases.

Chapter 18 – Four Cases

I leap from my bed. My cabin door opening has me rolling to the floor, porthole window side, sidearm raised at the intruder with my bed as a shield. My mind is racing.

"At ease soldier. Nice reactions, you might have lived," Hunter says pocketing his master key card.

He throws the empty canvas army bags on the bed and takes the blue 'sleeping / clean room' card, re-opens my door and hangs it on the handle, closing the door. I assume he's not asked for the room to be cleaned.

Hunter takes his pistol from me and checks the clip.

"How on earth did you get through security with this?" His sarcasm shows his power on the ship.

He slides it into his belt and turns to the cases.

"Why have you got all four cases?"

"Ronni has a roommate."

"No she doesn't," he states confidently, then "or maybe she does. Lucky guy."

He tips the contents of the first case onto the bed. Large plastic-wrapped bricks of one hundred dollar bills. Some broken into smaller bricks that need mending.

"Wow. It is real. A hundred thousand dollars a pack?"

I stand in awe then lift and tip a second caseload out on his and my bed is already looking full. We both stop for a moment and marvel at the enormous amount of money.

"You ever had to handle this much for Queen and country?" Hunter asks.

"Not this much, and I never even thought of taking a single pound for myself."

We tip the final two cases out, bricks bouncing to the floor until the bed is definitely full.

"This would give the cabin steward a heart attack!"

Hunter smiles, shaking every last piece of dry crumbled plaster from the case then wiping the inside clean. I follow his lead and we place the smaller cases in the larger ones. I stack mine on the top shelf of my open wardrobe.

"I don't know who she's sleeping with, but she can have two empty cases in plain sight. Just in case either yours or her room is searched," he says.

"Where are you going to put the money?"

Hunter recovers the canvas bags, and from inside he pulls a bundle of green plastic bags.

"Ten small bricks make a big one, maybe there's seven each."

"How about Georgie?" I ask.

"One more person to talk loosely after a glass of wine?" Hunter suggests. "What she doesn't know can't hurt her and it looked to me like she was having a hard enough time dealing with a much smaller sum."

He does know about the other cash. He may be right about her, but it doesn't feel right. He can see I am still thinking on it.

"We've dodged bullets for Queen and country, and now in the streets of South America. Now it's our time," Hunter persuades.

He's not wrong. We've both spent a lifetime avoiding death and its time to retire properly. Being discharged after 30 years' service meant I lost my pension, and why? Because I helped some children against orders. Retirement for me will be taking this to Syria and working on a relief campaign for orphaned children. This is more than enough, maybe even to fund a children's home back in the UK too, though they will ask where the money came from.

"Six, maybe seven million for three is not much different to five million for four," I suggest.

"This is the kind of money people kill for." Hunter flicks his knife open, slits the plastic. "She can't play that game."

As he wraps the green plastic around a million-dollar brick, I know he's right. Even knowing about this kind of money could be a death sentence. My cabin phone rings.

"Ee?"

"Hi dad, did you go out? I slipped out, got lost and was late back."

"You're lucky they didn't sail without you."

"They wouldn't sail without me! I have friends on the bridge," she jokes.

"Friends on the bridge?"

"Yeah. Friends. So much I need to tell you, can I come to your cabin," she offers.

"I'm just getting in the shower."

"I'll be there before you shower, it's kind of important," she insists.

"Can it wait until tonight? I have to do the Panama commentary, I need to get changed and go."

"OK. Sure. I just wanted to say hi, and see you before you did it," she says with concern.

"Hey. I'll be fine."

"I know you will, but I want to see you first," Auli'i insists.

"I'll come to your show later. Now stop worrying. There's nothing to worry about," I assure her, looking at the money which she can't see.

"Good luck, Dad. Love you," she says.

The phone goes dead, and it felt like something wasn't right. I think of ringing her back but Hunter takes the phone and dials.

"Ronni, come to Kieron's; E178."

"Ee sounded worried like something was wrong, maybe I should go and see her?"

"We need you here, this is going to take time. Even with three of us," Hunter says.

Working like a well-oiled team, one holds the bundle tight, the other binds it. The haul eventually consumes much less space wrapped properly. Twenty large bricks stacked on the floor and the bed is still covered in loose notes. All three of us stand looking at it.

"Didn't make seven each. I said we should have done a second run," Hunter says grabbing a handful of notes, maybe thirty thousand but it seems like nothing.

"That's way more than retirement money," Ronni suggests.

"I'm already retired," I offer, collecting a pile of loose notes, "Where do we keep it?"

Hunter lifts the end of my bed which hinges up, money flying everywhere, to reveal a blanket cupboard.

"Here? Me?"

Hunter bends, collects and throws one to Ronni.

"They may have been better in half a million stacks," she says swaying with the catch.

"I like that they are not easy to move," Hunter says.

Ronni stacks the meter-long green blocks neatly at the head end replacing blankets forward. I am left collecting loose notes from around the room.

"That was an upper body work out," she offers, finishing.

We stand, looking at the haul as the ship's thrusters power which means we are moving sideways away from the dock. Engines power up and there is a little vibration as they work against each other in a manoeuvre. We have to transit the three locks of Gatun before it gets dark, and I'm due to do a commentary. Hunter tosses the canvas bags in and drops the bed down and the three of us start to collect up loose change, maybe a hundred thousand each.

"I'm about to be late for my proper retirement job, I need to put a shirt and tie on."

"Open neck is fine on the bridge during the day. You don't want to look like a school teacher," Ronni says.

I pull my shirt off and turn the shower on but neither of them seems to take the hint.

"We're sailing."

"They'll be singing that on deck," Ronni says.

"Funny," I offer, as if it was a joke, to both of them heading for the door. Ronni turns.

"No joke, they'll be singing and waving flags. The great British sail away party. You should go and experience it."

"You're serious?"

She nods but Hunter stops her at the door and her smile disappears.

"One more thing."

He pushes the door closed, Ronni is pinned against it, he is in by the closet and I am in the bathroom. Three of us in a tight space as he produces another security picture from the airport. This one is a camera view of Ronni watching the Latin woman being searched. Ronni has been circled.

"The police came on board just before I came down. They asked if this was one of our guests."

"Well, I'm not, a guest," Ronni says concerned.

"Correct. That's why I said 'no'."

Chapter 19 – I am sailing

Now I've seen everything. The upper lido deck and bar are full of guests happily singing, 'Rule Britannia' obviously not getting its true slight against King George II's decision of a land army by his son Frederick, who was ready to take over and wanted a strong navy fleet. Sadly, the prince died before he could enjoy his right to the throne. Guests are massed against the rail overlooking the pool on the deck below, waving flags. I look up, expecting to see a flyover by the Red Arrows.

I try to get to the rail to look down at the lido deck inquisitive as to what is at the centre of this jingoistic rally but there's no way. The very merry guests are packed a few people deep. I go for the stairs to gain a view, hoping this doesn't turn into a conga, but even the stairs are busy.

Eventually, I get to see the epicentre. This explosion of excitement is emanating from Georgie on the sun-kissed mezzanine deck opposite, supported by her team, all in slacks, white shirts and blazers, doing a well-rehearsed routine, waving and singing. They all wear headset microphones so their hands are free. I'm going to ask for one of those when I'm on stage, I want my hands free to gesticulate.

The song ends, and the odd notes now tinkling in the background of her enthusing hype are recognisably the start of Rod Stewart's 'I am Sailing'. I'm sure there have been other versions, it can't be an original song, but he owns it now. The crowd cheer wildly; they know what's coming. Georgie and her team are now parading, that's the only word for it, down the stairs each side of their raised staging to the wooden edge of the pool, addressing all the guests. It's not a record playing, I can see a pianist and a band left on the mezzanine that Georgie has vacated. They are repeating the opening bars of the sailing anthem and watching for a cue. They will last for as long as Georgie wants and she is up to something.

"Ladies and Gentlemen, Boys and Girls, some of our fabulous entertainers are leaving the ship over the next few days. I want you to welcome, the comedian from Havana, Cuba. Manuel!" Georgie shouts up, and waves to a smart looking man with a moustache who has appeared at the front of the mezzanine stage.

"Come-on down Manuel," she shouts.

Manuel runs down the steps and joins them around the edge of the pool, arms waving, hips gyrating with each step to show his Latin dance sexuality.

"And one of the West End's most talented singers, Elaine!"

Elaine walks to the front, beaming, and waves.

"Drink, Sir," a waiter asks me.

I'm so tempted to join this party and enjoy myself, but no, I wave him on with a smile. Not a sailing type wave, a no thank you type wave.

"Elaine, come on down!"

Elaine trots down the stairs and joins the team on the other side of the pool, but Manuel is stealing that show. "Let's have a big round of applause for Elaine and Manuel!" Georgie shouts.

The crowd oblige with cheers and applause, they really do respect the work the entertainers put in, or there is an alcohol-fuelled pack mentality at work, well primed so nothing will fail. Except maybe me who will, very shortly be giving quite a dry commentary through the locks. Seeing this show from the crowd, I might just start with the line, 'had Britain continued to be part of the original plan for the canal in 1843, it might have been called The Atlantic and Pacific 'British' Canal, and been bigger, and better'. Wow!

"And, there is one more entertainer I want you all to meet, because you'll be meeting him very shortly as he takes you through the Panama Canal with his expert knowledge…"

Georgie shouts turning my way, arm up and pointing straight at me.

How did she see me amongst the crowd? Hidden on these stairs? The world has stopped. A sea of faces turns to me in slow motion and I freeze. Embarrassed, I hear nothing but an echo of cheers fading to a low dangerous note.

"Let's give a great seafaring welcome to the wonderfully handsome, charismatic, military hero, Commander Kieron Philips! Come on down Kieron!"

She didn't just do that, did she? Am I now waving and smiling? The first lesson of undercover work is to blend in, act like a local, be seen as a local, never be seen at all, though I might not give them Manuel's Latin hips. I think I'm going to be singing along with Rod any minute; I remember now, it was the Sutherland Brothers, they sang the original it's their song my inner self protests.

Chapter 20 – and quiver

Life on the bridge of this cruise ship is far more sparkling, spacious and polite than a military ship, but there are similarities. So much so, I'm fearful of becoming too familiar with the crew. If I was making crew announcements on a military ship, officers would pour a pint of milk down the back of my pants, tie shoelaces together or much worse to sabotage my speech. Even though we have slowed right down, the lock system is getting closer far too quickly. I look from the huge sea gate of the canal to the sheets I've hardly even scanned since printing them from the computer, up to those officers who I seriously consider will be testing me before we've gone through the three chambers. I can tell, I'm being ignored professionally by them all.

CRUISE SHIP HEIST – OCEAN ATLANTIC

As I spread my notes out on the sill below the newly cleaned huge windows of the bridge, the Captain begins an announcement. "Ladies and Gentlemen, it is the 'Cap-it-ain' speaking from the bridge."

He has a way of adding an 'I' between the 'p' and the 't' and making the 'ain' sharper than reality would have it. I guess it is his stamp, his trademark on the announcements he makes. My eyes are fixed on him and the wry smile he speaks through. I know something is afoot.

"To say we have a real treat is an understatement; not only are we all about to transit the Panama Canal but to talk you through it, I hand you over to Commander Kieron Philips," he finishes.

A young officer now stands before me holding the Captain's microphone, which I am obliged to take. A little earlier than I had expected.

"Good afternoon everyone, and how lucky we are to have a pleasant sunny afternoon for our partial transit, because this side of Panama has four times the annual rainfall of the United Kingdom, and when it rains here, it buckets down! Today it looks like we can head towards Gatun Lake and sunset with a cocktail on deck with no need to consider wind or rain."

I am really performing for the Captain as I walk across the bridge to check the other side, microphone in hand. I pause because I can't be expected to talk continuously, can I?

The Captain nods, and I'm not sure if it's to me or to his crew. How much would I need to pay them to leave me alone to read my notes? I turn back to the other side of the bridge. My notes have gone. I've been concentrating on looking out of the window, on my first words of introduction, and someone has taken my notes. Not one of them offers me any eye connection. None of them are looking my way, not the Captain, not the officers and certainly not the local pilot. I turn and look out of the wing of the bridge back down the ship to the road bridge we just sailed through.

"We just passed what will be the third bridge that will span the Panama Canal. It will be known as the 'Atlantic Bridge'. The other bridges the 'Bridge of Americas' and the 'Centennial Bridge' are both on the Pacific side. The Canal, the road and the railway were all built to get to the Pacific and were in part fuelled by the gold rush. This new road bridge is a double-pylon bridge, double-plane, concrete girder, cable-stayed bridge with a main span of 530 meters, and two side spans of two hundred and thirty meters."

I slide the switch on the side of the microphone to off again and look to the officers for corrections as that was all done from memory. None are being offered, I am on my own and this whole transit commentary will have to be done from memory. I wonder how my vacation ended up being such a challenge on every front.

"Wind is a factor here, the tugboats you can see either side are shadowing our progress to the lock gates in order to ensure we're straight and on target. There's a call for bigger and more powerful tugs as the new canal extension has invited bigger cruise and container ships through that are affected more by the wind." I continue. "Whilst this ship has side thrusters if used they would disturb the water in the inlets too much, so tugboats are preferred and can do the job far more easily. You'll see the gate to the first chamber opening ready for us. In the middle of the forward two lock entrances, you will see a pier jutting out towards us, with the first of a number of small trains that we will become very familiar with. These are known as 'mules' and are not there to pull us through the locks. The ship's own forward thrust will perform that duty; the mules are there to keep the ship safely in the middle of the canal."

I slide the microphone switch off again for a moments breath. Just as I refuse to look for my stolen notes, the crew are ignoring my loss. The next section needs no explanation, even if I did have my text. I step forward and take in the engineering, which whilst basic and predictable like so many huge industrial feats from the late nineteenth century, it defies the lack of modern utilities we'd require to do such a job now. I raise my microphone to speak but am beaten by Captain Feldman on my right who whispers a reminder to me.

"Don't forget to tell them about the death toll, they love those figures," he offers.

Another officer leans in. "The height of water rise."

"And don't mention the drug trade," another says.

"No," agrees the Captain.

I'm being put through my paces as their day's entertainment. I can't take much more of this, so I switch the mic back on,

"The locks are not here because the Pacific Ocean and Atlantic Ocean are at different levels. Sea level is the same. The object is to cut through from coast to coast, through the mountainous rain forests, where water runs down from great heights and forms many small lakes which are much higher than the sea. To excavate this huge area all down to one sea level would still be impossible today, so the three chambers here at Gatun, will raise our ship in stages, eighty-five feet to the Gatun Lake, formed between 1907 and 1913 by the building of the Gatun Dam here in the Chagres Valley across the Chagres River. Then, it was the largest man-made dam and the largest man-made lake. And now our Captain would like to say a few words," I end passing him the microphone and smiling.

As he takes the microphone the crew on the bridge applaud briefly before he switches on and adds a few tales of his own. I'm sure not every lecturer is treated this way, but then not every holidaymaker has a shoot-out with a drug cartel as a day excursion.

My cruise has only just started.

Chapter 21- Crows Nest meet

The Crow's Nest bar is just above the Captain's bridge with similar views but it is now dark, beacons and lights shape the edge of the huge lake. Guests are relaxing with a drink and chatting, having had dinner. I have a gin and tonic, sitting alone by the window between two groups. A jazz ensemble plays in the centre of the upper level and it is a relaxing end to a crazy day.

I don't know how relaxed Ronni will be feeling right now, though I doubt she's overly worried about her picture being with the local police. My picture was on most wanted a few hours earlier, tomorrow it could be Georgie. She won't be as calm about it.

What I'd like to do, is to take the money from under my bed and hide it somewhere else, maybe in a lifeboat. Not that it matters, because if they kill me in order to get to the stash under the bed, I won't be alive to miss the money or laugh at them if it were not there. The band finish and a host enthusiastically announces that it will shortly be quiz time.

My chair's close enough to the group at the next table for them to instantly adopt me as an extra team member. Maybe they think I look like a quizzer or someone with knowledge. I can certainly answer questions on the canal, though that might be considered unfair. I see Auli'i wandering around the bar and it's my excuse to escape until she hurries to me and plants me back down, sitting on the arm of my chair.

"Oh good, you're in a team. I love quizzes," she says.

There's far more enthusiasm for a beautiful young girl joining than there was for me, and I can see a few wondering if I'm the British tourist who went and found a younger foreign bride. I need to engage, I always do, and before Auli'i can give her wind-up version of being my young wife. She has a wicked sense of humour when it comes out to play.

"Auli'i is my daughter, she's in the company theatre show. My name's Kieron."

Names are fired back from around the table, but impossible to remember. Jill, the lady opposite me, re-crosses her legs. Her focus implies she has more questions for me and in a guise of trying to relax and be sociable. Having ducked earlier connections, I must relax and not treat everyone I meet as a potential enemy. Auli'i certainly is inclusive with her overlarge smile and I need to learn from her innocence.

"So your father is here to see you perform? How nice." She smiles at Ee.

My brain fights to know how to react as my mouth opens wanting instructions. Auli'i jumps in.

"No, he's here to find a wife, my orders."

Three women around the table and one man put their hand up as volunteers, but not the one opposite, she is being very cool.

"Auditions later, and any help gratefully accepted. It can be an arranged marriage; he has no say! You deal directly with me." she offers.

I'm amused but speechless, she's made them all laugh and joined everyone, like a true entertainer. I have no need to respond.

"Well, he's joined the right group. We're all cruisers travelling solo," the man on my right addresses Auli'i, and I wish I had paid more attention to their names.

He now focusses on me.

"Kieron."

"My name's Tony. You should join our gatherings."

Before I can speak, the elegant lady opposite, whose name I do remember, Jill, continues her interest in Auli'i.

"Do you get to have time off, see the ports, go on excursions?"

"Yes and no and yes," Auli'i says in a way that she must have done before.

It's a practised answer to a standard question that she must have to fend off, like my pet hate, 'have you ever killed someone?' 'Not since this morning', I think I would have to answer, not sure that would go down so well. Let's hope the question's never asked.

"I'm working tomorrow," she beams, "but as a group leader on an excursion. You know, hold up the paddle, follow me, then count the lost guests."

They laugh and the quiz starts. I've escaped.

Someone in the group writes the answer before I've digested that there was an actual question. The host is repeating it again, as Auli'i is asked a follow-up question.

"What tour are you on?" Jill asks.

"The Panama Railroad, but don't ask me questions, the local guide is there for that," she answers.

"What are you doing tomorrow, Kieron?" Jill asks.

"Is that question worth two points? Because I do know the answer!" I say though I'm actually oblivious to the quiz at this moment. "I booked a local tour to visit the Emberá or Choco Indian tribe in the National Park area of the Chagres River."

Auli'i laughs at me. "Predictable," and she hugs me with one arm.

"I never saw that offered," Jill says.

"It's run by the tribe; the tours were founded by a woman called Anne who married a tribesman," I explain. "So, I'm hoping they are genuine and informative. I love learning about nations and people."

"Too much info, Dad, you are boring them now."

"No, I would like to have done that, I haven't booked anything yet," Jill answers, and Auli'i picks up on her interest with a shot. She stands up and encourages Jill to stand, then turns for me to stand.

"I used to have to do this," she says, "being matched up for a possible marriage when I was a young girl." Auli'i is eyeing us up and down while Jill plays the part by linking my arm.

"So, can you get me on this tour?" Jill asks.

"The villages are pretty deep in the rain forest, you have to cross rocks and streams," I explain.

"I can do that," she says. "I have some lower heels!"

Jill turns her ankle and that is the second time today I've seen very expensive shoes being underused.

"Well you can only get there on their traditional canoes and you must be a good swimmer." I continue to try and dissuade her.

"I can swim." She smiles.

"I now pronounce you…." Auli'i stops.

Georgie comes between us and breaks us up. "Hey, he's my superhero."

How have I become the centre of attention? Jill takes being trumped well but she has me fixed in her gaze.

"Are you enjoying yourselves?" Georgie asks the team.

They all nod and Georgie turns to me for a quiet moment.

"Where did you get to this morning?" she asks me.

"I walked around town, then came back, a little stroll around the pool, then did my commentary." I lie.

"I missed the commentary, sorry," Georgie plays.

"Well, I think, if you're lucky, it gets repeated on TV," I offer.

"Don't you learn fast?" she says, leaving.

I enjoy her cheek, perhaps to the annoyance of my arranged wife to be Jill, or maybe I'm reading too much into that.

The quiz finishes and it turns out, even as a combination of nationalities and talents, we were not clever enough.

As I lay on my money built bed alone, I reflect on the day. Even if I were to consider staying on the ship in the morning, it is now complicated, I'm taking Jill with me. That sounds stupidly risky.

Chapter 22 – Chagres River, Panama

Jill and I meet for breakfast. We exchange shallow pleasantries and overcome the awkwardness of an arrangement made the previous evening after several drinks. It could have been worse, she could have come back to my cabin and I would've lain awake all night worrying about her sleeping on the ship's most expensive bed.

"I'll feel bad if we get ashore and they can't take you," I admit, but that's a minor concern. I'll feel a lot worse if I'm arrested the moment I step ashore.

"Nonsense. If that happens, you'll do the tour, I'll look after myself. I'm a fully paid-up member of the solo cruisers club. I've done the induction on travelling alone." She gloats as we head down in the glass lift on the side of the ship from lido deck where the buffet is. It would have been a much more formal affair had we met at one of the restaurants for breakfast.

Stepping into the lifeboat tender bobbing at the side of the ship, she's excited looking at the lush green coast. My eyes are everywhere, hoping that deep in the rainforest will be a quieter day than yesterday's city tour. I want no trees made of hundred dollar bills, today. I'm on my own with absolutely no back-up or kit.

Tour buses line the shore, no police, no gunmen. Our bus is the smallest and looks the most local, to put it politely. On it, the green and white artwork says 'Classic Bus' which I guess was state of the art when it was manufactured, maybe back in the sixties. Our group were mainly with us in our tender craft, a few were earlier, and the last four are walking up from the lifeboat that docked behind us, which gives me time to ask about my plus one. Jill gets lucky, the driver radios ahead and adds her on to the days' list. She duly pays, and I feel awkward, but paying for her would be equally awkward. There are barriers best not crossed today, after one evening I have not had a chance to make any compatibility judgements, or am I over thinking this? The coach journey is upriver and takes about twenty minutes, occasionally cutting in from the shoreline and through dense vegetation, then stopping at a low bank by shallow water. This is where we start to go back to a time far beyond the art-deco bus.

We are fitted with a modern amenity, lifejackets, then sat in one of a few very long, carved dugout canoes. They are untraditionally powered by small modern electric outboard motors, very eco-friendly. Ronni would approve. The boatmen are almost naked, causing similar comments to those I'd expect on the way to a hen party, not that I've ever been on one. I'm sure these migrated Choco Indians are used to it and deliberately dress to impress. They probably wear denim on days the cruise ships don't come in. Today, I've no doubt that their lack of dress code will be enforced throughout the village.

After all of us tourists, a few supplies are loaded onto the last canoe with a local man. We cut through the early low mist hanging above the still water as we travel through silence up the Chagres River, our Tarzan-like boatmen paddling to assist the small silent motor for over half an hour. Looking back, as I do from time to time, I consider that the supply boat never catches us because neither the driver nor his assistant is in costume. The Chagres is the only river in the world, that with the aid of the manmade canal, flows into two oceans. The journey itself is a treat, we see many birds, such as herons, egrets, and osprey, as well as fish and turtles in the water. By the time we slow down, the banks are dense with rainforest jungle.

"It feels a bit 'Apocalypse Now'," Jill says to me.

I nod. "Except this is a Colombian tribe displaced in Panama, so it's unlikely someone is going to hold a gun to our heads." I look around the jungle, lush in different hues of green. I realise I would never see a sniper, I would never see a bullet coming.

"This is so nice of you to take me out," Jill says.

Chapter 23 – Supply boat

Our lifejackets are left in the canoes that have been pulled up the shore, just a little, indicating this is either not tidal or someone else is tending the boats, but I can't see anyone. The beach, which is dark sand with a few scattered pebbles only has our footprints. I am not encouraged to lay down and relax on the blue beach towel I brought from my room. I'm still looking over my shoulder and I know I should relax and enjoy this, I am now on holiday. However, I wish I had that automatic weapon with me.

An Indian guide wearing a huge number of bead necklaces and a lone bright red codpiece addresses us with a huge smile. His teeth, like the ship's crew, are perfect enough to make any British tourist jealous.

"Welcome. The Emberá people live here long time. Before this country is called Panamá. Long before our neighbours land is called Colombia. Long before the first Spanish explorer arrive here."

I'm hoping long before the drug trade.

"We have people in Brazil and ancestors from Polynesia. Over 30,000 Emberá people in Panama; most in the Darien region, but many groups between here and Panama City in the west." He waves his arm up and points.

"We live here in Gatun. Proud to share our village, culture, music, dance, food and medicine with you. Follow."

This is exciting, seeing life so different from our own. The jungle is fascinating. The other guests move off quickly but I take in the surroundings, following last, always keen to have everyone in front of me. I turn and look back for the supply boat, but it is nowhere to be seen and I suspect it has taken another way in. This scenic walk will give us a chance to see the land that they know well, and the stories all add to the drama of living here in the jungle.

Ten minutes of hiking inland turn into twenty. I could spend days here, pitching a tent and making camp. I bet night time in the jungle would be a fantastic experience, full of the noise of insects and frogs. We cross a bridge that no one on earth would insure as against accident. We see the occasional toucan and many wild parrots, then stopping to swim in a waterfall for those who brought a towel and had bathers under their clothes... Or in Jill's case her bra and pants which have gone transparent. I pass her my large towel as she steps from the water but she appears to have no embarrassment, maybe she doesn't know they have gone transparent. I cannot be the one to tell her, but if she keeps opening the towel as she dries herself I might have to. I look around, and I am the only one treated to the view so I decide to let her continue and hold it as she redresses.

Eventually, we pass the first houses, built on reinforced stilts, about eight feet off the ground at the side of a small estuary, where the supply boat is being unloaded. There is another way in. I look up to see the green mountains from where water must sweep down in the rainy season. That explains the stilts.

Deeper into the village is a large communal open-sided hut with music and dancing.

"Do you think this is put on for tourists?" Jill asks.

"Yeah, but I suspect it's based on hundreds of years of tradition."

The music stops abruptly, encouraging us to move in, pure theatre. A row of youths step forward together and deliver an address, each having one line, like half a dozen detectives in an episode of Criminal Minds.

"Welcome to our Village."

"We ask you to join our music and dance."

"Share our food."

"Then explore nature with us."

"Many plants are natural medicines."

"May help you with an ailment."

"See basket making and weaving."

"Our masks made from palm leaves."

"Carvings from Cocobolo wood."

"Which you call Rosewood."

"Nut carvings."

"Tattoos… that will wash off."

"Eventually."

At which, they all laugh on cue.

"Massage and shamanic dance."

"And please play and swim with the children."

A drum roll builds and the kids all part. An elder steps forward and takes centre stage. Jill grabs my hand and squeezes it. I convince myself this is driven by the atmosphere, nothing more, but I do feel an awkwardness when she doesn't let go. I wasn't expecting such a tactile response.

"You call us Choco or Katío Indian," he begins. "But we are Emberá, from the Choco region of Colombia. We never use Choco, we are Emberá. This is our land; we have never been forced away from our land, or into schools, or made to change language by government."

"Panama recognises seven unique ancient tribes and protects our land as 'comarca', like reservation in North America. We have been here on this island for centuries, this has always been our land. This way of life is the way it has always been and always will be," he finishes and they all beat their drums.

A younger warrior steps forward, with an even wider smile,

"Tourism is fun for my family, but also necessary to buy food, books, modern medicine and gas even though the motors on our boats are now powered by the sun with solar power. So, we thank you for coming to see us. Enjoy!"

The music kicks in and warriors with added war paint stamp in rhythmically and encourage all the tourists to dance, but it is mainly women who rush forward, and it now it does looks a little like a hen party. Dancing is not my forte, so I scan the village built within nature, the reason I came. Huge trunks, chopped to dovetail together, bound by vines. I look for signs of modern bolts hidden, but they don't appear to have been used. I'm soon surrounded by keen young children who've not developed the inevitable boredom our western offspring seem to find in family and tradition. They're all smiling and happy.

"Where do you learn?" I ask.

"School!" they all shout.

I'm led away by children, totally enjoying the freedom and experience. For years it was a rule never to be led anywhere by children; it would be a trap. But here there is no malice, this is a trade they are learning that will last as long as the ships visit.

School is another open hut, but this one has solar panels on the thatched roof and a stack of large batteries sit in the corner. Nothing and no one escapes modern technology. Supplies from the canoe are being laid on the carved wood table that would sell for a fortune in any major city. The children's innocence evaporates and they vanish, so I sense someone is approaching behind me. I turn slowly and greet the man, in normal dress, who I'm sure I remember from the supply boat. He is waving the last of the children away and they obey.

"Fruit, fried plantains, fresh fish. Simple," he whispers to draw me in. "They cook in their homes on logs, placed on a bed of dirt."

There is a tension as he talks and I sense he hasn't really come to tell me about the food. This is not an innocent meeting. He produces the now two famous printouts, but these have Spanish writing on them and a phone number. One of Ronni, one of me. Both have the Latino woman circled.

"Why is there a reward for you and your wife?" he asks, taking out his mobile phone and nodding back towards Jill, who is dancing without a care in the world... I can't let him make that call.

Chapter 24 - Reward

"Put your phone away, I'm not going anywhere. We're stuck on an island," I order, taking his arm firmly, bending his thumb back against his wrist just enough for him to feel the need to comply. I keep the pressure on just enough to lead him, walking with me towards Jill. I focus on her, nervous. This is why I was single, why working agents never marry or are quick to divorce. Relationships are like ships in the night, when and if they ever happen for soldiers. Jill places me in a new space.

We watch the dancing for a moment, then Jill spins on a drum beat and sees me. I'm beckoned to the dance floor. I smile and refuse politely, waving her on to enjoy herself.

"Let's look at that picture of yours." I take the one of Ronni and hold it up. "That's not my wife!" I hand the picture back leaving him looking at Jill. "And we're on holiday. My wife's not that woman," I say pointing at the Latino woman who has been so much trouble since the moment we met.

"Why is there a reward? For what? For her? Not us, we're just tourists enjoying a tourist attraction, which…" I pause, closing in on him, "will never have visitors again, if an innocent man and his wife are arrested on it. It would be television news all over the western world, this tour will be finished. These villagers will starve. Who do I see about getting my money back for your ruining my day? Is this your tribe?" I ask him.

"No. I sell them supplies."

"Not any more. You'll lose this customer, then all your other customers when they hear what you did. You will be finished."

At last, he's starting to look worried.

"The reward for this lady in both pictures is not for us! You've made a very dangerous mistake."

He looks up at Jill bouncing towards us in time to the beat.

"This is a fabulous day out!" she says, leaning in and kissing me on the cheek, perfectly on cue, selling our innocence.

"What's your name?" I ask putting him on the spot.

"Carlos Aparicio," he says, now embarrassed.

"Come and dance Carlos, he won't dance, he's boring!" She is trying to pull him onto the dance floor.

"Carlos has a supplies company, what's it called Carlos?" I ask.

"Aparicio Supplies," he says, turning to see me holding up my mobile, and snapping a picture of him and a perfectly posed Jill.

"Posted online, Carlos, with British tourist Jill, at Emberá tribal village."

Jill spins away taking the invitation of another warrior, and I am alone again with Carlos.

"We were warned about kidnapping in South America."

"No, not me. I no kidnap tourists," he says.

"Good."

I may have turned the tables, and worried him, but I know it's me who's really in trouble.

The music stops and there's a surge towards the school hut, which is now perfectly decorated for lunch.

"You know what we say in England?" I ask him.

He shakes his head, 'no', totally confused.

"Let's think about this over lunch." I start walking towards the food as Jill catches me up and grabs my hand. I'm rather glad she came now; I have a foil, who I treat every bit like my lover, although this romance might backfire on me later as this escalation is not a considered one. I have not had the chance to get to know Jill or consider how I feel about her since our meeting last night. This is definitely the arranged marriage Auli'i was talking about. More a union of necessity than a marriage of convenience.

The people from the tribe eat with us and regale us with details about their simple everyday life. They point to the stream, which is where they bathe. The larger river, where our boats are, is where they catch the fish we're eating. I keep Carlos next to me as a local tribeswoman talks about her life to both of us, and it is obvious she doesn't know him. I guess he never spends time here.

"We grow plantains, bananas, corn, sugar cane, rice, beans, and yucca root." She smiles.

"And are tourists totally safe here?" I ask to her surprise.

"Yes. Most safe," she defends.

"Some places in South America, tourists are kidnapped," I say.

"Not here. We are peaceful people."

I surprise Carlos by grabbing his paper printouts, he makes a late move to retrieve what is now being torn in half under the table. I show her the section without me in.

"Carlos was telling me this lady has gone missing. Maybe stolen. He was looking to see if she was here."

What is said next is all in a local language, which I can't translate, but she calls others, he defends himself. In the minor disturbance, I lift Carlos' telephone from his pocket without his knowledge. He stands, motionless as a group of angry warriors gather around us.

"Her, she's lost," I say. "Carlos wants to know if she is here?"

As the picture is passed around, one Indian obviously knows who the woman is. He passes it back to his friends.

"Wife of King," he says.

They all look at the printout, Carlos looks with a new concern. I now know she is the wife of a king and I want to know a lot more.

"You thought the Queen was here, Carlos?" I ask him, trying to sound genuinely concerned. "I didn't know Panama had a Queen."

"Wife of 'El Rey', boss of Colombian drug cartel," another Indian explains to me.

They all seem fearful and concerned as they recognise her and I know I have enough momentum to close him down.

"Carlos thought, because she was in the airport with tourists, she might have come on this tour to the Indian village?" I ask, but what I'm really wondering is why the wife of a drug lord was arrested. Who would dare? And the walls of money flash through my mind, what a huge coincidence.

The warriors shake their heads slowly, it's a no, she's not here. They know everyone on the island. I bet you can't move here without them knowing.

"Well. If she's not here, can we enjoy the day?" I wrap up.

Inside I fear that this whole thing will not be over until I'm far away from South America. She must have been running away with the cash. Maybe the dead man on the plane was her minder? Did she kill him to escape then get arrested for a caseload of money? That seems daft. That seems far too obvious a mistake for her, the wife of a drug lord. The whole story makes less sense the more I find out, or does it? Is this drug cartel looking for her and twenty million plus damages? What I do know is that we can't be connected to any of it.

I choose some food then circulate looking at the masks, hats and baskets with only one interest; I'm looking for a piece of metal wire, but metal is not a local product. I glance over at Jill and see that the guests sitting with her hold the modern answer; they're looking at their booking papers, which are stapled together. I join them.

I squeeze in next to Jill. Taking my actions as a show of affection, she stands to encourage me to sit so she can perch on my knee. We seem to have got very comfortable together very quickly.

"May I?" I ask, taking the sheets. They explain the tour in detail, but I'm not interested in the content. My thumb has slipped under the staple and as I hand it back, I palm the metal clip. Behind Jill, I remove the back from Carlos' phone and take out the battery. Her closeness is an ideal cover. I grab a thick leaf from my plate to insulate my fingers as I hold the metal staple across the battery terminals. It glows red as it shorts all the power away. It burns through the leaf and I almost drop it, but the colour goes, meaning the power has lessened to zero. I refit the battery back into the phone and try to switch it on. It flashes then goes dead. Now Carlos can have his cell back, it's useless.

Jill's pulled away by a young girl. "I'm having a two-week tattoo," she shouts back over her shoulder.

"Where?"

"Somewhere sexy," she teases.

"I'll never get to see it," I say, standing.

"Oh you might," she says and I realise things have gone too far.

"I had the most amazing massage," Jill tells me, sitting between my legs in the canoe home, laying back on me. "And I bought this," she says, holding up a small bag of powder.

"Drugs?" I ask.

"No!! It's holistic. It's a mixture of medicinal plants and natural remedies blessed by a mystical ritual."

Then, through the trees, I spot blue lights flickering in the distance before we turn a bend and see police cars lined up, all with swirling lights. I was not expecting a welcoming committee but I realise Carlos could have borrowed anyone's phone to ring ahead. Despite the lack of clothing and pockets, the tribe's people all had cell phones.

Carlos is in the front of our canoe and not giving anything away. I have managed to keep him close throughout the afternoon, but as we near the shore, it becomes very obvious I haven't kept him close enough.

I have no disguise with which to camouflage myself, other than Jill, my new wife.

Chapter 25 – Blue lights

Disembarking, it seems like this could be my lucky day. We are guided away from the police, towards our small classic coach parked a hundred yards further on. It looks like there's an investigation in progress. An area is taped off and police dogs are sniffing, but not sniffing for me, and no one is checking faces against a picture. Carlos does not appear to have created this problem or have any desire to call them over. His body language suggests he is wary of the police and he walks on deliberately trying to blend in with the tourists. Then I see Hunter, in his officer whites, leaning on a police car with another officer whose uniform has a slightly different trim. They stand with two old, unfit police officers sporting an embarrassment of medals on their breast pockets.

I now understand. Carlos' phone might not have been working but mine was, and the text I sent Hunter as to my potential problem must have been delivered. He gives me the slightest of nods, which could be to any of the ships' guests, but I know this elaborate charade is designed to escort me safely back on board. The two ship officers step towards the front of our group.

"Any of you guys on the Sea Zoo?" Hunter asks, using the nickname for the ship. There's pride as they respond yes, Hunter smiles rubbing his hands together, "Good, I can go!" Hunter walks up the line greeting everyone and ensuring they had a great day out. He stops at the tour leader.

"How many did you have?" he asks, looking at the clipboard. The guide points to a figure.

"Twenty-six. Good, all here," he says re-counting and catching my gaze just long enough for me to have signalled distress if I need to.

"We can follow this last bus back?" he says to the local officers, but it's not really a question.

Our small coach is tailed all the way by the police car, and behind that is Carlos, in his Aparicio Supplies van. I have no idea how he has done this, but Hunter is smart and I am ready to be amused by the tale when I'm safely back on board.

With both the ships in sight, our bus stops and empties out. The police car lets the two officers out, they shake hands, laugh and split towards their respective tender stations. These booths must be standard, as both ships have erected a simple twelve-foot square easy-up shelter with the ship's name and company logo printed on the canopy. They are about a hundred meters apart and must come out at every tender port for the lifeboats to ferry to.

Jill and I are at the back of the group, who are now interrogating Hunter.

"What was happening back there?" a guest asks.

"There was a report that a tourist might have been in an incident, a jacket was found with blood on it. The local police jump to attention if any tourist might be in trouble, they called me down as I'm the head of security for the ship. I've got one more tour to come back; coach of thirty-eight, all safe and we'll be first to the locks this evening." He smiles.

"Whose jacket was it?" a guest asks.

"I don't know, but the police should have known that none of our guests would've been wearing a cheap jacket like that!" He laughs.

Every member of the cruise ship's staff has a little entertainer about them.

"And none of you would have been carrying the 44 Magnum that shot him five times," he says dramatically.

"He was dead?" a lady asks.

"Shot five times, of course he's dead!" her friend adds.

"We don't know…the dead person just left the bloodstained jacket behind." Hunter shrugs and they all seem confused.

"How do you know it was a 44 Magnum if they didn't find the gun? Or a body?" another guest asks.

Hunter shakes his head slowly, looking at them.

"You're all making stories up quicker than me now. By dinner, it'll have become an angry mob with machine guns, and the brave officer from security, Hunter, that's me, fought them off with his bare hands!" He acts incredulous, and no one believes him now.

"Could it have been a crew member?" one of the guests suggests.

"Who?" Hunter asks.

"In the tawdry jacket," a male cruiser adds.

"How did you know the jacket was tawdry. Wait, were you the shooter?" Hunter teases and the entertainment continues.

"The crew have nicer clothes than some of the guests," another cruiser jokes with an edge. "Dress code is slipping."

"They certainly have better teeth," another says.

"We're all employed on our ability to smile." Hunter beams deliberately all teeth.

I know the jacket was a plant. Clearly, Hunter staged everything to have a police presence. Maybe even got blood from the kitchen. All for my safe journey back.

Our empty tender boat manoeuvres to the edge, Hunter's show is over. Jill and I reconnect for a moment. I can finally relax, I've survived. More importantly, she has and luckily she has no idea how she's been used.

"Would you like to have dinner tonight? I want to say thank you," Jill whispers.

Is this what real life's like?

"I would, but sadly I can't," I admit. "I'm working."

"Working?" she asks. "You're not a passenger?"

"I am but I'm guest staff. I do the commentary back out through the locks," I explain, as plainly as I can.

"You're the Canal expert! I thought I recognised your voice. At least I'm not being refused because you have a wife." She grins and pecks my lips.

The crowd starts to move. I look back and see Carlos going for his phone, which is still dead. I see him curse, then look up at me, knowing he's been played. He points angrily at me, shaking his head, then runs his hand across his throat, threatening me. Hunter sees it too. Luckily Jill hasn't, she is moving towards the boat and I follow.

"Trouble?" Hunter whispers.

I nod enough to say yes. Hunter watches us board the tender and waves us away. I don't look back.

Chapter 26 - Commentary

"A partial transit of the Panama Canal doesn't mean we enter the canal in one piece and only some of us manage to get out. However, many workers did go in to earn a wage and never came out. The death toll is estimated at around 28,000 due to violence, disease, and poor working conditions during the many construction attempts connecting the 51-mile journey. The Panama Canal shaves about 7,800 miles off a sea journey from New York to San Francisco and avoids the dangerous rounding of Cape Horn at the tip of South America."

I've showered, dressed and am commentating the ship's passage all before sunset. Bringing Jill with me to the bridge has saved me from the practical jokes that would no doubt have gotten more extreme now the Captain and his crew know I can take them. Her presence gives for an amusing atmosphere between me and the officers who know exactly the card I've played.

I, on the other hand, don't know how I've managed it. Jill looks radiant in a beautiful long silver dress, cocktail glass in hand, looking out at the lit Gutan locks below. The diving front neckline shows a tempting line on her breasts and the new tattoo that goes down further along with every officer's imagination.

"You left these behind last time," a young officer says to me handing back my first notes, just as I'm about to raise the microphone again.

He's lingering, he's been set a test, like a gang initiation. I notice his trainee rank from his name badge 'Junior officer Bachvarov'.

"My notes are just back up." But I take them and move my new ones away from him. I guess he's been challenged to steal my new notes or swap them, but he's blown his chance.

"I wear a covert earpiece, everything's been pre-recorded into my mobile. I learnt that when showing the Queen around the Royal Yacht Britannia," I tease.

He walks away slowly to report back and, will no doubt, be chastised for repeating the stupid tale if he believed it and dares to. Even I am way too young to have shown the Queen round her own yacht. I take the microphone again.

"The lowest toll ever paid through these chambers was thirty-six cents back in 1928 when Richard Halliburton swam the Panama Canal. That's about twenty dollars in today's money."

Jill is impressed, which is a danger. We'll be through the locks soon and will make it in time for our table in the Asian restaurant Jill has reserved. I'm looking forward to it, I didn't eat much at lunchtime, what with Carlos and the phone.

"It takes about eight minutes to fill each of these chambers on the way in, going up. The way out, going down, is about the same time. The fastest transit of the whole canal was by a U.S. Navy hydrofoil, The Pegasus, in two hours and forty-one minutes, Pacific to Atlantic. The average time for a cruise ship is about eight hours, but they normally add a stop in the lakes, as we did today."

I switch the mic off as I see the reflection of the bridge door open in the glass. Georgie is dressed to kill. I turn and smile, she smiles at me but her eyes have already flicked left and seen Jill.

"Georgie!" I announce with a start, embarrassed. "No sail away party?"

"You're the party tonight, where's your uniform?" she scolds.

"Uniform?" Jill asks, not wanting to step aside for Georgie. "You're not crew, though."

"No, we don't let army boys come to sea," the Captain chimes in.

"I like a man in uniform," Jill says cheekily, teasing the bridge crew as much as me.

"Me too," adds Georgie exciting all the young officers.

"I didn't want to out-ribbon the Captain," I joke.

The Captain smiles the comment away and I realise I feel very at home on the ship, I wonder if all ships will be this easy. Not that the last two days have been a walk in the park.

"I came to see if you wanted to have dinner, but it looks like you already have a date," Georgie says.

"I can check my diary," I tease. "But it's filling up quickly."

"Why don't you join us?" Jill offers, but I know she doesn't mean it. Georgie knows too.

"I'll wait 'til he's in uniform." Georgie winks. "Maybe we can do something tomorrow?"

"I'll see if I can move things around."

Although I've only known her two days and she's my boss, I'm already bonded to her, I know her darkest secrets. Or at least I am until she finds out there's another twenty million on board. Georgie leaves, and I ease over to Jill.

"There's something about her, I can't put my finger on it." Jill smiles.

"She's the boss?" I suggest.

"It's not that," she says touching my hand.

"She has superpowers," I reveal wistfully.

"She does? What are they?"

"I don't know, but her cabin steward told me. Not that I was in her room, well, I was, but for business reasons," I fumble. I've dug an unnecessary hole and I am only saved by a phone ringing. This is not just any phone ring but an important one and everyone in the room turns.

The phone is beside the main chair behind the two officers driving the ship. That is the Captain's line and the one he alone has to answer. As he listens, he looks very concerned and everyone watches him wondering what has gone wrong. "I'll be straight there!" he says into the phone, then "hold this position," to his officers. In passing me rushing to the door, "It appears we have a number of stowaways."

My body goes cold and my muscles tense. The relaxed state of play between two women did not last long, it never does. This sounds like the inevitable second wave of gunmen sent to complete what the first loan one failed to achieve and what was missed in the jungle. They will have pictures of me and Ronni. For the second time today I wish I was armed with an automatic weapon and at least wearing a vest, whether that is normal on a cruise ship or not. I have to follow, I have to assess the strength of the enemy.

Chapter 27 – Stowaways

The officers on the bridge have to stay because they form the required complement required to drive the ship, even though it is not going anywhere. Each of them is keen to follow the Captain, but none have been ordered to do that, and none know the problems that have gone before over the last few days with an associated body-count or collateral damage. Uninvited, but unable to stay left behind, I excuse myself from Jill and follow the Captain now about half a dozen paces behind him. Knowing I'm unarmed I look for anything to use as a weapon at every turn, but there is nothing. I have to hope that Hunter and his team have also been called and he can palm me a gun as he did before. To my surprise, the chase moves straight outside to the deck where guests are running away in distress. The Captain moves in the other direction, to the right and climbs up to the sun deck. I am now right behind him but this is a strange vantage point for any gunmen to take unless they have taken hostages.

At the top of the stairs, he stops. I stop behind him and whilst relived that it is not a team of South American gunmen, I am totally bemused by yet another new scenario for me. I could not write what each day of this cruise is bringing, no one would believe it. The deck is swarming with bees. A number beyond any comprehension have inhabited one particular sunbed, and another large number are exploring a slatted vent. Other huge numbers race around in circles like a special effect straight out of a horror movie. Hunter is there with two of his officers and they are bemused at the ships' new guests who appear very determined to stay.

"This is a new one on me," the Captain relates. "Get Officer Ronni Cohen up here because there must be a protocol for this."

"You think, sir?" Hunter growls.

"Bees will be protected," he replies.

I wish I was, whilst this is a let off I am feeling more vulnerable now.

"There will be a correct way of dealing with them. We will have to do whatever we do, properly. But passenger safety comes first," Captain Feldman continues moving over to Hunter's side and they both look at what must be hundreds of thousands of bees. I invite myself to stand close to them, although I'm not one of the ship's team. The Captain looks back at the three hundred meters of his ship where many guests still stand at the rails looking out, some are still sunbathing some are watching and filming him with their phones.

"We can't go sail forward, with the possibility of sending the bees backwards, scattering them over the whole ship. They have to be contained and dealt with here," the Captain suggests.

"I have ordered stage smoke to be brought up, and the fire team to get suited in full protective clothing," Hunter Witowski explains.

"Let's clear all the decks." The Captain orders turning back.

While we all look at the possibilities, we wait for compliance, fire, and decks to be cleared it is obvious the passengers' safety comes first. Subduing the bees or allowing them to migrate to the rest of the ship is surely a risk that cannot be taken. Many of the passengers are very old and the effect of bee stings might be very serious. But what if this is a diversion, a release of bees so we don't notice a team of stowaways? Now I am getting stupid, none of that drug cartel has thousands and thousands of bees standing by to attack.

Officers are clearing passengers off the decks as the fire team arrive in full protective suits and carrying CO_2 cylinders. The bees attack a deckhand and he screams with the stings. A suited fireman goes and collects him from the deck and passes him down to a medic.

"OK, the suited team can move in as soon as the rest of us are inside," the Captain orders.

Hunter and I are the last two plain-clothed civilians on the sun deck, he waves at the fire crew and they advance, blasting the bees with the freezing CO_2 that leaves a white residue and thousands of frozen bees littering the deck.

"Let's sweep them into buckets and get them tipped off the back, not over the sides, they could get drawn in and defrost in a cabin," Hunter announces to his team being clear and precise. Ronni arrives in a breath-taking dress but it is all too late, the bees have been dealt with the only way they could have given the need for passenger safety. The three of us exchange looks and I am not sure whether the solemn tone of our meeting is us knowing it could have been a swarm of gunmen looking for their money or that there are many frozen bees about to be thrown from the back of the ship. The survivors of the swarm leave the deck and head back towards land and the dark cloud over the sun deck has lifted.

"I don't think I'm dressed for this," Ronni states and leaves.

"She means it's my paperwork," Hunter shares with me, "Years of cutting edge training. Bees!"

He raises his walkie-talkie, "Good to go Captain."

Was that the first hint from both of them, that ship life is not always as rosy as it looks.

Chapter 28 – Hot spice

The Asian restaurant has a different feel to the buffet, which is the only place I've managed to eat at so far. Mood lighting, hanging beads, it's modern yet classic. It's quieter in here, and the food gives a distinctive spicy aroma. People talk in whispers and the service we're afforded is instant and personal.

"Could we have a bottle of Sula, white, please," Jill asks the maître d' who seats us. "The coldest one," she adds.

"I'll inform your wine waiter; his name is Sai," he tells her. "Tonight, you will be taken care of by Ragini and Shivam."

I like it that Jill's an independent woman, as well as having considerable beauty, she has hidden layers. I don't have any good female friends. Such a woman cruising alone has to have a story to tell. The Captain was intrigued too, that was obvious. Why is she travelling alone? I'm wary of asking too much in case it leads her to reciprocate and ask questions about me in areas I've only shared briefly with a therapist. If in danger defer to the bees.

"Do you know anything about Cartagena?" I ask.

A waiter attends us with a plate that doesn't look like food. Two small round Swiss rolls, only large enough for a Tom Thumb character. He waits until he has our full attention.

"Thank you, my name is Shivam." He pours water on the swirls and they rise, each like a phoenix, expanding into a hand towel that he offers first to Jill.

Throughout the ship, you're encouraged to sanitise your hands, especially before eating, but here, this cloth extends to the forehead and if I was not in company, I'd be tempted to cool my neck. I'm sweltering from a combination of temperature, unexpected events and intoxication, though not from alcohol, from Jill's poise and control.

"Good evening, my name is Sai." The wine waiter has appeared, presenting Jill with her ordered bottle or the wine list. It is a nice touch to show she still has a choice. She looks at me to check I'm happy with what she's chosen.

"Sure, I don't know the wine, but that's a reason to try it."

Jill feels the bottle to check the temperature and the waiter pours a little for her to taste.

"Sir, madam has made a good choice. Sula wine is from our largest wine producer in India. Mr Rajeev Samant, the founder, is a distant cousin of my wife. He only started in 1999 with his first cuttings of the Zinfandel grape smuggled into India from Northern California. The legend is that cuttings were nurtured in the lower decks of a cruise ship all the way home to India. It may be a little far fetched, but he now has 1500 acres in Nashik and nearby Dindori. Recently, they won silver at the Decanter World Wine Awards for this Sauvignon Blanc," he says, without taking a breath, no doubt the tale could be even longer if the restaurant was not absolutely full. We both stifle a laugh, thank him and he leaves us to it.

CRUISE SHIP HEIST – OCEAN ATLANTIC

"So you asked if I know anything about Cartagena. The answer is no, except that it's a city in Colombia," Jill offers.

I taste the wine and it's easy on the palate, maybe too easy. I'm not used to drinking much, not used to relaxing at all. Not like this. I down my whole glass of water.

"-and other than what I saw on Narcos," Jill adds.

"From the chef." Another waitress appears, waiting for us to us pause for her to describe the pre-dinner nibbles, then Shivam leaves us menus and they retreat. At this rate, we'll learn more about the restaurant staff this evening than each other, perfect. I try the food, it's delicious.

"This is amazing. I read that this chef was the second Indian chef to win a Michelin star."

"It's my favourite. I look forward to it as one of my cruise treats," Jill shares. "I guess I'd never have booked this to eat alone, so thank you. Us solos are a group... We even have a chat group."

"For singles, like a dating site?"

"Not at all, no. We all love travelling and don't have a problem being single."

"That sounds very grown up," I add, enjoying the thought that I might fit in somewhere in the outside world.

"It's run by a cruise resource site called Cruise Doris Visits, though I don't believe there's actually a Doris. Maybe it should have been called Dorothy Visits."

"Dorothy?"

"It is a term used for some of our group. But maybe they were being deliberately clever using Doris. Anyway, they have all different chat groups for ships, including our one for singles," she explains. "It means we can travel alone, but then get together to eat in restaurants, go out on walking tours... friends without benefits." Jill smiles and sips her wine.

"Good old Doris!" I say. "And Narcos?"

"It's a TV series I was glued to about Pablo Escobar."

I shrug, I've never heard of it.

"The drug lord," she explains.

"A documentary?"

"No, a drama, all about his ruthless killings of everyone who dared upset him, politicians, police, FBI, anyone."

"Tourists?" I ask automatically.

I have been warned in so many ways against going ashore tomorrow.

Jill shakes her head with a smile and goes back to the menu, then she adds the bullet…

"Not unless they cross him."

Chapter 29 – Doris Visits

The starter is so good it steals all the conversation, but as our plates are cleared, Jill hits me with the personal stuff.

"So what uniform was the lady 'superhero' referring to?" Jill asks.

"Georgina is head of entertainment on ship."

"But you call her Georgie?" she says with an edge.

"Oh, everyone does."

"And your daughter has the most beautiful olive skin, where is her mother from?" she pries.

"Well those are two very different lines of conversation, which one would you like first, or can we talk about Cartagena?" I try.

But Jill waits, her eyes fix on me, her perfectly formed lips seem to move very slowly to a curious pout. How much should I share with her? I'm treading water, I have a whistle and a light on my lifejacket, and I'm not seeing a use for either. I'm lost at sea.

"I was in the army, boring ceremonial royal duties but never important. Interesting for about half an hour, which has to stretch to two forty-five minute talks on-ship, so if I tell you now, I'll be spoiling it." I sidestep.

"Or... you could give me the super quick version now? Then I can stay on deck sunbathing while you toil in the theatre," Jill says not giving up.

"And my daughter is adopted, though not officially. She turned eighteen too quick for the need."

"There is always a need isn't there? What about inheritance, making her next of kin?" she asks.

"Good point, but I have nothing to leave. I like that she calls me dad... So, Cartagena?"

"Does she know her real parents?" Jill asks with a more solemn tone.

I could answer this but is it mine to share? You don't own your children, I certainly don't. I ponder as to what I should tell. It is always a conundrum especially as I don't want this solo cruiser night out to get too personal. That could give her the wrong idea.

"She recently turned nineteen. She's been dancing on the ship just a few months. She loves dancing. She gave herself the name Auli'i after the actress who voices Moana. It's a kids film, she dreams of being in western movies... I never met her parents."

"Where's she from?" Jill continues.

"You're not from immigration, are you? I hear they like to do this kind of job on expenses rather than sit in the boxes at airports." I'm trying to change gear.

"No, I'm a benefits investigator permanently assigned to cruise," she throws out full of sarcasm then shakes her head just enough. "Is she a refugee, how long has she been here?"

"Here, in Panama? Just a day," I answer.

"With you, you do live in the UK?"

"Are you a journalist?"

"No, I write computer code; it's nice to talk to real people," she shares.

"That sounds interesting," I say because I genuinely like geek stuff.

"No, it's really not. Tell me why a grown-up girl chooses a name from a cartoon at the age of what sixteen, seventeen?"

"Do you watch kids films?" I try.

"You won't distract me!" she insists.

"It's the plot, a teenager sailing dangerously to safety, and whilst sailing she discovers her identity. My daughter sailed," I offer but Jill is not yet fulfilled. So I add. "To safety, up the Euphrates."

"In Syria?"

"Unless they've moved it."

"Wow, you adopted a Muslim refugee, that's brave and wonderful," she congratulates me.

"Some might say stupid. It cost me my pension. And, she's a Christian. Ten percent of Syrians are Christian."

"And you were in Syria?" she continues.

I nod.

"On ceremonial duties?" she mocks.

"Did I say ceremonial? Yes, I did. I was one of the first into Iraq in 2003, part of the coalition. Forty-five thousand troops. I did all the parades at all their palaces. Then popped back to our Palace, then back again," I play. "Do you know how important Islamic and Syrian scientists, mathematicians and doctors have been to everything we know and use today? And how we deliberately belittled their intelligence while stealing it all during the crusades?"

She nods, knowing I'm trying to dodge talking about myself, about Auli'i. Her face is a human can opener, all the right muscles twisting into me. She missed her calling, I've had worse interrogations behind enemy lines.

"If you ask me if I've ever killed someone, I'll have to kill you... Now Cartagena or the new tattoo that vanishes cheekily away into the unknown."

"So she was on a boat with her family, and sailed into Iraq?" she continues, undeterred after the slightest of re-boots.

"Not exactly. She lived at the other end of the Euphrates, in the Raqqa province," I reveal.

"I don't know it..." she says, prodding for more.

"The river side of the Tabja Dam, which stops Lake Assad from flooding the valley. Its strategic importance means there'll always be fighting there. Problem is, no one knows who is fighting who, or why. When it was taken by I.S. in 2013 her parents were killed. She ran, dodging bullets at her feet, with other children, some who never made it. Those who survived hid in her father's fishing boat. She was the oldest. And look the rest is really hers to tell."

At last, Jill relents. "OK, we can talk about our day in Cartagena and the tattoo stretches round to my back, no reason."

I've been dodging verbal bullets here, but tomorrow they could be real. More death and destruction.

Chapter 30 – Under Clay

Shivam begins to serve our main dish with a flourish and of course, he has a story to tell. Jill likes stories, and to be honest I do too. He breaks open the clay crust on the meal I ordered, lifting it away to be sacrificed to a side plate. Underneath is the chicken biryani and it smells incredible. It's not what I was expecting.

"It's a pie?"

"Dum cooking. Traditional Indian cooking. The food is sealed under clay. Here we use pastry to keep all the aroma and flavour in, so when we break it, you are the first person who is presented with all that flavour," Shivam explains with pride.

He takes other dishes from his small trolley and lays them on our table.

"To compliment, you have yoghurt, chilli, lime, and mini-poppadums. You also have a lentil dish."

The smell is amazing, but the food is even more spectacular and for a while we are silent, exchanging smiles and nods as we eat. The wine is a perfect match for the food.

The sun is going down on the distant empty horizon, a vanishing red ball surrounded by a pale blue halo. It all works to create the perfect atmosphere. I could grow to enjoy cruising, though I wonder if this wouldn't all become so familiar it would be sinfully taken for granted.

Jill sits back with the menu and smiles like she's won a prize. I'm full, any more food seems impossible, but Jill picks up the dessert menu.

"Desert choices; 'Chocolate Textures', which is chocolate truffle mousse."

"I'm not really a mousse man."

"I've not finished," she pouts. "'White Chocolate and Mint Sorbet with Mint Chocolate Soil'."

"No, not convinced."

"'Cardamom Bread and Butter Pudding with Ginger Custard'..." she says nodding her head 'yes'. She is encouraging me to choose it.

I shake my head, 'no' so she continues.

"'Blueberry Bhapia Doi, Yoghurt and Berry Mousse'. OK, I know, you're not a mousse man. So, it'll have to be, 'Khatta Meetha Teeta', which is, a chilled mango and passion fruit parfait with chilli glass," Jill says.

"And that's not a mousse?"

I look up to Shivam who steps forward, seeking permission to speak and Jill nods.

"Not a mousse, sir. Cream is whipped with sugar, and set in the fridge. Egg yolks whisked with icing sugar until pale, then we add mango and passion fruit. They are then folded together. That is just the beginning. It ends being set in a perfect chilli glass. All assembled with the utmost artistry."

It would seem rude not to order it after he's gone to so much bother to sell a dish, which I am assuming more than one person has spent much time making.

Auli'i suddenly appears, rushing up to our table.

"Dad! There's been a chemical attack back home!" She's shaking. I pull her down onto the chair that Shivam slides in next to me and hug her close. She has gone cold.

"Are you sure?" I ask. "Those weapons are outlawed. They wouldn't risk the reprisals."

"In the Eastern Ghouta region. I have relatives there who have been texting. People are dying everywhere."

Auli'i holds up her mobile phone.

Jill stands and helps Auli'i up.

"Come to my room, let's see if we can find out more."

She leads Auli'i away and I follow, nodding our thanks to Shivam. I take out my mobile and dial a number I haven't used in a long time.

"It's Kieron… I hear there's been trouble."

Jill looks back having heard me on the phone, her face is full of a million more questions.

Chapter 31 - Outlawed

Jill must do very well from writing code; she has a suite, and it doesn't look like an ordinary suite, it looks like the best suite on the ship. She sits on the sofa comforting Auli'i and they both look to me for answers.

"Put the news on," Jill suggests, and I find the remote. Her large TV comes to life with the ship presentation of a previous lecturer.

"That will be you in a few days," she says.

"I hope I won't be that dull," I say watching for too long, I know that they want the news. I skip through the channels but there's nothing about Syria, I know they will have less than I do. I switch it off.

"I rang a few friends on the way up here. Television will just have hype and well-worded press releases with no real detail. They normally run library footage, cameras won't have gathered there or released material yet."

"What did you find out?" Auli'i asks.

"Forces have been mobilised to supply equipment and experts to the area. There are casualties."

"You're not a ceremonial soldier are you?" Jill asks.

"I know someone in the VCD."

Jill looks at me, questioning.

"Violations Documentation Centre, they record alleged violations of international law in Syria. They're responding. Bombs have been dropped that appear to have toxic substances. One hit a pastry shop in Douma. The White Helmets are in there," I explain.

"White Helmets?" she asks.

"Syria Civil Defence rescue workers. That's all standard procedure."

"That sounds like a much longer phone call than our walk up a few flights of stairs," she digs.

"They told me as quick as I just told you. It is what it is. They're in, they can smell toxic fumes, they're guessing it is chlorine…" I say, not sure whether to continue, "…they can see dead bodies foaming at the mouth. It needs to be tested and confirmed."

"Kieron!" she scolds, gesturing I should protect Auli'i.

"Jill, Auli'i has seen more atrocities than we can imagine. Sensitive, is telling the truth." I hope that I'm right, though Auli'i is as upset as I have ever seen her.

"It's OK Dad, you're right, I know what's going on. Friends text me every day. I can't share with them how lucky I am. I can't send them pictures of my life, of this ship. I can't. I ran and ran until I'd left them all behind. I feel so guilty."

"You can't feel guilty for wanting to live," Jill says.

"Douma is near my auntie's in Damascus. We have family there. Children will be dying, as my friends did. Dad, can we use some of that money to help?" Auli'i asks.

"What money?" Jill starts, but she is offered no answer. "I have money. I can help."

"That's very kind of you, Jill. But, we've got a little money. Money's not the problem, the problem's bigger than money."

It's easier to say that than 'we've more than a few large ones stolen from the drug cartel of the merciless killers you mentioned earlier'. Add to that, the need to smuggle the money around the world, then behind enemy lines to attempt to do things that few governments and few aid agencies want us to. If I were to offer full disclosure, I should tell her that there might be a gunman on the ship after me, and almost certainly tomorrow in Cartagena.

She doesn't deserve this on her holiday. Auli'i doesn't deserve this in her life. I force a smile, lost.

Chapter 32 – More news than the news

I hang up my phone. Jill and Auli'i look across the suite to me, waiting on my every word,

"An area called Martyrs' Square's being sealed off and the Syrian-American Medical Society is moving in. It's bad. They fear hundreds may have been killed, but it's not the area your family's in. It has the footprint of a chemical attack; respiratory distress, central cyanosis, burnt eyes, blue lips and foaming at the mouth. It's going to get very ugly now because someone will have to retaliate."

I can see Jill now wonders who I really am, but she knows I am a soldier. She knows I have been in Syria.

"Why don't you go back to your room? Auli'i is fine here tonight," Jill says.

This is a very strange situation, but I think Auli'i needs the maternal comfort Jill has volunteered and I leave pondering how I would have dealt with Auli'i alone, or Jill alone in her suite inviting me to see where the tattoo went. She would most definitely not have followed me down to my officer's room, in the lowest passenger deck on the ship, near the crew area.

I take the stairs down and as I pass the theatre Georgie is there talking to a dancer. The dancer leaves, Georgie turns to me.

"How is she?"

I am shocked that Georgie knows. Other stage members come out and pass us giving us stone-faced smiles. Everyone knows. This is such a tight community.

"Let's talk in your cabin," Georgie suggests.

She leads me down another flight of stairs and the short distance to my cabin, which has the number on the door and a plaque which I've never noticed before, 'Gen. Man. Ent.' I point to it.

"Does this mean I'm using your room?" I ask.

"No," she says following me in. "It means your room is allocated to my department. It's always the guest speaker's room."

The door slams closed.

"So, how is she?" she asks again.

I wonder if she's actually worried that she might lose a dancer tomorrow if Auli'i asks to fly home from Cartagena. She picks up on my pause.

"Auli'i, not your girlfriend," she clarifies.

"Jill's not my girlfriend, she's just another solo cruiser. Auli'i's shook up, but fine. She'll be OK by morning," I answer.

"Tough kid. Tough dad," Georgie says.

Expecting her to leave, I ease to her side so she can pass, but she stays put.

"Aren't you going to offer me a drink? We're partners... and I'm intrigued. How does a girl from Syria get to call a soldier dad?"

Maybe we should go to a bar, but Georgie has just sat on the edge of the bed, on top of twenty million dollars. She is going nowhere. I definitely need a drink and she seems to think my room might be stocked.

"I don't even have water; do I have a fridge?" I ask, still not knowing the room.

Georgie bounces up and opens the cupboard under my desk.

"No, you don't have a fridge." She picks up the phone and dials. "Ankur," she says into the phone. "It's Georgie. Can you send a bottle of Billy Billy to my 'guest speakers' room '5335', with two glasses? On my account."

I had no idea what to expect from a cruise but to date, none of this could have been predicted. None. I was expecting entertainment, singers, dancers, shows, food. Maybe even late drinks in a cabin, but I feel shell-shocked. Georgie bounces up again, looks in the other cupboard.

"Good, at least you have a safe. Have you got your money in there?" she asks.

"Safe from the bees?"

"You know it's just short of a million dollars. What the fuck do we do with a million dollars?"

"Well, you just treated me to a nice bottle of wine," I answer.

"It frightens me," Georgie admits.

"You took the money at the airport, you started this," I accuse.

"I was genuinely trying to find an owner for the case until I saw the same case at customs being opened and it was full of money. That explained why it was so bloody heavy. I was worried in case it was stage kit. I turned and went back to the toilet and checked it. The case I had was full of money too. What was I supposed to do? It looked like millions... I've never had money. I just couldn't leave it."

I can see that she needs to unload, someone to share with. I can see how vulnerable she is under that tough managerial exterior, the confident woman who can walk on a stage and greet a thousand people. It's an interesting combination. I'm learning more about Georgie each time we meet, and there's a magnetism she has which is maybe why she's so brilliant on stage.

There is a knock at the door. The wine is here. This is going to be a much longer night than I expected.

Chapter 33 - Big glasses

Either the glasses are big, or the bottle small, but somehow we've nearly finished a bottle and I'm explaining how the Arab uprisings in Tunisia, Egypt, Libya and Bahrain turned from major protests to Syrian Army intervention back in 2011. Escalations make people form into groups, turn against each other and then foreign governments work out who to support to attack the other. Madness becomes mass casualties, children become parentless and refugees flee for their lives. Time for a new bottle?

We, on the other hand, have become very relaxed sitting opposite each other at each end of my small bed, our legs intertwined. I have no idea how that happened either, but it is easy being with Georgie.

What am I doing here, wide-eyed, a little legless and a lot confused? In three days I've met four women; dodged the wrong one at the airport, been on the run with this one, found a military buddy in Ronni, then chased to an Indian reservation with Jill. Jill, who is wonderful, but Georgie puts a spell on me and I've no idea what I'm doing.

"I like soldiers." She smiles.

Does she? We've both ditched our empty glasses and my fingers slip her shoes off.

"I know, I would have been happy with just her shoes." She says gently having no intention of leaving.

I play with her bare ankles, as her shoes fall to the floor. My toes are in the warmth of her upper thigh and our eyes are locked in silence. I need to command an assault but this is so alien. I grab her ankles, pull her behind the knees, and draw her into me. She makes it easy and I've no idea how my emotional pocket is being picked but we kiss. We kiss deeply, passionately and longingly. It's quite some time before we part.

"I never do that," Georgie says.

"Me neither," I say.

"No. You don't understand," she repeats.

"Never fraternise with staff?" I ask softly.

"Oh no, not that at all. A ship is a virtual rabbit warren of affairs."

"What then?" I ask.

"I don't date men."

Now I understand the smirk from her cabin steward.

-

It's early and we've slept cuddled together all night. She eases herself away starring at the scar on my right shoulder that runs from neck to the top of my arm. She touches it, her hands are soft.

"I have to go to work," she starts, "are you going to risk Cartagena?"

I'm still half asleep and for a moment I'm wondering if she means with Jill, now I've slept with her.

"They had your picture and they want their money back."

She stretches slowly into her clothes hiding my view of her beautiful naked body, a vision that I hope will stay with me for some time. Last night, we slept on a bed of money. More money than anyone can afford to lose, and I still find it hard to understand how we found that shop with the walls made of dollar bills unless the whole block is shops and houses made of money.

"They're after a woman, the wife of a cartel boss. She got on the other ship if she survived. They will have gone after her now, I'll be fine," I say with stupid false confidence.

Georgie pauses at the door.

"OK. We agreed to have dinner tonight."

"We did?"

"As I was leaving the bridge last night, you were going out with Jill."

"Jill. I was."

"You have a short memory," she says.

"No, I remember."

"Good. Enjoy Cartagena. Stay safe. See you later."

Chapter 34 - Cartagena

CRUISE SHIP HEIST – OCEAN ATLANTIC

It's hard looking Jill in the face after she spent the night playing mother to my daughter, while I was sleeping with another woman. She and Georgie could not be more different. Auli'i's with us now and we almost look like a family. It's the disguise I need to feel comfortable walking through the charming, narrow cobbled streets of Cartagena.

Blooming bougainvillaea overflows from balconies of the pastel-coloured, colonial influenced buildings as we stroll in silence. Jill is perfectly dressed, in tight white sixties-style trousers, high-waisted, and short enough to show her ankles in fashionable heeled shoes that she manages effortlessly on the uneven ground. Paired with her tight pink top, she has a Sophia Loren look about her that sits perfectly in these surroundings. Her hair is tied in a scarf and she could easily be a local. Auli'i links arms with her and they both walk like dancers.

Turning into a plaza, the bright sun hits them as quickly as the hawkers trying to sell them bags, hats and sunglasses. I stride forward, closing the distance I had left to admire them both. The hawkers back off; it might be the military stance, the six-foot-plus frame, or to those who can sense it, perhaps I still wreak of danger. After two series of sessions with my therapist, he admitted that when we first met he was scared stiff of me; that takes years of training. We walk towards an alfresco bar that will allow us to gaze at the bright yellow walls and towering domes of the huge cathedral 'St Catherine of Alexandra'. It can be seen from all over the city, but this is an ideal spot from which to observe it.

Like so many historic cities, Cartagena de Indias is built around a perfect harbour, a place where ships must have sought safe haven from the weather, then traded back and forth. America to Europe and back again. Trading routes that still exist for fruit, nuts, coffee, bananas and of course drugs. There has to be an endless number of stories that have played out here since it was founded around 1533, and now it's so peaceful, full of tourists, enjoying the new trade of the mega cruise ships.

A table is offered and no doubt Jill will have asked for her preferred bottle before sitting. I join them after carefully looking round to ensure we're still not being followed or tracked. The day seems all too perfect at the moment. We have come to the very people that have been chasing me and I am hiding in plain sight. Rose wine is poured and I clock two policemen standing by their motorbikes chatting.

"I would love to see the cathedral," Auli'i says.

"Sure," I say, looking at Jill, who agrees. "And what would you like to do Jill?"

She looks over to a smart looking carriage drawn by a pair of horses. "I'd like to take a tour. After the church, if we have time."

We sit there drinking, unrushed. Auli'i is fixated on the cathedral. "I haven't been to church in a long, long while."

"What was your church like?" Jill asks.

"Strict. I learnt to sing there. It was Greek Orthodox, the Eastern Church of Antioch. I used to be scared of the black robes. Then the troubles split our town into religious factions, fighting each other; family against family, friends against friends. When my family were murdered, I left. There were a few of us with no reason to stay. When we got to Aleppo, we went into a church for help. We were all split up and they found me a family who gave me a room, but they made me work hard to pay for it. Then I decided it was time to leave for good… I wonder how I'll feel going inside there."

"Cathedral, then carriage tour around the old town. Let's do it, we may never come back."

I'm definitely not coming back. I stand and search my pockets to pay the bill the waiter is holding, but realise all I have in my pocket is a roll of one-hundred-dollar bills. I manage to separate one.

"We only take pesos, señor," the waiter says.

"I've got this," Jill says, positioning to pay while gaining local knowledge for the large tip she is adding.

Chapter 35 – In plain sight

There's a saying, 'I need a moment'. I've never understood it before, never considered it. However, standing in this city, made beautiful by the hard toil of the 10,000 slaves imported each year... their bloodshed and abuse deserve a moment. The bloodshed just over money. We all stand looking back at the Cathedral, digesting what we have seen but my mind is of current greed and guilt. The huge opulent arches, white and bright. An 18th-century gilded golden altar with hand carved sculptures. It's a show of wealth that holds no comparison to the dark oppressive churches Auli'i described. But all these places of worship mark the cleansing of one race and the start of a new power, and their beliefs being forced on others. With slaves to be converted and baptised, the church would have been busy. Mixed emotions rage for me as they no doubt do for Auli'i, as we've both stood within the fighting caused by opposing beliefs and witnessed the slaughter. There is yet another guilt, the guilt of survival.

We turn and walk amongst other tourists down towards San Pedro Claver Plaza, then along by the government buildings as our waiter kindly directed Jill. The square at the end where we will find the carriage rides is visible.

"I need to go into the bank." The hundreds are burning a hole in my pocket, I need to go and get them split. It's possibly the worst place to risk revealing large bills, here in the centre of the world's drug mafia, but surely the numbers can't be listed. The list would be so huge that no one could compile it.

"I have enough local money, there's no point in changing more and being left with it," Jill argues.

"Just in case, I can always leave it in tips on the ship."

Am I testing these notes deliberately? The ship is close enough and my cover good enough to escape. I step into the bank, there's no turning back now. Anyway, I'm a tourist out with my wife and daughter. Should I bring them into the bank with me? I stop just inside the outer doors and stand next to an equally tall, but a thicker set black security guard. I look at a picture on the wall, marking time.

"That's the Banco de España senor, look it says 1908, I was just a young boy then." He laughs. "Reckon there's another Cartagena over there in Spain. Looks pretty don't it?"

"It sure does," I agree.

I open the door and call to Jill.

"Great picture on the wall here!"

As Jill and Auli'i walk towards us, I show the guard the one-hundred-dollar note.

"Will they change this to local?"

"Colombian banks like big notes. You'll be fine with those, change as many as you like."

I don't know why I certainly don't need the money but I change three.

"Could I send money to a Syrian bank from here. If it was cash?" I ask the teller.

"Yes, senor. We can send it anywhere, we just don't guarantee it arrives." She smiles cheekily, counting out my Pesos.

I breathe a sigh of relief. I have got away with my first cash exchange… and I have an idea.

Chapter 36 – Cash laundry

Plaza de Los Coches is a large square of four and five-story colonial buildings, hotels and offices. The carriages wait by the bearded statue of Cartagena's founding father, Don Pedro de Heredia. Jill is trying to find a particular driver she has been recommended by the waiter, but she is not there. The choice is someone very demonstrative and with an obvious sense of humour. The girls climb in, and I am helped up last as I negotiate the price and pay him up front.

"You let us get on and off, no rushing then I will pay you the same again when we stop."

The deal is struck with a fee that means everything to the driver but is just play-money for me now. As the carriage pulls away Jill is consumed by the sights, and I lean over and whisper to Auli'i,

"Can you get the bank account details of your relatives, so we can send them some money, for food and medicine?"

"The banks have all been destroyed."

"There must still be banks, in Damascus."

Auli'i texts on her phone to find out for me. Banks may be destroyed, but mobile phones survive.

"I feel like Don Pedro is judging me, each time I ride past him! So, mis amigos, what do you know about Cartagena?" the driver asks us.

"Nothing," Jill admits.

"Good, I can tell you a bunch of rubbish." The driver laughs. "My name is Inigo Montoya."

"No, I saw that film, you're not him!" I counter.

The driver turns. "Good, I like you. We will have fun. What have you seen so far?"

"The cathedral," Auli'i says, enjoying herself.

"Which Cathedral?"

"The yellow one," Auli'i shouts.

"OK! We do the other colours."

Not all carriage drivers are the same, and so far today we have been lucky. He has added a loudspeaker down by our feet, and he wears a head microphone. A mixture of new and old that works for us all. The slightly elevated position in the carriage, and not having to concentrate on where we are going, all makes for a very different experience. Jill is making us laugh doing little queen waves and Auli'i is copying, though I'm not sure she understands the origin of the humour.

"The white cathedral!" our driver announces, "Cathedral de San Pedro Claver. While others got rich from the slaves, he went and helped them, cared for them, fed them and gave medicine. He was born in Spain, went to university in Barcelona, and came to Colombia in 1610."

"I think he's our kind of guy, don't you?" I say addressing Auli'i and she hi-fives me as we all get down from the carriage. I pass our driver another small note, but this time he refuses.

"When we complete, Senor. I will take you all the way back to your ship. My day is your day."

Back on the carriage, feeling we've had our fill of churches, the driver continues his easy patter,

"We are now in the centre of the old city. This is the naval museum of Columbus, opened in 1992 to commemorate the 500th anniversary of his finding this side of the world. We can stop if you like museums?"

He glances back and both my travelling partners are shaking their heads 'no'. I could have stopped, had I been with Ronni or Hunter, we may have found it very interesting, but we continue.

"Now, this you will like. For me, the most beautiful place in Cartagena, Plaza de Santa Teresa. Please take your time, my time is your time."

We took more time than we should, but our driver was still there, though we did have to wake him. Our tour continues and the driver's performance is peppered with stories based on the city's bloodthirsty pirating past, both inside and outside the fortress Castillo de San Felipe de Barajas, which was on my to-do list. It's one of the strongest forts ever created by the Spaniards during their colonial period, that was kick-started after the ethnic cleansing of Spain by Catholic Monarchs Queen Isabella I of Castile, and King Ferdinand II of Aragon, and it has a Palace of Inquisition. We also see Plaza De Bolivar and the Gold Museum. We're exhausted, but before we return to the ship I ask him to take us back to my bank.

Inside, I see the same bank teller who remembers me, and I offer her the bank details Auli'i has been sent, which she claims to understand and she types the details into her keypad.

"How much would you like to send?"

The question is priceless, I have no idea just how much to risk. "Is there a limit?"

"No, senor, just a fee."

"Five thousand dollars," I say then count out the money just under the counter ledge.

"Do you want the fees taken out of that, or are you paying them separately?" she asks.

"I'll pay them."

The form is printed out. She signs, I sign, my passport is scanned and it appears done. It all seemed far too easy. I am smiling inside, walking on air, I am alert, watching front, back and centre, but the test has been a success, and now all I have to do is get out of dodge.

Outside, I climb back into the carriage.

"To the ship, driver. And don't spare the horses!"

He thinks that was a joke, so do the ladies, but it wasn't. It has been a great day. I tip him handsomely, and I'm still glancing back and forth as we show our cruise cards and go through the port gates into the secure area.

It all appears to have gone without a hitch and tonight I can enjoy a glass or two with Georgie, as promised.

As I follow Jill up the gangway, she turns back.

"Why don't we have dinner tonight, the three of us?"

Chapter 37 – Let's have dinner

"Georgie. The good news is Auli'i's fine. The bad news is I'd like to rain-check our dinner. Tonight's awkward," I say, waiting for the unknown.

"OK."

That was too easy. Is she upset? Am I in trouble? Should I say something else? I don't get a chance, Georgie, who must be working, is efficient.

"Tomorrow, no excuses. It's a formal night and you'll be in full dress uniform," she says seductively and hangs up.

The ship's moving and I appear to have left Cartagena behind just as smoothly as I've postponed Georgie. She then appears on the public address system welcoming people back on board and listing the entertainment this evening. Now I know why I got off so easily. I check the mirror on the way to the door. I might not be in uniform tonight, but everything still has to be perfect, it's a military thing. As I reach for the door, the phone rings.

"Kieron Philips," I answer.

"Even though dinner's off, might you get lost and find yourself in my cabin later?" It's Georgie, with the cheek in her voice I love.

"I've no idea where it is, so I would be lost."

"Nine-seven-two-five. Not before eleven thirty," she says and the phone goes dead.

CRUISE SHIP HEIST – OCEAN ATLANTIC

I wander into the sports bar where Jill has suggested we meet for a pre-dinner drink. Tonight there's a magician on in the main theatre and his billing is based around his success on a TV talent show. He sounds amazing and I like magicians. I like all sleight of hand, whether done by politicians, spin doctors or my old military superiors. They all make reality disappear and you learn to love the tricks for what they are rather than resent them.

Thirsty, I order a beer, one thing I forgot to do during our day out was take in water. I should know better, but in these new surroundings, my guard is dropping. The glass dips below half full before I put it down. I guess you can take the man out of the army, but not the army out of the squaddie.

Jill glides in like a goddess in a chiffon dress that looks like it has been made around her and I smile like a Cheshire cat, trying to keep my eyes off the tattoo and what the dress might or might not be revealing. As wonderful as the image is there is just something about her, which for me says friend, not a lover. How have I been so lucky to meet two, actually three with Ronni, wonderful and very different women? Ronni should never be left out of that group because she looks amazing during the day and very special in a dress, plus she can handle a weapon. I like that. Jill has not arrived with Auli'i, which is good, because Jill and her getting too close would complicate what's already going to be a sensitive few days ahead.

"Would you like a drink while we wait for Auli'i?"

"Perfect Gin Cocktail, please," she says to the waiter.

"You look great." I compliment her, knowing that going too far will add to a growing problem.

The barman starts to elaborately make her drink, and it suddenly hits me that Auli'i, who's so desperate for me to find a partner, might have set me up. Are we going to be alone? That could be embarrassing.

"There will be three of us, won't there?" I ask Jill because she's had more of my daughter's ear than I have today. Jill turns to me and I sense a problem. I imagine us out as a couple being caught by Georgie, I imagine all kinds of complications somehow more daunting than a gunman looking for me and his boss's wife.

"No," she says, "not three."

Has Auli'i tricked me into a date with Jill? All the years of depravity, serving king and country behind the lines and missing out on life now thrust me into warp-speed catch-up; treats thrust at me so fast that the universe cannot schedule them apart?

"Four," she says.

I relax, not two. Then after my moment of relief, I panic. Georgie? Have she and Georgie been talking, working out who knows what? Jill's face doesn't give anything away. I fill with a new kind of worry. One I have never considered before. I look at her and search for an answer.

"Auli'i has met someone, and she wants to introduce you to him. So there'll be four of us and I hope you're as excited as I am."

I'm shocked and relieved at the same time. What should worry me more than my daughter having a boyfriend or that she told Jill before me? My glass must have a leak, it's empty and I'm too embarrassed to order another.

Auli'i enters, looking stunning and dragging a young man with her. I've no idea how to react. None. I've never prepared myself for this moment, and as I look at the young man beside her I realise I know him.

Chapter 38 – The trickster

"Dad, this is Christophe," Auli'i announces. "He's a cadet officer. I wanted to tell you about him, but I hadn't found the right moment."

"Sir," Christophe says, duly shaking my hand.

I recognise him. He's the sailor the crew sent over to steal my notes as they heckled me on the bridge. My poker-face must have left me as I look at him accusingly.

"I'm sorry about yesterday, Sir," he apologises.

Auli'i turns sharply, unaware of his secret. He couldn't have introduced himself to me in front of his captain, and I guess telling Auli'i might have caused more concern about tonight. Why a sailor? Why not someone from her own department? How did this come about?

"Do the crew know our connection?" I ask.

"They all knew, they knew you didn't know I was seeing Ee… that made it worse."

"You played it well, Christophe, I remember the torment of my early years. It's nice to meet you."

"Thank you, sir," he says, and I'm trying to place his accent.

I see Auli'i relax, though she's a little confused.

"A drink here, or shall we go through?" I ask.

"Let's go to dinner," she suggests, indicating for Jill and me to lead the way.

Jill takes my arm. "He seems very nice," she whispers.

And behind I can hear Auli'i asking him what we were talking about as they follow us to the restaurant.

Le Jardin de Palermo is different from the Asian restaurant. It's lighter; the tables and chairs are green, posing as garden furniture. The design, from the prints on the walls down to the napkins, all hint at Italy. The waiter offers menus and introduces himself briefly as the mix is more complex tonight.

Yesterday's waiters put on a show for Jill and me but tonight, as four, our unit is not looking for outside distractions.

"Do you think the fish is fresh?" Jill asks.

"There's only one way to know a fish is fresh-" Auli'i offers, and we all look at her. "-to catch it yourself."

Jill and Christophe find her answer amusing, but to Auli'i, it was a memory and I notice she is hurt.

"Auli'i is our expert fisherman," I explain.

"My dad taught me to fish. He preached, 'if you can fish, you'll never starve'." She pauses. "And I didn't, starve." There is silence then she corrects herself. "My real dad. Not that you're not real." Auli'i hugs my arm.

"I'm real alright, and as concerned you're all grown-up and have a boyfriend as I'm sure he'd be."

"He'd find all of my new life a challenge, but I like to think he'd understand."

"I'd like to have known him."

I'd have liked to have met both her parents, they raised a special girl. I've never discovered much about them through her as she rarely speaks much of the past, but tonight she has a suitor that wants to know all about her.

"He would tell tales of the Euphrates, so full of fish he'd only have to work half a day. That was before fishermen got greedy and used dynamite or electric shock to catch fish in bulk," she says. "So, I think I'll have fish tonight, for my dad's hard work."

"Me too," agrees Jill.

"But then some fishermen used poison; Lannate or chlorine powders, which killed the fish, making them float to the top. If you ate those fish you'd be ill… Maybe I won't have the fish."

Christophe joins the conversation. "How can you eat a fish that's poisoned?"

"You don't."

"But how would you know?"

"They turn blue," Auli'i says.

"Where are you from Christophe?" I ask.

"Bulgaria, Sir. The lads call me Uncle; they think it's hilarious."

"Uncle?"

I'm distracted noticing Hunter on the other side of the ship, with a female officer. They're both dressed in officer whites but look too close to be just colleagues. Le Jardin de Palermo fills the space surrounding one loop of the Atrium on deck eight. He must be almost a hundred feet away, directly across the beam from me, his partner has her back to me. Is it his wife? Didn't he imply he was single? Seeing them in the distance is making me uneasy. Is it that he's not watching over the ship and keeping us all safe?

"Me neither, I didn't get it, Dad," Auli'i says.

I force myself to re-join their conversation. It feels like I've been adrift for hours looking across at my partner in crime, but it was seconds. Get what? I try to reconnect to the here and now.

"Uncle Bulgaria. Apparently, he's a Womble," explains Christophe.

"Yes, of course. Adopt it, own it, and they'll soon get bored. Uncle's a good nick-name."

"I have. They all call me, 'Uncle'." Christophe smiles.

He's smart. I like that, but I'm so distracted by Hunter. I need to get up and speak to him. I'm sure he said he was single and it doesn't look like it. He might be able to keep quiet about nearly seven million pounds each but can she? They seem locked in a romantic conversation.

Jill has noticed I'm distracted, she's looking around the circular balcony to try and see what is stealing my attention.

"It's nothing."

"You had that serious look you had back in Panama at the tribal village."

She's beginning to read me too well. The waiter rescues me by taking food orders and comes to me last.

"I'll have the chicken romaine with salad to start."

"Sir, please help yourself," he says, leaving.

The salad buffet will get me to the other side of the ship and closer to Hunter and his mystery lady. As I look across the room, Hunter is also up from the table. He and his lady are leaving. The atrium offers no direct route; just a drop to the dance floor on the deck below. He's heading towards the exit. I move off quickly towards the food, trying to get to him before he goes, but as I round the rail there's no way I can catch him or fall into his peripheral vision. His arm is around her waist and they've both got their backs to me as they head towards the sports bar beyond.

My blood runs cold, it's her hair, I recognise her hair. Surely it can't be the woman from the airport? The wife of El Rey?

Chapter 39 – The King

Rarely have I eaten anything, even a salad, so fast. I'm sat wishing for the main course to arrive. I've been the absent father, I should focus on being at the dinner table with my daughter and the man she has introduced me to.

My chicken is placed before me, the others all have fish and I can see them checking the colour. Auli'i starts to eat which seems to give confidence to the others to start.

"The fish is great, it tastes fresh. It was just the chlorine attack back home brought back so many confusing memories," she says.

Auli'i has rarely said anywhere near this much about what happened back home. I've never asked because I've never been sure how much she would want to talk about it, but Jill is inquisitive, and Christophe wants to know everything about her. I can see it in his eyes, he cares for her in a way that's hard to understand as they've only been together weeks, months at most.

"We don't know how lucky we are living in the west, not ever having been near a war," Jill says.

I look at Christophe and see his arm move. I know he's taken her hand under the table and I feel secure knowing she's moved her life on. I feel someone else sharing the responsibility of Auli'i with me and know that one day, maybe soon, I'll be replaced and my short term role as guardian will be eclipsed.

"But you have terrorism. Bombs on buses and trains," Christophe says to Jill.

"We do, but I don't feel that's the same. What do you think Auli'i?" Jill asks.

"You're right. It's different. You can't imagine hearing huge thuds that shake the ground like a giant stamping through your village. Soon to have those fears replaced by the choking smell of sulphur in the air, explosions splitting houses. Then you're forced to run, jumping over people burning in the street. You learn never to look back, just to run, but never straight. Snipers shoot at your feet, maybe just for target practice. Why else would they shoot at running children? You run and run so fast your lungs empty and by the time you breathe back in, you've grown up. And you realise that you're not just an adult, but the only adult left in your family. You run and you never stop running because you've nothing left. Nothing to keep you there. My misfortune was in the end what saved me. Had I still got family, I would never have left them."

I'd never heard her speak like that, but I understand it. I understand what made her so strong and independent.

"You're very brave." Christophe smiles at her. Auli'i shakes her head, no.

"So do we eat this fish or not?" Chris says to lighten things. I like him. I like him a lot.

"Eat the fish," she says smiling. "And the one thing I still take with me everywhere is my net. The fishing net that my father gave me and taught me to throw out. The one that kept me fed, is the first thing I pack. And it is in my safe –"

"I am not sure I ever learned the knack of throwing that net. You should always keep it safe," I say, and stand feeling I might be able to escape for a moment, "Would you mind if I went to the bathroom?"

I'm allowed to leave, but the last place I'm going is to the bathroom.

Chapter 40 – The atrium

The atrium has a second loop, a figure of eight and is split by a drop to the art gallery a deck below. Our side is the café, the other side is a sports bar and casino. To the right are chairs and tables with flat screen TVs on the wall, to the left coin machines flash wildly, almost hiding the blackjack and roulette tables. At the far end is the cocktail bar with stools all along the front, not one is available. My eyes scan the casino area quickly, as I remember Auli'i saying staff can't gamble. Hunter is unlikely to be in there. They're not at the bar, and I don't see them to my right although I can't see behind the high bench seats that run down the centre making an island.

A football match is on all the television screens around the bar. I'm not aware what game it is but my impression is that it's important as a full crowd is engaged. I don't think Hunter would have been able to waltz in here and find an empty chair anywhere, but I have to check. Time's escaping. My free pass from the dinner table has a limit. I walk between the chairs and television screens quickly. I go to the bar and circle back down the other side, through the casino towards the cashier's desk. Hunter's not in here.

I re-join the table as the plates are being cleared.

"So where did you go?" Jill asks softly in my ear.

Christophe and Auli'i are chatting, no doubt he's discovering more about her.

"Bathroom," I say.

"No, you didn't. The bathroom is below and the stairs are here in the centre of the atrium. You went into the sports bar."

My, she is attentive. I've not had to answer to a partner before, so this is all new. Surely there's a toilet facility in the bar? But I notice guests leaving that casino section and rushing down our adjacent atrium stairs and I know I've been caught in a lie. She knows it too.

"I know this ship very well, I know you less well, but I know there's something going on," she says.

"I saw Hunter, head of security, I needed to thank him for helping me with my Panama Canal notes. He was eating over there, he left and went out that way. I thought I could catch him." Most of my answer is true. Jill's nodding her head. Maybe I'm safe.

"So... do we leave those two alone now?"

That's a great idea, but then I will be alone with Jill and I need to find Hunter, with whichever female officer I've mistaken for the wife of El Ray, then I've got a date back at Georgie's room.

"I would think that your friend walked through the bar, past the cabins on the eighth floor and down the stairs at the back to see the second show of the comedian in the club on the deck below. It would save him walking through the promenade deck," Jill offers, pleased with herself.

Her hand has unnervingly found my thigh as she leans in. She's a great detective, but dangerous. It's time to move.

"You two have a great evening. See you tomorrow." I smile and I mean it.

Following Jill is a pleasure, she walks like a ballroom dancer, her body flowing effortlessly. We pass the casino and the same people appear to be fixed in the same positions, tapping their money away.

"I see you're on at eleven tomorrow, in the theatre."

I'd forgotten that tomorrow is a sea day, a workday. Tonight guests can stay up late and enjoy the many entertainment areas of the ship, but I should refrain, I'll be on stage performing in my parade uniform tomorrow, then in the evening on show at dinner- with tonight's overnight date- in my dress uniform. Tomorrow I'm a ceremonial soldier again, and hopefully, with South America behind us, the warrior soldier will finally be retired, again.

We enter the elevator area, but Jill saunters past the lifts and towards the stairwell. It is only one floor down. I follow, but at the top of the stairs Jill does an abrupt stop and turns knowing that I will concertina into her. I have to hold onto her so as not to push her down the stairs with my momentum. She is clever and dangerous.

"So, my room tonight or yours?" she asks.

"I daren't, not tonight. I have to prepare for my show tomorrow and be up, fresh, focussed and presentable."

"I wanted to show you all of my tattoo before it vanishes. I like it."

"I think I might get to see it around the pool tomorrow if you are wearing a bikini."

"I don't take defeat easily. Tomorrow?" She breathes so close to my cheek I can feel the words as well as hear them.

"I promised I'd have dinner with Georgie tomorrow night. It's a formal night and she wanted to dine with me in my ceremonial uniform. Sorry. I'm not trying to avoid you."

I am, and I don't think I'm doing it very well. My uniform is ready, my act needs no preparation.

"Then have dinner with her tomorrow night, and come to my room for dessert afterwards."

Not waiting for an answer, Jill turns and walks down the stairs. I follow. Is this my introduction into the gentle life of cruising? A few million, gunrunning, local honey on tap, local mafia with guns and a full dance card?

We turn into the nightclub and just inside the entrance are Hunter and the woman from the airport. She is the one I was shown in the picture, who Hunter told me I was seen with. Who the Emberá Indians told me was the wife of Panama's biggest drug lord, and who is now wearing navy whites.

I smile, slip my arm around Jill and walk past them with a nod. Maybe they're both undercover drug cops, maybe I've fallen into an international sting. What other answer is there?

"I thought you needed to speak to him," Jill says.

'I do, but this isn't the right place."

Powering into the venue, we both walk into Georgie at the bar, how could she be missed? She stands tall in heels and is wearing a red dress with a line of white buttons all the way down the front.

Her eyes drop to my arm around Jill's waist.

Chapter 41 - Nightclub

The nightclub is awash with colourful dresses, but all the men are dressed in standard black dinner suits. All but me and Hunter behind me in his officer whites with stars on his epaulettes showing he is security. It shows how unfair it is on the sexes, if the ladies also had one standard dress in one colour, red maybe, it would be so much easier. Mrs El Ray in her junior officer whites would still stand out. I wish I was somewhere else. Anywhere else, safe with Auli'i. They can keep the money if it's still there and that I'm beginning to doubt that. I've no idea what's going on but I'm feeling used. I've spent years managing units and working behind lines and I end up being used on a cruise ship. I have been had and had again and Witowski has the cheek to complain about having to be a bee wrangler.

I turn and look for Hunter but he and the woman have gone. I won't get my answer tonight. Not unless Georgie knows, not unless she's in on it.

"Are you having a wonderful evening?" Georgie asks with a loaded grin.

She has that leading, threatening smile you see in American horror movies, so polite, but the audience knows it is false, something is about to go wrong. I seem to be in a freak show.

"Yes, fantastic," Jill answers for me.

I prepare to speak but I'm rendered helpless by a lack of anything sensible to add.

"Have you been to dinner?" Georgie asks Jill as if I'm not even there.

"Jardin de Palermo."

"I trust it didn't disappoint?" Georgie angles.

"Very nice."

"And do you have plans for later?" Georgie fires.

"I hope so." Jill smiles.

"I trust they won't disappoint," Georgie says starting to move away, looking at me.

"No one will be disappointed," I add, reaching for Georgie's shoulder to stop her.

"Yes?" she says waiting.

"Did you see the woman Hunter was with?"

"No," Georgie says. "I didn't. Sorry."

Georgie leaves and Jill stands before me, waiting.

"She didn't see the woman Hunter was with," I fumble. I feel empty, waiting for my brain to catch up. I wonder if she can see the buffering wheel rotating in my eyes with the caption, 'please wait'.

"I gathered. But why would she have, and why do you need to know?" she asks.

"I am good with faces, very good, and she looks like someone I met once," I share.

"Obviously not…" Jill pauses. "…as good with faces as you thought."

"No. Old age. No wonder they retired me out. What would you like to drink?" I ask edging towards the bar but my escape is stopped by an efficient waiter. He will bring me everything I need, except answers, excuses, and a disguise.

"Hendrix and Fever Tree please," Jill asks.

I give him my card.

"Double madam?" he asks, dutifully upselling.

"I think so." She smiles.

I nod holding up two fingers, indicating I'll have the same. Not because I fancy a G&T, but because I don't have the space to think.

"I did Hunter a small favour. Apparently, I'm looking after something for him. Don't ask me, I don't know what it is," I start with no second verse worked out.

"But surely, rule number one is don't take anything on board for another person?"

The problem with Jill is that she's far too clever. She roots out problems and decodes the errors. It's what she does for a living, plain and simple. A cog in my brain turns and an error message flares up. I must not disappoint tonight.

"It's not about what was brought on board so much as the room I'm in. I'm in an officer's cabin, a staff cabin. Nothing like yours. I look out of my window to see a lifeboat, nothing else, just a lifeboat. It appears to be used for storage and he had loads of stuff stored in my room and asked if he could leave it there while I was on board. Which is fine, as I've very little. But if I'm storing his stuff because he's had a female officer move in, then that is taking a liberty."

I pause, congratulating myself. Now I need to change the subject in order to avoid further investigation.

"Do you know, much of Syria has had no water or electricity for two years, and many of the civilians are trying to escape. It's not easy with a family and trying to carry possessions."

"What made you think of that?" Jill asks.

She's clever, sensing a glitch in my control code, understanding what has caused it might lead her to a fix.

"That I travel light. But Auli'i left her home with nothing. Having nothing was what totally freed her." I'm pensive as the drinks arrive.

"I will bring your card in a moment, Sir," the waiter says leaving.

I can see Jill about to say something, so I jump in. "I don't normally drink gin. I must have been totally distracted."

"Why don't we just go back to my room and fuck?" Jill says. "Then you can prepare all you want."

I nearly choke. Twice I've had to dodge this bullet in a matter of minutes. I guess the biblical version of denial is three times but I need to escape before I'm challenged again.

"We, er, we agreed tomorrow. After my staff dinner. And to be honest, I shouldn't be drinking a double gin tonight. I can't do my show in the morning if I have a hangover," I admit. "It is my first one on a ship and I'll be judged on it."

I could drink this drink and hers like a shot. I need to drink it, but now I can't. Avoiding my glass, I notice Tony and the other solo cruisers Jill was with when we first met at the quiz waving to us. The singles. They have a table.

"Look, your friends, the solos, are waving us over. They have a great table to watch the act. Take my gin, I can't drink it. Mustn't drink it. I'll go and prepare my show. If I don't find you later, then we can agree to rendezvous tomorrow."

"Can we?" Jill says looking at me sternly.

She could be a man crusher. I like that. But now it's time to go. I hand her the glass, peck her on the cheek and turn. Is there a disaster behind me? Am I about to be shot in the back? I dare not turn and look.

Chapter 42 – G&T

I'm normally good with numbers and letters, but there's no answer when I knock. Is it the right door? Do I stand outside and wait? Left here exposed, I could be seen by more of her colleagues than is good for either of us. Do I go? Has she changed her mind?

I walk to the end of the corridor and hover like a rookie on a bad stakeout until my patience wains and I press the elevator button. My deck is way below hers. The doors open and there she is, we're face to face.

"Where's your friend?" Georgie asks.

"I managed to lose her."

"Shame." She turns into her corridor. "I told you I like women and she's interesting."

This night could not be more confusing, but I follow awkwardly, hoping I'm doing the right thing.

"It was a dinner for me to meet Auli'i's new man, a cadet."

"I know." Georgie turns to me as she stops at her door. "Jill's very attractive, for an older lady," she says backing in.

I follow and catch the door before it slams, letting it gently make that slow metal click. I did not want it announced to all the neighbours that she's back for the night.

"Who was the female officer with Hunter?"

Georgie shakes her head. "Didn't see. Why?"

It's my turn to shake my head 'no' and contemplate the madness of the suggestion. It bugs me, I don't normally get faces wrong. The woman at the airport is etched in my mind.

"What?" Georgie asks again ducking to the floor level mini-fridge. The light goes on as she opens the door. It is packed full. This is her living room, kitchen and bedroom for months on end.

"How long do you do on board?" I ask.

"Long enough for you to come back a few times, most of your audience changes every two weeks."

"Most?" I ask.

"We have a few who almost live on board. No idea what they see in it."

"Aren't you supposed to be more positive?"

"I am. It is great for a holiday, but those of us who work here look forward to getting off." She smiles, pouring two gins, then adding tonic.

"It's worrying you... the woman with Hunter?" She focusses.

"I apologise. It is and it shouldn't distract me."

"Let's get it out of the way. Who was she?" Georgie asks.

"That was my question. She looks like the woman arrested at the airport."

"The drug smuggler's wife who we thought would be dead?"

"It sounds crazy. In officer whites, sounds too crazy."

"More than crazy," Georgie agrees. "Why would he be with her? How would she get on board? Well... he of all people could get anyone on board and put anyone in officer whites."

It's an outrageous idea and all I offer is a shrug in agreement. I sink my gin having missed out on the one I ordered with Jill just minutes ago. I hope she's not ringing my room, or worse, knocking on the door.

Georgie's glass is also empty. She is slowly unbuttoning her front fastened dress, bottom to top, staring me straight in the eyes. This is an act of perfection; had she started with the top button, she would have ended bent at the reveal stage. The dress waves open and closed to reveal a lack of underwear. The mood has changed. Georgie is a magnet and her eyes steal me. The last button is released and her dress drops off her. She stands naked in heels as if it's a party trick she knows well. I feel I should applaud but I'm spellbound, stunned and excited. Too excited to react but she is waiting.

"It would look better in the shoes you had your eye on."

"I agree, and you think they're on board."

Georgie steps forward and we kiss. I see nothing, but feel myself being led to the bed.

Chapter 43 – Red shoes, red seats

A morning, which could have been filled with embarrassment and awkwardness, has energy driven by schedule. Georgie has duties and I need to go and prepare. I'm on stage at eleven. Seeing I'm dressed and restless way faster than her, still naked, she frog-marches me to her door.

"I'll see you tonight, full dress."

I linger in the corridor, wishing to be caught by Manesh, wishing to through his perception of Miss Georgie upside down, but he is not there. I walk swiftly, double checking the time I've allocated myself before I'm due on stage. I'm already looking forward to this evening, wondering just how enticing Georgie will be tonight. Then my mind flashes to Jill. She said solo cruisers were just friends. Allowing each other to dine out, dress up, but she's expecting to see me after dinner in her room and I can't do that. I've let that solo cruiser friendship go way too far and unless I am reading it incorrectly she wants to be more than friends. Even friends with benefits is not an option. I stop at my cabin door, I have no cruise card. I double check my pockets. Did I leave it in Georgie's cabin? No. My mind races back. Damn! The club last night. The waiter will have returned it to Jill, who will ... No, will she be inside? My stomach sinks. I raise my hand to knock on the door, but I can't do it. I can't face her.

"Hello, Sir"

I turn and see my cabin steward looking at me from his utility trolley just two doors down the corridor.

"Kayan! Good morning. I thought I heard you inside," I say to excuse my standing outside with raised hand, "I've left my key inside, would you mind letting me in?"

He attends like a shot, the door lock is released with a solenoid click and I'm free to go inside.

"If I was working inside, sir, the door would be open, always."

I open the door slowly. I breathe a sigh of relief. Jill's not inside. The bed is still down and made, I need to get back on schedule. I check every detail of my parade uniform in my mirror. I open my bag to see the computer, double check the charger and adapter to go from its side port to a VGA connector, which they stressed I bring, are both also there. My magic clicker and its receiver are in their folder, there's nothing more to do other than leave.

The unlit theatre's velvet seats are an empty sea of dark red bumps. There's no engineer in the sound box yet. Two passengers wander in slowly lost with too much choice as to where to sit. Eventually, they choose, nowhere near each other, to no doubt strain in the dark to read the 'Ship's Daily' which they both have. I walk to the front. The huge empty stage gets bigger as I approach, and the lectern smaller and lonelier. Where's the screen? I look back to the sound desk for an engineer, then at my watch. I was told thirty minutes before, which I imagine is the start of his shift. I'm early. I climb the six narrow steps onto the stage and stand by the lectern. I plug the charger into the power socket, then into my computer, and seat it firmly behind the retaining ledge on the lectern. The machine is on, but the small green light on the charger is not. It's on via battery and that could be my first disaster; there's no power to the lectern and I don't want battery failure.

A small sound-lead already plugged into the lectern fits into my sound-out and the role of VGA cable on the floor connects to my adapter for a picture. If only there was a screen and a working projector. That's it, I'm ready. I look up and my audience has already gone up by fifty percent, a third person is walking in. No, they must be confused, they're now walking out. At least my engineer has arrived, lights flash on in the sound booth at the back of the auditorium. He waves to me.

With nowhere else to go I wander up to his control area. A huge sound desk and an impressive light desk. The project comes alive as the screen starts to roll down on its electric motors. He may think he's clever but I can also operate everything from here with my clicker.

"You have audio?" he asks.

"Yes," I say clicking the slides forward to a video clip with sound.

The engineer checks his fader, desk, and cables. "No, I have nothing. Is your volume up?"

I return to the stage passing my audience, now almost in double figures. At this rate, I could entertain this crowd in my room, well Jill's room, rather than this 1,200 seat theatre.

My volume is up, I remove the lead from the side of my machine and hear it play on my internal speakers. I put it back, then check the other end is plugged into the lectern. It's not. It's unplugged just enough not to work. The sound kicks in as I re-seat it properly. Was that an accident or low-level petty sabotage? The engineer gives me the thumbs up, but I hold up the mains plug to indicate that I've no power. I'm going to double check everything that could disrupt my show. He is on his way down with my microphone and I will watch him do all those checks. The waiting is blacked out in my brain.

My introduction by Adrian, Georgie's number two, marks the point of no return and I approach the stage to very full applause. God bless the uniform. The rest should be easy, I've spoken about all these things before and I know the show works to hardened soldiers, male and female, but who knows how it will go down with this crowd?

"Good morning. Thank you for coming! I know there are many wonderful activities all over the ship... those who are expecting line dancing, sorry you are in the wrong place! That's in the atrium, and handicraft is upstairs in the crow's nest."

I look out the audience, well-spaced, making it look busy. They giggle, but it's not them I'm concentrating on. My scan of the room sees Auli'i and Christophe. Jill is in with her solo friends, and finally, I spot Hunter, standing in the dark shadows at the back. Maybe he thinks I can't see him, but I can and the woman next to him is unmistakably her, Mrs El Ray, I'm sure it is.

Chapter 44 – Looking out

"When you ask for a little Cheddar Cheese after dinner tonight with your coffee, you're asking for the most popular cheese in the United Kingdom, and the second most popular in the U.S. If only someone owned a patent on it, but Cheddar

Cheese is not even a 'protected designation of origin' in the European Union. Neither the cheese nor the name demands a royalty. Shame, as America consumes around one-and-a-half million tonnes a year, and Britain about three-hundred thousand tonnes a year. It was made popular by war! In the Second World War, it was known as 'Government Cheddar'. During rationing, most milk was used to make one single kind of cheese, almost wiping out all the other varieties."

I must have gone on too long because I sense movement in the wings behind me and I can see the pianist from the lounge bar upstairs standing at the side of the stage holding music. Some people are already leaving, the dash has started, and a new crowd is forming where Hunter was standing in the shadows at the back. Not a bad place to end; war and food.

"Enjoy dinner tonight. Please stop and chat if you see me around the ship, and I'll be back with more odd tales on the next sea day."

There is decent applause, so I must have done OK. Stage Crew are already pushing a grand piano on the other side, background music has started on the address system and the screen is rising. I close my computer but a crowd is forming at the front trying to catch my attention with questions.

Hunter is nowhere to be seen. No Georgie either, so she hasn't watched my show. Auli'i comes up onto the stage and helps dismantle my computer. With the piano locked into position, one of the stage crew is straight in remove the lectern and another is taking my microphone and belt pack. I feel like a quick-change artist.

"You're all welcome to stay for choir," the pianist announces to the auditorium, testing his microphone. Guests laugh, those leaving and those staying, the next section of entertainment is about to segue seamlessly on.

"Shake a few hands before we go," Auli'i encourages, holding my computer and cables, but encouraging me to drift slowly away and backstage.

I move to the front against the traffic of guests allowed to climb the side stairs onto the stage now the screen has been raised and safely docked. They are arranging themselves into a curved tiered formation. Thanking each of my guests will intrude on the choir, it's obvious I'll have to finish earlier next time. Assuring them I'll do questions and answers next sea day, I escape backstage with Auli'i.

"Where's Christophe?"

Auli'i points and I look towards the piano where Christophe has joined the pianist.

"He's in the choir?"

"He loves it," she says, putting my computer in its bag. 'You were great Dad! They'll want you on all the ships."

"Thanks. It all went so fast."

Not only did my act whiz by, but the choir is now singing to a small audience, only a handful, but there are people watching the rehearsal. Steps at the back of the stage feel like they lead deep into the pointed front of the ship. There are clothes rails, all full of costumes and a large trunk flight case with the label on, 'Musicals 3: Props'. The labels suggest it's been sent from a production house in Skipton, North Yorkshire of all places. Programming logistics must be as well organised as moving crew around the world to meet ships, picking up supplies and fresh food, and finding docks to berth in.

"You've got the secret."

I'm listening, a touch concerned at the word secret, while looking at the trunks. I see one labelled, 'Transfer to the Ms Sea Highway in Lisbon'. Auli'i is waiting with the door into the dressing room open.

"What are you looking at?" she asks.

"The trunks."

"What for? Do you need one?"

"What secret?" I reflect back to the first question while shaking my head 'no' in answer to the trunk.

Has she read my mind? Sizing up a stage props box to get millions of dollars moved.

"You appealed to the female audience, not every male presenter does. Your show works for everyone. You were perfect." She beams.

"I would hardly call it a show."

"It is, and you got a bigger audience than some evening acts," she says, which is a nice compliment as she knows what goes on. I doubt Adrian or Ricardo would tell me that, maybe not even Georgie, if daytime even passes her desk.

I follow Ee through the dressing room and I get to see where she prepares for her shows. Pictures are all over the dressing room mirrors, but hers has a familiar picture of the two of us pinned on it, though most are of her and Christophe. I'm glad I still have one.

"What do your cousins actually need in Syria, apart from money?"

That stops her.

"Anything could be sourced from Damascus or Turkey, so there's no need to ship things in trunks, Dad." She's trying to second guess me.

She doesn't know that I could fill that trunk with money if the twenty million were all mine if it's still there. If Mrs El Ray has not been and got all her money back while I'm not in the room.

I've got a lot to sort out before I can be sure any of it is mine.

Chapter 45 – My share

"You need something to sell after your show. The singers sell DVDs... you could write a book!" Auli'i suggests, opening a backstage door into bright sunlight.

The wind on the promenade deck hits me as hard as her left field suggestion. This is the crew way to get in and out of the theatre, avoiding the need to go past all the guests, I guess technically I'm not supposed to use it.

"Just write a book?" I question.

"Yes," she says marching me along the deck against the fresh breeze.

"You said you needed to earn some money."

"Maybe not now," I let slip.

"You got a job?" she says stopping firmly on the deck outside the door at mid-ships.

"Maybe, maybe I have some money, maybe, to do something, possibly like a children's home. And it would give me a salary."

From one can of worms to another, this is a conversation I should never have started until I know where I stand. She allows me inside and walks me to a free table from the row that lines the side of the ship looking out to sea. She sits.

"Is it a charity job? Is the parcel you gave me to look after money? How much is in my safe?"

"No," I offered hesitantly.

A waiter attends us efficiently,

"Would either of you like a drink?"

Auli'i shakes her head and he leaves not really expecting a sale, he can see she is staff by her lapel badge even if he doesn't know her and he must do.

"How much did you transfer to Damascus?"

She had not taken this too seriously until now. She knows I spent a lot of money getting her to England and through school and that I was running on empty, but it has never been quantified in any way.

"Hmmm, maybe I could write; novels on missions behind lines do well."

I'm grasping for time or a conversation change. I really need to go and see Hunter and find out what's going on, I liked him, but now I don't trust him. First I need to go to my room and make sure the money is still under my bed. She can see I'm deferring.

"If that is money in my safe, it's a lot of money."

'If only you knew', I think.

"I'd like to go down to my room and dump the computer. Maybe we could have lunch together?"

"Let's," she says bouncing up.

"Maybe you should check it's still in your safe," I offer. I need to separate us for just enough time to accomplish my mission and the best way is to give her a mission.

"It was this morning," she says turning down the stairs.

It's not worked. I can't lose her and she follows me to my room. Kayan, my cabin Steward is there, which is a relief as I still don't have a cruise card. He opens the door reminding me to visit reception and we enter. I take the computer to my dressing table and place it next to the kettle. Auli'i opens my wardrobe door.

"You have a safe. So, yours must be full for you to give me that parcel... that's a serious amount of money." She is probing.

I could lift the bed, expose the green bundles and reveal it jokingly, 'no this is a serious amount of money', but it might not be there and then she doesn't need to know.

"Do you mind if I use your toilet?" she asks.

As the door closes, I reach for the bed and heave it up, pull the blankets forward a little to expose the green plastic of the blocks. My lungs fill with relief; the money is still there. I close the bed fast, not re-covering the plastic blocks. I straighten the sheets and then turn and sit. As she opens the door, I stand.

"Lunch?" I ask smiling, knowing I still need to question Hunter.

Auli'i stares towards the safe.

"It's empty if you want me to take it back I can, but if people think I have something the temptation might be too great. It is safer with you."

She nods. "Let's go back up past the theatre and collect Chris. Choir will have finished."

We wait outside the theatre looking through the flow of exiting guests who seem to have been enthralled by the choir and are no doubt heading for the buffet. Auli'i leans into me,

"So... if they are all twenties-" She holds her hand up to imagine the size. "-that's thousands."

"Genuinely, I don't know. I never opened it, it was an unexpected gift."

Christophe appears last, laughing and joking with Adrian the choirmaster.

"They seem close friends."

I let that escape when it should've been a restrained thought or phrased differently. The morning's caught me off guard. The whole cruise has.

"Yes, he was a little fluid, bisexual until he met me!" she announces proudly as if she'd won him over.

Chapter 46 – Embarrassing silence

Lifts are always silent, and for me, this is an embarrassing silence. A conversation is unfinished, though Auli'i doesn't seem embarrassed in the slightest by her boast. Is bisexual what Georgie was suggesting? It was never this fluid in the army.

Arriving at the buffet, a tray is handed to me with a serviette, knife and fork. We split to different areas to get our food, either the hot counter, salad, cold meats or some other more complicated selection. None of us takes much and we meet at a table by the window near the door we came in. It is away from the main seating area and where some of the crew seem to sit, though there is no segregation. These must be the crew who have buffet privileges. A guest approaches our table and turns out to be my first fan, she expresses a gushing glow of thanks which is both welcome and encouraging.

"If only I'd a book to sell," I offer sarcastically to Auli'i after the guest has left.

"So how much money does this charity have and what is it for?" Auli'i asks.

Now a third person knows, Christophe.

"Nothing's definite yet, and it is not an official charity. I helped someone, they have offered to help me. But whether they will or not is hard to pin down. So far they've given me some money, and the problem is its cash."

That has met with silence from Auli'i and confusion from Christophe, who I appreciate, seems to think it's not his place to speak.

"And they have demanded I say nothing. If the money couldn't be put to good use, I wouldn't have taken it."

I'm grateful that we're eating as it's stopped the potential barrage of questions, or has it? Ee has stopped eating again and is thinking.

"When you said you were sending my friends some money, I thought maybe fifty or a hundred pounds."

"Let's see if it gets there."

"How much was it?" she asks.

"Five thousand dollars."

Auli'i's hands drop to the table.

"Five thousand dollars! Oh my God! I need to call them."

Auli'i grabs her phone, a rather poor habit at the dinner table considering it can hold up to seven thousand germs and viruses. It makes hand washing on entrance obsolete. But I'm not sure she should be spreading this news just yet, it will spread like a virus but the money may never get there making it fake news.

"It may never arrive," I offer, to stop the leak from spreading.

"It will get there. You did it at a bank!"

"I did it in a bank, in Colombia. It's a country that has been known to defy all standard rules. So let's not get excited."

"I hope it does get there, imagine what they could do with that-" she stops herself, "-but why so much? Why thousands?"

"Because if all the money I have gets taken back... let's say my benefactor loses all his money in the casino and demands it back, then that sum is safely in the hands of people who need it. I can show him the transfer slip and say he's lost that bit."

"A gambler gave it to you?"

"It was definitely a gamble the way it was acquired. Easy come, easy go. I might try another transfer tomorrow from St Vincent, just to make sure they get it. It might be different there."

"As much? Oh no, they won't know what to do with it. That is if the bank in Damascus will give it to them..." She's now looking worried.

"Exactly. There are lots of potential problems to face before we're home and dry."

I continue eating my lunch, aiming to finish and excuse myself as soon as I can. Maybe now that she has Christophe to spend her time with, and has more than enough to think about, I might be free to go. Christophe seems nervous, I can see he is waiting to say something, so I turn and engage him with a look.

"I think the Captain is going to invite you to dinner, sir," he says shyly.

"What makes you say that?"

"He said it to me in passing, you being here has brought me to his attention which has been a good thing."

I can understand how that works. Any connection opens a door and I hope mine remains positive for him. I smile and excuse myself, leaving before I can be questioned further.

"Dad!"

I heard the call, I can't ignore it, I turn and walk back with a smile.

"Can I open it?"

What can I say? The damage is done. I think for a moment, but it is probably only seconds. Before I can answer, another fan grabs me; the uniform is a homing beacon to those who saw me. Enthusiastically, she spends what seems an age telling me about her experiences of rationing in the war. I am going to have to develop the art of listening. She eventually leaves, grateful to have shared her story. I look at Auli'i waiting for an answer, then at Christophe. Is he wondering if he is involved in something the Captain may reprimand him for?

I shrug ambiguously, why not? And I escape before it is translated. Maybe it is time there was an audit done.

Chapter 47 - Audit

Crew quarters are strictly forbidden to passengers, which for me means no-go anywhere from deck four or below. The security office is down on deck four at the opposite end to the officer's mess where I had breakfast with Georgie. I've already broken so many rules, but I'm in uniform so no one will question me.

Hunter's busy with two officers and his office door is closed. A closed-door normally means a dressing-down or a secret briefing. As they're both standing at attention, I would wager they're in trouble for something. It may be a cruise ship but it's run with the military discipline of a service ship.

Hunter knows I'm here, he's seen me. Like in so many areas of the ship, there's a chart of pictures outside pertaining to Hunter's department. His picture is at the top, Hunter Witowski, head of security. He has three lieutenants in a very predictable format below him. One's Caucasian, and he no doubt will be Hunter's right-hand man. Of equal rank are two other officers, one I suspect Indian and the other Malaysian. These will be the officers he uses to communicate accurately to the many Indian and Malaysian crew employed on the ship. Under them are officers with designated areas of control. Nowhere do I see Mrs El Ray. That's not to say that each and every security person is on this list, they can't be, my guess is there's quite a team under him.

The door opens and the two officers leave.

"Very smart. But your uniform carries no favour here I'm afraid, you know how it works," Hunter jokes as I fill the doorway.

I know very well that whilst delivered jovially, Hunter's telling me I've no standing on this ship. He grabs his mobile phone off the desk and turns to his assistant.

"I'm at lunch."

I've already had lunch, but apparently lunch, like breakfast, can repeat itself. Hunter leads me to the restaurant where the Maître d' sits us at a table for two, by the window and away from the guests.

"You enjoying your holiday?" Hunter asks me.

"I don't quite know how to answer that, but it's certainly been a new experience."

"Your commentary went very well, as did your talk this morning." He congratulates me. "So far you're having a very positive cruise."

I smile. "How do you know my talk went well?"

"It's measured on a few things, and one of them is being reviewed by Georgie. I guess you'll be alright in that area."

He's been keeping an eye on me, and he obviously knows I've some connection with Georgie, or maybe it's just our shared bounty he's referring to.

"So, Mrs El Ray that I was seen with at the airport…" I stop to see how he reacts.

"South America's behind us. If a gunman was after anyone, they'd have made their move then jumped ship to a waiting boat. Or if they were stupid they might have tried to board us, but we have LRAD."

"LRAD?" I ask because it is not a term I am familiar with.

"Long-range audio device. It would blow their eardrums at two thousand meters. We're clear. I can't see them risking anything this far away. Trust me, I sail this route regularly. I know it. I know them. Relax."

Even though I don't know this part of the world, I understand his logic. I get now the police arrest at the airport and the payoff. I bet it was for them to dress her as an officer, be one of the three police officers who ran on while we concentrated on hiding money and watching the hull being painted. I never saw, but I would lay money on there only being two police leaving the ship. I am dying to ask but he has ended that line of conversation. I can see how he knows this cruise route well, back and forth, and might know Mrs El Ray. What I can't understand is why she or they would choose this cruise to jump onto? It is not the most direct transatlantic cruise home?

"It all makes sense," I lie.

"Good."

The waiter takes our order and I would like to be able to enjoy a relaxing meal but I'm someone who needs all the T's crossed and I expect he knows I won't retreat that easily from the answers. Hunter focusses on me again.

"I think the company will ask you back. You've done South America now; you might want to try some other routes for a while," Hunter suggests.

"Do you fancy a glass of wine?" I offer.

"On duty. But by all means, you have one." Hunter waves the wine waiter over.

"White or red?" Hunter asks.

"White, lunch time."

"Leave it with me." And he has a simple exchange with the wine waiter. He offers his cruise card and I don't suggest I pay, we can both act like multi-millionaires, at least that's what he's implying.

"I only ordered a small glass because it gets warm quickly here. But, if you like it, let me indulge you with a bottle."

I need to ask, I need to know who is involved.

"Perfect. So… Mrs El Ray was one of the three police officers, and is now on the ship because it's heading east as the season is over?"

Hunter moves his head slightly not to disagree, he's not going to add to my calculation.

"Is Ronni in on it?" I ask because it had to be asked.

"No one needs to know anything," Hunter says, "no one does. We're all winners."

"Except mine and Ronni's pictures are with her people, and they appear to want her back."

"I've been meeting up with her for a while, so they could very well have mine too."

"No. You're too smart for that."

"If only," Hunter ends.

Chapter 48 – Chess game

Two people play three-dimensional chess though three layers of boards. The manoeuvres on this ship are like a complex online shoot 'em up video game, with players entering from all over the world, trying to outwit each other. I can't believe Ronni was not in on it. I can't believe we stumbled on that house with walls made of money by accident. I don't want to believe I was the disposable new guy, but I can see how a trained expendable team member on the ship was more than fortuitous. That blows away all my confidence in being involved with this, I might have stayed alive but they won't have been expecting to split the money. Am I over thinking this? Was having a military guy on board for this leg of this cruise an accident or planned? I was meant to do the New Orleans segment, then they asked me to change last minute. I thought it was odd asking me to commentate on the Panama Canal when I knew nothing about it.

The queue at reception is short and they quickly replace my lost cruise card for me, allowing me to purchase anywhere on the ship again. It's amazing how easy it is to get that card once you're in the database and how much it means. As long as my face matches the image the card displays on the ship's system, I can get on and off at any port without a passport, I can buy anything and go anywhere. I guess in the future it could move to fingerprints if ships weren't so worried about hygiene and the bacteria stored on handheld devices.

I wander into the 'Crow's Nest' bar, high on the ship looking out to sea. What a glorious space this is in daylight. I'd been here in the dark for the evening quiz, but now I can see it's a huge lounge. I sit, look out at sea and collect my thoughts. The wine waiter attends and I wish I knew the wine I had at lunch.

"You don't happen to know the white wine Hunter Witowski, head of security, drinks. He just bought me a glass in the restaurant and I don't know what it was."

"I will find out, sir," the waiter says and scuttles away.

I wonder what he's going to do, ask someone who might know, dare to ring the head of security, or ring the wine waiter in the restaurant? Whichever way, the sheer will to get things right, has to be appreciated. These are people who will survive the inevitable replacement of humans with robots in the workplace, those with a willingness to work efficiently and cheaply. Professions that exist to break rules may go first. There are robots on the ship, I've seen them. Cruise robots, all called Pepper, who will help you with directions, tell you what is on the menu in all of the restaurants, help you find all the photographs taken of you or dance with you if you don't have a partner. I haven't had to interact with one yet, but they can converse efficiently in four languages.

A large glass of wine is brought to my side, which is a surprise, as I never actually ordered it or gave my cruise card.

"Compliments of Mr Witowski, sir." The waiter says, placing my drink on a circular paper napkin. The last thing I want is for Hunter to feel I'm on his payroll, not even for seven million dollars. I lift the glass and look at the wine. When someone offers you something, whilst thanking them, ask yourself why they're offering it. This is a nice wine and I wonder if he's watching me drink it. I scan the ceiling, find the nearest camera and toast him. I look back around to see Jill arriving into the bar and she may have thought that gesture was for her.

She approaches, stands by my table and presents me with my old cruise card. The waiter must have returned it to her last night and she would have signed for the drinks on my behalf. I pull out my new card.

"Snap."

"Where were you last night?" she asks.

She obviously means after I left her. For someone who went to great lengths to tell me that her solo cruiser friends were all happy to stay that way, she has got very close. I guess I should have noticed the change in gear.

"I went to your room," she states.

"I wasn't there."

"I know that."

She wasn't there this morning and surely would not have stayed long with a luxury suite to go to. My bed didn't look like it had been slept in, but then the steward might have made it. This is quickly becoming awkward.

"Oh, I went to the theatre after the show was over, I wanted to have it to myself. I stood on stage and went through the bullet points of my show in my head."

"I thought you might do that... so I went to the theatre, but it was closed."

I'm thinking on my feet here... "There's a door into the stage from the promenade deck, it's marked crew only so I snuck in there."

"No, I got in. It was dark. Empty."

"Well after nosing around backstage, I wandered around the promenade deck going through my lecture over and over again."

Christophe rushes in and saves me because I'm not sure I could deflect another question.

"I've been looking all over for you. Sir, please, Auli'i needs you."

I neck my wine before following him, it is a military reaction. But my eyes and brain are working in those stolen seconds. He's in civilian clothes and is not wearing his badge, probably two breaches of code. That means there's a big problem. He seems very concerned, and my thoughts are that she's been hurt defending the safe.

"Should I come?" Jill asks.

Christophe stops. "She asked for her father," he says hesitantly.

I can see from Christophe's face that we need to go and he does not want Jill.

"Her room's in a prohibited crew area. I'll ring and leave a message on your phone. Excuse me," I say.

"Don't forget our date after dinner," she calls after us.

I follow Christophe, who's striding away fast, something is wrong.

Chapter 49 – Something's wrong

The cabin door is open just enough to squeeze in, no more. It's awkward. Christophe follows me in. The room is lit by just the bedside light and Auli'i is sitting on the lower bunk bed, crossed-legged with piles and piles of one hundred dollar notes.

"Dad. What on Earth have you got into?"

"How much is there?" I'm expecting a million, not sure why I ask.

"I've counted eight hundred thousand dollars so far."

At a rough guess, there could be almost the same again. It seems a comparatively small sum to worry about given the overall picture, but I can't say that.

"I don't know, I was given it, I never opened the package." Which is true but not an excuse.

"But you sent five thousand pounds to my friends, you must have opened it!" she exclaims.

Everyone's a detective. I can see how the police break you down and trip you up. Christophe is shell-shocked, I can imagine he's wondering what has he got himself into? I'm wondering that too. Just how much danger is this young sailor in if Hunter or Mrs El Ray finds out that he's in the loop? How much danger is Auli'i in?

"Look, here's the problem. The money was acquired by someone else on the ship, it's not mine. However, inadvertently I was there, I knew about it, and I was given a small cut to keep absolutely silent."

"A small cut!" she breathes.

Then both of them are dumbstruck.

"But…" Auli'i starts and has nowhere to go.

"Auli'i, sweetheart, the biggest task is to wrap it back up and completely forget it. Don't mention it to anyone, because I don't know who else is involved in this. You can't know who might mention it to the wrong person."

"Is it crew?" she asks.

"The more you know, the more danger you're in. Best you wrap it up and forget it."

"But why's it in my safe? Is your safe full? Is your room full?"

"Because I'd expect it to vanish from my room if I left it there. That's why I transferred the money yesterday, that's at least one bit they can't get back. I'll transfer some more in St. Vincent tomorrow because that might be all the help we can offer."

Auli'i picks up a handful of money and holds it out. She looks at me with sad eyes, questioning eyes, as if I have let her down in some way.

"You don't need this, do you? There's more."

I reach out and take the handful of notes, I quickly try and count them.

"It's ten thousand," she says.

"That might be too much to transfer in one go, maybe two banks. And just before we leave the island, because I am seriously worried they discover a trend."

"But you have more?" She is still curious.

"I do have another parcel hidden but I've got no idea how much is in there." I'm desperately trying not to lie more than I have to.

"You must have opened it to get your spending cash out?"

"There were some loose bills, that's what I transferred."

"Loose bills! It must be from a crime, Dad!"

"Not that I did, I saw it brought onto the ship, which is itself against all rules. This bought my silence, but I don't know what in."

Auli'i starts to wrap the money back up, Christophe who has been silent this whole time, steps forward to help but it becomes obvious it's not going to go back together.

"I'll go and buy some tape," he says.

I stop him with my arm. Maybe a touch too firm because he is leaving with far too much speed.

"No. We can't risk someone seeing you buy tape. Pack it the best you can."

"How much trouble are you in?" Auli'i asks me quietly.

"I'm still trying to find that out. That's why I said I don't know how much money I have yet."

"They might have given it to you to keep quiet while you're on board, but will demand it back as soon as you leave," Christophe adds.

He's sharp. His Bulgarian upbringing may have given him some street credentials, or he's watched a lot of TV.

"No one's at risk as long as we don't talk. I'm trying to find out more, but I'm new on board."

"I'm scared," Auli'i says getting off the bed and forcing the money into the safe,

"I better change the passcode on the safe now, or my roommate will see it."

But something hits her and she turns to me sharply.

"But if she can't get in the safe… she'll call house-keeping."

Chapter 50 – Wrapping tape

Georgie has her head in a computer in her office which I've not bothered to find before and I've never seen this side of her work. In order to find binding tape from a source that big brother's not watching, I need to disturb her under the pretence of checking on our date tonight, which I hope is still on. It's not the sex, though that's magical, it's her, her confidence, her ability to be in control. I lean in until she senses my presence and lifts her head. She's in work mode and her look is not in any way a romantic smile, but it softens and evolves just a little, which makes me feel special. I return the smile and hope she feels that maybe I've brightened her day.

"Have you planned somewhere?"

Georgie shakes her head slightly. "I have to introduce the act at seven thirty, thank them and close the first show at eight fifteen, introduce them again at nine thirty, and close the show at ten-fifteen."

"Are you asking for a rain check?" I ask. I can't see any tape as finger a pair of scissors on the edge of her desk.

"Not at all, just explaining what I do between courses and drinks; my life. Informal meal in the wine bar works best, it's next to the theatre and I can be in and out."

"So, seven forty-five?"

"I like a man who can work a schedule out." She winks.

"And in a uniform?"

I'm hoping this evening will roll into another night of romance and experimentation, I just have to explain my absence to Jill.

"Did you say you've opened your parcel?" I ask.

Her smile evaporates. "I'm still feeling so guilty."

"Me too, I just had a peep," I offer.

"Frightening amount." She nods.

"Around a mil?" I say, meaning a million. She agrees.

"Have you got some tape so I can re-seal it?" I ask.

Georgie opens her desk drawer and tosses me a small roll of clear tape.

"You could've afforded to buy that," she teases.

"I didn't want to be seen buying it."

She narrows her eyes at me, questioning my move.

"Hunter," I explain quietly.

"Do you think he'll ask for a share?" she worries.

"I don't think so. I don't think he has the right to ask."

"Hmm… Uniform," she demands, and I nod, we do have a chemistry. "And leather pants!"

That catches me out.

"Joking." She pouts.

I nod again and leave.

"But they do sell them in the shop!" she shouts after me.

I know that was a joke. I put my head around the edge of her door.

"And well done this morning, you only got one complaint!" she adds.

"Complaint?"

"We all get complaints, there are professional complainers who try and get free vouchers and money back for any reason."

"What a way to ruin your holiday. What did they complain about?"

"They found your lecture harrowing, they suffer from PTSD."

"Then we should talk, me too," I offer.

Georgie's face changes, it is that concern that I might be ill? I can see the cogs turning behind her eyes.

"No, I don't think they actually know what PTSD is and you would throw them over the edge, so no introduction," she warns me then returns to her work.

Her entertainment office is an unrecognisable door hidden near the theatre entrance by the stairwell. Passenger stairs only go up. The only way down to a lower deck is through the crew door, which I take to find my way back to Auli'i, it should be easy, if only for the Captain coming the other way.

"Sir," I offer, almost automatically.

"Bit off-limits for you Witowski," he says quite rightly, not to scold, but it's a corrective measure I respect.

"My daughter's been under the weather; concerned dad. Want to boost her up so she makes the show tonight."

"Good man. Would you join me and a few others for dinner when we start the crossing? Do you have a plus one?" he asks.

"There's still time! Can I get back to you?"

"I hope Auli'i's feels better and you can relax upstairs and enjoy the cruise, upstairs," he smiles.

"I'll be straight back up, sir."

We part, me going down, him climbing, and as the stairs turn we face each other a floor apart.

"Good show by the way," he says, leaving.

"I didn't see you in the audience, sir."

"It was on television this afternoon. A man with your talents could be very useful."

I look up but he's gone. That was a strange thing to say, 'A man with your talents could be very useful'. Is he in on this? I shake it off. Maybe I'm over-analysing things.

I lean into Auli'i's room, just enough, ensuring no one and no corridor camera can see my handover. I excuse myself from the prohibited area and take the crew staircase back upstairs to safety. Having spoken to the Captain, what I want to do is talk with Ronni and Georgie. If there is a whole team working this woman's escape, that twenty million has got to be sliced up a number of ways, not least including hers. I'm surprised it's still under my bed.

The stairwells are next to the elevator shafts, which is where I am. There's a house phone on the wall next to the lift, which reminds me I need to update Jill on my daughter's condition. At least she's not involved. I call her.

"Hi, Jill."

"How is she?" she asks.

"She'll be fine by show-time. Lovesick I think, not that I'd know about that sickness," I offer, dipping my toe in the shark-filled water.

"No?" she questions.

"That's why I like your group of solo cruisers, close friends, no ties. It's a wonderful free spirit you have."

There is a slight pause. We're playing a very dangerous game of chess. I can't sleep with her tonight or any night.

"Nothing's ever free," she responds sounding a little downbeat.

"You're right... I wonder if I'm expected to buy my boss dinner tonight, or we go Dutch?" I add, to make the water even muddier.

"You'll have to tell me," she demands; I know she's pushing for the expected late night debriefing mentioned earlier.

"Why don't we meet for breakfast? I'll fill you in on my possible long term employment prospects after my first critique. Do you have plans for St Vincent?"

That was a well wrapped but harsh cancellation.

"It's our last beach stop. I'm going to lay in the sun and drink cocktails, with friends," she says firmly. "I thought you might be with me."

That's sucked the air out of the space. I need to think before my next move. I need to be brief, definite, but upbeat.

"I'll look out for a group drinking cocktails."

"Well let's see if you can make it," she ends.

I put down the phone.

Did it stall her advances or was that all too easy? Does anything add up? Should I trust anything or anyone? If Mrs El Ray is on board, why is the money under my bed?

Chapter 51- The bed

Dressing can be so therapeutic when it's an automatic process. The ceremonial uniform requires no decision making, well maybe one; ribbons or medals, but even that is obvious. The actual medals would not be appropriate. The rest of the dress is always the same; it goes on in the same order and has to look the same. I've done it enough times for me to be in autopilot, and it allows my brain to work through what has happened and who might be involved. It is always best to focus on and rework the actual facts and I have not had the time to do that until now. Why did Ronni hang back and watch the woman at customs? Was she a wingman for the woman?

What was she doing because the magic is always done before you think, and what you see is just to make you forget what the planner doesn't want you to remember? I need to replay that whole event and work out how involved Ronni is.

A woman was held and searched with Ronni, she had no money. The police were looking for money. The Latina woman was arrested and they found the money hidden in plain sight. They arrest her, dress her as police and get her on the ship. Ronni deliberately ignores them, calm as can be as she keeps a payoff.

I need to speak with Ronni.

I click my cabin door closed and my stride lengthens, as it always does in this uniform. Ceremonial Uniform does something to your stature. I'm still re-running every move in my mind… As we worried about a small sum of money in a case, three police boarded the ship behind us. One of the police was Mrs El Ray? I remember thinking one was female from the way they ran but I never really looked, I didn't want them looking at me. That was that the trick to ensure we never saw her get on, that was why the money was such a gift. Nothing has been an accident. We were played. Does she want it back? Maybe. Maybe every last dollar. I'm meeting Georgie in the wine bar by the theatre, but it's Ronni I need to question.

I arrive at the wine bar, one of my favourite areas. It's like a very elegant foreign officers' mess. They're never this big in England but abroad they can be quite special. As I order a beer, there's a steady flow of guests going past into the theatre, which means the evening's entertainment will be starting soon. There's no need to look at a watch, the end of that stream means we have hit seven thirty.

Georgie appears looking wonderful. She stops and stares at me,

"Wow. Impressive!"

"No, it's you who's stealing the night. You look amazing," I mean it. I am struck dumb for a moment, when I should be offering her a drink or a seat, given her limited periods in the bar. Her aquamarine dress hugs her body and twists as it goes down around her shoes. How does it hold that shape? How does she walk in it? I prefer my mind being full of these questions. Her hair is up off her face, she is wearing full make-up and lashes. In the corner of my eye, I see Jill and her friends rush past and Georgie turns to see what I see. Jill's not sporting a smile, not now, she doesn't wave, doesn't stop and she is gone to think about her next move in this crazy war.

"Shall we sit?" Georgie asks moving to a table.

"Can you?"

"I'll manage," she flirts.

A waiter attends as they always do.

"The Merlot, please."

Georgie goes to hand her card but I offer mine.

"Not tonight. This is my privilege."

The waiter takes my card, I signal another pint and he is gone.

"What did I do to deserve all this?" I ask, still inhaling her beauty.

She crosses her legs with the twist of the dress and sits mermaid-like. This dress won't just magically drop off like she managed the other might, this dress looks like it took a far more complicated assembly.

"The uniform and the rank are playing their part," she says raising her phone and taking my picture.

The waiter is back with the drinks and offers to take her phone. Georgie moves round to me, he carefully frames his shot and then fires a number of pictures as if it were a semi-automatic. It all continues to be so unreal.

"So what rank are you, what did you actually do?" she asks.

I am wearing blank epaulettes as I am in someone else's domain.

"You don't know?" I deliver a little pointedly as she picks up on the tone.

"Why should I?" she asks, a little less flirty.

"It seems that Hunter in security knows more about me than is available on Google, even the Captain seemed to know my rank unless I'm reading that incorrectly."

Her head tilts, she is acting puzzled, demanding I continue.

"I was due to join the ship a week before I did, I was actually looking forward to New Orleans. Really looking forward to it. But my trip was changed to this week, even though I know nothing about the Panama Canal."

"You seemed to know a lot. You did the commentary."

"Who has access to advance crew and passenger lists, and booking of guest entertainers?" I ask.

Georgie shakes her head, shrugs.

"Who could have seen me, my title, and changed me to this week?"

"I'm not following, you're perfect for the Panama Canal. It was obvious."

"I'm also perfect to help with the heist of a lot of money."

"No, you didn't really play a part in that. In fact, I did all the work there, though not intentionally. I'm not even sure why I have to split it three ways." She grins, without too much malice, though she's hard, "This money is a key to my escape."

I can see that now she has found this prize, like me, there is no way she will let it go. She may have been one of the dance troupe twenty years ago, has climbed the corporate ladder and now been trapped here a long time.

I study her far deeper than before. She is maybe forty, I can't be more than ten years older than her. I am convinced she has no idea about the twenty million. I suspect she would feel betrayed that she's not in on it.

"Did you ever really see the woman whose bag you ended up with?"

"No. Well, a glance when she was arrested, but not really. I was looking at her shoes as much as her."

"So you wouldn't recognise her again if you saw her?"

She shakes her head. "But, I'm not likely to see her, she was arrested."

"By the police," I add.

"And possibly dead by now."

"The police boarded the ship about the same time as we arrived from the airport. What if the woman was in a police uniform? Three police boarded, two left. She could be on board."

"Were you dropped from military intelligence?" she teases.

"Maybe, but think a minute, I was in that branch for a reason, for a long time. Were we used at the airport? Was that money deliberately left to distract us?"

Georgie now looks worried. Her mood has changed to one of serious concern. I don't want to ruin the evening, but I do want to get off the ship alive, and if possible, I want to do it with some money. It seems Georgie knows very little if anything. How much should I reveal to her to get her onside?

Georgie stands.

"Order any three dishes off this menu, it's great," she says handing me the tapas menu.

Georgie waves over a waiter and indicates her choice but the waiter seems to know it. I select three, and he leaves to key in the order.

"That will arrive magically as I get back from the theatre." She shouts back leaving.

"Exactly your style. Well organised, nothing left to chance. Who changed me to this week?"

She stops for a telling moment. Not Georgie, she is thinking hard.

"If that woman is on the ship, she'll want her money back," Georgie muses.

"Maybe not," I offer, knowing there is a larger sum standing by.

"Oh she will," Georgie says, annoyed. "We're being played… I'll be back."

She turns on her heels and marches off, with a definite edge to each of her powered steps, worried about her cut. My thought is that the big money has been left with us knowing we can say nothing because of the smaller sum we have already accepted. Already guilty, already involved. But, none of it are we ever meant to keep or share.

Chapter 52 – Serious concern

The crowd swell out of the theatre and fill the bar. Georgie wafts back in with her show smile on and the food arrives all like clockwork. She sits, now armed with an answer she has been pondering while gone.

"Hunter gets a list of everyone due on board. He pointed you out to me, said you'd be perfect for the Canal."

"I'm not surprised at that. The woman whose bag you took, who is the wife of a huge drug baron, is on the ship. Working in his department."

Georgie is tight-faced, she knows none of this. "These prawns are to die for. Not that I want to die any time soon, especially not poor." She bites into the giant fried prawn leaving me wishing I'd ordered one until she reaches over and feeds me the other half. Then she leans back and studies me as if I'm a puzzle.

"Why would he want you on board? You have the ability to see what he's up to. I never did."

"How does a huge organisation move me, at short notice from New Orleans, to the next section of a cruise?"

"Every speaker wants to do New Orleans, it's easy to fill, but fewer want the Panama Canal, it's a tougher gig. Loads of schoolteacher types, but they're boring. Panama is often filled at the last minute, or Hunter Witowski has to do the Canal commentary – we know he can do it."

"I bet he's good."

"But it's never as special when someone from crew does it. A handsome military hero like you makes it special. His words, not mine. This time he didn't want to do it, suggested you."

Georgie stops to take a bite, her mind is working overtime.

"How can you fly home with a million dollars in cash? You can't. Hunter will suggest you leave it on the ship, in his care, until the ship is back at Southampton where you can meet him. He can make things happen. It's now divided by four, maybe even five, why? Why would he divide it so easily?"

Her insight into the ship is useful. It's my turn to think, because I have far more than one million, or do I? Has Hunter no intention of sharing?

"I don't want it back in the UK. Well, not all of it. What are you going to do with yours, if we get it?"

"I would like a small house on one of the Caribbean islands." There's a determination about the suggestion like she's dreamt and fictitiously planned this all out before. She does not want to lose the money.

"Which one?" I ask.

"Bequia."

"Don't know it, it's not on our route. It must be an island you don't see often?"

She ignores my question.

"We need to spend the money now, to keep it. I could jump ship with this kind of money. Although, even if it's enough for a house, I could be left with nothing to live on. I would need to work. A million is not enough," she decides.

My previous assessment was right, she has had enough of this life. I wonder how many years she has been at sea? Could she really change her life now?

We finish our food, though our enjoyment of it has been demoted. I have more than enough money to cut and run. She's definitely not been in on any of the second plan. But I wasn't in on our second bounty before the day it happened and Hunter clearly hasn't filled me in on everything now with the Mrs El Rey on board.

"Do you think Ronni is in on whatever plan Hunter has?"

Georgie thinks for a second, then stands. "Let's invite her up and ask." She strides to the bar, reaches for the bar phone and dials. If Hunter is in the office, he has to be watching this. She returns to the table.

"Hunter could be watching us now," I offer.

Georgie picks up her glass, "We're moving to the corner."

The tone of the evening has moved as far away from romance as is possible and I'd like to get it back there. Now comfortable at our new table, I lift my cruise card, we order some more food and two Wine Trios. These are ornate trees of curved metal that hold three different wines and six glasses. Mine are three different reds and hers are three sparkling whites. They are all on my card, Georgie has had her alcohol quota and the computer will apparently refuse her more, maybe she doesn't care though, because I'm getting the distinct impression she's one foot out of the company. I may also be terminating a civilian job I've only just started.

By the time Ronni joins us, we're both in a lighter mood. Georgie checks her watch.

"How timely. I have to go and introduce an act. Back in ten minutes." Georgie leaves.

"What's the problem?" Ronni asks.

"Seeing as I don't know everything that's going on, it's hard to know there is a problem."

Ronni tilts her head slightly, encouraging me to continue. She has a million in the pot.

"You knew about the airport," I state as if it were fact.

"No. I was told there was some intelligence on a local drug bust so to watch myself and look out for Georgie."

"And if you got into trouble?"

"Call Hunter." Her tone suggests a little defence.

"You never thought that was strange?"

"He's head of security. It was South America!" Her voice raises slightly, she's getting a little angry.

"And we find three or four million dollars. How strange?"

"I guess it is. But I wasn't expecting that."

"And what of the woman?"

"Didn't know anything about her."

"Seriously?"

"Seriously. And I'm not sure we should be talking about it here." Ronni stands to leave.

"Ronni, give me another minute. Why did you turn right out of the dock in Panama?"

"The same reason you did?"

"I had no reason. I noticed you being followed, saw you were in trouble and stayed on your 'six'. I also noticed Hunter was watching you from the gangway and I thought it was me who engaged him to follow you too, but he was wearing a vest. Were you? Now I guess he planned it."

Ronni sits back down. We both take a moment to breathe, maybe she is beginning to understand there is a serious question to address.

"Hunter had shown me the picture they had of me at the airport. Said I had been implicated and was in trouble. He wanted to get to the bottom of it. Said we should address it."

"How?" I ask.

"I needed to be cleared. He said he got the picture that morning. We hatched a plan to flush out whoever was behind it."

"A plan?" I ask.

"To see who would follow me."

"Don't you think that was a stupid idea?"

"No. We assessed that they couldn't have many men here, and the gunman they sent to the ship that morning was an amateur. I might have been a scientist, but I have been trained and seen action."

"Amateurs are dangerous."

"I was wearing a vest." She pauses. "You missed that."

"I did wonder why you had boots on. OK, so who gave you the directions, and why that particular house?"

"Hunter picked the route at random, and we agreed on a derelict property in case he lost me. That way he would know where I was drawing them too."

"He picked it at random?" I ask again.

"Yes, we found it together with online maps, street view. A rendezvous house in a derelict area," she says, thinking.

"And the house just happened to be built of money?"

Ronni stops talking. I can see her rewinding events and re-examining each moment. She hits a thought that she needs to share.

"He shouted 'what's that in the wall?' How could he see?" she asks puzzled.

"He also happened to have the local gun he seized that morning on him, so we could use it and leave it," I add, "and I wasn't wearing a vest. I was expendable."

We're interrupted by Georgie coming back. "Nearly done. In thirty-five minutes', it's show-over, good night all and off to bed."

Ronni stands, "South America isn't over?" She asks.

"Not at all," I say flatly. "I fear it hasn't even started."

Chapter 53 – Time for bed

Georgie watches as I run my fingers under the drawer in my dresser, lift my phone to look for marks, pull the TV forward to see if it has been tampered with, check the lamps.

"We could go to my room. I have drinks and snacks," she suggests.

"Just checking for a trace of a bug."

"Taking this a bit far aren't you?"

I shake my head and continue searching.

"Let's go to my room."

I toss the things off the bed and lift it.

"Why would he bug the bed? To listen to us having sex?" She laughs.

"He could learn a lot from you! I have. No, I'm cutting you in on what I might have, if anything. It'll buy your house in Bequia." I pull the sheets back and exposed the row of green blocks.

"What?"

"A million dollars in each block."

Georgie is lost for words, she looks confused. Her mouth has dropped open seeing the top of stacks of blocks.

"How much?" She gasps.

"How much is a nice house in Bequia?"

"I've never actually looked."

She pulls out her phone, an instinct to search and find out.

"No. No trace."

Georgie turns to me and kisses me. "Life was boring until I met you."

"I don't need the blame for this excitement. You cruise ship types live a far more colourful life than I ever did."

We kiss, enjoying each other, and she does that magic trick again. She somehow unclips her dress and in one quick movement, it drops off her shoulders. The dress that looked to hug her all the way down, drops to the floor and she stands there naked.

"In Bequia, it's so hot, people never wear clothes," she teases.

"I don't remember that in any fact sheet. But, to be honest, I have no idea where it is," I admit.

"You might just be lucky enough to find out tomorrow. With a little loose cash, we could charter our own boat and be there in about forty-five minutes, then we either come back or just call in with our resignations."

"That sounds tempting. But it might be a little early if it's that close to South America. We don't want visitors, not even Hunter or Ronni. Let's go there, take the money if we can, bank it in order to buy a house, and then get back on board," I suggest.

"That sounds risky, leaving money behind like that."

"Once we take it off the boat, we'll never get it back on. It is a gamble. Unless we bury it in the sand and keep a pirate map."

I slam the bed back down. Push Georgie gently over onto it. Georgie lays naked on the bed. She has the ability to put a spell on me, to make me weak. It is a feeling I've never had before. I join her and we start to roll in the sheets.

"Pickett fence?" she says, kissing me again.

"I think you can have what you want."

"Bougainvillaea?"

Life is too perfect. We make love on my million-pound bed, and everything seems too perfect.

Sunlight bursting through the window wakes us both up. I reach up and close the curtains and we roll over in each other's arms.

"Won't you miss the stage, entertaining?" I ask her as we lay side by side, and feel the motion of the ship gently rock us.

"I could have a club, a restaurant, organise tours… or do nothing. We just have to get the money off the ship and to the island without being seen. Because Mrs El Rey is going to want it back."

"This isn't hers," I said pulling myself up.

I have a number of ugly thoughts swirling in my head, the main one is wondering how involved Mrs El Rey is, and will she make it impossible to keep any of this money. My mind starts to plot and plan. I think of using the canvas bags under the bed to carry some money off. But a vision hits me from last night when I checked the blocks were still under the bed. They were, but the canvas bags were not laying on top. I leap up.

"Jump up," I say.

"What? What is it?" She panics.

"There's something wrong."

Georgie leaps up and I lift the bed.

"The canvas bags have gone."

I pull the blankets back. The eight long blocks we can see are real, but the next three are just green plastic badly wrapped around lifejackets, covered by a blanket. Lifting them reveals that there are no blocks underneath, but piled blankets. The canvas bags have gone, and twelve blocks with them.

"Shit." I've been double-crossed.

Chapter 54 – St Vincent & Bequia

I run a teaspoon handle down the plastic, cutting into the green covering, a blunt blade. The parcel opens to reveal neatly packed one hundred dollar bills. I check four of the eight blocks that remain.

"Eight million! That's amazing," Georgie says.

"It is," I say, but instead of feeling great about it, I'm feeling like I've lost something. I have, I've lost twelve million. I sit staring at the lifejacket wrapped in green plastic that masqueraded as blocks of money.

"How much were you expecting?" Georgie asks.

"There was twenty million under here, the others must have taken most of theirs and left me with my share."

Georgie has come alive. "Our share!" she jokes.

"Hey, it was you who was questioning why you had to split the three million we got in that case."

"I was joking," she says. "But it was my case."

I feel the ship engines change thrust. It is a noticeable power change, both the sound and the tension of the ship are different.

"This is not right."

"It's fine, the ship is powering onto the pier. We've arrived in St Vincent."

"No, the money's not right."

"They've left you with your share," she states as if it could be perfectly logical.

"Then why wrap a lifejacket to make it look like a money brick?"

"Good point. That stinks."

"And I was told I would have a third, just under seven. Eight is wrong."

"And how much was I to get and who are they?"

I have to pause and think because I don't really know the answer.

"Hunter, Ronni, and I went to a safe-house in Panama, which turned out to be not so safe."

"You never told me," she barks.

"No. I was on someone else's mission; as planned and contrived as the set-up at the airport. It's all becoming very clear now."

"You should've told me!"

"I don't think I was meant to be involved, it was an accident I was there. But I'm sure they were glad I was."

"You still could have told me, you work in my department."

"Do I? It seems I've been under Hunter's direction since the day he changed when I join this ship."

"I need to talk to him," Georgie says, in what can only be a power play she cannot win. None of this falls under any ship rules.

"Slow down. Let's think about this. People get killed just for knowing about this kind of money, I'm worried about my daughter. Even though this is not right. I've been robbed. Maybe he's been robbed too."

"Then you need to ring Hunter," she suggests.

"Not yet."

I'm thinking hard. If they are taking the money brick by brick and hiding it somewhere else, am I due to be left with any? Does Ronni know? Does Hunter know? Is this her people and she is double-crossing him? Filled with more and more questions, I feel the need to act. To make some of this money safe.

"Let me think of a plan. Get dressed, come back."

"You'll run away with my money." Georgie pouts.

"Your money!"

Georgie starts to pull the aquamarine evening dress back up. Watching her dress is as sexy as watching her undress. Her perfectly carved figure is that of a much younger woman and is no accident, she must work hard at it.

"How do you keep so thin?"

"I teach Zumba, you should come."

She fastens her dress and looks a million dollars even without her make-up.

"The walk of shame I was trying to avoid." She grimaces.

"There's no easy way out is there?"

"No, someone will see me."

"I meant for the money. Bring your passport when you come back," I add. "We may be going to a bank."

"We may never be coming back." She turns at the door, "and the million in my safe?"

"No, leave that, this is a big enough problem. If we can't place the money safely ashore, we'll need to smuggle it back on ship and we don't have Ronni or Hunter to help."

"You'll think of something. Military intelligence," she tosses over her shoulder as she leaves.

Dressing, I consider our options. Two people knew about that haul, Hunter and Ronni, and I see no reason they would replace blocks with fake ones. If Hunter took it to re-split the money with Mrs El Ray, he would just tell me, or at least make proper green blocks. The cabin steward has regular access to my room, and any replacement cleaning staff when he is off, the amateur ploy is more likely to be theirs. Anyone of them could have stolen some bricks and left the disguised lifejacket.

I might have a big problem if it's not Hunter and we have lost twelve million. I have to confront him and report a potential theft. He'll look at the cameras and see who stole the money, that he can do easily, but if they've stolen twelve million, then why not all of it? I can only guess that they wanted the crime to remain unnoticed until they got away.

How do I play this dangerous game and stay alive?

Chapter 55 – Time to play

"This is your Captain speaking from the bridge, and it looks like you have a fantastic sunny day ahead here in St. Vincent. As my officers have told you, there will be a drill this morning. All passenger-sea-going ships have to perform drills each week. Today we are simulating a fire in the engine mechanics workshop, I repeat this is a drill and you need not take any action. However, should you wish to join in and learn more about maritime safety, you may do so when you hear the seven short alarms followed by one long alarm. If it was me on holiday, I would go ashore."

There is a knock at my door. It is either the cabin steward or Georgie. I turn my television off and the captain goes quiet. I open the door and I can hear him again in the corridor address system. It is Georgie.

"I've put on something for the occasion, a bright yellow life jacket that no one will notice."

"Come in." I close the door behind her.

"You know what this is?" I ask her, pointing at the lifejacket she's wearing. She tilts her head, sure she knows what it is.

"It's bright and obvious, but perfect. Take it off!"

She removes the jacket and I take it from her. I stab the lifejacket with the handle of a spoon, fast and hard in the seam of the buoyancy block at the front, then the same at the back, I then rip the material enough to pull out the buoyancy foam block.

"It won't float now," she jokes.

"I think I'm up against it with time, so help me."

I hold open the lifejacket and indicate the smaller bricks of one hundred dollar notes lying next to the foam. She passes them to me, and I squeeze them in. Then, in the space at the front I push a wedge of foam in, to plug each side and pick my one up.

"Here's one I made earlier. Now, from what's left, fill your pockets with what you can. The rest goes back under the bed."

The ship's alarm goes off. A screeching sound, seven uncomfortable blasts followed by one long blast.

"For exercise, for exercise, for exercise only." The ships public address system announces.

"Right, got your passport?"

Georgie nods.

"That's our cue then. Cruise card, lifejacket, passport and as much money as we can carry."

There is no time to think, but at the door, stop dead then turn back and see the other life jacket covered in green plastic and the foam blocks on the bed.

"Nearly made a page one error."

I push the foam into the rear of the shelf at the top of the wardrobe, making a false back. Then I slide the lifejacket back under the bed and drop it.

"Should whoever stole it come back, should Hunter look, it looks fairly sane. Like maybe I don't know. If Hunter comes into check he may see one life jacket."

"This is often a single occupancy room so one life jacket is not totally odd."

"Should he even wonder where the other is he will be more worried about the missing money. Hopefully, he won't find the foam blocks, they would tell a different story."

The two off us walk swiftly from the cabin, in plain sight, both trying to make light work of the nearly forty-pound bright yellow lifejackets clearly stamped 'crew'. We head down to deck four, the front of the ship, and instead of following the rest of the crew on drill and mustering to their stations, we buzz out. Cruise cards against the infrared scanner at the exit like all the tourists. No one questions us.

Walking down the pier in the sunshine feels euphoric, even better with Caribbean music being beaten out on a trio of tin drums. Girls in Caribbean carnival-style dress dance around two men who are high on stilts. We keep going, through the duty-free shop and out into the world, free to negotiate the hawkers selling taxis and tours.

Our target is easy to spot. His handwritten cardboard sign reads 'Private Boat for Fishing and Tours', and boasts a picture. It looks seaworthy, and the guy looks like an old sailor. Neither may be true, but we do have lifejackets now beginning to weigh very heavily.

"Do you go to Bequia?"

"You bet I do, but, if it's just two of you it be a bit expensive."

"Two of us, and don't worry, my wife is paying."

He leads off with a big grin, taking us past a number of bustling warehouses and shops that do not seem to appeal to tourists.

"I would like to think my wife would pay for me, but I have no idea where she be. Me name is Wilson. You seen the main island here, St. Vincent?" he asks, looking round to make sure we are still with him.

"Are you suggesting we do a different tour, Wilson?" I tease him.

"No brother. I get the rum on ice and we can sail," he says.

"I tell you what. You get us across there fast, we'll drink when we get there. Get the rum on ice for the return journey."

Georgie is one step behind me and she's silent, my guess is she's still thinking on her words, half said in jest, that if we buy a house today it could be the last she has seen of the ship, her friends, and all her belongings.

We walk along the dock past a few working boats and some small pleasure boats. I would not suggest going to war in any of them. Not even Churchill would have used these in the D-day landings. He stops by one, and it's definitely not the one we saw pictured on his sign. I point at his picture he's still holding at his chest.

"Dat boat sunk my friend, I got me this one for a while and she is a great ship," he says, looking less like a sailor every minute.

"This is nowhere near forty feet, so it's is not a ship," I say.

"No, she a boat and you are going to love her," he says climbing on board and turning on his ghetto blaster. He reaches to help us on board, but for the moment we are both fixed to the dock.

"The best thing brother, she very cheap." He back-pedals, waving his hands for us to grab.

"We don't need cheap," Georgie says to me.

I turn to him. "Can this get as far as Bequia?"

"It got me there once, and today the sea is as calm as a birthing pool," he says with charm.

Georgie shrugs. "This is getting bloody heavy."

"I thought you were the fit Zumba teacher."

I step on board and put my arm out for Georgie. She looks around the boat then back at our huge ship no more than two hundred yards away across the water, the one she calls home.

"Is this the last I ever see of that ship?" she asks.

"No sister, I will get you to the beach and bring you back." He almost sings his reply while starting the engine, which makes every noise but does not sound like it is singing. It sounds rough. He turns up the music then casts off ropes and before we know it we are chugging out of the bay. He loops the steering wheel into a rope hook and scampers around the rear of the ship shaking fuel cans, but they all appear empty to me.

"Wilson, do you need to stop for fuel?"

"No brother, this ship knows its way to the little island," he says, finding one that still has some gushing inside and grins like a pirate.

"Me not drunk them all."

His joke is far from funny, if it is a joke.

"I've got money if you need fuel."

"No brother, we get the rum on the other side. I'm going to get you there fast. No stopping."

If only I could believe him. We may have acted too hastily with our need to escape.

Chapter 56 - Bequia

The site of Bequia is welcoming, even from a long way out. At least we know we could swim or row the rest of the way now. The water shallows a long way out and becomes a picture for any snorkeler. Georgie begins to relax a little but not completely, she has been tense all the way over.

"You OK?"

She dips her head in reply. "You have dreams, you say things, then what if they come true? What am I going to do with a house here?"

"Neither of us have answers to that yet."

"I can't just leave the ship."

"And we aren't going to. I have a daughter expecting to see me later."

That produces a small smile, but everything we are doing is worrying.

"So we are going back?"

For me, it's about making the money safe and it's certainly not safe on the ship. Our boat docks and Wilson is immediately in an argument with a local. It will be about money, about the right to taxi and moor. I palm Wilson two one hundred dollar notes.

"Fill this up with fuel, get it seen by an engineer and be back here on this dock by three o'clock," I say privately to him.

He looks at the money and beams. "Yes, sir."

I can smell his breath. He has been drinking heavily.

"Sober," I add. "That's an order, sailor."

Georgie climbs out of the boat, hugging her lifejacket. I step out and follow.

"Leave your lifejackets. They're good here with me."

"We've got them," I say, realising how daft it is to carry a lifejacket into town. Up to now, we've not turned a single head with the bright yellow buoyancy aids. Inland they will draw attention. However, there is no way I am parting with this money.

"You thinking of getting a different boat, man?"

"No, you be here, we've paid you."

As Georgie and I walk down the short jetty towards the small town, as sweet as it is, it fails to look like it will have an estate agent or a bank. The sign outside the post office is handwritten on wood and infers it does everything but is written as a child would. We could be in the wild west. I guess I need to get used to local Caribbean islands, but the plan of entrusting them with money has started to worry me. I turn back and look out at the peaceful sea, at the boats to assess the wealth here. Money exists here, not new flashy money, these are older, large conservative boats. I turn back and look into the hills at the houses and ask myself; are these distant generations of families hanging onto money earned in slavery, or is this an island that attracts new money. We will find out and fast.

"You have a favourite spot?" I ask her.

"Jack's bar. Everyone loves Jack's bar. It sits on the most pristine beach, Princess Margaret Beach. I've walked over the hills to it and the houses on the coast roads are spectacular. But are we making a mistake?"

"Who knows?" I say honestly, then lean into her, "who cares, it's play money."

We approach the town to see a few taxi drivers and rather than take the first, I look at the cars. We need air conditioning, and we have to look like we have money.

"You want to see the turtles, man?" the driver of my chosen car asks.

"I want to go to a property agent, have you got the morning to stay with us?"

"Fifty dollars, man," he says quickly, with no idea that I need this deal more than he does and the price is not an issue.

We climb into the car and he drives us no more than a few blocks, we could have walked. We stop at a small property place that claims to rent holiday homes. I can see from the window display that he is way off base but he insists on walking us in. He high fives them. These are his friends, and as much as I would love to chat with them and hear about the island, my clock is ticking.

"You looking to stay on our beautiful island?" Is the greeting we get from a very cheerful lady.

"Not exactly, we are crew off the ship. We're looking to buy here if there are no restrictions. A group of us want a house on the hill." I turn to Georgie for support but she is running out of faith and steam.

"Above Jacks bar. Looking out to sea," Georgie eventually finishes for me very flatly.

That has slowed the lady down, and I can see the cogs turning. She is desperate not to lose a commission, but I'm guessing she doesn't have what we need. She retreats behind her desk with just a word.

"Expensive," she says, seemingly giving the word far more syllables than it actually has and stretching them out. "Very expensive."

"We know they're expensive. We know the island. But we have little time before we need to be back on our ship."

"Million dollars?" she asks, to gauge our status.

"We expect that. We either spend it here or another island, but our group wants a good deal."

She collects a black handbag and sits a hat on her head as if she were off to church then she leads us to the door.

"My name is Sylvie; it is the only name you need to know in Bequia." She turns to her young assistant. "You mind the shop." Sylvie turns back to us at the door. "You can leave your lifejackets here." She moves to take them off us, but the last thing we are going to do is let her feel the weight.

"No, we've got them thanks. Just in case we rush back a different way."

She doesn't take that as easily as Wilson did, but not because she is insulted, she is suspicious. Sylvie is a no-nonsense powerful African lady who can smell a deal.

Fanning herself only seconds out of the air conditioning, she moves to the front passenger door, sitting up front with the driver who has just got into the car. She leans into me as I open the rear passenger door behind her.

"So, how much money you got stuffed in those yellow vests?"

"Enough," I say because this needs to be progressed not argued.

"What wrong with the bank?"

"If we find somewhere, it can go in the bank, if not, it goes in a bank on another island. It was won betting in the casino, and I would rather not take it back to the ship or I might lose it before the next island."

She leans in even closer to me. "It is not going back to that ship. If the casino is that big, you can win some more."

She looks up and sees Georgie watching her. Georgie doesn't like to be excluded, Sylvie notes that and nods.

"Big ship, miss."

"Big ship, which is why it stopped in St Vincent. We can go back there if you can't help," Georgie explains across the roof of the car, trying to nail the conversation closed.

The Lady is soft but firm, as if she had been insulted and needs to just put us straight. "This is St Vincent, sister, a special little part of it."

Georgie doesn't take lightly to being told anything, so is fast to hit back. "Shall we go somewhere else, Kieron? I'm not feeling a deal here."

"We're working on that sister, working on that. Us and God have a plan," Sylvie says and she gets in the car. Georgie and I do the same.

"You call me Sylvie, now we are all friends," she settling back into her seat and crushing into my knees. "Trust God and Sylvie."

"Is that two people taking commission then?" Georgie asks.

"God's work is free, you just pay me and I thank him."

Chapter 57 – God's work is free

After climbing a steep incline, the car levels out and coasts around what is probably the only coast road. We pull up outside a beautiful house. The grounds are a little overgrown but colourful, revealing it might have been on the market a while. The wood and paintwork all look good and it has a huge balcony on the first floor. It doesn't overlook the sea, but Georgie turns to me and gives me the first proper smile of the day, it must be ticking all the boxes of her dream house. Sylvie is out of the car quick enough to observe us both.

"Sylvie knows what you want. So, are we friends now?"

"Kieron, the taxi's going!" Georgie panics.

I turn and start to sum up how vulnerable we are carrying this much cash in the middle of nowhere, Georgie being the most valuable thing I have here and what makes me vulnerable.

"He get key for Sylvie," Sylvie reassures us.

Words should never re-assure anyone, but we have a job to do and the time is vanishing fast. The house has a small 'For Sale' sign on a post just inside the fence, which she sees I have noticed. I know it's not her company, I remember seeing the name of 'Sylvie's Properties' hand painted above the little shop.

"You let Sylvie help you save money, it's been for sale long time and now it don't rent."

"What's wrong with it?" Georgie asks.

"It doesn't overlook the sea and others do, is what is wrong," I add as a negotiation.

"Two million dollars is wrong with it," Sylvie admits.

"And why won't anyone rent it? Same reason, no view?" I ask.

"People like new, luxury, not old school. Inside needs Sylvie's touch. Needs a new kitchen."

"The kitchen's no good?" Georgie calls back from a side window she's looking in. "Looks good from here."

"Kitchen works fine, but it's not the kitchen for this house. You put new kitchen in, Sylvie get that old one. We gonna be great friends."

"Can you fix the house up?" I ask.

"My man's on the way to talk with you."

I wander back into the road, there's not a car to be seen or heard. I notice two other houses for sale on the road down towards the beach.

"Trust me, if you have cash to convert, this is the way to do it," Sylvie says, knowingly.

Georgie is looking through another window, while Sylvie makes another call on her mobile phone, so I duck back under the hanging bougainvillaea and walk down to the first of the other houses for sale.

This house has tailored grounds but looks smaller. I peer through the windows and see it is quite lavishly decorated, and from what I can see of the kitchen it looks state of the art. It seems odd that three houses so close together are for sale. I walk further down the road and find a third house with a great walk-around balcony on the first floor, a fantastic feature, but possibly a security nightmare. I look through the windows and again it looks modern, with new decoration and fittings. I can also see that it's occupied and an Englishman rushes to the door on seeing me.

"Hi, can I help you?"

"Sorry, I saw the 'For Sale' sign."

"We've rented it for a month. It was for sale last year and the year before," he explains.

"I'll leave you alone. Sorry to bother you." I turn to find Sylvie waiting for me in the path.

"Hi Sylvie!" the man in the house shouts to her, "My tap's still not working."

"Can you see water?"

"Yes, but-."

"Then it works. Don't worry, my man is arriving soon." She waves at him and the door is closed.

"You like that kitchen?" she asks.

"Yes."

"Sylvie did that."

"So why didn't you get his old kitchen?"

"I did, it in my house, your old kitchen will be in my mother's house."

We both step back onto the hill and are confronted by the most glorious view down; a line of trees, beach, pale blue sea, and the view beyond of forever cascading colour. I hear the taxi return and park outside the house, with a newer smarter car behind it on the corner.

"I told you to leave it to Sylvie. Your key arrived."

"It's not my key, Sylvie."

"Unless you taking that lifejacket back to the ship, Sylvie is going to do some laundry for you and we going to be very good friends."

"How do I know I can trust you with a million?"

"Unless you wasted your time packing that jacket with one dollar bills, you need to trust me with a lot more than that."

"What's that one selling for?" I point to the house below us.

"Two million dollars."

"But the one up here that needs gutting is two million!"

"Every nice house on the island is two million."

We walk up the road together towards the house and I fear that if she clocked our money that fast, Hunter should be as clever. He's paid to be, has trained to be. My only saving grace is that we carried the lifejackets off the ship during the lifeboat drill. Here, exposed on dry land with these two obvious bright yellow lumps is different. Sylvie is right, I don't want to have to try and smuggle this money back on board, not even in a lifejacket. It might be Sylvie's lucky day, she already knows too much.

Before I know it, there's a pick-up truck behind the newer car, with a team of men in all holding gardening tools. Already we're drawing too much attention. Also waiting for me back at the first house is a very tanned and upright English man.

"Hello. William Hart, estate agent. Would you like to leave your lifejacket in my car?"

"No. If you saw the boat I came over on, you would hold on to it tightly."

He gives a knowing laugh. William has read nothing into it, which amuses Sylvie as she wags her head at his stupidity.

"So you are interested in this little number, fantastic prospects," William says which, is estate agent talk for it 'will cost me a fortune'.

"He was interested until I showed him Orange Blossom down the road. Seems I brought me up the wrong estate agent." Sylvie laughs and hugs William. It is obvious they are good friends.

"You know that's on our books too now, so I can send for the key and we can look at that as well."

"William, me got that key in me pocket. And the next one too, me tenant is home waiting for a leak be fixed. And me thinks, both the owner needs to sell now so would take one and a half cash. Me talking cash," Sylvie announces.

I walk away and leave her to it. I know she is horse trading even if William is one step behind.

"This one would be much more reasonable," William suggests.

"The only reasonable thing I can see, William, is to buy one get one free. This one needs so much work," she says.

I can hear Sylvie doing a great job as I reach the house, looking for Georgie. Not that it's her money, it's no one's money really. I was thinking of setting up a children's home. I also need a pension after the army rescinded mine by discharging me, but everything has gone adrift. Georgie's with a tall black man and they are redesigning the place, both waving their arms animatedly. Her wave turns into an enthusiastic beckon to get me to join them.

"Kieron, this is Ryan. He has great ideas. He did the other houses on the hill."

"I had a look at the two next door."

"Me do them. Pleased to meet you, man." He grins and shakes my hand very firmly.

"Pleasures mine. If Georgie is happy, I'm happy."

I glance at Georgie, she does look happy at last.

"Me could get very excited here, very excited." He turns to explain his dreams for the house to me, but Sylvie is behind me.

"Ryan, me need you to fix the leak down the road then come back and see if we can do somet'ing here," she says.

Ryan high-fives her as he strides out with a great smile and an understanding. He shows Sylvie instant respect like the tenant down the road did, she obviously is the woman to know. I watch him instruct his men in the pickup to down their gardening tools and take a box of small tools down the road. There is a very noteworthy system of command here and while we are holding cash it all works. Georgie takes a moment away from Sylvie to lean into me and whisper,

"I love it."

Maybe it is the atmosphere, the sheer hysteria, but there is something in her eyes that screams wedding bells and life together. I need a time-out because this is almost a first date and we're already buying a house together.

Chapter 58 – House of cash

Having convinced William that this could be a cash sale today, Sylvie left him behind with a list of phone calls to make and suggested he join us in Jack's bar on the beach. She is staying close to the money and doing the client manager job superbly. I can see why Georgie loves it here but can you get tired of paradise?

Jack's is a beach restaurant with a true Caribbean feel, black wood chairs and tables, cloth napkins and silver cutlery. It all looks very special just above the sandy beach and the sound of the gentle waves mixes with the music. Glasses of water are poured, and we are offered menus. This is not going to be cheap, or quick, this is for the people who own the boats I can see bobbing in the bay, and who rent the houses up on the hill.

Sylvie is at the bar on her mobile and I have no idea who she is calling now, but she is busy closing a deal. She turns and smiles walking back to the table.

"The white boy no understand finance, but me teach him. He got the fancy shop and a boat from his rich family, and me have the little shop and a small house, but me rent the houses he can't." Sylvie tuts smacking her lips together which is wonderfully expressive, and she sits down.

"You still holding onto them yellow jackets." She smiles.

I nod. Mine is on my lap wedged between my legs and the table. Georgie's was hanging off the chair but she gathers it and squeezes it onto her lap.

"Me tell him, come back when you can close the deal at no more than two and a half million for both them houses, me don't care how you split the money between them and he get some commission. So, are you buying and do you have that cash?" She asks, leaning in.

Georgie and I have not had a moment alone to catch our breath, and in these surroundings, it would be hard to do. Three of Georgie's dancers come into the bar for a drink and acknowledge her. They may have seen the yellow lifejackets, if so, our story could be getting more complex.

"How are you going to do this?" I ask. "This is cash I won gambling and I don't want to lose it."

"So you have two point five?" she asks again.

Just answering that question could get me hijacked, me and Georgie both killed and no one would know why.

"How much to do that house up, nicely?" I ask.

Sylvie shrugs as if there is no answer. "One hundred thousand makes it a palace, but up to you. You can spend less."

Her mobile phone rings.

"Sylvie." She listens, then without covering the phone, she speaks to us. "He says two point seven and we have to go to the bank today."

I look at her hard, this is a crazy deal but we have to close it fast because it's approaching one o'clock, and the ship sails at seventeen thirty hours. We have four maybe five hours then we need to start moving back. This is no time to really weigh up our options, we have to act fast. Maybe we will be dead in days. What the heck, I nod. Sylvie rolls her phone back to her mouth.

"He says two point five in dollar bills is all he has. Close the deal or we going to have lunch and they sail away." There is another pause. "Done!" Sylvie listens for another minute then she waves at the bar.

"Me ordered fresh lobster and white wine, then we go to a bank." She smiles.

"Oh my God! What just happened?" Georgie asks, and I feel her gripping my thigh. I like that we are a couple. If I am getting the right vibrations, she is quietly elated and feeling safe now it is over. I am sure there is still much to do though, and I'm eager to see the deal finalised and this money gone.

"We could skip lunch and get on with business?"

"No, me got to get a whole team together to make this happen, and be more successful at it than your England cricket team." Sylvie beams.

"Our football teams doing alright now," I protest, as the wine is poured.

"Me only see cricket!"

Sylvie is on and off the phone, demanding people jump to her attention. I eat and drink, hoping it's not my last meal and I'm not going to be mugged and dumped in a volcanic sink hole, if they have these here, all these islands must have come from volcanoes. If that were to happen, everyone reading the story, if the true story were to get out, would say how mad we were to be on a Caribbean island with such a huge amount of cash. And I suppose they'd be right. Sylvie puts her phone down.

"You just bought two houses for two point six million dollars. I hope you have it because if you do, me is going to eat very well for a few weeks," Sylvie says, as the wine arrives.

"I thought it was two-point-five?" I ask, but why does it matter, I have no idea how much money is stuffed in the jacket.

"I said me going to eat very well. I saved you two hundred grand, least you can do is share the saving!" She smiles.

I really don't know how much I have and it's not going to get counted here. We left the ship in a rush and never counted it out. I probably have two hundred thousand in my cargo shorts, because I've tightened the belt as far as it goes and they are still falling down. How embarrassing would it be if we didn't have enough? I look out to sea, trying to remember the bricks I broke down to pack this morning. I must have three million plus. I look out to sea and wonder; if I have more, how do I leave the rest of the cash here? I can't send money to Syria in case some clever banker links us to the transaction. It is not just about laundering drug money, which is what it must be, sending money to the Middle East would raise an eyebrow if not a few terrorism alarm bells. Then we have the lifejackets, will anyone remember seeing us leave with them, will they expect them to go back? Should I find a boat shop where I can buy proper foam to mend them? Hunter sees everything, he will ask why we took them.

The food comes quicker than expected but eating is only easy for Sylvie.

"We need to discuss the work you want to be done in the house and how you pay," Sylvie asks.

"That is Georgie's department." My mind is racing, trying to justify a genuine use of the lifejackets and whether they go back to the ship. When they finish talking interior design, I step in.

"I need a picture of the two of us at sea in kayaks."

Sylvie smiles, the cogs turn. "To show why you bring lifejackets?"

I nod, we all know.

"Then we go now," Sylvie says, checking her watch.

"Best to do it here," she says. "We need time to make things work. This is not New York."

"No, not here. Somewhere quiet, no ship's crew."

I slip Sylvie a bill from a roll of hundreds in my pocket. That is the first time Sylvie has seen any cash. Until then we could have been on one big stupid ego trip. She hands it to the manager.

"Put the change on my account."

We rush up the steps to the road and wake our waiting taxi driver, who is in a deep sleep. Sylvia seems to be anxious about something and I'm hoping it is time, she has taken to checking her watch, and it worries me more and more. Has she set a trap for us? Are we to be snared somewhere on the road at a predetermined time?

The car spins around and he drives faster than before. The delay going to a kayak photo-shoot seems daft now, but I'll have the picture of us using the lifejackets if I need it. It is also a test for Sylvie, a test of her compliance with our needs. A test she appears to be passing, as we drive off the road into the trees by a sandy bay where somehow a kayak is waiting for us. The great thing about the plan is that although I have to leave my phone and shorts, (which have a considerable sum of money stuffed in the pockets) on the sand, the lifejacket won't leave me. The fluorescent yellow beacons are fastened around our necks, weighing a tonne and bang into our bodies as Georgie and I run down to the water's edge. Sylvie follows, holding my camera phone. The driver is entrusted with guarding what we have left behind. If only he knew, his honesty might be tested.

The water is so warm and inviting, it would have been great to have come here and relaxed like I'm sure Jill is doing, wherever she is. I did say I would try and find her, for all I know she could have seen me, I have been rather blinkered. I hold the Kayak while Georgie struggles to get in, nearly tipping it with the weight. I try to get in unaided but it's impossible. I join the two canoes side by side and have Georgie hang onto both and I manage to get in. I have my back to the beach for just a few moments and I panic to turn back around. To my relief, Sylvie is still there with my phone taking snaps. She is just in the shallows, gentle waves over her feet. She is motioning that we need to go further out. I paddle backwards and try and pull Georgie with me, who banks slightly as a jet ski comes powering in and creates a wave. In a moment of zero coordination, we tip over, top heavy and hit the water.

The lifejackets have no buoyancy at all, but fill with water and encourage me to sink. I fight against the weight to get my head above water. I kick down, where is the bottom, which way up am I? My legs find the bottom. I hold the sides of the lifejacket so the money can't escape. Then I see Georgie, struggling underwater about fifteen feet away. I dig my legs down and push, but each step is hard. I try to lift the lifejacket, to get rid of it, but I struggle with it and can't manage. I can see her choking, taking in too much water. I power through the water, each stride taking too long, sapping power from my body. When I reach her I dive down, grab her torso and heave, our combined weight is huge, it is an effort to save her from drowning and I can see her gasping for air and filling with water. I try and release the lifejacket but it is tied and fixed. I balance my weight, bend my legs and lift. When she is above water we hug each other. All I care about is her safety. She is worth far more than three or four million. I hold her up and squeeze her hard until she breathes again.

"We're not meant to have this. It's not worth it?" she splutters.

"Nothing is worth losing you. But there's no turning back. We can be independent, we can do good things."

The Kayak owner strides easily past us and through the sea to collects his boats. The photo shoot is over. Sylvie may have our pictures, but the money is soaking wet.

Chapter 59 – Wet money

In this heat, drying our bodies is almost instant and dressing is not a problem, but we are now carrying two huge dead weights. I could ditch the lifejackets for a better method of carrying the money, but if the plan goes wrong or they won't take wet money we will need them to get it back on ship. Then again who turns down a few million just because it is wet?

Although we bought two huge towels that wait at the beachside, the amount of water that can be retained in bundles of money is beyond the scope of towelling. The bank might not like us dripping wet, but they certainly don't seem to mind this strange business opportunity.

The pictures on my phone are an embarrassment to lifejackets, there are only two worth keeping, the rest are deleted. Sylvie might be good at many things but photography is not one of them.

The two bank officials look at the piles of wet money, now stacked on towels laying on a table in their back office They start to open the sealed packs of one-hundred-thousand, packs I've never opened but am guessing hold one hundred dollar bills throughout. Some release water, some are dry. The first step is separating the dry notes to the easy process of a counting machine.

"This is a deal for two houses. Seller demanded cash," Sylvie says and no one argues with her.

We separate two and a half million in dry dollars, all counted and correct and it's piled onto a small tea trolley.

"They can take the wet notes and save our bank a problem," the main bank official suggests.

The dry money is covered and wheeled out with us following. I hold back and from my cargo pocket I take a sealed one hundred thousand dollars and hand it to Sylvie. She puts it into her bag.

"Your commission, as agreed, right?"

"You make someone a good husband. If missie there say 'no'." Sylvie points to Georgie, "you come back and see Sylvie!"

Sylvie has no idea Georgie and I have only known each other just under a week. We catch the others up as they enter another room, where Sylvie introduces us to a well-suited black man.

"Meet our solicitor, Senior," Sylvie says.

"Madam, Sir," he greets us in a deep voice that could get him an overnight announcer's job on Radio 4. He shakes Georgie's hand then mine. He lifts the cloth off the tea trolley and looks at the money.

"So, this is two point five million, for the two properties?"

Senior turns to the two other men. "These are my colleagues, solicitors for the vendors. Gentlemen, do you need to see the money counted or will you take the bank's word for it?"

They look at each other and agree. "We will need to see it counted."

"Then we will have some tea and make ourselves comfortable. First, we sign the papers," Senior suggests.

For all we know they could be Sylvie's relatives, but they spread paperwork across the table, and two chairs are supplied for Georgie and me to sit on. Papers are slid back and forth and explained as we sign. The bank manager watches blankly and signs when required, as does Sylvie. I photograph them and the documents, I've no idea how I could use this if it went wrong, but again, best to have the pictures.

"William Hart is driving the owner and his wife, they be here soon," Sylvie tells the manager. "It is their money after they sign and you can deal with them."

"Thanks. We don't need to meet them. We can go back into the other room and deal with some outstanding business," I suggest.

"Senior will stay and ensure your money is split between accounts and all fees are paid. We can leave," Sylvie confirms.

Senior shakes Georgie's hand, then mine. "I'm here on the island, whenever you need me."

The bank manager nods. I shake hands with the other two solicitors and Sylvie leads us back to the first room, where there is still a pile of dry money and a lot of wet money that we need to account for.

"We need to open a bank account each, with this money split between us," I suggest.

I offer my passport and Georgie offers hers. I put my arms around her and hold her in front of me, my head next to hers, watching the wet money being stacked.

"We now own two properties together," I whisper.

"Weird," Georgie replies.

"You reckon between this lot they could marry us now too?"

I have no idea where that came from, or if I meant it. My arms across the front of her feel her heart stop, the world stops as she slowly takes in what I said.

She turns to me. "That was a joke right?"

There is a long pause. "I've never been known for my humour."

"Well, it made me laugh."

She is making light of it, but she hugs my arms around her and there is a connection.

"And we need an escrow account with Sylvie's company, which should have one hundred thousand dollars put into it that Sylvie can draw on. Let's suggest up to five thousand in any one week without authority, a larger sum needs either of our approval."

I look to Sylvie for agreement and she nods.

"How much you got left now, Mr Philips?' she asks.

"Guess they will tell us."

Sylvie picks up a few particularly wet one hundred dollar notes.

"You know you didn't have to go to this much trouble to laundry your money." She finds hilarious.

Neither of the bank officials finds that funny.

"This is all straight forward sir, except wet money cannot be machine counted. I will need to have it manually counted. I don't have the staff and the bank is busy."

Sylvie pushes the manger to the door. "You go look again, me think there was some staff hiding."

She is not gone long when she comes back with a young female bank worker, who seems embarrassed by the million or so in wet money on the table. She would've fainted if she had seen the tea trolley. She sits and starts to count.

A younger male employee then enters with the second official. He too is amazed by the amount of cash which to us seems trivial now.

"Holy shit!" he lets escape.

"Nathan," she senior bank member reprimands.

"Sorry, Sir."

The returning official hands us the forms for our accounts, but the circle of people who know about the money we have and possibly where our properties are is expanding. We will be village folklore by morning, and no doubt famous by the weekend. I hear a camera phone click and immediately reach out and snatch at the mobile phone of the young bank worker behind me who has just snapped a picture of the remaining million or so. He cowers away in fear and the atmosphere in the room has changed in an instant.

"Sir, what are you doing?" the manager says to me. "We can't have violence against any of our staff."

I turn the phone over and show the manager the picture of the money. I turn back to the kid before the manager can speak.

"I posted a picture, that's all," he says nervously.

"I was just trying to stop you."

I turn back to the manager handing him the phone.

"All his friends and their friends know this bank is holding all this money overnight. People die for that kind of money. Buildings are burned down for that kind of cash."

"We must move it to another branch," he says.

"Someone might knock on his door tonight, prepared to rip his limbs off to find out how to get into this bank whether the money is here or not because he just told the world it's here. Sylvie, can you help sort this out?"

They have no idea the problem this could cause. I walk out of the room, it is all I can do.

Chapter 60 – Chinese whispers

After an exchange of curt whispers in the main body of the bank, where I offer to pay for a guard overnight, and more importantly one on the kid's house, Sylvie calmly suggests she will handle everything and we agree to talk later on the phone.

Back in William's taxi, I leaf through papers; including the management contract with Sylvie's company, bank papers, and a statement for the escrow bank account with her. There is paperwork for our own bank accounts too and initial deposits of three hundred thousand dollars each with further sums to be advised. Lastly, there is an agreement appointing our solicitor who we have left back at the bank watching two scared youngsters count the remaining very wet money.

"Me don't think you could do all that in five hours without Sylvie." The car stops, we have arrived and we are about to part.

The bay looks calm, yet I feel anything but calm. Sylvie stands next to me and is quiet for the first time. Maybe she's worried about that slip by the young employee.

"If this works out, we might ring you again to do some more laundry," I say, a lot softer now.

"My mother did laundry all her life, she was a very proud woman."

I find myself kissing her cheek. She may be the first honest person I have met on this cruise. Georgie and I leave without having to deal with the little stuff, she will pay off the taxi driver. A fast boat is waiting for us, again settled by her, and she will pay towards our other boat which has apparently been kept in the repair shop needing severe work. It may even be condemned. She is going to see what she can do to help there. Our stormy visit has affected a whole community, and she is going to control the rumour mill somehow. This must be how the rich live, a paid service to fix anything in life, they just leave, as we are, but if all goes well, we will be back visiting Bequia as owners. As the three of us walk from the taxi down to the speedboat, I put my arm around Sylvie.

"What a day, eh, Sylvie?"

"Oh, happy day!"

"You sure you will all be OK?" I ask her as I step into the boat.

"This is a safe island Mr Kieron, it my island," she boasts.

"If it was Jamaica, someone would already be after that money," I suggest, maybe wrongly.

"This not Jamaica. This is Bequia, and you live here now as my neighbour. I'll be seeing you," she waves as we start to pull away.

"Make sure my tenants behave," I shout back as the boat swings around and powers out to sea. Georgie waves too, but is silent. I turn to her.

"What's up?"

"The way you looked as you snapped for the boy's phone. I thought you were going to kill that boy." She pauses.

"Never."

"But you could, I saw it. You changed, your eyes, you became a different person."

"I was trying to save him from being killed. People do kill for less than money."

There is a lot more going on in her head, I can see it, I have seen it before. I know what's coming even though there is a silence between us now.

"Have you ever killed anyone?" she eventually asks.

The question inevitably comes up, and no one loves the answer, no one believes the lie.

"I was trying to stop a picture going out on social media. I snatched because speed was required. By the time I got the phone, I bet it had already been shared. Imagine that was a kid with a loaded gun pointed at a friend. You have to react fast. My friend, your friend, would be dead. Today I was too slow."

"No, we should have explained the situation to everyone before it all started."

I have to bite my lip because that is the approach the new generation take from behind their safe opinionated desks. It is harder than ever for a young soldier to return home and have his work discussed.

"You're right. The problem is, this is such a complicated thing we've got involved in, we don't have time to plan. Who'd have thought that today would end with us owning two houses in St. Vincent?"

Georgie stares straight ahead, defying the air the boat powers through, ignoring her hair being blown behind her and wrapping around her face as we bounce across the sea. A great day that should have ended in joy has a nasty edge to it, plus a rush against the clock. In an envelope now stuffed down the front of my shirt is a wad of paperwork. In my pocket, I have two broken deflated yellow lifejackets that I couldn't leave on the small island where they might be found and used as evidence, or for blackmail. What do I do with them now? Where can I lose them? I look back at the small boutique island getting smaller and smaller, fading away, and turn forward to the ship, which I hope will start to get bigger very soon.

I slide over to Georgie, put my arm around her and her head sits on my shoulder. Have we really bought a life together after knowing each other a week? Or are we now penniless after being scammed? I wonder how much houses do cost on that island and if we've just been conned, or whether we have made some friends for life. Who knows, who knows who you can trust? We both still have over a million each in our cabin safes. What a mess.

The ship is getting closer and all we have to do now is board with incriminating paperwork that no one will take or read. Maybe it's time to ask Hunter if he has been taking money from under my bed. If not, I will be informing him we've been robbed.

In for a penny, in for four million.

Chapter 61 – Hot air

Our boat cannot pull up on the same dock as the ship, because the ship is in a bonded area for immigration and customs. We have to dock away from the ship, near where we left this morning by the fish market, and rush along to the port gates. No one is working at the dockside now, people work early here when the ships come in and before the sun comes up. The boat slows down. I check my watch.

"Perfect timing, forty-five minutes to boarding."

"For you. I'm late. I have to put on a smile and run the 'Sail Away' party. Dance around the pool, wave a flag."

"A life you didn't want to leave behind."

I get a disapproving look from her as the boat docks and we are offered a hand to jump ashore.

"I should call you up to dance and sing with the rest of the Ents' team."

"No thank you."

I can tell Georgie is still not happy, still worried. She sees me as a killer now, not a soldier.

"I'll run ahead. You don't need to rush do you?"

She's gone, without an answer, without a smile, without the warmth that was there when the adventure started. I look around and see the passengers walking back towards the ship

CRUISE SHIP HEIST – OCEAN ATLANTIC

and I decide to wander the other way. I don't need to get on that ship. In fact, if I could catch Auli'i and Christophe they don't either. I wonder how many staff they lose at each port. How many people wish to swap Asia or wherever for the Americas?

The food and tourist markets are closing, the streets are easy to cross and I walk without purpose up a hill. I see children running around in a side street, a school must be turning out. They all look so perfectly groomed in their identical school uniforms. Blue jackets, white shirts, grey skirts and pants. None of them looks bothered by the heat or dishevelled, all of them are smiling. Not one is checking a mobile phone. Society here has taken a different way forward.

I look at the building they are leaving, and it is the most incredible ornate gothic-pillared church courtyard. If I had found this in Rome, or Greece I would not have been surprised. It's like a feeder school you might find in Cambridge, but then it was no doubt built after the colonial invasion. I walk around as if time doesn't matter, reading notice boards and taking in the amazing Hogwarts-like surroundings. Old greying stone, a fountain, vines, and the entrance to the main church.

I stop and take in another noticeboard with a thermometer drawn on it, and it is half-full. It's renovations to the building, roof and to equip a technical area with computers. For a moment I wonder if such technology is exactly what they should avoid. They are a quarter of a million Eastern Caribbean Dollars short. A nun leaves the church office and passes me with a friendly smile.

"I look at that every day. Looking hasn't helped yet," she quips.

"Would you like me to try and help?"

"Please. It is the medical centre I want to see here." She says pointing at the small section of all their ambitions on the board.

"If it only saves one life," I say.

"Exactly," she agrees.

"If I can find a way of helping, would you send, let's say a quarter of whatever might appear, to a similar children's charity in Syria?"

"I like it when I see a little of God in people," she says. She looks deeply into my eyes, I can't help feeling she looked further than that.

"Some people have to play God or life would not work,"

She turns and walks away without judgement.

I pick up my phone, photograph the plea for help and send it to Sylvie. I walk away from the building and down the hill, dialling her number and hoping to see the ship reveal itself from behind the dock buildings, if it is still there.

"Sylvie, I have an idea that might just keep that young banker alive."

"No one gonna kill him," she shouts.

"Hear me out…"

We talk as I walk back down the hill until I turn the corner and see the dock road again. The ship towers above the buildings now. I speed up knowing I've been frivolous with my time, there are only twenty minutes to boarding. After Sylvie, I ring Georgie as I start to run.

"Georgie!" I start enthusiastically.

"Kieron. Can we do this later?" she says, cutting me off and I stop dead. I hear the cold tone in her voice and I feel everything we had has gone. I look back towards the church where I wasn't judged, but I am standing outside a bar.

I find myself in the bar, ordering another whiskey. I haven't drunk spirits for a long time. I reach the bottom of the glass, and here they are fast to refill. My twenty minutes is up. The ship is blowing its horn, but I can't face my broken relationship with Georgie. I can't face her questions, and it's not easy for anyone to understand if they've not served themselves. We are trained to kill, given permission to kill, it is your job to kill, though no one wants to do it. Tour after tour after tour in war zones, dodging mines, spinning round in the dark and shooting before you are shot. The one thing that gets shot is your life, your perspective on humanity. But nothing hits you more than when you get home, when you are asked over and over by anyone you get close to, 'have you killed someone?' Then relationships are broken, a line has been crossed. It's not just that they won't like the answer but they become addicted to the questions.

My glass is topped up. "Thanks, buddy."

"Is that your ship, man?"

"Yes."

"When the bighorn blows you need to drink fast, very fast."

"Thanks."

He leans into me on the bar. "And pay me before you run because me don't want to shoot you in the back, no?"

I look up at him.

"You could, we all gotta die sometime," I say slowly.

He sees something in my eyes that makes him back off, something that didn't make the nun back off. She could see I did what was asked of me. It's something that few people get to see because I never mix with people when I get this low but I guess Georgie saw too much.

I pull a one hundred dollar note out and pay him, I don't want to finish his drink. A man who runs a bar should be your friend and but I think he would soon be asking me the wrong questions too. I bet he never gets asked have you ever killed someone? Or the next question, the one that I can't take.

I step out into the sunlight and squint. If I miss this ship, that's it. I will be spending too much time in that bar. There is no next stop for the ship, no other Caribbean island to catch a short flight to. The ship is now crossing the Atlantic. Next stop Madeira.

A rubbish cart is emptying fish ends, vegetables, and trash. I toss in the spoilt yellow jackets. I look down at my cruise card, should I throw that too?

Chapter 62 – Ship has sailed

Leaping the closed port gate is easy, but the gangway from the dockside to the ship has gone. As I accelerate to the still open shell door, I see the gangway has been drawn into the ship and the crew are inside stowing it. No crew are left on the quayside. Ropes are being released by harbour staff and the door is being readied to close. The side thrusters are working hard to push the ship from the pier.

"Too late!" the Asian security guard shouts, "too late!"

The crew activate the shell door and I hear the motor start up. I turn and run away from the ship screaming with the pain of failure, then sharp turn back and run at the ship. My legs mimic the power of the ship's side thrusters. I run focused on the steel, and I don't care if it is the last leap I ever make. Few can understand making those life and death decisions, but the last few hours have sent me back there. The nun did.

Shouts and waving arms can't stop a man in mid-air. Screams bellow from inside and then there is the bang of my limbs against steel and I hang on in pain, looking up at them. They freeze, every one of them, then panic spreads and they're pointing to the closing shell door because it's still coming round on me. I can see it. I will be crushed. Typical. No matter how much training they do, no matter how many 'man overboard' drills they do, nothing prepares them for the unexpected. We had the same in Kuwait, the first time I took men to the Middle-East, we had to go through houses, clearing room after room. Making choices of dummies, friend or foe in training. They were never ready for what they met, women and children shooting at them. Faces up close and dangerous. These faces are just as lost and I am left hanging, no one knowing what to do.

"Stop the door!" I shout.

I can see them shouting at each other, I can't hear much until the motor silence and the door stops just above me. My world begins again. One guy is on the phone, probably to Hunter, who will be on his way down and I will be arrested. Damn whiskey brain is crashing in on me now! And I have the house paperwork on me, giving away the day's work if I am searched. I am done. Can I refuse to be searched? I think of the lifejackets, I need to get rid of them. There is only one thing for it, let go and drop into the sea. I take a deep breath and let go with my right arm. It swings down as I feel for the two empty lifejackets, but where are they? I check all my pockets as hands grab at me and wrench at my body, anywhere they can grab. I can't escape. I suddenly remember I tossed the jackets in the trash, my head is spinning.

I am pulled up, each of my ribs dug by the edge of the steel as I am pulled on board then I'm dragged to my feet and handcuffed. The shell door is closing now, far too noisy.

"What? I have a cruise card. Let me go, I'm a guest!" I argue but it's too late. A door opens and Hunter steps up to me.

"What are you doing?" he asks me in amazement.

"Testing your men, as you asked. They were a bit slow to react, but they all passed," I try.

Hunter leans into me, I know he can smell I've been drinking. "Testing? You need help!" he whispers.

"I just helped you, big time."

"I'm not a psychiatrist, but I do know this is not a test."

"It's a test based on the reality of FIBUA training. Fighting in built-up areas," I reply quietly just to him.

"This is a ship, we don't fight on board."

"It's about reality shocks. I've done this crew a favour, given them a real training exercise, one that takes them from the relaxed plodding drills to having to actually think fast," I slur quietly, then summon up a loud and clear. "They passed!" I am soft again, for his ear only. "Now you think quickly."

"Take him up to my office," Hunter barks.

"I think I've broken something, maybe a knee cap, maybe a leg, a few ribs," I say, acting as if I can't stand alone. "I think I need medical attention first."

That one always works, he will have to allow me medical care if I need it. That always takes the sting out of any reprimand, even footballers know that.

"Sit him down, get a stretcher, take him to the medical centre," Hunter demands, leaving.

I have escaped another bullet. I will be stripped, examined, maybe X-rayed, and then taken to Hunter, maybe even the Captain. I guess dinner with him is off.

I'm sat firmly into a chair and I scream in pain, half for effect and half because it really does hurt now the alcohol and adrenalin are both wearing off. I watch the door finally close safely. Two medics arrive in green jumpsuits, lay out the stretcher, and lift me on. My mind swirls. I either feel seasick or drunk. I want to put one leg on the floor, but I can't because the stretcher is moving and my leg is supposed to be broken. In fact, it might be.

The medical centre is clean and far too bright. My clothes are removed and dropped in a box. The envelope of documents thrown on the pile with them, perfect. That is the separation I needed. I'm covered with a gown and the two medics gently work their fingers up my bones.

"Ouch! That hurts." I say, no acting required.

I see the two guards just outside the door stand to attention. Is the Captain about to enter, or Hunter. Hunter, I can blackmail with my knowledge of Mrs El Ray and his heist of money, but the Captain… that could be awkward unless he is in on it.

It's Hunter.

"How is he?"

"Lucky, don't think anything's broken, but he's bruised, as you would expect."

"OK, give me a minute," Hunter says, and they leave him alone with me. As the door closes he hand clasps my neck. "Bloody idiot. What's going on? Can't I trust you to keep your head down?" He tosses my head to the side, releasing me.

"Good job my neck's not injured!"

"Not yet!" he threatens.

"Am I blowing open your plans for a stowaway and all that money under my bed?"

"I'm moving that straight away, you can't be trusted. Well, you had better be trusted to keep your mouth shut," he says leaning into me.

"So, can I go now?" I ask, and he knows he has to let me.

"Why did you do that?"

"Mental battle scars; I'm still under treatment, anxiety, mood swings, violent outbursts and disruptive behaviour, which in the main is under control. Something, some pressure must have triggered it. Can I speak to someone about what I have been through since I joined the ship? Images of gunmen shooting at me again."

"No, you can't. It's bullshit."

"It's not bullshit!" And though it's not the whole story, what I say next is uncharacteristically honest. "I'm still trying to deal with a lot. I start to get friendly with someone who asks me questions I don't want to answer, can't answer. Have you ever killed someone? Do you like being asked?" I throw at him.

"That shit will never leave your head, never, no amount of treatment, no amount of time. You just have to lie and learn to lie well. No one will understand anything we do, anything we've done." He fires at me.

"Like the bees. Don't mention the bees," I add.

"Stay in here until they have checked every bone in your body and filled out every piece of paperwork they can find." Hunter storms out and I'm relieved I handled that so well.

The medics come back in and begin dragging over a portable X-ray machine. It is like being in a war zone. It appears that I have broken nothing, except protocol for boarding a ship. The door opens, and Georgie comes in.

"What on Earth?"

I beckon her over. When she gets near I whisper, "Take the envelope out of my clothes box, hide it well under your dress and get it out of here."

"You're slurring. You're not well."

"No, I'm drunk, there's a difference."

Georgie goes to my clothes box, takes the large envelope and tucks it into her top just as the door bursts open again. Hunter is back with twice the ferocity. He is far from happy.

"Clear the room, please!" he barks.

The medics and Georgie leave.

"Is that me too?" I say cheekily as the door closes.

"The money's gone, where is it?" he snarls in a panic.

"No idea, I've been out all day and they brought me straight here."

Hunter opens the door and two security officers come in.

"Bring him to my office when he's cleaned up."

Chapter 63 – Where's it gone?

I am sobering up fast by the time I reach the security office. Predictably, Hunter is watching videos of the corridor outside my cabin. This confirms he's not in on the theft.

Every time the cabin steward goes in and out, Hunter watches and re-watches each frame then moves on. So far it is not them. It's hard to tell day or night, other than with the flow of guests and the clock on the bottom corner, the lighting is the same. Jill comes into frame and enters my room. Hunter goes back and freeze-frames.

"Who's she?"

"One of the solo cruiser guests. Jill Cohen. I bought us some drinks and left before I got my cruise card back. She gave me the card back the next day but I had already got a replacement."

That will never be enough and he's going to ask the obvious. I'm not sure I'm up to interrogation about my love life.

"So where are you?" he asks.

Knowing he can look at the cameras I can't lie, he may as well hear it from me.

"I left her in the bar and went to Georgie's room," I admit.

"Georgie's?" he asks, just as surprised as her cabin steward was. "You must have something special. It won't work with her, no matter how much treatment you get."

If only he knew we had bought a house together and almost settled down. It's a good job he can't read minds. Hunter continues to spool on. Jill is in my room for ages before peeking out of the door then ducking inside again.

"I can't see your attraction personally, but you're in one woman's room and another woman is waiting in your room for you to get back."

"But I don't go back," I admit.

"A bit stupid, considering?" Hunter says taking a break from watching and swings round to his computer. "Jill Cohen," he says as he types.

Her picture pops up, the ID picture file that every security guard sees as you check in and out.

"By the way, I'm not checked back in on board yet," I say, producing my security card.

"I not sure whether you'll be thrown overboard unnoticed yet." But he takes my card, scans it, then hits some keys and eventually goes back to the screen of Jill as he hands me back my cruise card. He switches the file to her account, showing the price she paid for the suite. Shit, she's rich. I can see her home address, the date she booked and some other details he has on her preferences.

"She doesn't always travel solo," he muses, then looks at me. "You seriously didn't know the money was gone?"

I shake my head.

"I only went back to change this morning, I was there no time and went ashore. How could she move that much money out of my room? It took me and Ronni and four large cases to get it in. Not that Ronni was much help when we got on board."

Hunter turns back to the video desk and starts rewinding. A man comes walking down the corridor and knocks on my cabin door looking back and forth. Hunter freezes the video. "Who's that?"

"Another one of the solo cruisers group. I think his name was Tony, maybe Tony Kaye," I answer, trying to remember.

Hunter spins round and pulls up his details. Then he flicks back to Jill's details.

"They travelled here together. And I was given notes on them."

"What notes?"

Hunter turns around and operates the video, he writes down the timecode on the security footage of when Tony Kaye goes into my room, then he fast forwards until the two of them come out, dragging three heavy canvas bags between them.

"That is sixteen million, some weight they're struggling with," Hunter says.

"Sixteen? We had twenty," I state.

"They left four," Hunter offers.

"Why?" I ask, seeing our alibi play out. Hunter has checked my room and seen only four million remaining. Little does he know they took twelve and left eight; I took four of it myself.

"They can't carry what they got." Hunter points at them struggling on the screen.

Jill stole my money.

Chapter 64 – Jill?

After watching security footage all evening, we ascertain that two bags were dragged into her suite and one bag into Tony Kaye's balcony room mid-ship.

"Guess they couldn't carry it all," Hunter says. "But they did well to move that. One hundred and sixty kilos."

Hunter brings up a list of times that people log off the ship with their cruise card, a search reveals that Jill was one of the first off. He punches the time in and watches the security footage for that time. Jill strides off looking a million dollars in flat shoes and a beach dress. She descends the gangway with a beach bag that could carry a million dollars, or a towel and sun cream. Then she is out of vision. He runs the pictures back and stops it, then prints a picture that shows the bag clearly.

"You've gotta love a thief that dresses like that," Hunter says.

Swinging back to the screens he finds the time Tony Kaye is logged out through security, again punches in the time code to see him getting off with a small backpack slung over his shoulder, a water bottle in the side pouch. Hunter prints a freeze frame.

"Our blocks were forty inches long, they've broken them down. Maybe a million in there? The bag doesn't look heavy enough for two million. But what could he do with it?" he asks, turning to me.

I shake my head. That bag could well be a million but what it really means is my four million may be home and dry. I've amazingly been given a golden ticket.

"Can you jump to the time they came back on board?"

I don't want him to spool through and see Georgie and me leaving with lifejackets.

Hunter does the same process and we assume their bags are now without the cash.

"You going to pull them in?"

I really want to ask for a couple of painkillers, not that the medicine would know whether to deal with my head, my knee or my hip.

"Not yet. We're five days at sea now before Madeira. No one's going anywhere. Priority is finding the money."

"What's left of it," I add. "But how could they bank it? Banks have money laundering rules."

"You're in South America. It's the banks that launder money, they just take fees," he offers bluntly. "We may have lost some of it, but I intend to get the rest back."

Hunter is silent for a few moments. He has a way of carrying his authority. Aside from the Captain, I shouldn't think there is anyone above him. Maybe the Hotel Manager, maybe those two sit up top and Hunter is one of the next levels down.

"I thought you were trustworthy," he says, blaming me.

"I left my key in a bar, how does anyone know the room it connects to?" I defend.

"She did. What's gone should come out of your pot," he says.

"Why?"

"Why did she go to your room?" he argues.

"Because she wanted to fuck me?" I offer.

"Exactly. See my problem? Why does a woman who is going to a room for sex start to search under the bed?"

I like Hunter, he's clever. I need to be far more on the ball because civilians are tricky too.

"Maybe she wanted to hide under the bed and surprise me?"

Hunter is not impressed with that and thinks I am still drunk. I probably am. Jill has turned out to be a dark horse and I'm now in rewind, flashing back to each of our few moments together. I strain my memory; ordering a double Hendrix each in the wine bar, I was trying to avoid her to get to Georgie, and we were talking about Hunter and the Latina woman. Jill was inquisitive as to why I was worried about who Hunter was with.

"I told Jill I had done you a small favour, that I was looking after something for you."

"Why would you do that?"

"Let me run with this, I said to her I didn't know what it was. She said, rule number one, don't bring anything on board for another person."

"Go on," he encourages.

I'm not going to speed into this, I've always thought Jill was far too smart to be interested in me. I have been sheltered in the army from all these tricksters outside. What was Jill up to?

"I remember thinking that her need for detail and answers was because she roots out problems and decodes errors. She works in IT."

"The fuck she does! Go on," Hunter demands.

OK, Hunter knows something about her, if he didn't before, he has read it on that file.

"I told her I didn't bring anything on board for you, but that I had an officer's cabin. I told her I look out to sea, or could if the lifeboat wasn't there. I said I had stuff in my cabin that was not mine because it was an officer's crew cabin and I had not objected…" Then I can't resist asking, "So, she doesn't work in IT?"

"No, she's a criminal. Red flagged in my system."

"Not important enough for you to stop her coming on the ship?"

"She knew your room, Kieron, why?"

"I was ditching her to meet Georgie. I was just trying to avoid her advances. So what has she stolen from ships? It can't be money, she can't have known there was going to be money. Who would have known that?" I ask.

Hunter is silent, he knows that I am joining dots.

"If…" I start a little more carefully and with more thought. "If your 'Latin lover' stowaway, had all this planned, and sent you to collect the walls of money from that drug safe-house, then she may equally have employed a thief to steal the whole amount from you…."

Hunter is silent, he is no longer watching tapes. He's looking at me and I can see the concern through his poker face.

"File says a jewellery thief and her suspected crimes are executed off the ship. Big diamond shops in the Caribbean, but nothing proven. Opportunism is not her style," he says unconvinced.

"Seems like we've both been duped," slips from my mouth and I may have gone too far.

Hunter flicks his pen in his fingers. He's not as on the front foot as he was.

"Did you mention my room number to Mrs El Rey?" I persist.

He doesn't come back with an immediate reply, but eventually, he draws a box. In it, he writes, 'Deck 5', then below it, 'Cabin E178'. Next to the box, he writes his name, my name, Ronni's name, and Georgie's name.

"You slept with Georgie, she knows, right?"

"No. All she knows about was what she was involved in."

Georgie is not going to appreciate more complications, I can see our relationship being over before we start, and then having to split the house and property, when technically she wasn't even due half. That's an ugly thought, but as true as Georgie suggesting the suitcase money shouldn't be divided into three. I hope I've been fair throughout all of this strange windfall.

"I may need you to keep Jill Cohen busy while I personally search her suite, and I don't care what you have to do with her, you do it. We'll find the moment." He pauses. "I never mentioned your number to my friend," Hunter finishes.

He goes back to his four names written down. He lightly crosses out Georgie then reluctantly writes down Maria Isabel. Now Mrs El Ray has a name. Then he writes down Auli'i, and my blood goes cold.

"She'd know your room."

I can't reply to that because she could know my room, whether I had told her or not. Hunter then writes down Christophe Bachvarov.

Chapter 65 – The scam begins

Life is not easy, and money is not easy. Even lottery winners sometimes have their lives totally ruined. I've read that they're offered therapy from the start, and I've already given my therapist a hard enough time without this. Her treatment and my recovery are, according to her, 'complicated', by my desire to build a court case to get my pension back from the army. Her theory is that therapy can't really begin until the court case is settled. More interestingly would be to test whether her opinion on her ability to be effective might well change with my ability to pay a private fee.

I drop my clothes and gingerly get into the shower. I did slam myself into the ship. Bruisers to my knee and leg are now gaining colour.

My long shower is therapeutic, and it delays the work I need to do. The chaos Hunter made of the room should not be the cabin steward's problem. I eventually get dry and fix the room. I put the bed back, no longer the most expensive bed on the ship. I must remove any thoughts of knowing Jill is the thief, then repair our friendship, and keep her busy. I also need to mend things with Georgie. Five days at sea might not be enough.

I appreciate wearing casual clothes. My body feels too bruised and battered for formal attire, and the attention it brings. I'm not going to have a drink. The way I feel now I may never drink again, however, I do need to eat. I don't want to go into the dining room and share a table with guests who'll eventually start to interrogate me about my job on board, then the usual questions. No, not tonight. I go to the elevator and take a lift to the Lido deck, I'm going to dine alone in the buffet.

I look out at sea and remember I was looking over the edge when I saw Ronni being followed. I wonder how many guests would have been looking over to see my jump, I would guess not many. Georgie conducting the sail away party would've been a greater attraction in the centre of the ship.

I wander into the buffet. The food is excellent and there's a whole tray of grilled tuna steaks. I fill my plate and find a seat by the window. The sky is red, the start of another magical sunset. I can fully understand the attraction of cruising for the ordinary unpressured guest. I eat slowly, dreaming of eating fresh fish and seafood on the balcony of my new house.

I open my phone and without thinking panic that I haven't switched roaming off, because roaming on board is so expensive. Then I remember, I don't have to worry about money anymore so I look at the pictures of the two houses. One features Georgie, so genuinely excited and I realise just how much she means to me. She means more than any amount of money. I need to tell her, I need to tell her how special she is and how much I value our friendship. To suggest more could scare her off forever but we do have something special. Even if it has to be friends with benefits, I can take that, she has actually taught me about intimacy. I'm not sure I want marriage and children, just to be friends would be enough.

My plan for tonight is first to go to Auli'i's show and catch up with her and then find Jill. I'll ask if she had a great day and apologise for not finding her. If I do have to get naked with her she'll see the bruises. Maybe I could say I got hit by a car. No, no, I can't do that.

Georgie catches up with me on my deck seven ramble; the walk that runs between theatre and nightclub and has every amenity in-between. The walk that almost all guests do many times a day. Georgie looks machine-like, in work mode,

"I have a small problem-" she starts, and my face opens up to show I'm listening but I'm fearful that this could go anywhere. "-The next speaker has just cancelled, meaning at the moment there's no replacement joining in Madeira, where you are meant to get off. Could you stay on if a replacement can't be found? It would only work if you can offer some other talks. I can get someone to help you and you can use the office internet. Obviously, I'll encourage them to find a replacement if they can."

There is something about her phrasing that hurts, something about her manner that cuts into me, it's too polite, like she could be talking to anyone.

"If I stay on, I promise to be good, on and off stage," I say. She smiles and is about to power away, but I call after her, "And I'd love to spend more time with you, you are a very special person."

Her smile remains fixed and I watch her as she gracefully walks away, in a simple dress she makes look like a masterpiece. I have a lot of work to do.

I'm early at the theatre but don't have the popular desire to sit at the end of the row in case the ship sinks, so I find a spot in the middle, ready to watch Auli'i again.

The show is fantastic, but Auli'i is not there. Now I wish I was at the end of the row. Now I want to be first out.

Chapter 66 – Where's she gone?

I don't have crew privileges and am not allowed in crew areas. The Captain was clear about that when he saw me below decks, but nothing will stop me going through the side door to the stage. The stagehands recognise me and make no comment, but the cast has cleared. No doubt they are getting changed to go and relax, but I am far from relaxed. I can't walk into the women's changing room, so I go backstage left, knock and enter the men's changing room.

"Hi, sorry, excuse me, I'm Auli'i's dad, is she alright? She wasn't onstage."

One of the young performers turns. "Yeah she was, you didn't recognise her," he says with a smile, "I can't tell you more, I would be thrown out of the Magic Circle."

They all laugh and my panic starts to dissipate. I want to know more, but I don't need to know here and now.

"Great show. Even better now I don't know what I missed."

I turn and leave, heading for the quickest route out but I'm caught. Georgie is walking backstage.

"What are you doing here?" she almost snaps.

"I can't tell you, I'd be thrown out of the Magic Circle," I say, and march past her.

I can feel her eyes bore deep into my back, but I refuse to slow down or turn back. That's probably wrong but I think she needs a cooling off period.

I stand at the top of the theatre stalls checking my phone. I've paid for the WiFi package so I should use it even if I'm not one of those who apparently check their phone one hundred and fifty times a day. I have a text from Sylvie, with a link which annoyingly will not open. The name infers it's a link to the island's local news website. There's obviously a story but I can't get it, the internet is slow. I walk out of the theatre, refresh the page and wait whilst looking at the board of all the stage cast. Roger is the name of the singer who relieved my panic about Auli'i and gave me the joke I used on Georgie.

Auli'i bursts out from the stage door,

"Hi, Dad," she says and kisses me. "Where were you today? Did you transfer any more money?"

"No, sadly I wasn't able to do that today, for many complicated reasons. Did the money I sent arrive?"

"No, but it was only two days ago."

Just two days ago? What a roller-coaster I've been on, it feels like a month has passed.

"So we've got five days at sea, what do you usually get up to?"

"We rehearse, do drills and enjoy the ship. It's just like living in an apartment block. Well, no. More like student digs."

"At least I have my own room."

"Or have you been up in the suite?" she delves.

"No!"

She grabs my arm and walks me away. "Let's go to the club, there's a late night comedy show. 'Loopy'. They're always good unless someone takes their children in, then they ruin the night."

"Is the late night show an adult show?"

"Yes."

"Then why would anyone take their children in?" Seems a sensible question to me, but obviously, a lot of parents don't agree.

"You think you have heard every excuse then another one comes up. Those parents don't understand the damage they do."

"Damage?"

"Yes, because then the comedian can't do their act, and then they get complaints that they didn't do a late night show," she explains.

"Then why don't they just do the show?"

"Because then the audience will be offended that they did such a risky act with children present, and they complain very strongly about that."

"Why doesn't the company police the club entrance?"

"They try, like enforcing the dress code, there is always someone."

We make the back of the ship in what seems like no time. It's easier to walk at this time of night when there are fewer people moving about. Georgie sees us enter and catches us. Auli'i says hi, not knowing anything of our relationship.

"It's busy tonight. Can you not take seats the guests may need, please?" Georgie instructs and walks off.

"What's got her goat tonight?" Auli'i says, turns and sees my concerned expression.

"No…" She grimaces, "no, not you and my boss?"

Chapter 67 – Late night Loopy

There were no children in and it was a terrific show, the likes I'm not sure I've ever seen. An adult show, so controlled that even the cruise ship audience could not be offended. Though I can understand why it would not have been performed if there'd been children in. We're standing by a table against the back wall of the club and I was so enjoying the show, I didn't notice other members of stage cast join us.

"You found her! Keep an eye on her, she disappears that one," Roger, the guy from the dressing room says.

"Yes, thank you. Your Magic Circle membership is safe," I reply to him.

"But yours isn't," I hear Georgie say from behind me.

I turn to her and she has half a smile. Maybe I am being let back in.

"Look, I am really sorry about today," I start. "We were both under incredible pressure," I say softly, seeing that Auli'i is looking at me in amazement, which is rather off-putting,

"I hope we can talk tomorrow. Excuse me a moment while I reprimand my little elf-like daughter."

I step beyond Georgie, the Elastoplast has been applied and lingering longer could be awkward.

"Dad. That's Georgie!" she whispers to me, "You can't. She has a partner."

"Partner?" I question.

"Yes. Who works in the spa. You are way off base."

I'm speechless. There's so much I want to say but can't. I'm hurt by the fact that Georgie has a partner.

"On board now?"

"Maybe not now, she might be on leave, but she's around. She'll be back soon even if she's away."

I can't help but turn and look at Georgie, who is talking with other staff. The comedian who was on stage is approaching and about to join her. Rollercoaster? It is perpetual motion. I turn back to Ee, I wasn't going to drink tonight, but I flash my cruise card to a waiter.

"Her name is Bedriška, she's Russian, frighteningly tough. Rumour is she's KGB. I can see the parallel with you." Auli'i smiles.

"I'm not frightening!" I defend.

"Dad, you were trained to be frightening. I like that you're tough… What about Jill?"

Ignoring her question, I order a beer and Ee orders a drink, but I'm in a daze. Maybe I can understand a little more of what was going through Georgie's head today. We've just bought a house together. She must be cut up about what to tell Bedriška, who, if she's away, cannot re-board before we dock in Madeira. I've got five days. Five days to do what? Break up a relationship, or sort mine out? Or, just be the foil for a cabin raid on Jill.

Georgie turns then beckons me and Auli'i to join her and the comedian. With my arm around my daughter, we step in. I wonder if he's heard the joke about 'the compliance officer, the security officer, and the retired officer'. I'm so glad I'm not still drunk.

"This is Batman," Georgie says, and I'm confused. The comedian shakes my hand.

"Great gag, great gag. Wish I'd seen it. Name's Paul," he starts but has no intention to leave a gap for me to speak. "Apparently there are a few good films of it trending on people's phones. I nearly put it in my act but the management doesn't like that. But you're a hero now. You could be a YouTube star!"

I must be being talked about... 'Batman', I'm not sure about that.

"It was a military thing," I mumble wondering if I'm going to make things worse, but it appears I'm the talk of the ship so that might be impossible.

"Military, eh? This is a civilian ship! Are we being commandeered?" he asks.

His rhythm and punctuation hit features all the words that need a drum snare. He also smiles to the point of laughing and it is contagious. Funny guy, but it is all a cover, he has a secret that is far from funny and if I had longer and I cared I would try and discover what it is. He is taking a breath, my turn.

"Actually cruise ships are commandeered in war and crisis, and they have to be ready," I answer, knowing that has happened in many wars from World War Two to the Falklands. "Training can become very staid, very routine and without any real sense of panic. I specialized in military training. The crew were put to a real test, to see if they coped or would need counselling afterwards." Maybe I've gone too far, maybe I'm digging a hole. Georgie is keeping very silent. She has good ground to think it untrue. Paul leans into me.

"So what's next? We're not going to hit an inflatable iceberg on our way across the Atlantic are we?"

The group laugh. He's permanently on show, no off switch to his act almost a Laughter-Tourette syndrome which I feel is covering something up.

"The thing is Paul. You don't mind me calling you Paul, do you?

"No, it's my name."

"Good. If you knew what was coming next, then it defeats the nature of the training," I say.

"So, I can't know what's coming next?" he asks.

"None of us can. I certainly have no idea what is going to happen next."

He looks at me as if I am just spinning a yarn, and I think of how there is a major drug baron's wife on board and twenty million dollars of her money, that someone else has stolen and behind that are all my other problems and he then sees something that stops him laughing. He can read people after all.

Chapter 68 – What is next?

It appears the Captain may have had words with Hunter on his new training methods. That's just one of the stories in circulation that I heard from the young fitness trainer in the gym. Still, in my workout clothes, I sit eating my breakfast and reading the daily one-sheet of news delivered with the ship's daily itinerary. Thankfully, I haven't made the front page, the only mention of me is that I'm due to lecture at eleven o'clock. Maybe I can relax in the unknown for a while, life may be back to normal. I sit at the window, half-gazing at the mesmerising ocean, half reading the news back home which seems so distant and irrelevant.

The public address pings. It must be nine o'clock because it is the officer of the watch with his normal morning update. The weather will be good which means most people will be out on deck absorbing rays and not watching me in the theatre. A waiter passes with two silver jugs, tea or coffee. I accept coffee, I have time for a second cup before I need to go and rehearse and change into uniform.

The public address pings again, it's the voice of the angel who has me more confused than all the money I'm trying to juggle. She can make a whole ship smile. She's powerful, yet I've glimpsed moments of her vulnerability. She's private and yet totally public. She's professional yet sexy, and she has just paused for effect to say that there is a change of schedule at eleven o'clock. That's my time, that's when I should be giving my talk.

"Not to be missed, in the theatre at eleven o'clock, I have the honour of presenting a special show," she begins, "I will be interviewing a number of very special guests."

I have been taken off the programme. The Captain must have intervened.

"We are lucky to have on board the very unassuming, but high ranking military special operations commander Kieron Philips."

No. Where is this going?

"As much as he can speak, within whatever official secrets act he is bound by, we will have a chance to talk with the man who you all know tested our security yesterday with a leap from the land onto the ship, our unwanted stowaway."

OK. I think I get what she's doing. There is no such thing as bad publicity, everything can be spun.

"And there will be more, much more because he will not be the only military hero on stage, there will be other surprise guests. Join me in the theatre for a once in a lifetime show. Then at twelve on the top deck, there will be open Deck Quoits…"

My mind switches off from her voice. I'm to be interviewed on stage by Georgie with a special guest. I wonder who that is. I figure it will be the Captain, but know, if it were to be the Captain he would have to be announced. He would be far more important than me. He can't possibly be the special guest because he would have to be the star and she has just given me a hard to beat headline. I finish my coffee and move outside into the sun.

There are already towels on sunbeds, which is so not allowed. No one is allowed to reserve a sunbed on the ship, in fact, you're entitled to ask for the towel to be removed, but people try. It's going to be a perfect day for sunbathing, a chance to relax and absorb some vitamin D, not watch me being interviewed. Though with that announcement I might just get an audience.

I climb the stairs to the mezzanine deck above, that circles the pool like a balcony. I walk circuits, taking in the view. There's something quite special about the ocean. Maybe I should have joined the Navy, but then they don't get too many flat sea trips around the Caribbean. I can half relax knowing I won't be doing my talk, today might even be fun. But who is the other guest? My heart sinks. Maybe I'm to meet her girlfriend across the stage, that would be a chat show to remember. Two special operatives, one military, the other a female KGB agent who now works in the spa. That would be a confusing advert for the spa. Could this late change to the show mean that Georgie is dragging out my performances so I can stay on board past Madeira? My mind has gone from empty theatre to full theatre, from Captain to KGB, from my guilt-ridden drunken return to the ship to hero.

I remind myself I'm working today and shake off my pointless daydreaming. It is already time to get ready for work, time evaporates faster and faster the older I get.

When I get back to my cabin, my bed has once again been upturned but I can relax for I have no money left to guard. The message light is flashing on my telephone. It will no doubt be Georgie telling me of the programme change. I check it, it's not, it's Ricardo. Technically I answer to him on a day to day working basis, he is the production manager. The message is to wear my parade uniform, nothing else is required.

Chapter 69 – On parade

Stagehands are busy setting up, this is obviously a last minute change at the start of their shift. I previously had a lectern to one side of the stage and a big screen in the front. Neither is there, these guys are working to a different plan. There are five seats in a semi-circle and handheld radio mics on each chair. It is more like a TV chat show set up. The mini orchestra has been set up on the rear of the stage, but they can't be on with us, or at least I don't think so. They work to their full working hours as it is, to pull them in before their rehearsals at 4pm would cause problems. It must be there ready for later, it does make a good backdrop and the lighting will no doubt leave it in the semi-dark. Maybe they will flood it with colour for dramatic effect.

There is already an audience, so I dare not walk to the front as I'll become the pre-show. The last thing I want is questions when I have no idea what's going on. Who are the five chairs? Me, Georgie and three others. I still don't think it will be the Captain, but maybe Hunter. Hunter is becoming a permanent fixture in my life and I guess if this whole thing is about my leap and security, then it makes sense he will be here. I guess I will be briefed and there will be a company line, a script to stick to.

Rarely do you get to witness things running like clockwork as much as on a ship. The theatre has been filling, but it must be about five to eleven as guests are now flooding in. Either that or someone has called a lifeboat drill because this is a major muster station. I smile duly at each passing guest, standing at ease by the sound and lighting box door at the back, waiting for some form of direction. Georgie marches up next to me, faces front, smiling and repeating 'good morning' continuously, as a robot would but oozing far more charm. I wonder if the cruise company know just how fantastic she is, and how lucky they are to have her, or, whether they have a cupboard full of Georgie's that they roll out as required. Somehow I don't think so, I've seen her assistant manager and the other hosts, and like all commanders, she has that x-factor you cannot explain. She is a superstar.

"Behave," she warns me then marches off towards the stage leaving me at the back. At the front, she does the same, somehow connecting with each and every one of the vast audience. I have not seen the theatre this full before, even for an evening show.

The lights in the auditorium dim, but there's no orchestra, no drum roll. Just Georgie. She walks up onto the stage and smiles, and welcomes everyone,

"You all know by now, that we have an action man on board." There is some laughter, and she pauses with a smile that holds them all where she wants them. "Ladies and Gentleman, please welcome, Commander Kieron Philips."

I automatically start down to the stage. It is certainly not a short walk because the theatre holds over a thousand people and it appears to be full. Everyone is applauding. I take the steps to the stage and as I walk to the semi-circle of chairs I mock a limp, exaggerating yesterday's injury. It gets a laugh. Georgie hands me a microphone and invites me to sit.

"Sorry, I'm not a footballer, I won't milk it."

That gets me a second laugh.

"While I've got you on your own," Georgie starts with a tease, and all I can think of are the things she has been doing to mesmerise me when we have been alone, "Are you bound by some official secrets act?"

"Yes," I draw out the word, "but nothing covered by that would be in the slightest bit entertaining, so I don't imagine too much of a problem. However, if a team of men in black drop down onto the stage by ropes and drag me away… you know I've gone too far."

"Or the dancers have got up early," Georgie adds, which gets a laugh.

"Why would the dancers want to drag me away?"

We've made a good start and I have no idea where this might go or whether she's just filling time. I guess I try and entertain until she focusses me elsewhere.

"So, no juicy secret stories?"

"Well…" I tease, "I know a great story from World War two, and thank you but no, I was not there! It's one I obviously can't be tied to by any secrecy, as it's pure hearsay. Judge for yourselves…" I turn to the audience and try to connect with them, "Have you heard the one about board games in the ration packs sent to prisoners of war by the aid organisations?"

The audience shakes their heads and thankfully seem interested, so I tell them the story of how escape route maps-made of silk so they didn't rustle in the silence of night- and other useful items like compasses were hidden in the trinkets of the Waddington's game 'Monopoly'. And how real money, in foreign currencies, was hidden within the game's money.

"It is up to you whether you think it holds any reality or it's just a wonderful marketing campaign, but I love the story."

I look back to Georgie.

"Fascinating, as was your first lecture and your commentary through the Panama Canal, which seems ages ago now. So much has happened."

Did I imagine it, or was that look held just a little too long to be an empty remark? I could stay on this ship forever if this was my lot.

"This is my first cruise, and I really can say I never imagined how action packed it would be."

That is the truth, but they will never know why. I scan the audience again, more relaxed I can make out faces, people I have seen around the ship, and there in the middle is the familiar group of solo cruisers, Jill and Tony Kaye are amongst them.

"We have some other military heroes on board, let me first call our head of security, Commander Hunter Witowski."

There is applause for Hunter, he enters from side stage and gives a little sensei type bow to the audience. I can see he has seen Jill sitting with Tony in the middle of the stalls. He turns and kisses Georgie on the cheek. We shake hands and hug. It feels like the opening to the Graham Norton Show, except we have not all been chatting away beforehand in the green room.

"Sorry, I can only stay ten minutes, I have a team to address," Hunter apologises.

I like him, I like his directness and control. I think we could be mates if it was not for the very strange position he has taken to be involved in the safe transfer of Panama's drug Lord's wife.

"Oh, that's a shame, I won't get to find out all the dirt." Georgie laughs.

No, I think, you won't, but I know he is charged with getting her money back. He turns to me and I know what he's up to. Having seen Jill and Tony here, he has two cabins to search. I am not sure why I should help him because I don't feel we will ever see any of the money. Other than the small matter of about three million dollars which they may not be able to trace.

Chapter 70 – Let's play

"Tell me; when you boys get together, is there an element of 'let's play'," Georgie teases, getting straight to the point.

"No," Hunter says firmly. "I don't 'play', not when lives are at stake."

"No, he's absolutely right." I feel I'm a guest watching what is going on and repeating.

Hunter looks at the audience. His big frame and commanding spirit must be a huge hit doing the Panama Canal commentary, he didn't need me on board for that.

"I hope you all take the lifeboat drill very seriously because if you ever have to do it again, which of course we hope you don't, but if you do, it might be in a panic. My crew mustn't panic. But it's hard to be sure whether they will panic or not because nothing is real in a drill. Kieron and I both trained as servicemen in real situations, so as I had Mr Action Man with me on the ship, we decided to put some of the crew to the test."

"Wow," Georgie enthuses. "What an opportunity."

"Yes, and they all passed, so you should all feel very safe," he enthuses.

I nod and smile reassuringly, watch and repeat.

"What if you hadn't made the jump, fallen in the water?" Georgie asks me, and I guess I have to join in now.

"They would have had to rescue me, that might have been another test, as I could have pretended I was drowning. However, that was not what I was asked to do."

I turn to Hunter with that last line, it is back to him.

"Certainly not," Hunter adds and stops looking at me, neither of us wants to go further with this which makes it an amusing game.

"So, if it is not a rude question, how old are you? I mean, that leap is not the act of a retired military man," Georgie probes.

That makes me happy. That is a personal question and she is checking me out. I would love to ask her the same question, but the difference between us cannot be much.

"That is covered by the official secrets act," I offer.

Georgie smiles at me as the audience laugh and she notices a man with his hand up. "Yes, Sir. Sorry, we don't have a roving microphone."

"If they all passed, doesn't it show the drill was completely unnecessary and there was no need to frighten guests?" he bellows.

There is always one, or two, who have no idea or could have done it all better.

"It was definitely necessary because while some reacted fast and calmly, I observed others who watched the more experienced crew take control and react. They are all better placed now for having been there and seen it," I say confidently.

Hunter nods his head firmly, this is a cooling mission we are on and it must have come from above. I can see he has more to say so he must have been directed with some form of script.

"We chose the side of the ship because everyone would be on board and few passengers would be able to see it as most of them would be at the sail away party. It was a perfect plan. I do apologise if anyone was frightened, but from all the posted films I've seen, it seems like most people found it funny because they seemed to think it was a drunken passenger," Hunter concludes.

Georgie turns to me again and I wonder if she has a list of questions.

"Didn't Tom Cruise get hurt doing a similar jump to that?" she asks.

"He wasn't available for this job," I say.

The audience laugh and it could be a case of job done, but we there are still two empty chairs onstage and we are barely ten minutes into the forty-five-minute show.

"Will you be telling us about any of the special training in the remaining lectures you have with us?" she asks.

"I will touch on what I can," I say.

A few hands have gone up with questions and I can see Hunter is itching to leave. He has less than half an hour to search two rooms, presumably alone, because I've just spotted Ronni waiting in the wings, about to fill a chair. I guess Maria Isabel El Ray, or whatever her current name is, could help Hunter. He is putting his microphone on the floor to leave as Georgie points at a lady in the middle who stands up,

"Have you ever killed anyone?" she shouts, and the room goes silent.

Hunter glances at me, he knows I'm not best placed to handle this question right now. He sits back down and grabs his microphone again. "Well, this is not a normal cruise ship conversation! But... as you've asked, let me say this; corporal punishment is not allowed in the United Kingdom. People feel it's too extreme. But as a voter who elects the government, who appoint police and judges, you are part of the machine responsible for any punishment or war and the consequences. Has war ever killed anyone? Yes, throughout the whole of history, and yet the voting public is rarely asked if they have killed anyone. But as a voter and taxpayer, you are no less on the front line, no less responsible, and it's why no soldier should ever be asked."

I stand up and shake his hand. He is a friend, I know that whole performance was for me, to stop me having to answer that question. I know he has to leave, so I thank him in an off-microphone hug. "That might be better than any therapy the army ever gave me. Thank you."

Hunter hugs me and whispers, "I need more time."

He leaves to applause. I sit down and Georgie points to another guest for a question.

"Why were you thrown out the army?"

Hunter doesn't turn back. I am on my own.

Chapter 71 - Discharge

The idea of this session must have been to make things easier, the Captain can't have expected this. The guests aren't pulling any punches, I can't see Ronni backstage anymore either, maybe she's made a break for it.

"Four seats on stage, I have two more guests," Georgie says calmly, "Commander, can I bring on someone who can help you answer that?"

Shit. I can't answer that easily, who does she have? No, I know what she is going to do and this is where the trouble starts. It is how I got into trouble, how I went off mission, off-plot, off-grid. My mission here is to keep this going longer than the allocated time, but the collateral damage it could cause personally is unacceptable.

"Georgie, I'm not sure that's fair," I say, hesitantly, but you can feel the tension, the audience is gripped.

"Ladies and gentlemen I want you to put your hands together for a truly incredible young lady, who is a valued member of our stage cast, Auli'i." Georgie stands and applauds and the audience joins her. I am in shock.

I stand and applaud, watching my daughter bravely enter from the rear of the theatre, slowly, with complete confidence. She waves as she walks up onto the stage. I'm angry, this is a complete invasion of her privacy. I hug her. "Are you sure about this? I am prepared to tell this without you having to-."

Auli'i hugs me and silences me. I can feel the confusion; do they think she is my child bride? I turn to the audience. "This is my adopted daughter, Auli'i and I am so proud to watch her on stage here on the ship. I am full of guilt that she needs to relive any of her pain to answer questions put to me."

Auli'i collects her microphone, she is a performer and far stronger than me, she takes this all in stride. "I am honoured to call this man father. He stepped in after my own parents were slaughtered, even though it cost him his commission, his pension and everything he had worked for all his army life."

Auli'i finishes and we could close the curtains now, leave the audience wanting more, but she calmly turns to Georgie who is still standing, they hug and take their seats.

"Before we start, your name is spelt A U L I, an apostrophe, and then another I, is that right?"

"Owl as in the bird, Lee, then another e. Owl-lee-e. It's Hawaiian."

"But you are not Hawaiian?"

"No, my features give that away! I'm Syrian. It was not my birth name," Auli'i explains.

I need to stay on mission, to lengthen this show without exploiting Auli'i to do it.

"This is like Surprise-Surprise, who is the fourth chair for? My old boss? My long lost grandma?"

"I didn't think of her!" Georgie laughs.

"I can see Ronni waiting in the wings, should we bring her on?" I ask.

"Good idea," Georgie says, standing again.

"Please welcome my final guest, a female senior officer and marine scientist, Ronni Cohen!"

Ronni walks on to applause, but I can't help feeling she has rather become the undercard and the audience are gripped to know more of the main story. Ronni sits and takes her microphone.

"I would be proud to have been dismissed for what you did, Kieron. I've got a lot of respect for you," Ronni says and starts another round of applause.

I nod my thanks, I'd really rather not go into more of Auli'i's story but I check my watch, Hunter has only been gone ten minutes, he is unlikely to have even got to Jill's room and I can see her getting restless in the audience. Maybe I'm just panicking, but I can't let her go.

"Georgie?" I start then she turns to me expectantly. "I've met someone on this cruise, who has been exceptionally generous to me and more importantly to Auli'i through what have been a few very difficult days with the new attacks on her friends and family in Syria. As Hunter has vacated his chair, and we have a spare seat, would the guests like to have a fellow passenger onstage who can ask questions on their behalf, because she's gained more of an insight into our story?"

Georgie turns to me; she can't say no. I turn to Jill; I have trapped her. I am not sure either is happy but Jill is not the kind of woman who waits to be invited. She stands and becomes the centre of attention. There is a magnetism to stardom that is many a person's downfall. It could be the start of Jill's.

Chapter 72 – The story

Ronni's story is fascinating, and Auli'i was truly excited by the good work she did as a female enlisted marine biologist, and now does as compliance officer on the ship in an industry facing new regulations. I watched her listen to every word about the company's special programme to train and promote women into positions traditionally held by men. Ronni wishes to excuse herself as she has more work to do than there are hours in the day, and the spotlight is back on us.

A glance at my watch shows that the forty-five-minute slot is nearly finished and Hunter has had thirty-five minutes. My guess Hunter has started to search Jill's suite. He knows the room well, so he should easily find the money which the security videos tell us went in but did not come out. He may have commandeered a cleaning trolley and filled it with the money that they struggled to carry. Then he'll be on his way to Tony's if he's not already there. I look slowly at the three women sat onstage then scan the audience who are gripped. Jill has started asking questions which Ee is answering diligently, unfazed.

"We seem to need a little more time Georgie, is that possible?" I ask.

"Look, everyone, it is twelve o'clock, I know we have gone way over, but shall we say another fifteen minutes and I will close?" Georgie suggests and the audience audibly agrees.

Given not that many will come to the front with questions, Jill will be held here. Tony, on the other hand, may be able to leave, I need to trap him in. I sense a gap in the conversation. "Can I say a big thank you to a little group of people, the Solo Cruisers. As a group, they are there for each other and they have extended that courtesy to me and Auli'i. Jill is one, and who else is here?" I pretend to scan the audience. "Tony! Tony, please stand up. Malcolm, Sue, Mave… all of you solo cruisers give so much support to each other and those cruising alone and for the first time. Thank you."

Hopefully, that'll get people talking to him after we finish, delaying his exit. I am not sure Georgie liked me inviting Jill onstage, and it looks like she is falsely clapping the group. She is working to a directive, but so am I. She turns to me,

"So tell us, Kieron, were you actually court-martialled?" she asks me and I know it is a reprimand.

There is silence and I can see Georgie looking at me, wanting to know the answer, privately and for the audience.

"Would I have preferred my career to have gone behind a military desk, into my fifties, and beyond rather than into cruising around the world. Yes, probably."

I can see that has not in any way answered or avoided the question.

"But I had not cruised then, I had not seen this side of life. I had not met all of you. And I am now blessed."

No, they are still waiting, they want the dirt.

"We were sent to Syria as part of a United Nations effort to keep the peace in a nation that was torn apart. It was a job I was sent to do in Ireland, back in the early eighties when I first joined up. Syria was different, never have I seen confusion and so much pointless death. Cities lay so destroyed it's unimaginable, snipers shooting at running children for target practice. Auli'i was not exaggerating. I had to go off-grid. I went rogue. I was outside my remit and was helping displaced homeless, parentless children who managed to stay alive. I wasn't the only one, but I went beyond my remit without permission. I started to help children cross into Turkey. Then, I brought Auli'i to England. I was still serving; my ageing mother became a mum again. I broke so many rules that there was a pile of books to throw at me. The barristers acting against me didn't want me setting an example in any way. I found myself facing time inside if found guilty when I had just left my mother with a child she was not expecting. I took a plea deal to walk away. I lost my career and my pension and I'd do it all again."

I hug Auli'i. Then there are some questions we jointly answer and a lady in the audience suggests I should write a book.

"That's funny, my daughter has suggested the same thing. To be honest, I've found it hard dealing with all I saw. I was lucky enough to have some basic therapy, but today, all of you, allowing us to tell our story has been the best medicine ever. Thank you."

Georgie has to call an end to the session just twenty minutes over and recommends that everyone come to my next lecture tomorrow. I am left wondering how to follow that but

I have a mission to continue the delay. I have to give Hunter more time.

Jill is mobbed by the crowd, she is going nowhere. So is Auli'i, who everyone seems to have fallen in love with. I can see Georgie is the only one avoiding the crowd and making a fast getaway.

"Georgie?"

"I'm busy."

"What's wrong?"

She turns sharply and there is a curt conversation between us where she lets off steam.

"Hunter was meant to stay."

"He's busy."

It is awkward for me to say more.

"I'll give him busy! He takes over my department, books you for his use. He takes you on missions without my say so. I bet you're working for him now. He needs to respect me!"

"Hunter." She blasts into the phone turning away and there is no way I can stop her without causing a scene and I can see Tony and the others with a clear escape route. I am torn.

"Hunter!" I can hear her start as she reaches the side of the stage.

I head for Tony and the others and catch them.

"I just wanted to thank all of you, you don't know what a support you've been."

I make sure to make a public fuss of Tony and put halt to any progress he may have wanted to make beyond the theatre. He's stuck with me and all the attention. This is going to be a long goodbye.

I glance behind them to see an angry Georgie come off the phone and march up the side of the theatre. I guess he has hung up on her which means he is busy or pissed. He is above her grade. I hope it means he has found the money and is in transit. If he is still looking we're in trouble. The clock is spinning now, not just turning.

Chapter 73 – Lunch everybody?

Georgie heads straight for me. I can't let her say anything that would draw attention to Hunter that would highlight him being the man missing at this time. Georgie has a serious edge. I have to turn it all into part of a general conversation.

"Captain's idea?" I ask.

"He thought it was the best way to diffuse the situation. I would say it's made history, it'll be blogged and chatted about. You should write that book. I've got things to do. I'll find you later, we, we need to speak."

The smile is unreal, but many of hers are and she has a way of getting away with that. Georgie makes her escape, leaving Auli'i, Jill, the solo cruisers and me with a small crowd. No one has picked up on the edge and Jill always likes Georgie to leave. It takes some time for the crowd to disperse and I see the comedian Paul watching us from the back of the stalls. He has noticed, he is watching, he watches everything. Observation is the heart of comedy.

"Lunch everybody? I'm starving after that," I suggest.

The last few of the audience leave us and we walk out, Paul is there to stop us,

"Very impressive, but I can't see the comedy in it."

"Because there isn't any?" I offer.

"There is comedy in everything, I just haven't seen it yet."

The solo cruisers all recognise him, and I am forgetting the barrier between star and guest because they have very keenly joined us.

"Join us for lunch, dear, we'll help you find whatever you've lost." Offers one of the more camp members of the solo group.

"I will. I normally only eat in my cabin."

"We need you to come out of that."

Paul is whipped up and I am no longer the centre of attention as we walk towards the elevators.

"Why don't we go to the restaurant? Eat peacefully. I think you've earned it," Jill suggests feeling she can command this period in time and it is perfect for me allow that. I keep her busy without sex.

"Me? You did it all." I turn to Tony. "Wasn't she marvellous? She saved my bacon."

"I guess I did. I think a few people have worked hard at that," she adds but I am not taking the bait, she doesn't need to know one more thing about me and I'm focussed on my mission.

"Let's take the stairs," Tony suggests, and they all move off. I pause on the top step.

"Shall I get Ronni and Hunter paged and tell them where we are?"

It's not as if anyone can refuse, so I turn back to the house-phone by the elevator and dial reception, watching them slowly turn out of sight.

"Hi. Can you page Officer Ronni Cohen and Officer Hunter Witowski and say the theatre party are dining in the aft restaurant. It's Kieron Philips from the entertainment department. Thank you. Oh, and it is urgent, very urgent.."

Lunch in the restaurant is very civilised. The buffet is great, it has fantastic food, excellent views, but this is a decadent treat.

"I never get to do this," Auli'i gushes. "Technically I'm not allowed in here, but I guess like my father I like to break the rules sometimes."

That gets her a laugh. I squeeze her hand. "Are you OK?" I ask because she has revealed a lot in the past hour.

"I'm amazing. Not only was it good to share, but they really seemed to care. I lost a family, I can't get them back, but telling the story can bring more awareness to the cause and can help those people still in Syria."

"It's turning a negative into a positive."

"You sound like my therapist now, Dad."

"We must have the same one!"

"I think all therapists are the same," Jill says.

"Dad. Let's write that book together," she suggests, leans in and kisses me on the cheek.

"What a brilliant idea," Jill agrees.

"No. That is your book. I will help, but it is yours and it can only do good."

"You can write a foreword for us, Jill, you'd be great at that," Auli'i adds.

Jill enjoys the attention and seems relaxed but then she still thinks she is a good few million better off. What happens after lunch may be a different story.

I watch Paul observing every exchange and moment as they are revealed, but I can relax about his intervention because I know, one word to Georgie will control his act. This is not comedy. He has no idea what he is playing with.

Lunch drags on as it apparently can on at sea, and then we retreat to the Crow's Nest where it continues with after dinner and early evening cocktails. Paul has now left, that is one less worry. I have certainly succeeded in keeping Jill and Tony occupied. Auli'i eventually stands to leave and I remember she has a show.

"Hey, Ee. I never saw you on stage last night, but I was told you were there. What did I miss?" I ask.

"You saw exactly what you were meant to see," she says and she's off.

"What was that about?" Jill asks.

"The big dancing magic show. I never saw her, but she did something and I would like to know what it was."

"Oh the magic show, we missed it." Jill sighs.

"It was all illusions and disappearing, and I obviously missed something, or maybe I didn't."

"There are probably lots of things you're never meant to see," Jill adds dangerously and smiles.

There is no excusing she is a thief but I told her I was looking after things in my room that were not mine. She appears to feel comfortable that she has not stolen anything from me or Auli'i. Not that I have a clue what's going on. I am not going to take her cunning for granted.

Jill orders another round of drinks.

I have avoided alcohol today and I decide to excuse myself, "I need to get out of this uniform."

Jill stands and pecks my cheek. "I've been trying to get you out of that uniform all cruise."

"I think I should go and change," Jill announces and I feel in danger.

"You know, I'm pretty shy," I whisper and leave first. I feel her after me so I have to be fast and hopeful.

I walk through the long wide art-filled corridor leading from the Crow's Nest, past a card room and a wedding chapel, which I will be avoiding.

Hunter is waiting for me at the end, I won't be able to avoid him. If she is behind me, it will be quite a meeting of minds. I feel her breathing behind me, catching me up.

Chapter 74 – The stash

"You know; some things you can never put back in the box. No matter how you try," Hunter starts, aiming it at me not her. "You had the easy public version, now the company dressing down.

"I was hoping to do the dressing down," Jill says unashamedly.

"Later," he offers to her. He then firmly fixes on me,

"let's go and have tea."

This is not a request, it's an order. He leads me to the lift.

"Saved your sorry butt again have I?"

I don't need to reply. I might have only recently left the restaurant but it appears sea days can be all about eating.

The Maître d' sits us at a table by the window away from anyone else. Tea is welcome, the sandwiches and cakes we both turn away.

"So, what's not going back in the box?"

Whilst desperate to know about the money, I follow his lead. I'm keen to have my questions answered but the order is not important. He may have found nothing, he may never tell me the truth but I listen.

"I've been asked to talk to you officially by the company, I don't think it will be the last conversation but the Captain did a great job of wording everything back to head office."

"I guess he knows everything that goes on within his ship."

"No. Not all, and it needs to stay that way," Hunter insists. "Like all cruise lines, we work for an American corporation. They understand war, military heroes, and making money. So you're lucky."

"Lucky? I wouldn't have described my trip this far as lucky."

"You're alive, no bees stings, female stings, and you may have earned a lot of money. May have," Hunter repeats.

"Have I? Or does Maria Isabel want it all back?" I ask very pointedly.

Hunter eyeballs me hard.

"Do you trust anyone in this world?"

"My daughter. No one else. Not really. People can be bought."

"You don't trust me?" Hunter asks.

"No."

"We're doing the same job. You smuggled an orphan out of Syria, I couldn't believe the symmetry when I got the file on you."

"You're comparing Maria with Auli'i?"

Hunter gives the smallest of nods then explains in a low voice. "Two women, trapped, living in fear, one shot at, the other abused almost daily, both surrounded by killings."

"Have you told Maria the money's gone missing?"

"I will now."

"Because you have it?"

"Best no one knows it's been found. It will flush out whether she knew it was gone and who works for who. You don't need to know anything, you are just being used, right?"

Hunter is a great life-chess partner, but he knows a lot more about me than I do about him, though I don't need to read his jacket. I've worked with people like him for many years and can go with decisions. I change the subject, it is an interrogation technique, I still want answers he might give.

"That's not what the company asked you to tell me."

"Correct."

I pour another cup of tea, whatever the company has said could be irrelevant here, to either of us. I could take Georgie from this ship and Auli'i and set Christophe up with his own boat charter business in the Caribbean. Between us, we have two million in our rooms to live off, rent-free in the sun.

"Luckily for you, there was a rumour started this week on the chat sites, could be corporate espionage, it could be just some spotty millennial… That Norovirus had broken out on this ship."

"But it hasn't," I say.

"Doesn't matter whether it's true or not, we have to deal with it. Twist it, spin it, get it off the front page," Hunter says.

"OK. Wag the dog."

"You did that. You're currently trending. Stories about your antics on the ship are being leaked. All the press and publicity is focussed on this new story. You have cured Norovirus."

"I started another story last night in the bar that cruise ships have to be tested in case they are commandeered for war."

"Georgie told us, the Captain relayed that back, it was outed early this morning. The company is now acting against its own rumour and categorically denying that the ship is going to war. It made morning TV in the USA," Hunter says.

"Amazing nonsense." I shrug.

"Sure, but the news is nonsense as we know from our years in the military. What is important is that the ship has had more news coverage than we could buy in TV spots, and it's not over."

"You want me to jump off the back of the ship next?" I ask.

"No. But in your contract, the company owns your performance on stage, and Auli'i's, Georgie's, Ronni's and mine. Problem is they don't own Jill Cohen's, so she shouldn't have been up there," Hunter explains. "You blew it."

"OK."

"Although we both know why she was there, it could end up being embarrassing," he adds.

"If she is a thief she's bad publicity?"

"Correct. The recording of this morning's show has been reframed, Jill is cut out, snippets are with the press."

"And the bit about my dishonourable discharge?"

"Did you lie?" Hunter asks.

"No."

"Then don't worry. The English discharged you, the American public thinks you're a hero. We love all that. You're going to get a book deal, you are going to need to talk to the company lawyers. This could make your daughter and maybe you a star."

"And the Norovirus?"

"Gone," Hunter confirms.

"I know, but that I can cure Norovirus?"

"Let's hold that one back for a slow news day. The company is riding a fine line of free good publicity."

"I'm so glad for you. And the money?"

"On a quick count, four million is still missing."

"Wow! You did great."

"That makes me think they had someone working with them in St Vincent, and the plan was to get as much as they could to a bank. Maybe the same in Madeira, but Madeira is a whole other problem."

Hunter leaves an ugly pause, so unlike him.

"Jill will never have earned four million from a jewellery heist." I offer.

"No. She's been paid well. If she and Tony can walk away with that they've done well, if," Tony slowly adds. He wakes himself up,

"Back to the company message and you. There's a good chance you'll be setting up a company to test ship security, and you might just get a contract straight away."

"What if I don't want to do that?" I ask. I was looking for a quieter life when I took this cruise.

"I'll run it; it could be my ticket off the ship. You just do some publicity and we'll use your name," Hunter says.

"Like we are buddies?" I ask.

"Too early for that, right?" he asks.

"So, the immediate future. While you manage all of that for the corporation, who manages Jill when she reports twelve million stolen?" I ask.

"Who can she report it to? Why would she bring twelve million on a ship?" Hunter asks.

I drink my second cup of tea and pour a third.

"And?" I ask, to see if there is more.

"If she tells Maria that it's been stolen," Hunter ponders, "who does Maria report it to? She only knows me, and I don't know it's been moved from under your bed."

Hunter pours himself a cup of tea and I feel a need to double check the bullet points.

"Just a quick recap. The company want to make my daughter famous?"

"Correct, great story for the ship. They want her as their own."

"I get a book deal?"

"You and your daughter's story, you don't even have to write it," Hunter confirms.

"And I'm starting up a security company?"

"With me, partners, I get my share," Hunter adds.

"And I still get a share of the money?" I ask but Hunter hesitates. "And Ronni?"

Hunter is having to think this one through, something is bugging him. He is stumbling on promising anything.

"If we can get it off the ship and use it, we split it, however, we have to work it out, and it includes Ronni." He confirms. "Georgie wants to speak to you next, technically she's your boss. She'll get details and paperwork." Hunter stands, he's finished. I stand and we face each other.

"So where's the money?" I ask.

"Safe. Trust me."

"But we don't trust each other," I remind him.

"Correct," Hunter says. "No more pillow-talk."

My new partner rises as he is done, it is not feeling like a partnership yet.

"One more thing," I stall him with.

"Jill might think I have the money. That puts me in danger."

"There is that chance, but she stole the money."

"Maria El Ray doesn't know that."

"Good point," he agrees and leaves.

Chapter 75 – The setup

"We want you to stay on in Madeira where a small film crew will be joining," Georgie says to me.

"I want to move rooms," I attempt as a rebuttal demand.

"Move rooms?" she asks.

"It's all about respect, the company will understand that. Plus, I really want to get away from that bed. It has awkward bad memories for me."

Georgie slows down. I'm sure she can see my reasoning as well as my dig.

"But that's the most expensive bed on the ship." She dares to jest.

"Was," I correct her,

"And that room is still short of a lifejacket, but we can't be seen putting it back. My room is short of one too. We will sort it out at the next lifeboat drill." She thinks out loud.

"This has been quite a day so far, I couldn't have imagined any of this two weeks ago."

"You got to swan off and have lunch! I've had hours of negotiation with either the Captain, Hunter or head office," Georgie says.

"I wondered where you were. I missed you," I dare.

"Did he get the money back?" she asks, but the lift stops.

The elevator door opens and guests join us so the conversation ends. One guest turns to me.

"Could I have your autograph please?" she asks, scrabbling for a pen.

"It really is my daughter who is the star," I say as the lift stops again. Georgie holds the door open and waits for me as I sign. It's obvious the lady expects a peck on the cheek too and as confusing as my life has become I can see Georgie almost ordering me to comply. She then wants a picture and I realise why the elevators always appear busy. I complete the brief encounter with the lady and wave goodbye as Georgie lets the door close.

"A tip. It's easier to oblige and leave than to argue the toss," she says, as she walks me towards her office.

"Come and stay in my new cabin tonight? A tip. It's easier to oblige and smile."

She ignores my question. "So did he find it?"

"Apart from about four million which Jill apparently smuggled ashore-"

Georgie stops in shock. "Jill?"

"-Sorry, loads to tell. But I have been ordered not to. Jill took it from my room while I was in your room. Hunter has her on security film. He has her and her male accomplice taking bags ashore yesterday morning. He thinks they took it initially to their cabins then moved it ashore."

"Really?"

"Jill doesn't know Hunter has stolen the rest back, that is if she has discovered it's gone from her cabin. She won't know who took it, or who to tell."

"Who would take it, but you?"

"I was on stage with you and her, then I went for lunch with her."

"Oh shit, I didn't go to lunch. Who will she suspect? I never did trust that woman from the moment I saw her on the bridge with you."

"We should spend some time together later and talk further," I add.

Georgie lets me into her office, follows me in and closes the door.

"We need to discuss your show tomorrow, there are elements you need to include. Words and phrases you have to say."

"Can we have dinner together?"

Georgie has gone into work mode, she rounds her desk, putting a barrier between us, and sits down, placing her arms on the table. This is 'Boss Georgie' and I guess I have to listen, but I feel battle weary and I need to see Ee just to run everything by her too,

"Georgie. Can we call Auli'i up here? She's going to need this explained to her too."

"Ee and I were chatting while you were with Hunter. She's very bright. She knows she needs a break like this news story or she will end up on a ship until she is forty, like me. I have just had a break, she has got a better one, I convinced her to take it. She understood, she wants to be an actress. I love to see a powerful young woman who knows what she wants. She's upstairs in a communications room being interviewed by a ghostwriter in New York. Nothing can be used until the contract is agreed. They want you next," Georgie catches me stunned, "the machine is already turning," she explains.

"You're more important to me than fame. Can we be humans for a moment?" I want to hit the pause button on all of this.

Georgie softens. "All this feels so weird. I've still got a million in my safe and I co-own a house in Bequia with you, that's doing my fucking head in."

"Two houses," I correct her. "And it looks like we may have got away with that. Shit, Sylvie sent me a message."

I dig for my phone in fear that if the news is bad, if the kid from the bank was tortured and killed Georgie would never forgive me. I hit the link, but again, it will not open. I look up from my phone and Georgie appears in shock.

"What's up?"

She shakes her head looking like she has been hit by a tidal wave. "What if she thinks I have the money, what if I'm pregnant?"

Never had I considered pregnancy, I never thought to ask, rudely I never thought she could be. How stupid of me.

"You're not on the pill?"

"Bit late to ask. For either of us to ask. Why would I need to be?"

I am speechless. It's not something I've ever needed to consider and now, to be a father to a baby, approaching fifty, and she has to be close to forty.

"No," she says studying my stoic reaction. "I've not started my menopause. I am still very capable."

"I never meant to infer anything like, I just never thought, never…"

I am genuinely confused.

"Me neither. I haven't slept with a man since I was in college, and that is a long time ago." She is in genuine shock.

This is crazy. I thought the rest of the cruise had been weird, but to walk off the ship a father, a real father, to a baby that actually needs me is something I could not have in any of my wildest dreams have expected.

A very real dad. It's my biggest shock yet.

Chapter 76 - Dad

I'm trying not to make eye contact with Mrs El Rey but it's not like the cabin is huge. I guess it helps that she's standing to look out the window maybe avoiding contact with me. She knows who I am, but in reality, I have no idea who she is. Well, some idea, but she doesn't know that I have a clue. Her hair is up, she is wearing officer whites a team of stewards are clearing my room. My small case is packed and deliberately left open on the bed. I throw my few toiletries into the handbag and my folded suits are thrown on the bed.

"That's it, I really do travel light, oh the safe," I add.

I open the safe in plain sight, which only contains my passport and wallet. On top, there is a plastic shopping bag containing an unopened bottle of tequila that I'd forgotten I picked up in Colombian duty-free.

"Tequila! I forgot I had that in the safe. I'll carry that if you have got the rest."

I take the bottle and leave the passport and wallet in the safe and address the cabin stewards and security team as I leave.

"So you can move everything upstairs for me?"

"Yes, Sir," a cabin steward says.

"I will need my uniform for tonight."

"I'll be right behind you with it, Sir. Ready for formal night." He smiles.

"Best you take your passport and wallet, sir, we have everything else," an Asian security officer says.

I stay deliberately away from the safe now I am at the door.

"OK, just pass them to me and I'll leave the rest with you."

I have forced him to pass me my passport and wallet,

"You know, I really haven't enjoyed this room, I was always on edge," I say but that is for her.

"You have a much better room now, follow me, sir, my colleagues will do everything else," he says and we leave.

I hear my case being zipped and another closed, they couldn't hold any money let alone twenty million. As I stride away down the corridor, the others following behind, I turn and look back, confident that the female officer will not be with them. She isn't, as expected. She saw me and the luggage out and has stayed to check her money is safely hidden. My guess is that within minutes she will have discovered her fortune has gone even if she didn't know before.

Hunter has set this test on my timely change of cabins. She could ask why she was sent down at all, however, as far as she knows it was to protect her own money as I left. As far as she is concerned, Hunter, like me, has no idea that it's gone. The results of this test will mean she may start asking questions, or she knows Jill has it. Hunter will be watching every move she makes from this moment on. I'm not in a position to see this play out, but I'm pleased that Hunter has set it up so I have clearly been moved with nothing. I'm in no way connected to the money unless she thinks I've moved it before my relocation. Hunter will be forced to show her the security footage and then blame the real culprits if he truly is on my side. As long as he doesn't show her me and Georgie leaving with life jackets, but then, that was for a safety drill.

I arrive at the new cabin, and it's much nicer. Slightly wider, nicer facilities and a bigger screen TV - not that I've watched the TV since I arrived. The balcony is fantastic, a private space to relax. I open my bottle of Tequila and toast my new room, mindful I cannot get drunk again.

There is a knock at the door and I wonder if it's Georgie, come to congratulate me on my move. I dash enthusiastically to the door, only to find Ronni.

"You owe me a few explanations," she says.

Ronni can't help but touch my ceremonial uniform laid out on my bed, shoes on the floor in front of it. "This takes me back."

"No more than a stage prop now," I add.

"Was it any more back then?"

She is right, but she hasn't come here to debate the purpose of uniforms.

"I just witnessed an angry female security officer storm into Hunter Witowski's office."

"I wonder what that tells us?"

"I'd say it tells us she was a plant at the airport, we were helping the authorities with a drugs bust?" Ronni suggests. "The money was an accident."

That catches me from left field, I'd never ever considered that Mrs El Rey was one of Hunter's staff all along. That complicates what she and Hunter might be up to, together or separately which is way beyond my wildest assertions. I grab the two clean glasses and pour us both a drink. However, outrageous suggestions may seem they should never be overlooked. If it's true, if she was on some form of drugs bust, if that was bait money, Jill and Tony are the bad guys, and Hunter has just taken it. That makes Jill and Hunter effectively partners and both women are better actresses than I could have imagined.

"If that's the case, I've no idea what's going on, just when I thought I was starting to figure it out."

"What was your take on it then?" Ronni asks seeing I am struck dumb, and I can't say a word.

Chapter 77 – Dressed to kill

Dressed, but not to kill, tonight is the ceremonial dress night and Ronni has joined me for dinner after Georgie avoided the offer. I would have been far too overdressed for a single table in the buffet and attracted too many embarrassing questions at a shared table in the restaurant. I hope Auli'i will join us later. Technically, she can't eat above decks and I can't eat below, even with our new status. She can use the bars though, and she knows I want to chat with her.

"It is an unbelievable mess and I have no idea how to call it," Ronni says, now we have discussed Hunter, Mrs El Rey and Jill being the thief.

"Trust is hard at the moment," I add solemnly.

"I have eighty-fifty 'k' in my safe and I'd like to hold onto it," she says.

"Not more?"

"I put five hundred into a bank in St Vincent on the pretence it was for a house. I had to fill in loads of forms, but I felt the bother was worth making a chunk safe."

"Or losing it. That was a cool idea. I still have mine," I say.

"I would feel cheated if we lost a share of the bigger money I could have been shot for!"

Ronni is right of course, as mad as it seems, and as unexpected as the money was, we are worthy advocates of it and it would be a gross injustice for us to have been used at gunpoint only to be cheated out of it. Ronni is great company, easy to chat with, she is used to being one of a team.

"Do you trust Hunter?" I ask her.

"Not any more, not until he explains himself," she says and we both notice Jill waltz over. I pull out a chair.

"What a day!" I say. "Can I get you a drink?"

Jill shakes her head.

"I'm celebrating," I tease.

"What?" Jill asks flatly.

"New cabin, with a balcony. Not as big as yours, but very nice. It also looks like we've got a book deal."

"When did all this happen?" Jill asks.

"After we left you, Ee and I were dragged into the offices. She was interviewed for two hours, then I was... for half an hour, you can see who the important one is."

"By who?" Jill asks.

"Someone at head office and a ghostwriter in New York!"

"That is marvellous," Jill says. "Sounds like you won and I lost."

"What did you lose? Was it a mobile phone? Someone found a mobile in the theatre, I guess it's gone to a central lost and found area."

"It wasn't a mobile," she says. "Not to worry, I doubt it is in lost and found."

Ronni and I both sit poker-faced, both knowing much more than we let on.

"Have you eaten, do you want to join us?" I offer.

"I'll have a large glass of red wine."

The waiter brings a clean glass before he is asked and he pours from our bottle. We toast.

"To finding whatever it was," I say.

Ronni is quick to toast. Jill is slower.

"Was it in the theatre or the restaurant?" Ronni asks her.

"It could have been either." Jill pauses, "I could have left it in my room."

"I do that all the time. I think I have dementia setting in some days," Ronni says. "Hey, do you two want time alone? I can go."

"No, no," Jill adds. "I'll drink this with you then I have a million things to sort out."

"Hope not," Ronni jokes and Jill looks at her. "A million is a lot of things!" She laughs.

"A lot." Jill tries to smile then turns to me. "So I didn't know you wanted to be famous?"

"It's Ee I want to see with a future. An actress needs a career break. But she needs to be careful, I need to stress that to her."

"Yes. A moment of fame can lead to disaster," Jill points out.

"Yes," I agree. "Ronni and I were talking about that. We knew soldiers who won medals or credits, and then found colleagues to be jealous, others who felt they deserved something too. The prize became divisive."

"That's good advice," Jill says and waves. She has seen Ee approaching. Jill necks her wine and stands to give up her chair. "You listen to your dad's advice. I'd hate to see you hurt," Jill delivers, with an edge before leaving.

The waiter brings another clean glass for Ee, finishes pouring the rest of the bottle between the three of us and takes an order for another bottle. Auli'i is a good listener and takes in our gentle warning, unlike the one that Jill left with which I'm sure was far more sinister.

With Auli'i off to enjoy her evening, Ronni and I are left alone, but the tone has changed.

"That Jill could be dangerous, I'd keep an eye on her," Ronni volunteers.

"I never saw her as the thief, I worry what else I don't see coming!"

Chapter 78 – The quiet ones are the worst

Despite my luxurious new cabin, I had the worst night's sleep to date. It's still early, the gym's not open yet, but I'm up and standing in the breeze on my balcony, dressed and ready. Of all the things that have happened so far on ship, I've not been directly threatened or had my daughter threatened. Not till last night. Jill was clever, I'd only take her words as a threat if I knew that she was angry enough to mean it. I gave nothing away though, no reaction, though that will be tough to continue.

I work hard in the gym, punishing myself. I row faster and faster, my mind racing, my breathing hard. It's just day two of what will be five long sea days. I'm scheduled to do a lecture then a conference call, I pull harder and faster. The book could be written before we get to Madeira if this drama is over by then; it just needs focussed effort. I stop rowing and I'm sucking for air. The wheel spins at the front of the machine. My heart pounds.

I've hit a wall. The tribe in the backwaters of Colombia recognised the woman in the photograph as the wife of a drug lord, people have been after her, she cannot be a crew member. Unless our Maria Isabel was providing a distraction, working as the woman's body double. I need to see her name badge then have Georgie or Ronni to do a staff search and see if she is new, or has been staff for some time. Or worse still, the Latina woman has replaced a now estranged crew member and taken her identity.

I walk to the desk and pull a chemical wipe. I slowly clean the machine I have used, the handgrip, the seat and the steel middle bar as if I am wiping away prints and DNA. I bin the wipe and walk to the window towelling down. My heart rate should be lowering but my tension is rising. Surely, a crew member couldn't be replaced without friends knowing.

I decide against any uniform today for the lecture, simply because I could not face being called a fraud now my military discharge has been made public. Whilst the audience was tamed when Georgie was with me, today I'm on my own. The theatre is packed and I sense they're expecting more dramatic life-threatening stories, but my standard lecture is far from that. I skip a lot of material I normally use, jumping slides manually and changing what I am saying until only a blank screen is left. I have no idea what to do. These people have not got a clue of what goes on behind steel water-tight doors. No idea what's really happening on this ship. Just like the fire on the Titanic, no one knew and it sailed away with a coal bunker on fire. Safety chambers distorted rendering them useless.

I switch to a photo album. My Syria album is huge. I click and a picture fills the screen. A city with not one building standing. As far as the eye can see the city hangs broken with twisted cables and steel. Not one wall standing, every building fractured, in piles of rubble. Is this what they want to see? I sense their uneasy intake of breath as the slide changes. Foreground they have noticed the dead bodies, a child can be seen under the bricks and they are uncomfortable. I move the picture on, but they are not going to get any better.

"We forget what the generation before us went through in the Second World War, the blitz, the loss. We think we've moved on but history writes a repeating story. Maybe if our country as a whole was to object, to refuse to have their pension funds invested in any company making weapons, it might help reduce war zones. But while people profit from war, there is every reason for some to ensure conflicts continue."

I look at my blank screen, then back to the blank audience. I have gone too far. They don't want to be told they are cruising on the pension profits partly earned by death and destruction, that's unfair. I feel they want Auli'i and not me, and if I leave them with this, tomorrow's theatre will be empty. They want a young hero, not an old cynic.

"Auli'i is upstairs in a communications room telling her story to a ghostwriter, I'll be doing the same when I leave here. It seems her story has touched some hearts and made the news back home, maybe that will help change things. She will join me on stage tomorrow, and maybe she will reveal more of what really happened to her. Have a great day."

That was wrong of me. That was a low blow. I take a few questions but they are subdued, then I head down off the stage to where Jill has been watching. Keep your friends close, but your enemies even closer.

"Tame, compared to yesterday," Jill suggests.

"It just goes to show that unless it's a sensation, unless it's huge, no one cares," I suggest.

"Another working day?" Jill probes.

"I'd love to be doing a quiz with you all, but yes. Come up and sit in if you like, but you heard it all yesterday, you'll be bored senseless," I suggest to her.

"I will. I am intrigued by what goes on behind the scenes," she says. She's clutching at straws now, desperate to find her money.

"I love watching her innocent mind deal with all this. Auli'i is fast becoming a sellable face. Or is the brand just using her, and encouraging her?" Jill asks.

I haven't tried to dissect the two needs or work out the driving force, but Jill is staying. Being stuck with her means I can't research Maria Isabel 'El Ray'. However, Jill might offer a clue as to whether she is working alone or with a local team, and how dangerous she really is. I should be patient. There are four days at sea where nothing can happen, the Atlantic Ocean is huge.

"They've offered me a job!" I announce as we climb the stairs together, turning at each half flight. There's no way we would get a lift with nearly a thousand people leaving the theatre and heading up to the buffet for lunch.

"Permanent member of the entertainment staff?"

"No. I seem to have failed at that," I say, laughing it off.

"What then?"

"They want me to set up a security division and to be honest, it doesn't interest me all that much, but I think I have to go through the motions. The money will be handy and I guess it will give me something to do."

"Don't they have great security?" Jill questions.

"Yes, they do actually. The offer could just be to cover my antics when I got drunk and missed the ship," I confess.

"I guessed that wasn't pre-organised!" she exclaims. "Not that anyone in the world would believe otherwise now, fake news wins every time."

We land on B deck, where the bridge is. I stop and we stand a moment to regain composure. Whatever your fitness level, a dozen flights of stairs are a workout.

"They want to put an edge into the training occasionally, go from walking pace to running. Stop people casting a lame eye over paperwork, inventories, background checks. It's like training soldiers, when they do the same stuff over and over, they miss things."

"Take the job," she suggests. "Maybe all you need to do is set it up then let someone else run it."

"It's easy for you to say that, but everything today's computerised. I'm not technical like you. Maybe we could work together on this, your skills could come in very handy," I suggest, making it sound genuine.

"I doubt I can help you. Have a little faith in yourself. You know what you're doing."

We walk on to a room near the bridge, knock and I enter. Jill follows behind me, with a twist offering only her back and then sliding to the side of the room. It could be that she does not want to intrude, but I jump to the conclusion that she knows how to avoid cameras, and one is pointed at Auli'i.

If Jill normally avoids security cameras, why then, being so professional, did she make the mistake of dragging the money away in full vision?

CRUISE SHIP HEIST – OCEAN ATLANTIC

Our interview is cut short for a photo shoot which Jill decides to sidestep. I don't blame her, but throughout the afternoon I'm bugged by her blatant theft on camera.

We have not one, but three photographers who move Ee and me around the ship, each taking their moment to demand our eye line, each with a different style. The photo-session is incredibly intense, I've changed uniform and been in civvies, been up and down the ship more times than I can remember, and gone from hard sun to sunset and now I am tired. I am not sure I am offering the right face or pulling the right shapes for these photographers, I'm fighting with the pretty wild conjecture that Jill is either not working for Maria or has tried to double cross her by stealing it and not telling her. Maria was shocked the money was gone, Ronni saw her storm into Hunter's office. Or was that an act?

I am so tired from staying alert and smiling that I'm going to go back to my room, wake up that unused TV, pour a large tequila and order room service. That's my day over. I might, if I can summons the energy, do what Hunter did and try and write down a 'who did what and who knows what'; military level Cluedo.

I am in loose shorts and bare top when there's a knock at the door. Room service has been and I am not expecting anyone. It could be Auli'i, but she normally calls first. If I had a gun with me, it would be to hand, but I don't. I put my hand across the spy hole, a dangerous thing to do. Assassins wait for the light to go and then shoot through the hole knowing the target has their head there. No shot, I'm on a cruise ship, I look through the spy hole.

"Hello stranger," I say opening the door to Georgie.

"I've never been on a cruise with half the elements this one has thrown at me!" she exclaims.

"I should hope not."

She stands looking at me. "Do I prefer this look or the uniform? Hard choice," she says and we kiss. "Sorry." We separate and it looks like we are friends again.

"No worries," I say. "That is how all this started."

"What is?"

"Me saying 'no worries'. I tried to say it in Spanish and got it all wrong. The woman at the airport corrected me, and now she is on board ship working in security. Or is she?"

We kiss again and I know this is going to lead to trouble.

"I meant to buy some condoms."

"I meant to avoid you."

Chapter 79 – No cover

The phone wakes me. I look over and try and focus on it, but it's hiding behind an empty bottle of Tequila. I turn around, Georgie is sleeping like an angel. The phone stops.

The phone starts ringing again and I pull it over to look at the time displayed on it, it is ten o'clock. I leap out of bed. I'm on stage with Auli'i in an hour! I torture myself as to whether the clocks went forward, but surely that would reflect on the phone. The ship's phone has to be right. It rings again.

"Hello?"

"We've got a murder," Hunter says.

"Who?" I ask in a panic.

"Tony Kaye."

I sink with relief it is not my daughter.

The shower wakes me up, but when Georgie slips in with me, it wakes everything up.

"I thought you were worried about being pregnant!"

"One of the girls has a morning after pill I can take."

I am going to be late because I am enjoying soaping and washing every curve on her body.

I dress the fastest I can and trying to recover I almost run downstairs to the theatre, leaving Georgie in my room back in bed, wrapped in the sheets where she can't be found. It's her day off and she wants to relax.

The stage show goes much better today, with Auli'i by my side, and I rush out of the theatre as soon as I can. The corridor is empty except for Hunter's security guard standing outside what must be Tony's cabin. He lets me in.

Hunter is inside on the phone, and I gather it must be to the Captain. I take a moment to look at Tony's dead body. It looks like it's been a good few hours since the blood dried. Without touching him I can see he has bled out from mid-chest, maybe near his heart. It's a large wound, from a considerably sized knife. Hunter ends his phone call and approaches me.

"I can see only one conclusion," Hunter says.

"Natural causes?" I ask.

"Yes."

"It's like being back in service, employed to look in places none wants to look."

"Then say what you're told to say."

"Who found him?"

"Cabin steward," Hunter says.

"Has he been contained?"

"He's with one of my staff back at my office. I have another trusted man outside. That's as far as it goes."

"You'd better go back and check cameras. Send down a body bag. Laundry bags. I'll deal with this."

Hunter leaves me. I pull out my camera and take photographs of everything. I find and expose the single accurate wound, which is sideways, so the blade goes in between the rib cage with ease. I suspect a broad, very sharp kitchen knife. I take pictures then trace the wound to paper.

Hunter's man outside knocks, then hands in the bags Hunter has sent. I roll the body into the black body bag and zip it closed, then bag up the sheets. Finally, I wash my hands and arms and check myself for blood splatter. Drying myself, I look at the carpet and walls which have avoided any obvious blood spill between cabin door and the bed. My guess is Tony's mouth was covered with the murderer's left hand at the door, maybe punched first with the knife hand. He must have been shoved back onto the bed, stabbed then held down until he passed out. This was done by someone big and powerful, not that Tony would have been capable of much resistance to anyone knowing what they were doing. While I'm straightening up in the mirror I hear a commotion outside and I recognise the voice as Jill. She is the last person I want to discover me in here.

"The gentleman has Norovirus. He is in quarantine. He's sleeping. No one is allowed in," I hear the guard say.

He's done his job well. Jill must have left as the voices stop. A few minutes and I guess she will ring Tony's mobile. I doubt she believes he's sleeping. I dart to the phone. Not knowing the passcode, I force the back off and remove the battery. I wonder if she thinks he has been arrested. In which case, she will start to worry. The room phone rings and I stand looking at it, I didn't get to that one quick enough.

There's a knock at the door and the guard enters. "Sir, that is Mr Witowski on the phone for you."

"Are you sure?"

"Yes sir, I have him here on my handy."

I answer the phone but say nothing, just listen.

"Philips?" he asks.

"Yes. All done. Ready to move. Two bags of very soiled sheets. Mattress needs covering then moving, the carpet is fine. All photographed," I report.

"Good. Get yourself up here. My other men are on their way to do the get out."

I pull the phone cord out of the wall, then move to the bathroom and do the same for the extension.

In Hunter's office, Hunter has nothing on his screens, which surprises me.

"It happened at twelve forty-five in the morning," he says.

"Who did it?" I ask.

"No idea. Camera system went down at twelve-thirty, it was back working at five-past-one. I'd guess five minutes to do the job, the rest of the time to travel each way, to and from."

"No. They'd have been told to look for the money, another ten minutes at least in the room before they failed, so less travel, they must've been closer by," I interject.

Hunter nods. I present my traced template of the stab wound.

"Large knife, clean stab under the rib cage and up. There's no blood splatter at the door, or on the way to the bed, so his mouth was covered and he was walked to the bed before he was stabbed. The killer, whoever it was, knew what they were doing"

"Doesn't strike me as Jill, nor Maria Isabel. But I'd say it was a two-man job. I suspect Maria Isabel was in here, disabling the cameras," Hunter offers.

"Why?" I ask.

"She'd looked under the bed after you changed rooms to find the money had gone. She reported that to me. I was shocked, as you can imagine. So I searched security footage with her, eventually revealing to her Jill and Tony taking the money. She obviously didn't know the money was no longer in their rooms."

"Who is this woman, who are you involved with?"

Hunter takes a breath and slowly turns, he is not going to share more information, or maybe he doesn't know. Maybe that relationship is being tested.

"Let's not jump to conclusions. It's happened exactly halfway across the Atlantic, three days out, three days in. This could have been planned so no one can get to the ship, and the crime scene would have time to get corrupted. Maybe Tony and Jill have been driving this, let's keep an open mind."

Hunter measures my template etching and agrees a standard eight-inch carving knife would probably not be long enough.

Killing Tony and not Jill is deliberate. It infers Jill is the leader of the two and she's been sent a warning. Unless Jill did it.

"You know, this also suggests that we're never going to see a share of this money, none of us."

Chapter 80 – No payout

There is a way of looking at people, even in a crowd, which makes them feel you looking at them. That's not to say it always works, but someone who is scared, on the run, hates being hit with that look and fear shows on their face.

We have a few clues. A large carving knife, wielded by someone powerful, accurate. Feels more like a Latino hitman planted in the predominantly Asian kitchen staff. If Jill is not running the show, she may well be pressured to give up the money with the threat of her partner being dead. We need to neutralise that threat.

The kitchen is in full swing as we walk through with the head chef there is a sea of faces. Our presence does not mean any of them stops work; trolleys are loaded, ovens are opened and closed, trays lifted in and out. The chef shouts for quiet.

"Yes chef!" they all reply, and continue working in silence.

"Is anyone missing a large knife?" he shouts.

"Yes chef," comes from over in the meat area.

Hunter is off in that direction with the chef, while I watch everyone react, this is a two-man job. I want just one show of weakness because someone near that position or with access to it must have taken the knife. Someone has had to come to work today and act normally with a guilty conscience. There is no point in running until there is somewhere to run to and we don't hit land for three more days, he or she, will be here.

I sense movement on the other side of the kitchen and I follow it. Years of training tell me when to make a sudden noise that triggers a run. I stamp, move forward, and a tall man tosses a trolley and pushes his way through the staff. I'm after him. I hear Hunter running from the other side of the kitchen and the chef shouting for a clean-up.

The man throws more trays and twists barrels into our path, he does all he can to avoid us. Chef is going to be very unhappy at the loss of food. Our man bursts out into a public area, the restaurant, with guests seated for lunch. It is then that we slow for a moment, assess then accelerate, and in a double swoop pin our target to the ground. Hunter's handcuffs are out, the runner's struggling hands pinned behind him and he is lifted away as kindly as we can. We have an audience. The Maître d' cleverly begins to applaud loudly and the waiters are first to follow, then the guests join in. This will no doubt be my next lecture; the hardcore training on the ship continues with excitement in the restaurant.

With a body in the morgue and a man now in the cells, the question is how many people is Maria working with, and does Hunter know where she is? Is this a situation he has lost control of?

Hunter checks the agency log for replacement staff who joined anywhere in South America and they are all called into his office one by one. No one is absent from that list and few look like they could be of any use in a snowball fight. Hunter and I sit back in our chairs and take a moment.

"So Maria Isabel is temporary agency staff?"

"It looks that way," Hunter says.

"I didn't ask how it looks," I persist.

"At the moment, she is in no way implicated."

"Nor are you."

"I have a dead guest-" Hunter starts.

But I interrupt him,

"-Natural causes. Let me guess, a heart attack?"

"It is better than announcing that I have his killer in a cell."

"Shall I just leave you to type that report up? I have media duties."

"You think you're safe out there?" he asks me.

I stop at the door. "What was your deal with her?"

There is a long pause and I don't get the feeling that he wants to share that information with me. The pause turns into an awkward silence, only broken by his telephone ringing. He might be expecting me to leave, but I feel I deserve an answer. He can see I'm going nowhere so he answers the phone.

"Witowski." After listening, he replies, "I'll be right down." He replaces the receiver then holds my look. "Auli'i is missing. Not at rehearsals, not seen since she left her face to face with head office."

My blood floods with adrenalin, hate, and fear.

Hunter jumps to his feet. "I'll go through crew deck, check her room then meet you in the theatre. You take promenade deck. This could be something totally unrelated."

But we both know it is not.

Chapter 81 - Missing

I'm walking fast, looking everywhere inside on deck seven. I don't expect her to be outside, but I do open the doors and look to the back and front. At the Atrium, I stop, drop a level and check the shops, then back up and I head towards the front, trying not to show my distress.

In the distance, I can see Jill and Maria walking towards me, smiling. They are friends. We will meet in less than thirty seconds and I need to be controlled. I can't accuse them, I certainly can't attack them. I can't even let on that I know anything. I have to smile and it's going to take every skill I have because I want to kill them both.

"Hey!" I say, slowing to approach them. I look at Maria's name badge, 'Maria Belle'.

"Don't I know you? Have we met?" I play innocent.

"Yes." She smiles confidently. Then without changing expression or demeanour, her tone threatens. "You have twenty million dollars of mine and unless I get it back you will never see your daughter again."

She has just delivered the threat I was dreading and she's full of smiles. She is someone who has played this game at the highest level and has no morals about killing. Threatening her will get me nowhere.

"No. It was at the airport. You were arrested?" I ask, still playing confused. If I refuse to take the message in, she will need to deliver it again. Maybe she will lose her cool.

"I don't have time for this, nor do you, and your daughter certainly doesn't."

"Sorry?" My mind is racing. I hit out with the only thing I can come up with. "Is this another publicity stunt?"

"No," Maria insists firmly with that huge violent smile, the smile she shot me at the airport. I see it all now so clearly, why are Hunter and Jill mixed up with her. Outwardly, I refuse to accept it, though inwardly I believe every word.

"Jill. Tony's looking for you. In the Atrium. Said he thought he had Norovirus, but it was just a dose of the squirts." That is the only play I have.

"This is not a game," Maria snarls and she drags Jill away.

What a nasty toxic piece of work. Jill looked confused about Tony but said nothing. I turn and watch them go but they never look back.

Explaining it all to Hunter and Georgie in the theatre is a very sobering affair. He has to report to the Captain, who in turn has to tell head office that their new star appears to have been kidnapped and threatened. He is still holding back and it is him I want to attack but he seems fully on my side, what would I gain? I guess we all knew this would not end well, but now we're at the last chance saloon, the most important thing is finding Ee.

Hunter and I both know that running around is a waste of time and that we have both covered one floor each quickly.

"Nothing on promenade deck except Maria and Jill walking from the theatre towards the atrium," I explain.

"Nothing on crew deck either, it's busy, too many people who could see a struggle or someone moving a body," Hunter says.

"She's not dead," I snap.

"Sorry, I don't mean body. Auli'i would have gone to her room, front of ship, after her interview. She is below the theatre. She would then go up to the stage via the front crew stairs. No reason for her to deviate."

"She finished in communications early and was fine. She's always early, the first to arrive," Georgie adds.

"She's somewhere on the stage then, under it or above it. They wouldn't try and move her," I suggest.

CRUISE SHIP HEIST – OCEAN ATLANTIC

The three of us power up and walk together through the empty auditorium. We enter the stage door and arrive at the side. From the wings, we look at the show being re-blocked with one person less. I can't see anywhere they could have hidden her. Hunter looks up.

"They couldn't have carried her up there," I state.

"No, but they could winch her." Hunter runs to a steel ladder by the wall. "There's one the other side too."

I run through the dancers causing confusion, leap on the ladder on the other side and climb up as fast as I can.

"Clear the stage, workers in the fly loft," Ricardo shouts taking control of the stage area and his staff.

From each side, we kick through the rigging but she is not tied up here.

"Not on the stage, not above the stage, she has to be under the stage," Hunter shouts to me.

I instinctively grab a rope, twist it around my leg and slide down. Hunter is a fraction behind me. We run and jump down under the stage onto the platform under the floor. Our phones light up the under area but I can see nothing. I stop. My head darts round towards the dressing room. There's a trunk. I pull at a padlock on it.

"Who's got a key for this trunk? Key! Now!" I shout. Stagehands appear from nowhere and try their keys but none fit.

"Someone's switched the padlock. That's not one of ours," Ricardo says.

"Get all the keys, try every key you have, Auli'i is in here!" I shout even louder.

I turn to Hunter who is on his mobile phone,

"Bring the large bolt croppers or cutters from the engine workshop to backstage now. Fast!"

The dancers have all stopped and are grouped around us.

"The chests are airtight, they're sea chests. She won't be able to breathe in there!" The stagehand panics.

Another stagehand tries every key from a big bundle, but none work. In a panic, I try and pull at the hinge. I look for ways to unscrew it or break it. The chest is fool-proof and my heart is sinking.

"Where are those bolt croppers?" Ricardo demands in his communicator.

"Come on!" I shout.

"Engineering is on the way. Let's think, she might not be in there, where else could she be?" Hunter asks me, holding my head and focussing me. "Where else?"

"Hunter. She's in there. The padlock's been changed! The stage crew don't know this padlock."

"Bolt cutters are on the way," Ricardo relays having been on his mobile. "But these trunks are watertight. Airtight!"

My heart is beating out of my chest. I climb the stairs two at a time to the stage searching for help. Paramedics are running down between the seats in their green suits with their emergency bags.

"She's locked in an airtight trunk! Have a defibrillator and oxygen ready," I shout, desperate for the engineers.

"Bolt croppers!" I shout.

Two engineers come running through the theatre carrying tools.

"Hurry, please!" I shout.

They run up the steps to the stage, over it and drop down, everyone has parted to let them in and I am right behind them. They look at the padlock and open the bolt cutters, but as hard as they push they can't snap the lock. I try. Hunter tries. Nothing.

"Step aside!" The other engineer demands and his angle grinder kicks in, cutting at the padlock sending sparks everywhere. It snaps and drops to the floor. Watching the lid open is a torment. It is too slow. She might not be there. She might be dead.

I see a glimpse of her hair. She's there. My arms dive in and pull her up. I see her eyes above the gaffer tape crudely covering her mouth. I rip it off and heave her out, assisted by Hunter and I lower her to the floor. Her body feels limp, lifeless.

We part to let the paramedics in. Her clothes are ripped apart, another starts chest compressions. The third places pads either side of her chest.

"Clear," he shouts.
The medic stops the chest pumps he had started. The machine fires. Nothing. I'm holding my breath. The paramedic resumes chest pumps.

"Clear!" the third shouts. The chest pumps stop, the machine fires again and she is charged back to life. She gulps in a breath and the oxygen mask is placed on her face.

Hunter and the engineers cut at the tape that binds her arms and legs. Auli'i sucks air hard. She is alive and I drop down to the floor. She must have been just seconds from death.

Chapter 82 – Seconds from death

"You're made of tough stuff," I declare to her.

"I had every faith you'd find me," she says to me.

The dancers ease in and touch her shoulders for reassurance. She turns to them, realising almost everyone she now knows is here.

"He got me out of far worse than this you know."

I look round, sure that they must think this is a publicity stunt because it's too far-fetched to be real. Then I look straight at Hunter, who can't worm his way out of answering my questions about Maria any longer, if not for me, for the Captain. He will have to write a report. Hunter squats down to her level.

"Can you tell me who did this, Auli'i? We don't have a camera back here, I need a description," Hunter asks her.

"We do," Georgie offers. We turn our attention to her. "We have technical cameras and show cameras. The technical camera is left on most of the time." She has Ricardo take Hunter away to show him.

"No posting any footage. None of you. I will be back," Hunter shouts back over his shoulder.

The medics proclaim Auli'i well but advise her to rest. The ordeal has not affected her the way it would most others and she's determined not to take the night off. The rehearsals to block the show without her naturally stopped as her rescue began and they're all now out of working hours if they are to perform tonight. Auli'i's girlfriends lift her up to the stage and help her stretch out, watched by the medics.

Georgie walks me to the edge of the stage and we both study Auli'i trying to shake off her cramp. Showtime is drawing closer and the stage has to be reset. The stagehands wait for Ricardo's cue to begin work. Ricardo waits on Georgie to give him the go-ahead to start but she waits.

Hunter re-joins us. "Not the best of cameras, and it is dark, but the picture is clear enough to show Maria and two Latino looking males who we didn't see on the roundup of local staff.

"Her team runs deeper. This escape of hers has been well planned," I accuse.

"She can't dance tonight," Hunter says, looking at Auli'i doing steps.

"Why?" asks Georgie.

It hits me that Auli'i is now our 'high-value asset', my daughter is being used. I've spent my life manipulating governments and politicians at the behest of our leaders and never got emotionally involved. Now, for the first time, not only do I have 'skin in the game' but the actual HVA. These are terms I never thought I would own. I re-enter the conscious world seeing Hunter talking, but I know what he is saying, I know he is playing her.

"They need to think they still have her," Hunter states.

"Surely they'll think she is dead?" Georgie asks.

"They wouldn't know the trunk is airtight. But, we've obviously missed some of the Latino crew joining the ship, and while they're out there, they're dangerous."

"But you interviewed everyone?" I stop. I realise the ship does this circuit every other week throughout the Caribbean season which lasts four months.

"I need to go back further, previous cruises, this has been planned for a longer time than we thought. My guess is they are all from the same agency but joined us weeks earlier. She can't go on tonight, Georgie."

"What do they want?" The stagehand asks, the obvious question everyone will ask and that we don't want to answer.

"Gather round, everyone," Hunter demands, ushering everyone who has seen this rescue or knows about it to come close. "Everyone, quickly!"

"Why did they do this? What did they want?" the stagehand repeats.

"Auli'i has been getting a lot of attention on the ship recently because of her story. Her story has a value to the company, which she has gone along with, but then you discover the high price you pay for attention and fame. Auli'i, maybe it's time to rethink allowing your life to be public, time to lay very, very low. All of you, never be alone," I stress.

The message is as mixed as my thoughts. Fame and jealousy pale behind death threats. The crew are silent, it seems like they have bought that story, but I know Hunter is involved in something rotten. I turn to him accusingly and he can see that.

"You all have to swear to absolute secrecy on what you've seen tonight. Not a word said anywhere. Georgie, I need a list of everyone here, I will share that list with the Captain. Any mention of what happened tonight will mean an instant dismissal and your name will be added to a blacklist that gets shared with other companies. We have a life at stake. Do you all understand the scale of that?" He scans the group. Everyone in the group nods in agreement.

"If anyone does not understand, or does not wish to comply, please raise your hand," Hunter demands. Again the group all agree. "Auli'i is safe from another attack while the gang think they still have her held for ransom. If they see her on stage tonight or hear she has been rescued they will come after her again. You can't dance tonight Auli'i."

"We can't do that show one short," Roger, the lead singer explains.

"I don't care. Get the asset safe," Hunter demands.

"She is not an asset. Her names Auli'i," I snap.

He knows I am on his back now.

"She is a high-value asset to those who want to bargain with her, and we are in South America, they don't play fair. Let's make her safe, keep her safe," Hunter demands.

Hunter says that to everyone, but he is spitting it at me to make a point. OK. We make her safe but I will want answers. He knows that.

"How much did you rehearse without her?" Georgie asks.

"Not even half, the second half of the show is more complicated too. Everyone has a role to play."

"I know," Georgie says, thinking.

There is silence, everybody deep in thought. Georgie looks at her watch; time is running out. Hunter has his own job to deal with while Georgie worries about entertaining the whole ship.

"The kidnappers are going to want to move her later on," Hunter says.

"They would need a forklift truck to move that trunk," the production manager chips in.

I understand the importance of dealing with all these problems, but my concern is the safety of my daughter knowing Maria is a very dangerous enemy lose on the ship, leading a gang of unknown size. Hunter has his phone to his ear.

"Get me a GPS luggage tracker, a selection of padlocks with keys and bring them backstage. In a bag, no one sees what you are doing." He ends the call and turns to us. "No one touches that trunk, from now on, that belongs to security. No more prints. No one goes near it."

"OK, crew, set the stage as if the show is happening, remember what Hunter Witowski has said, no one speaks of this, not even amongst yourselves," Georgie demands.

The huddled group gets smaller, just dancers, singers, the Production Manager, Hunter and Georgie.

"There's a way!" Auli'i starts.

"You can't go on. I want you locked away somewhere safe," Hunter insists.

"-I can go on, but all of you need to join the Magic Circle," she enthuses.

Roger tilts his head and smiles, he has caught on to her idea, he drifts towards the stage and starts to count movements back and forth demonstratively. Ee moves next to him and they exchange whispers. Hunter looks uneasy and makes a move to towards them, but Georgie stops him.

"They have to listen to me!" he says forcefully.

"Leave them a moment," Georgie insists.

I round and stand next to Hunter and we watch them hatch their part of the plan. They both turn back to us.

"It'll work," she says, nodding to Roger who agrees smiling.

"All of you get ready, it is your 'half-hour call' and you're behind," Georgie says.

The company rush off knowingly. No one needs to explain to them, they are as one, and their panic has turned into excitement.

"No discussing this!" Hunter shouts after them.

His head snaps back to Georgie, the Production manager and me. We are reduced to four, all thinking hard, all waiting for each other's developing plans to be shared, and Hunter and I wish to know what all the real entertainers seem to know by instinct.

Georgie turns to Ricardo. "Ee will need some help, see if you can lend a hand and let me know if I need to delay the start."

Ricardo strides towards the dressing rooms, leaving just three of us. Georgie can sense the uncomfortable tension between Hunter and me but she has her own department to run,

"Excuse me you two. Please don't kill each other while I'm gone, but I have to put a dress and a smile on. The latter may be harder." And she leaves.

The stagehand appears next to Hunter and gives him a USB stick.

"It's all on there?" Hunter asks.

The stagehand nods.

"Do not wipe it off your system until I give you the clear. Do not let any of your crew speak to anyone about this, you hear me?" Hunter demands with a desperation that I've not seen before.

I can never trust him. I have no instinct that he is ever on my side. Hunter is on his own side, fighting for his professional life. He has a dead guest, a man in prison, others lose about the ship and one of his staff was kidnapped and threatened. He is toast in any security world. He knows he owes me; he is in my debt professionally and personally. There is no excuse for putting my daughter's life at risk. I need an explanation and an apology.

"You got one more mission left in you?" he asks.

I'm struck dumb by the sheer nerve of his request for help, unless he means apprehend those after Auli'i, but that goes without saying.

"Mission?"

Hunter pulls out his smartphone, punches the screen and passes it to me. A film plays. It's a woman, gagged and bound to a chair. A gun is held at her head. I look up at him.

"They have my wife. They've had her for weeks," he says.

"Where?" I ask.

"Madeira. We live there. I need her back. Alive."

"How old is that film?" I ask, wondering if there is any chance she is still alive.

"I get proof of life daily. I demand a different Madeira newspaper or I kill Maria. And I will!"

"I'm in," I say without question.

Chapter 83 – Joint Mission

I moved cabin again last night. I'm now in a two-bedroom executive suite near the bridge. It trumps Jill's suite but I'll never be able to boast that fact to her or anyone else. Auli'i is asleep in the other room. We were up most of the night talking, a real bonding session. Last night she told me about traumas she has never spoken to me about before and maybe I can understand why she wants to act, to hide behind characters. We bonded even further and I will support whatever she wants. Whatever dream she has and for whatever reason, the quest is a therapy that is working for her, this has been a major threat which to her has appeared as just a blip on the way. There is no way she can ever go backwards. Her life will never be ordinary.

I'm expecting Hunter to join us in the room for a progress report over breakfast. I'm also expecting a communications team to come and set up in the sitting room for book interviews here with Auli'i, so she doesn't have to leave the cabin. It is a safe prison for her for the remaining two sea days, then we dock in Madeira and everything will change. Even tomorrow could be dangerous because we sail within helicopter range of the Canary Islands. Who knows what will happen, a huge major shipping corporation won't think like the military even if they did know what's going on and they have not been told the half. Hunter and I have to find his wife and time is running out.

There's a knock at the door. My mind starts to wager who will have made it here first. Maybe the Captain will swing by, it seems our proposed dinner will have to be delayed. I move to the side of the door and raise my hand up against the spyhole, rubbing the door to make a gentle sound. There is no gunshot so I risk looking through and see Ronni. Why is she here? Can I trust her? Who can I trust? I don't have a gun, but feel I could disarm an attack as long as I stay close to her. If a hostile opponent might be armed, never give them the distance required to draw a gun, or get too close to be stabbed. I open the door slowly and scan her from top to bottom, looking for the shape of a concealed weapon anywhere where it could be drawn from. Nothing, but then I missed the vest on her carved frame before. I smile, following her just a pace behind.

"We're having breakfast together," she announces.

"Are we?"

Ronni has been involved since the start so could well be a Trojan horse.

"Hunter is on his way." She walks to the open double doors and looks out to sea. "Nice room. Great balcony."

"Yes. Did Hunter say how long he would be?"

"No. How's your daughter? Is she still asleep?"

I worry about this being a fishing expedition to find out where Ee is. I've no idea how deep Maria's web of infiltration goes, who's been employed, who has been coerced.

"No idea if she was able to sleep."

Ronni sits herself down on the balcony. There is another knock at the door and now I have a problem. As soon as I give Ronni distance she can draw on me, go to Auli'i, but I need to open the door. I slide the glass balcony door closed behind Ronni.

"I want to keep the air conditioning in," I offer and she doesn't flinch.

I go to the door with an eye on Ronni all the time. My hand covers the spy whole and I push the door, no gunshot so I peep at the spyhole, and it's a waiter. My paranoia is really setting in. I open the door slowly to let him in.

"Leave the trolley, I'll do the rest."

He leaves. I close the door firmly then inspect the whole trolley. I have no idea what I might find; listening devices or a bomb, but I only see food and realise how hungry I am. I'm not sure when I last ate.

"Can't we eat out here? It's lovely!" Ronni shouts.

"We could be overheard."

The phone rings. I pick it up. It's Hunter.

"Meet at my office. Three men just took water and food to the trunk, so they've no intention of killing her, but they couldn't get in. That put them in a panic. Two from last night and one other, all three joined two trips back, same agency. I need you down here."

Ronni is watching me as I put the phone down.

"Hunter's office."

We both grab a croissant and leave, me making sure the door is closed firmly.

"Hunter said three men went to the trunk to feed her. They couldn't get in," I explain.

"They wouldn't. Last night Hunter and I took a forklift truck and stacked another trunk on top of it filled with stage weights. Both are padlocked. There's no way they could move it or get in," she explains as we get to the lift.

"Excellent move. Now we demand proof of life and give them a problem."

"That will be amusing," Ronni smiles.

Not for Hunter, I think. Ronni doesn't know.

Chapter 84 – Proof of life

Hunter pulls the blinds closed in his office.

"They used the phone backstage and dialled what is obviously Maria's cabin. Then it looks like they've been given an instruction and they don't like it. They failed and left," Hunter says showing us the footage. "At least the phone system revealed the cabin she is hiding in."

"Why can't we just go and get her?" Ronni asks.

Hunter doesn't answer that, Ronni needs the piece of the jigsaw that I have. It is not just about Auli'i. There is a knock on Hunter's door that saves him having to answer. He nods to me; I open it and Hunter's two trusted guards enter looking fresh. I close the door behind them.

"Thanks for coming in early," Hunter says to them, and hands out a printout of the three members of this gang. Two gang members we know from being with Maria when she took Auli'i. The third is new. Plus there are close up though grainy pictures of each.

"They're currently down on deck four, loading bay trying to steal a forklift. I had the supervisor disable the trucks and clear the area before they got there. I guess they'll jump start it eventually. They'll want to go to the stage dock, get the trunk and move it to a bay in the warehouse where they can access it. Slow them down as much as you can. They won't be able to open the trunk because we swapped the padlocks. But, if they get as far as trying to open it, arrest them. I don't want them to know she's not in there. This is important, do you understand?" Hunter asks.

"Yes sir!" they reply.

I open the door for him and the two guards leave at speed, I turn back and Hunter has handed Ronni a folder of pictures of his wife, held in Madeira.

"Who is this?" she asks.

"My wife."

"Where?"

"I am hoping Madeira. All their demands are for Maria to be allowed safe passage to Madeira. Maria and money," Hunter states.

"Name?" Ronni asks.

"Elaine," Hunter answers.

I never once asked him her name. That does now make it more personal and that is always dangerous. All three of us have the same information now. Ronni slides the pictures back.

"It's an attic room, a considerable building to have an attic that size. I can do more work on that," Ronni says.

"But we can't arrest Maria," I state.

"Not while they have Elaine," Hunter says.

"Let's keep the focus on Auli'i, while they think they have her as an asset, the pressure is off Elaine," I say using her name. "I would demand proof of life."

"Good idea. But another reason we can't let them open that trunk is that Ronni and I moved the sixteen million into it last night," Hunter says.

"My, you were busy," I add, turning to Ronni.

"I wasn't told I could tell you," she explains.

"Do we trust each other yet?" I ask.

"Hard to expect rational behaviour when you have skin in the game," Ronni says.

Ronni looks at Hunter and I know she is thinking he has to control his emotions to be trusted. She must think the same of me.

"I hear you. Let's not use her name. She's our HVA," Hunter agrees. "Ee is safe now."

"Agreed. Again, a very high-value asset," Ronni closes.

"Let's clear this up. The Captain's up to speed about Maria, about her and a gang having my wife held at gunpoint. About the kidnap attempt on Auli'i, and ransom for safe passage and that we have found Auli'i and made her safe. He knows nothing of the money."

"How did he react?" I ask.

"No real emotion, no comment other than that he approves of the actions taken. I reported that Maria and all accomplices we know of joined via the same agency. He has reported the same upwards and a company executive will fly down from the States today to sort that agency out with local law enforcement. I need to bring him up to speed about the new gang member."

"The agency was probably being squeezed," Ronni adds.

"Are you in the clear?" I ask Hunter.

"This goes way above the Captain's head. He's reported that Maria joined days ago, that I noticed the problem because she didn't know basic stuff that her CV said she should. He has reported that when I questioned her, she told me to keep quiet and let her have free passage to Madeira because they had my wife and that there was a gang on board protecting her. He reported we're investigating while trying not to make things flare up. All true… kind of."

"You should be the ghostwriter on this book," I joke. Maybe I should not have.

"We all know it's the end result that will determine how this plays out for me, but my job is nothing compared to getting my wife back," Hunter says.

"Agreed." Ronni nods.

"What is the company doing to help with your wife?" I ask.

Hunter shrugs. "They'll have to share intel with some form of authorities, but hopefully they will tell them we have it contained. They have no real information, no access to my proof of life films. I've stressed no action, no helicopters, no boarding, no obvious presence at the dock, no press. They have no option but to let us lead from the ship."

"It could all go wrong if the local police get involved in Madeira," I speculate.

"Yeah. And I need to demand my daily proof of life film around four in the afternoon, with a local newspaper which I nominate, same as normal. You need to be on stage at eleven, the same as normal. We have to let the gang roam free until we know how to totally close them down."

"They think they have Auli'i, and that one of us has their twenty million," I say.

"But you said you showed Maria the footage of Jill stealing the money?" Ronni computes.

"I did. Maria was shocked but even if Jill has convinced her that as the money was taken for her, then stolen from her, I think Maria will take control. She will use the 'Auli'i in the trunk' card to control us and the money. I don't think she'll bother trying to see the security footage which has been destroyed just in case, and so no investigation can find out about the money," Hunter explains.

"Jill is now expendable to them," Ronni adds.

Ronni has definitely worked in intelligence somewhere, I felt that when I saw her on the plane and now I can see it.

"Jill was with Maria when she threatened that they had Auli'i. Jill never spoke, she was nervous," I add.

"Nervous and worried; she must know she has no purpose, but has to hang on then for passage with Maria or definitely be arrested," Hunter says.

"Jail time is waiting for her the moment she steps off the ship," I add.

"Jill is good for confusion. Let Maria think we want Jill and will offer her a deal, Maria knows that can't hurt her, she knows it is a stupid play, so let's make it." Hunter says.

"But…" Ronni starts, "… Jill can tell of the money, a thread we have never revealed. It can't be revealed. Is she not better left in the wind as collateral damage?"

There is a moment of silence. Ronni is as hard as the rest of us. Hunter breaks the silence,

"No, let's bring her in now. Split them. She can get away later."

"I'm on stage at 11am," I worry.

Hunter checks his watch.

"Loads of time. Tell Jill ten minutes in the café on deck five or she's doing time," Hunter says.

"I think I can be more useful trying to find out where that attic is," Ronni suggests.

"That's very dangerous ground, Ronni. Be too clever … My wife's dead," Hunter worries.

"This is all a deadly game," Ronni states. "No one actually asked me if I wanted to play. Not at the start, not at the end."

Chapter 85 – Deadly game-on

Pacing backwards and forwards in the deck five café area, I wonder if I should ring Jill and emphasise that I was not kidding about having her arrested. I lengthen my stride and head to the end of the café counter. I dial her number on the house phone. It's busy. She was told not to phone Maria, if she does she is dead. We guessed it would be the first thing she might do. I turn back and pace again, then turn to the counter and order two coffees and it occurs to me I'm still starving.

When Jill arrives, I appear very relaxed. Waiting for her is her preferred cappuccino, but she looks uncharacteristically harassed and her daily war paint is yet to be applied.

"What do you want?" she starts.

"My daughter back for a start. I thought it was a sick joke when you said you had kidnapped her last night, but no one knows where she is," I state with a touch of anger.

"I never said I kidnapped her," Jill insists.

"I heard the words clearly when we met. Are you saying she's fine? She's asleep in your suite and will be down in a minute?" I ask.

"No. I did not say that I'd kidnapped her. I had no hand in that. Maria was the one talking," she says carefully.

"You were with Maria, you two were together, she spoke for both of you. You've got my daughter held somewhere."

Jill sips at her coffee, I figure she is considering her phrasing, but there is no easy way out of this.

"What do you want for my daughter's safe return?" I deliberately change the line of questioning.

"Do you not know what's going on?" she asks.

"No idea," I say bluntly.

"You didn't know you had twenty million dollars in your cabin?"

"No! Where would I get twenty million dollars?"

"Maria wants it back."

"I'm not in that cabin, I got moved. I have no idea about any money and trust me, that sounds like a big enough pile that I would notice it was in my room."

We didn't want the money mentioned in this confession so I have to deny it.

"It was under the bed."

"Have you been employed to feed in some stories to beef up this book? Twenty million would fill the cabin, surely. Let's take a breath and start again. Is Auli'i hiding in the crew bar laughing? Because this is not funny," I say, angry now but having separated the money conversation out.

"No, this is no story, it's not funny. Maria demands safe passage for both of us."

"You should be embarrassed. My daughter, the girl you hugged when she cried, now has her life in danger because you want safe passage," I almost spit at her.

"Don't go there. This is business. Guarantee we are both let off midnight before we dock in Madeira, you get your daughter unharmed."

"I can't trust you. I don't believe any of this. I want a film, now, proof that you have Auli'i and she is alive."

"You don't get to make demands," she says rising from her seat.

"Safe passage and you promise I get my daughter back?"

"I can't promise you that." She shakes her head.

"But you'll try, you'll make sure she's unhurt?" I plead.

"I'll try. But I can't make any promises," she concedes.

"Then I'll, but who do I ask?" I ask standing.

"This is very serious."

"Kidnapping my daughter, that's serious."

"Me doing jail time is serious, so you know what you have to do," she says, determined to walk away.

"And I get Auli'i back?"

"Yes, get to it."

She has said enough and to stop her leaving I raise my phone to show her the conversation has been recorded. She stops in her tracks then notices a photographer who steps forward filming us. She turns to see Hunter and a team of female security guards walking towards her. She turns to me, shaking her head.

"You don't know these people. They killed Tony. They will kill Auli'i," she threatens, being lead away.

A cold rush of chemicals runs up my body and snags in my throat. Even though Ee is safe, I feel sick. I feel worse for Hunter, and his wife. It is hard to think of her just as an asset that we have to recover, alive.

Chapter 86 – Families living in war

I get through my lecture, going through the motions. It's my standard military talk on families living in war. The audience seems disappointed and I watch them leave wondering if I'll have an audience at all tomorrow for my next talk.

It's nearly midday. I could go and see Hunter and his ever-filling cells below decks, but I decide to head back to my room to see Auli'i. We can order room service and eat lunch together.

When I get back, she is awake, watching television in her pyjamas.

"I'm enjoying how the rich live. You know, I can't even hear the engines up here!"

I've no idea how she can still be so upbeat. She hands me a card. "Invitation to have dinner with the Captain tomorrow night, plus one. Shotgun that's me!"

"Let's order food."

"I just ate breakfast. There's cold egg, cold bacon, cold beans and cold kippers, now they will be even more special." She laughs.

I dig around the trolley and make myself up a plate of brunch, then spy a microwave in the kitchen area and place it inside. That gets Auli'i's attention,

"Dad, you can't warm kippers! The place will stink!" She moans.

"Too late. Did the communications guys not come?" I ask, eating alone.

"Yep, I did an hour with New York. They have a new writer on the team, he is far more dramatic. He said, just because it didn't happen like that, doesn't mean it's not true... it is like the truth doesn't count."

"Never does," I add sitting with my warm kippers.

"He wanted to know about me being stuffed into a box. Re-worded everything I said so it was twice as dangerous. Not sure I'm liking this anymore," she explains without taking her attention from the screen.

"It was dangerous. But they shouldn't be covering that yet." I say.

"Really? Tell him. He hates the photos we did, said they looked like cheap magazine press. He wants a new session with me being tied in a trunk, or attacked backstage or something," she says, again not moving.

"Is that a good show you're watching?" I ask sarcastically.

"No," she replies flatly.

Auli'i rolls over and looks at me.

"Do we have to do this book?"

"It might not be just about us now, it might have a different ending," I offer.

After eating, I sit looking at the sun bouncing off the peaceful sea, wondering how we will ever find Hunter's wife in Madeira. It is all about saving Hunter's wife before they expect to take Maria off the ship by launch tomorrow at midnight. I think they will speed her away towards West Africa. I can imagine her being lost in Casablanca, Agadir or Tangier. Maria and her men could all be arrested any time on ship, they are all being watched, but then we lose Elaine. Do anything wrong and we lose Elaine. Do it all right, we might still lose Elaine. I should go back downstairs and join the team, but the food hasn't given me the energy boost I need and I drift off to sleep.

The ping of the public address system wakes me with a shock. It doesn't normally come on inside the cabin. "It is six o'clock, this is the officer of the watch. Before I give my report, the Captain would like to give a special address.

"You may have seen some strange happenings in the last few days. I can now share some news about something we have been dealing with on this leg of the cruise from South America to Madeira. Intelligence warned we may have a problem, which is why we were joined by some special forces personnel, at least one of whom you have met on stage. This move was to ensure nothing would affect your enjoyment of your holiday, and I'm also pleased to report that at no time did they need to be armed while carrying out their duties."

"Oh shit," I say standing up to listen, "This is not good."

"We have rather full cells at the moment, so I would beg of you that you all adhere to the ship's code over the next few days, or you will be sharing a cell to Madeira with some very unsavoury people. Whilst I'm not at liberty to tell you any more than that our ship was being tested for use by a drug cartel, please remain assured that the dusting on your cakes is no more than sugar! Please do not be alarmed if and when tomorrow at some point we slow down and a helicopter joins us in the airspace above the ship. You will be asked to stay off the decks. The top decks, cabins and bars will be closed. This is to allow international agents to join us on board, and for the prisoners to be lifted away. Please comply with all requests and instructions. Have a good evening. I will now hand you back to the officer of the watch."

The public address system reverts to corridor only as I open the door to leave.

"Dad! Where are you going?" Auli'i shouts after me.

"I need to go downstairs."

"Not like that! It's a formal night and it is after six."

The noise of the shower drowns out any sound from outside. I guess I will get an audience tomorrow, but it won't be an easy lecture I ponder as I wait for the temperature to settle. My thoughts race to why this has escalated? Hunter's wife must either be dead or if not she is now in serious danger as the game comes to a close.

I hear the phone ring outside, followed by Auli'i shouting, "Don't get showered!"

"Why?" I ask.

"Captain wants to see you now," she shouts in.

I would like to have the pressure lifted from me for just one day of this 'holiday'.

The Captain's private office is a room adjacent to his living quarters, just along from mine. The call stopped me rushing into in full ceremonial dress. Ronni and Hunter are there waiting, the Captain has yet to arrive.

"She's still alive," Hunter says, passing me his phone. The film plays, and it is his wife, tied and gagged, looking very frightened. A newspaper is raised up to fill the screen. The date is circled but it doesn't need to be. The headline is 'Drug Gang Arrested on Cruise Ship heading for Funchal'.

"She die if Maria-Isabel is harmed!" is shouted, then the disturbing film ends. Hunter must be going through hell.

"The three gang members we pulled in, Maria's on the run, we think by herself now. However, we've lost her. She went backstage and never came out, we searched everywhere," Hunter admits.

"She can't show her face above decks, she knows there are cameras everywhere," Ronni says. "Shame she's not my size, I would have all her clothes."

"We're also watching the trunk. But I don't think the gang had a chance to tell her where they'd moved it to," Hunter says.

"She never came out?" I puzzle, "like Auli'i was never on stage. There's a trick, a simple trick. We're not in the magic circle, but I know someone who is," I say, going for the phone and dialling next door.

"Ee. Maria went backstage and never came out. What's the trick?" I ask.

"The blonde dancer, it's a neoprene painted face mask and a wig."

I relay that to Hunter and Ronni. Hunter immediately rings down and asks one of his trusted assistants to go through the security footage.

The Captain enters and all attention turns to him.

"How are you holding up, Hunter?" he asks.

"Holding, Sir," Hunter replies.

"Firstly well done, no cruise ship can be used to run drugs. The whole industry is looking at us and your good work." He shakes Ronni's hand, then mine before turning back to Hunter. "The chopper will be overhead at 2000 hours tomorrow, just as it gets dark. We will be just under 200 miles out. It's all confirmed exactly as you've requested."

"Thank-you Captain," Hunter says.

"Now, are you sure you're up to this?" the Captain asks all of us.

I have no idea what he is on about.

"Yes, Sir," Ronni says.

"Yes Sir," I add because I'm one of the team and whatever it is, I'm in.

"Good Luck." With that, the Captain turns and leaves.

"OK. So what is it I don't know?"

Chapter 87 – The plan

The sea is incredibly calm, mesmerising in the early rising sun. Maybe it's the calm before the storm. Today I know it will swing from cakes to flambé. I missed Georgie last night, but I would have been restless and unsettled. Sleeping the night before a big mission can be tough, but last night was impossible, my life has become about more than just me. This operation has high emotional stakes, for Hunter, and that means for us. I can see that despite his own problems, he looked out for my daughter, who's now sleeping like a log in the other room. For three ex-service people thrown together who never trusted each other, we didn't do too bad. Now we are committed in total trust. These bonds last a lifetime, sadly some lifetimes are cut only too short.

I'm spinning my lucky baseball cap on my finger, the one I always wear the day of a mission. I check my watch again but the time has not moved much. I feel empty inside. I'm avoiding my phone because it has downloaded Sylvie's news attachment and the 'open' button is tormenting me. I don't want to see a headline about a dead kid from the bank. Death follows me and it needs to stop. If he was killed for that money Georgie will never get over it, I'm not sure I could get over the death of another youngster. Tonight I need a clear mind, tonight I can't be wondering if his online post of the money caused hell on the island or whether Sylvie managed to work her magic. I flip the phone over.

'Top Bequia property management 'Sylvie's Estates' donates one hundred and fifty thousand US dollars to school' is the headline and I breathe freely as I read on,

'Found in the backwaters of their office when planting vegetables, was a bag of mixed notes, all wet and muddy. Sylvia Cardinal who runs the renting and sales agency on the island, says that she called the police immediately and took it to the bank for safe keeping. Mitchell Brown, the young bank teller there, said he had never seen so much money. "It was a mess of old notes, ranging from a one dollar bills to a one hundred EC dollar bill. I had to sort them out, dry them and count them.' The money, which amounts to way over one hundred and fifty thousand dollars, has been donated to the St Vincent School fund.'

If just a little good has come from this madness, then maybe it has been worth it. I would love to see the face of the teacher in the school who wanted me to have a word with someone. She will donate some of that to a Syrian children's charity. I send the message and link to Georgie.

It is too early to go to Georgie's office for my briefing, way too early. She has to give me a briefing on what I can say in my lecture, made up from political musings on what we told them is going on. But, I can't wait, my emotions are running too high. I stand and leave letting the door slam behind me, then I realise I left my baseball cap by the chair, I stop, old habits and superstitions. I open the door and re-enter to see Christophe trying to rush back to Auli'i's room, naked! I grab my hat.

"Morning officer Bachvarov."

"Good morning sir," he whimpers closing the door but hiding too late. I laugh to myself, take my hat and go.

Georgie opens her cabin door half asleep, I have woken her. Her eyes widen and I kiss her. I have missed her all night. She is ripping at my clothes and we fight with the sheets to entangle ourselves together. Forget the condemned requesting a last meal, you can keep the food. This is the one thing I needed to know before today starts, that I have loved and been loved.

"Do you want to brief me now?" I ask as we lay together afterwards.

"You've just been debriefed," she jokes kissing me again.

"Some new information has just come up," I tease.

"My office in thirty minutes. Go!" she insists.

"Be nice and I might have a present for you."

"What," she asks rising to her knees on my bed, breasts exposed. Such a great vision.

"It looks like you need some new clothes. I'll have them sent up."

I arrive back at the entertainment office in uniform with my computer, ready to work. Georgie is not there and Ricardo the production manager hands me a sheet of notes.

"Georgie apologises, but says she got stuck into something else, said you would understand," he says.

I nod. The notes from head office are all company lines, all very sanitised.

"Did you read this?" I ask.

"I did," Ricardo answers.

"Did you try and say them?"

"Good luck." He chuckles.

The show is once again packed. The audience is full of questions but what do I know about helicopters flying above ships? What do I know about the International Force that is landing? Nothing, and that is what they will ask.

"Thank you all for coming in today. Are you all looking forward to Funchal?"

There is a half-hearted cheer, they seem to be here for the headlines again.

"I'm sure you'll all be at the side of the ship tomorrow to film the police cars and the prisoners going off to be arrested. Don't forget to charge those phones and make sure you have enough space left in the memory. And stay away from the decks tonight, as advised. It will be dark before we get within helicopter range so there will be nothing to see. Now, before I start I can say nothing about prisoners, not any of them, for legal reasons, they have a right to a fair trial. I think, but they were arrested at sea so who knows."

"Where will they be tried?" someone shouts from the audience.

"I'm not sure how it works. But initially they might be arrested under Portuguese law and they will have to apply for extradition if their lawyers want them tried back home. I did hear that two elderly ladies are still doing hard-time in the Ukraine for stealing a pepper pot," I tease. Some of the audience laugh, some gasp.

"Have you seen the Portuguese Daily online news, claiming a senior cruise member's wife is being held hostage," a passenger asks.

"No, I have not seen that article. I cannot comment on what others write in the news. Young Auli'i was held hostage as you were told yesterday, my guess is that they have got that story second-hand and all wrong. The gang on this ship are all behind bars," I state.

"Where are the prison cells?"

"I seriously don't know, I've never seen them," I answer truthfully.

At the back, I can see Hunter and he has his thumb up. I know that means that they have trapped and neutralised Maria and are negotiating for the release of Auli'i who we know they don't have. The plan is on. My heart sinks.

I rush through the end of my talk, take a bow, they applaud and my ordeal on stage is over. My scheduled talks and commentaries are finally done and I think the company will be whisking me off to head office with Ee. Who knows. Those decisions will all be made for us. We will be entering a publicity machine if I survive.

Unlike Auli'i, I won't even be going as far as Madeira, but only three people know that at the moment and neither Auli'i or Georgie can be told.

Back at my cabin, Georgie is trying on every dress and every pair of shoes that have been moved from the room Maria was stowing her clothes in, to her.

"I want you to share them with Ee. No fighting over them."

"The shoes are amazing."

"You would look amazing in anything."

"Can we take them?"

"She was a stowaway on ship, she had nothing," I say smiling.

Chapter 88 – Team of three

The ship has slowed right down and the thunder of helicopter rotors echoes through the upper stairwell where we wait. Below us, in position, are all the ship's crew wearing their yellow 'crew' baseball hats, and lifejackets. They are stopping passengers from climbing to the upper decks. They will have seen helicopters above the ship taking medical emergencies away, but not a military operation like this. The lights on deck go out. Few will know what is going on, no one will see in detail, but the rumours will spread by tonight. I look up and see the chopper is stable, with soldiers dressed in black perched on the side runners. Then they jump, all four together.

There is a gasp from within the ship because their ropes can't be seen in the dark. They have no idea how they will land. Their ropes are running out of a leg pack as they work a swift abseil descent, far different to the versions taught on climbing walls. This is our magic circle; these are our tricks now. One soldier's rope drops and he collects it and runs towards our open door as we run out to the remaining three ropes. They are tying deep figure-of-eight looped knots in the bottom of their ropes. We are fully harnessed up, clipped on and the soldiers leave us. We rise immediately.

As soon as we are in the chopper, four more soldiers drop down. As soon as they land, their ropes are dropped to the ship. A co-pilot shouts,

"Free! Go, go, go!" And the chopper powers up and banks away. We watch the ship quickly become smaller and smaller. Ninety minutes from now, the chopper will be back in Madeira, everything is now against a clock. We are each passed a black bag which we dutifully open and check our weapon, a small automatic. There are spare clips, night vision goggles, a medical pack, a map, and radio units.

"We will listen across the radios. Keep the local police off your back if they cotton on, but they won't. And we'll be near," the Commander in the chopper shouts into the comms unit. We all put thumbs up.

"Don't get too near. My wife, my call," Hunter shouts, and the commander gives him the thumbs up.

We each reseal the waterproof bag, pull on survival over suits, zip them up and harness ourselves in. Ropes are fed through a speed descender that's attached to our front and leg pouches wrapped around our ankles and Velcro'd tight. They are attached to the rail above, checked and doubled checked.

Each of us in our own zone, each with their own pre-mission routine. This is the second mission the three of us have worked as a unit. This time we know each other, we have all gone over the plans of the building. An attic above an empty shop that Ronni found was taken on a short term let for cash just four weeks ago. The attic has been staked out and listened to all day and we know that it is the target.

"Coastguard confirms; a high-speed boat is on course to the ship. ETA midnight."

Hunter and Ronni give him the thumbs up. So far so good, that means probably the best of Maria's agents are on the way to collect her from the ship in return for Auli'i. It is all a ploy, we should be able to hit the house and get Hunter's wife with little resistance.

"Don't take the boat out until we give you the signal she's safe."

The commander gives Hunter the thumbs up.

The chopper starts to dip towards the island.

"We're making good time. T minus five!" the Commander shouts, holding up five outstretched fingers.

We all give a thumbs up, probably for the last time. The chopper flies in low across the sea then slow to a stationary position.

"Go!" the commander shouts, and he only needs to say it once.

All three of us drop, a controlled descent on the rope, then drop off the bottom into the sea. The landing always feels hard but is forgotten quickly. The ropes are being pulled up as the chopper powers away. The three of us gather in the water, ready to swim towards the shore.

We hear the thwack of a missile being launched and our heads turn sharply. The flare chasing the bird in the sky confirms it is under attack. The missile chases the chopper which pulls up and then drops right fast, nearly dipping into the sea. A second missile is fired. The pilot pulls the craft left and flies at the source. The first missile hits the sea and explodes. The helicopter flies up and dips down towards the edge of the cliff, guns blazing. There is an explosion over the horizon.

"Shit!" I panic.

"Let's swim," Hunter shouts.

"If that was the bird which was expected to take the launch out, there's nothing to stop it now boarding the ship," I shout thinking again of Auli'i.

"Swim!" Hunter shouts again.

Ronni is swimming ahead, and I level out and pump. The shore is near but it's been a few years since I've had to swim like this. Exhausted and gasping for air we all drag ourselves ashore, unzip out survival suits and step out ready. Hunter is checking his watch.

"Let's go, we have an hour."

Our heads are up, stretching our windpipes and looking at the climb as we sprint up. At the top, breathing even harder we can see what looks like a burning camper van, which must have been where the rocket launcher was fired from. Now we have stopped moving, the flashing tail light of the chopper can be seen heading back out to the ship. Auli'i is safe.

We find our car as planned, dump our stuff and power away. We need to hit the house way before midnight when her people have demanded to meet the ship to take Maria. They can't be allowed to even get close, so we need to rescue Hunter's wife before Maria can give an execution order, and she will.

Ronni and I drink water, check our kit is dry and breathe. Hunter is driven by pure adrenalin, he drives fast, he knows the island and the building Ronni has pinpointed. He pulls up and parks on the coast road."

"We're on foot now. Let's move. We have less than forty minutes."

Chapter 89 – In Town

It is early evening as we move through Funchal, people are strolling about, looking for restaurants and bars. Musicians are playing. We pass the old cathedral, lit up and open with people walking in.

"You think we could all come back in the morning and make deposits?" Ronni says, and points out the most ornate 'Banco de Portugal'.

"We'd need a flatbed truck," I jest.

"I know someone with one, I'll call him later," Hunter says, powering in front.

"Could you not have parked nearer?" Ronni asks.

"I could, but they might be watching nearby approaches, we are tourists."

We are heading into the town proper, alfresco restaurants are in full swing, some offering local music and dancers. Hunter powers on.

"Hunter, we're supposed to be tourists," I say. "Slow down."

Hunter stops and we look into a restaurant with dancing. A moment to catch our breath again but we are immediately greeted with the sales pitch.

"Come in. Traditional Fado music of Madeira, from before year eighteen hundred," the head waiter enthuses.

"It seems sad," Ronni says.

"Yes, it is about being poor, and working at sea. It is about loss and sorrow," he explains.

"Sorry, that's not the mood for tonight, let's go." Hunter spins round and is off.

"On our way back," I say, turning to follow Hunter.

"We have the best, the freshest fish. Come in for Madeira wine!" he shouts after us.

CRUISE SHIP HEIST – OCEAN ATLANTIC

Hunter picks up his pace again. He is focussed on one thing. Striding after him we find the start of Rua de Santa Maria. The doors are all painted or sculptured in the most modernist graffiti-like way causing people to stop and take photographs.

"This is our street. Ronni, the rental you suspect will be the other end," Hunter tells us. "I hope you're right."

We all do, but we shouldn't have paused because another maître d' wants to recite his menu and offer a table. As we walk away he throws in two glasses of free wine. Tomorrow I would like to be back here having dinner with Georgie, everyone safe, but first, we have to survive tonight and get the money off the ship without being arrested ourselves. This street is starting to look dangerous as the artwork gets more adventurous and quite ugly. Restaurant tables almost close the narrow alleyway. The crowds of people stopping to photograph doors, waiters engaging with them. This will be a hard route to run in a chase.

Once again we are briefly caught as tourists and I notice how far ahead Hunter has got.

"Hunter. Hold up!" I shout, and he allows us to catch him. "We're tourists, buddy. Don't forget our cover."

"Are you two ganging up on me?" Hunter asks.

"We're near, we need to take in the surroundings," Ronni says.

"How do you know we're near, have you spotted it?" he asks.

"Not yet," She starts, "but did you clock the two soldiers having dinner together?" Ronni turns and nods to a table outside the next restaurant.

"They could just be two guys out on a night out," I suggest.

"They're our back up," she says and we're both intrigued.

As I look again they are holding hands, then one playfully puts his finger to the other's lips to stop him speaking.

"Yeah, they're UN soldiers. Peace poppies," Hunter says, "can we move on!"

"I'm not liking this. I have a bad feeling." Something feels wrong, it is that we have to get out as well as get in.

"Hunter, hold up."

"We haven't got time for this. Their launch is on the way to the ship. The ship will hit it with L-RAD. As soon as they radio back that they have been attacked, my wife is dead," he demands.

"Finding your wife isn't the problem here, it's getting her away without a shoot-out. There will be gunfire. If she looks, beaten, maybe not fully clothed, like someone we might have stolen, we will be accosted. It only takes one hero in this busy street and everyone will all join in. Look at the collateral damage." Ronni offers.

"Let's assess when we're at the target."

Hunter speeds off fast but both Ronni and I reach out and grab him. We walk on slowly together, Hunter trapped in the middle, with Ronni hanging on controlling his pace.

"Look around, there are families everywhere. It could be a blood bath," Ronni says.

"Your wife might need a clean dress to change into to blend in," Ronni says turning Hunter into a shop with lace dresses for sale.

"She'll hate that," Hunter says.

"She'll love it. It will pull on easily. What size?" Ronni asks.

"She doesn't have your shoulders," Hunter replies.

"Is that an impolite way of saying she is smaller than me?" Ronni asks.

"Probably," Hunter answers.

Ronni turns and walks into the shop.

I buy a bottle of water, some baby wipes, and a chocolate bar for energy from the shop next door. I stuff them in my cargo pants and we head off again.

"I've just remembered what Funchal is famous for." Hunter stops us. "Fireworks! They have a huge Christmas and New Year display. No one will turn a head if fireworks kick off."

"Perfect. Now we have a plan," I agree.

"We will take a table where we can watch them, you go and find fireworks. And hurry up," Ronni says leading us further up Rua Santa Maria.

After just another fifty meters, we see the target. The rental property Ronni found, closed downstairs, windows and low flickering lights on the first floor and a small light in the attic.

We sit at a table outside a restaurant opposite, one shop down.

Chapter 90 - Fireworks

We are the only ones in so the waiter enthusiastically hands us a menu and lights the candle on our table.

"Some wine?"

"No thanks," I refuse.

"Water, still, sparkling?" he suggests.

"Sparkling. Love your building, what's upstairs, is it all original?"

"We have extra seating upstairs, but it closed tonight. The fish, fresh, fantastic," he sells.

"I must look upstairs, love these buildings, use the washroom. Then we will look at the food."

I walk inside, climb the stairs and look into the dark extra seating area that looks like it hasn't been used for a while. I go to the window and study the next building across the narrow alleyway and the attic above it. On the first floor, I can just see three men playing cards through the window. The table is lit by a candle, which may mean there is no power in there. I can't see any stairs to the attic. That is where Hunter's wife must be, at the top. I step back and look directly opposite, the roofline is ornate making it easy to cross, but I'm not sure the loft hatches will have been opened for a while.

"You like?" I hear from behind me, it's the waiter.

"Love it, love these old buildings. Ever thought of a rooftop restaurant? People love rooftop places," I enthuse.

"No roof garden," he says.

"It could be a fantastic conversion. Might be easy. Can I look?"

He hesitates, obviously never having been asked anything like this before. I walk to a door I suspect hides the stairs to the attic.

"No light," he says to defeat my request.

I have already pulled out my phone, switched on the torch and am climbing the stairs.

"Sir, I think you come down. The manager not be happy," he pleads from the doorway.

"Yes, could you go get the manager? Get him!" I urge, sending him away.

This space would never be wasted in a big city. The floor looks sturdy; the hatch is closed but some soft blue moonlight can be seen through it. I go to it and push it open easily. The wood is rotten on the hinges, so I hold it open and I look across at the other loft. It is actually open, for air? But there is no light inside. There is no access or clear line of sight from here. I can see the roof directly over the road and that restaurant looks even more dead than this one.

"Hello, Sir?" I hear from downstairs. I close the hatch and rush back down. I'm finished.

"You could have a fantastic roof garden restaurant," I say.

"No sir, we are selling. All this end sold, to hotel," the manager says.

"This side?" I ask.

He nods.

"You sold? We no have job?" the waiter asks, obviously hearing this for the first time, but he is ignored.

"If this is a hotel, there will be lots of customers from it, you should buy that one, the empty one over the road, and build a roof terrace," I suggest.

"Good idea," the waiter keenly agrees to his boss.

The boss looks across the way.

"Both for sale," he says thinking.

"How many rooms will the hotel have?" I ask.

"Sixty bed, maybe," he shares.

"Sixty couples, who will all want food and a late night bar. I would invest in that restaurant," I offer, walking downstairs. The manager follows me at double speed. I walk straight out into the street.

"Honey. I found a great investment," I say to Ronni.

"Have you 'honey'?" she says, completely sending me up, but they don't know.

"We go see my friend," the owner gloats.

He walks me across the road, Ronni stands and I beckon her.

"Don't leave your bag, honey," I shout back.

"Will our table be OK, honey?" she asks.

"Manuel, bring some tapas for my friends. Wine," the owner shouts back gesticulating.

We head straight upstairs, the waiter in the quiet restaurant jumps up in shock, like he hasn't seen people in days. He meets the owner of our place and they chat away in Portuguese.

We have a quick glance at the upstairs space, which is being used for storage. I take out the wipes, water and chocolate and hand them to Ronni.

"Bring her across the roof, clean her up here. Don't wait for us, take her to the UN soldiers down the way."

I lead her to the attic, moving items out of our way as we get to the hatch which opens easily. We look out to next door, there is a route across the tiles from here.

"No problem," she says.

I look down and see Hunter looking for us. I take a loose piece of stone from the roof and let it run down the tiles and drop to the floor below. He looks up and I signal him to sit.

"On comms?" I check with Ronni.

I rush down through the storage space and keep going down to the ground floor. The owner rushes to meet me at street level.

"I like it. What's at the back?"

"Kitchen, toilet," he mutters.

"No road? Access? A walkway? Is it joined to next door?" I ask as quick-fired questions.

The owner looks confused and a little worried. "Kitchen, no so good next door. Toilet, old. The fence is broken, doors broken and next door needs building work."

I push through regardless, it is a small garden. There is no fence to next door and steps to the first floor, which might hold someone's weight. I turn and go back out to the front.

"I will send my business partner over," I say leaving the shop and heading back to join Hunter. I pull out a one hundred dollar note and hand it to our waiter. "Save this table. We are going to have a walk. Bring me two beers, won't be long."

The owner takes the note quickly.

Chapter 91 - Honey

"Set Ronni?" I ask into my comms unit, as I fit the covert earpiece and tuck it behind my ear. Hunter is also listening.

"Set," comes the reply as I arrive outside and meet Hunter holding a small box no doubt full of domestic celebratory explosives.

"Hunter, go straight through to the back, through the broken fence. Start the fireworks. I'll go in the front, you go in the back?"

He nods in agreement.

"The guys are on the first floor. Your wife must be in the attic. I'll go up the internal stairs. You take the fire escape, be careful, those stairs look dodgy. Ronni will be across the roof before either of us. Over," I say to him and with open comms.

I hear them both roger into comms as the beers arrive from the worried waiter. Hunter downs one straight away.

"Water, please," I suggest.

Our happy waiter vanishes.

"Go, Hunter. Ronni, go when the fireworks start."

Hunter collects his box, powers into the restaurant and straight through. I turn and watch the target building next door. My water arrives, I drink the water and order another. He leaves and I move to the door of the target building and wait.

A whizz into the sky is our cue. The explosion of bangs is followed by my shoulder taking out the door. There is no resistance on the ground level, and I climb the stairs and turn into the room to see a panicked man at the card table grabbing for his gun. One shot and he is down, I cross the room to him, kick his gun away and shoot him again. I can hear Hunter fighting on the steps outside and then it sounds like the stairs collapse. I run to the rear opening and look down. I can't get a clear shot on the man. I let off three shots next to them, lost in the explosion of fireworks. They separate, and I shoot the man before he has time to react. I snap around and look up to where I hear gunfire in the attic.

"Speak to me Ronni," I say into my comms.

"One down, one behind the hostage. No clear shot. He has a gun at her head."

I slowly and quietly start the climb to the attic.

"Take the shot, Ronni, don't let him shoot her," Hunter says over comms, and I hear him running behind me.

"Firecracker in the street, Hunter," I whisper.

"Ronni fake a hit on the bang," I continue into comms.

"He's pulled her up to standing, she's shielding him, no shot," Ronni says.

"Gun hand. Take the shot Ronni," Hunter demands.

"Fireworks Hunter."

I reach the attic and I can now see him but I have no clear shot either. The firecrackers go off, Ronni screams as if hit, and ducks.

The gunman drags our hostage towards the hatch, getting closer to me though he doesn't know I'm there. The asset is gagged and held my side but is being very cool. I have no real shot so signal to her to keep silent. The Gunman has his weapon pointed out to Ronni. I shoot and wing his arm, the gun drops.

"Gunmen running in on your six, from the street," I hear Hunter saying on comms.

"Finish him, Ronni," I say, snapping round to below.

I hear shots above and shots below.

"One down," I hear from Hunter.

"One down, I have the HVA," Ronni shouts.

There is a shot behind me and I feel hot steel in my shoulder as I am spun into the wall, winded. More shots. I shoot forward to the second man then lose my footing and fall. I'm crashing to the floor.

I hear Ronni shout into comms, "Man down Hunter, man down. I am clear with HVA."

I straighten my body rolling this way, then that to scan the building front and back, upstairs to the loft even though it was given a clear and downstairs to the shop.

"I'm OK. Hunter, go to your wife," I say.

"In location two. She's good, cleaning up and changing her dress. Clear my way out. Again, clear my way out," I hear from Ronni on comms, then the voice changes.

"Hunter, I'm safe, I'm safe." I know that is Elaine.

"Go, Hunter. Clear the way out," I shout.

I switch comms to silent and I gasp in pain. I try to sit up, but the bullet has caught something inside and I buckle. I switch comms on.

"Right behind you. As planned guys." But I can't get up. I switch comms off and take a moment. I scramble in the bag for the medical pack and find the morphine, then self stab-inject in my shoulder. I gasp for air, shuffle backwards so I can push my back into the wall. I hear movement downstairs and know it is hostile because they're trying to move in silence. I squeeze myself around, forcing my breathing to quiet and I flatten out, gun poised down the stairs. I have little option than to lay and wait. The silence is deafening. I'm not moving. Neither are they, but I can hear them breathing, just as I can feel warm blood running inside my Kevlar. The bullet must be under my shoulder blade; it must have just crept in. It's been a while since I felt this, and there haven't been too many of them. I hear a stop, a step then another. I push myself to the wall side. I listen carefully. Will he be left or right? The split second could be the difference between life and death.

I blink, I feel myself about to pass out. His head flashes across the opening, I roll away instinctively. I hear his boots on the steps below, he knows he has me injured. I wait then roll back, eyes open and shoot. His head is the height of my gun and it explodes.

Killing at close quarters is never a shock, don't let anyone tell you it is. It's a relief. It's a relief because at that moment it is you or them and you have less than a fraction of a second to react. It takes no time to live or die, so it can only be a huge relief. Unless it's a child with the gun. Then there is never any relief. Never. My face to face was with Auli'i, neither of us could shoot. Both of us could be dead, but there has been a bond forever, a bond that will never leave me.

Chapter 92 – Winged and down

I must have passed out. Struggling to stand, and breathing again I look down at the dead figure on the stairs, making my descent difficult. No amount of therapy can ever make you forget war. This has brought it all back. Again.

I hear a commotion outside where a crowd have dared to gather. How do I escape this? I hoist myself back up, strength returning to my legs. I look down and the crowd looks like a lynch mob now they can see dead bodies. I can see men preparing to storm the shop, enthusiastic amateurs are dangerous and if one of them is armed, I will be dead. To them, in their fear, I am just a terrorist. I climb up to the loft. I struggle out of the hatch and crawl over to the other roof. I weigh up my options, none look good. Maybe this is the way I go, misery over. Torment over.

Then I think of Auli'i. Will she be fine without me? Has Christophe taken over? I think of Georgie, someone I love deeply, but she has a partner. I am surplus to requirements, just as the army said. I lean against the edge of the hatch; my pain has gone now. I feel myself drifting. I grab at the lump in my side cargo pocket. I pull it free in a haze, not sure whether I am seeing Auli'i's fishing net rolled in my had or being thrown out in Syria. Her most treasured possession that she gave to me. I know how to hold it, how to throw it, but my arm might not work. I look below and see Hunter's face just at the edge of the crowd. I can't hear him because I turned my comms off. He is signalling for me to cross the roof. I laugh, I can see his threat. If I don't move, he is going to risk coming back for me.

No. He has just got his wife free. He can't come back for me. I watch him go into his pocket, take out a jumping cracker and hold it next to a lit lighter. The sound of it going off will send people screaming. I guess I have to go. I pull out the net as he lights the cracker.

I step out onto the roof and spin the net exactly as Auli'i taught me. It spreads out like a parachute floating down. The cracker kicks off and panic hits, as the crowd is covered by the net and surrounded by gunfire.

I run across the roof as best I can, but my footing is not good. I slip, I am running too low on the roof pitch. I slip again. I know I'm not going to make it. I see Hunter move to the side of the narrow street to gauge my fall. I run and run, getting lower and lower until I fall right off the edge. I ready my legs, but I am in space, in free fall. Two arms grab me, the pain shoots through my body like electricity, and I wake just in time to hit the ground. My knees buckle. I am up and being forcibly walked before I can focus, and I feel two people holding me, restraining me. I look right and there is Ronni.

"We ordered you a beer," she says.

"Can you add a morphine chaser?" I ask. I look to Hunter.

"Bad?" he asks.

"Shoulder, the rest is mental."

"Fuck man, we all have that," he says firmly marching me on.

"Have you called in?"

"Oh yes. Maria has been arrested. The launch was blasted with L-RAD and boarded by the chopper unit. Coastguard will be meeting the launch by now."

They sit me into a chair at the restaurant next to a lady I don't know, but I do recognise the lace dress. I high-five her.

"Hi, Elaine!" I manage.

I hi-five Ronni but that hurts.

She laughs. "You want me to take that out for you?"

"Here?" I ask.

"No, that would be ridiculous, in the washroom." She smiles, encouraging me and taking the field medical kit from our bag.

"OK," I agree, having no reason to say no.

Ronni and I stand to move away, but the two male soldiers stop us.

"Can we go before the police arrive?" the first soldier asks.

"Knowing you two lovebirds were here, was such comfort," Hunter says.

"Why don't you come back to the hotel, meet the team, you have rooms there too," the second soldier offers.

"I need to get a bullet removed first."

"We have a trained medic that will do that. Although, he may be pissed by now," the first soldier says with a shrug.

"Yeah, let's go, I probably won't bleed out," I say and the banter I have missed is back. The love of a fellow soldier is instant.

Elaine hugs my good arm. "Thank you."

That means so much. This is a job where normally, no one ever says thank you. I could hug her.

"Careful! Blood on my new white dress," Elaine says.

Yes, she's a soldier's wife. She will like Ee.

Chapter 93 – New day

Dressed in the same clothes we left in yesterday, Hunter and I arrive at the dock after just an hour or two of sleep and far more than that spent drinking, to see a fleet of police cars along the dock, blue lights flashing. Ronni is absent without leave, last seen trying to tame a special forces guy in the early hours. Hunter's wife has been left to sleep at the hotel with a unit guarding her.

To keep it next to the dock and not snap ropes, our ship is still using its side thrusters to power against a brisk early breeze. The forward gangway is being prepared for the guests while the middle loading bay on deck four is being opened for our access.

"Can you ask the Captain for us to be allowed back on board?" Hunter shouts.

"Yes, Sir. Mr Witowski. How did you get off the ship?" the sailor shouts back.

"Long story. Two of us, Hunter Witowski and Kieron Philips."

"And officer Ronni Cohen," she announces, coming up behind us.

"Did you get any sleep?" Hunter grins at her.

"None."

"So they really are special forces?"

"I've only tested one of them… So far." She winks.

Hunter scans the crew now that he has his re-entry planned. The head of police and a special forces commander are walking our way. Hunter turns to meet them and I follow just in case I am needed.

"Good morning sir, Hunter Witowski, head of security. I will leave you in a moment briefly, to get back into uniform. We have two female prisoners, one highly dangerous. Four male prisoners, all gang members that work for her. One dead body, suspected murder weapon in a signed evidence bag."

"We don't get this with every cruise." The police commander raises an eyebrow.

"We do try to offer that little bit more, Sir," Hunter says.

The commander stays ice cold. The special forces commander mouths, 'no sense of humour'. Which is my cue to turn away. The loading bay gangway fixed, I see Georgie running towards me, arms out. She hugs me after a full speed collision.

"Aaagh!" I recoil.

"What? You got shot?" she asks concerned.

"A nick. Don't squeeze too hard… Ok, do."

She hugs me again.

"What were you saying about never having been on such a cruise?" I ask her.

"Yes. I need to find a chemist and get a morning-after pill that backdates itself a few days," she says.

"Or?"

"There is no or, I am too old."

"No. Never."

She looks into my eyes.

"It might be great news," I suggest

Georgie hugs me until a tall blonde woman comes and lingers right beside us. Georgie lets go of me to hug her, and they kiss. I've just taken another bullet!

"Kieron, this is Bedi. Bedriška." Bedriška offers me a very firm handshake and an even firmer look. "Bedi, Kieron has been my special friend while you were away," Georgie explains.

"Good. I am back. He can go now," Bedi says, and I realise nothing they said about her was a joke or exaggeration.

"I have lots to tell you, we're rich!" Georgie enthuses to Bedi.

"I am very rich, I have you," Bedi agrees then turns to me, "Thank you. Goodbye."

Bedi walks with Georgie, arm in arm, back onto the ship and she never turns back.

Shit!

Chapter 94 – Never look back

In uniform on the dockside, Hunter is organising a local forklift to lift the trunk from the edge of the loading bay of the ship, and spin it round onto the flatbed Ford he said his friend had. As is standard now, this man is paid with a one-hundred-dollar bill.

"I've hired unit nineteen which I think is the other side of the dock. Kieron will go with you," Hunter says, then turns to me, "Kieron?"

Before we can pull away the stony-faced police commander walks up to us with his arm up. "What is this? This is a secure area. Nothing gets moved without my inspection," he says.

"It's props, for stage, film, TV," I say to him as he passes, but it is Hunter he is interested in, not me.

I step out and follow him to Hunter who is at the back of the truck. The police chief would love to look in the trunk, but his frame is not one that will allow him to leap up onto the flatbed, or leap anywhere.

"This is evidence of the kidnap on board, the company wants it kept," Hunter says.

The police chief turns to me then to Hunter. "So what is it? He says stage props, you say evidence."

"It's both," Hunter says.

"Both? How?" he asks Hunter.

"It is the trunk -," I start but he turns and shuts me up.

"Him, I ask. Not you," he says pointing at Hunter then turning back to him.

Hunter opens his hands in a helpless shrug and points at me. "But it's him who knows," Hunter says, and I know he's winding the guy up.

"It is a stage prop. That was used in a kidnap, so it is evidence," I say.

"Ah," the policeman says turning back to Hunter.

"But," I continue, making him turn back again,

"The company is flying a film crew here to film the girl in the trunk, just as she was when she was …" I deliberately stop. It is a game of tag, with sixteen-million at stake, which makes it that much more fun, that much more dangerous.

"Captured. A reconstruction," the police commander says turning to Hunter.

"I'm not sure it is an actual-" I stall, twirling my hand and making the commander turn back to me. I shrug and look to Hunter.

"No, not really a reconstruction," Hunter says.

"More like a news item, publicity, television. They will get here tomorrow after the ship has sailed. So if the trunk was on the ship, it would be too late to film it," I explain.

"Wait here," the police commander states firmly.

Crowds are leaning over the ship, standing quayside, phones up and filming, but the TV crews and news photographers have the best view. The Police Commander walks to the front. He oversees Jill being lead to the first police car. With definite order he stops Maria from leaving, he turns and waves the armoured truck in. He then allows Maria to be removed second, with special services as well as police, to the armoured truck. He makes sure he is in the centre of every picture.

Ronni drifts back and joins us watching our catch be lead off.

"About this sixteen million-" I start.

"Three ways, right? Even," she says.

"It's not really even," I admit.

"You want more?" Ronni asks.

"No, I already took some, before it was taken from me."

"Now I trust you," Hunter says.

Ronni looks puzzled. She narrows her eyes at Hunter.

"He took about four million out with Georgie, sown into lifejackets. I studied the film for ages, it bugged me because the lifejackets just didn't hang right," Hunter says.

"Georgie might end up keeping that four. It's not clear at the moment," I suggest.

"I figured we'd have to cut her in any way, so it kind of worked. But I'm pleased you've been honest."

"Can we get it out of here?" Ronni asks.

"Just waiting for the police commander," Hunter says.

We all turn back and watch him as the last of the four men are lead out, to the last police car. He's parading like a peacock.

Auli'i comes down the gangway with two female minders who seem to be advising her. One walks over and speaks with the police commander, and we can see he is making the most of this on camera. The other leads Auli'i over to the flatbed Ford, dragging all the film crews with him. Two policemen help him to jump up, Auli'i jumps up too.

"Open please, for TV cameras," he shouts over to us.

"I don't have the key," Hunter shrugs and turns to me.

"Me neither."

The police commander looks around and then announces. "She was cut out with bolt croppers, bring me bolt croppers."

A special forces guy runs towards them with huge bolt croppers.

"Is that your guy from last night?" I ask.

Ronni nods.

"Stop him then," Hunter demands.

"He doesn't stop that easy," she says.

As he leaps on the flatbed and the cameras move in, I'm sure we've been defeated. "We ripped this money out of walls," I remember.

"You didn't, I bloody did," Ronni argues.

"We got shot at," Hunter says in defeat.

"No, I got shot," I state firmly.

It is like a nightmare unfolding in slow motion. The padlock is cut.

"I was gagged, my hands bound, my legs bound and I could not move. I was forced inside and locked in," Auli'i acts out.

"But I now have them all in jail," the police commander delivers to the cameras and the guests filming from above. "Come closer." He beckons the cameras in. "We take crime very seriously here in Madeira. One of the safest holiday destinations in the world."

"Gone. Dreams gone," I declare.

"After all we've been through," Ronni says.

"I went through a lot more, my wife was held at gunpoint," Hunter says.

"My daughter was kidnapped," I argue.

"So we can see," Ronni adds.

"What is your name?" the commander asks Auli'i.

"Auli'i, that's A U L I then an apostrophe, then another I, but it is said, Owl – lee – ee. You can call me Ee."

"This is painful, just get on with it," Hunter mumbles.

"Would you mind going inside again for the cameras, or is it too much of an ordeal?" the commander asks.

"I'll try. It won't be easy. If I get distressed will you help me?" she says softly to the commander.

"She's acting," Ronni suggests.

"I know," I agree.

CRUISE SHIP HEIST – OCEAN ATLANTIC

The lid is opened. There are gasps and each one of us has our head bowed, hands over our eyes, but the crowd go quiet. I peek through my fingers first and see Auli'i standing in the trunk. Hunter looks and immediately jumps up. He looks at me and Ronni and shakes his head, and we know, the money has gone. Hunter jumps down out of the way of the press.

"So, do we trust each other?" I test.

"I don't know," Hunter says, exasperated.

Ronni shakes her head 'no'. There is a cacophony of flashing light bulbs, cameramen shouting 'Auli'i' and 'look at me'.

After a lifetime of camera flashes, Ee jumps out and down to join us. The two media executives follow her.

"Do you mind if I have some dad time?" Auli'i asks them.

The two women eventually leave her alone.

"Press officers. Two! I can see them being a bit more demanding than I imagined," she says.

We all nod, confused.

"That was nearly a nightmare," Auli'i exhales.

"Why?" Ronni asks.

Auli'i is about to speak when a photographer is brought back by one of the executives.

"Just one last picture? He wants a shot of you all," she asks.

The three of us definitely aren't smiling. He takes his picture and the press officer gets the message and leaves.

"Last night the book guys wanted a still of me in the trunk. I found the trunk in the loading bay, someone had moved it. But it was locked. I found the key on your key ring in the suite, went down to get it ready for pictures and you never guess what was inside…?"

"Sixteen-million-dollars," we all say at the same time, and then stare at her.

"No, it was full of bloody stage weights. It took me ages to lift them all out," she says, angry.

C.S.C.I.

I am not sure what the other two are thinking but I'm confused and I am rewinding all the pictures of the prisoners being taken away, and trying to figure out if there was any way sixteen million could have been taken off with them. No, not a chance.

"Deflated?" Hunter asks.

"I've never been so down," Ronni shakes her head.

We look at each other solemnly. Auli'i theatrically throws her arms around our shoulders grouping us together.

"Guys lighten up. It was full of money, I hid it," she whispers. "Well, not all of it, twenty thousand to Syria, via the post room. Hope you don't mind. It might get there, I labelled the parcel 'books' and put some old paperbacks in."

We have a mixture of nods, amazement and horror she has done that.

"Where did you hide it?" I ask her.

"On the ship. What's my cut?" Auli'i smiles.

We all look at her.

"How do we get it off the ship?" she asks.

Hunter and Kieron are now partners.
CRUISE SHIP SERIAL KILLER

Commander Kieron Philips has just got past being unwittingly involved in a very dangerous heist on a cruise ship in the Atlantic. The spin produced by the cruise company to the media and public was that he was a special forces operative working with their own ex-CIA head of security Hunter Witowski to solve a drug smuggling attempt. Now thrown together by that story, another cabin door opens and this time dripping with blood.

They set up shop in Miami, but before the doors are open they are called to another ship in the Pacific where guests are being killed mid ocean. The nearest land in any direction is days away, it is a serious problem.

Almost none of the guests have any idea of the dramas going on until the rumours fill the chat groups and fake news spreads. Panic will certainly dig deep on a ship part way through a one-hundred-day world cruise.

DORIS VISITS

Is a cruise resource site on the internet and YouTube, giving port guides, ship tours, and other cruise advise. It has been used by many researchers, and the films are often re-broadcast, like the films on Liverpool shown by Liverpool Live TV. You will see they are our research.

Stuart St Paul – writer

Stuart St Paul's first screen play was the subject of a million-dollar deal in Hollywood, initially with Trimark Pictures it then bounced around a few studios and saw prospective cast changes from Jean Marc Barr to James Caan, to Dolph Lundgren to Christopher Lambert. It became an empty but steep learning curve. With the same offers to buy the second script he completed, The Scarlet Tunic, he and his then producer, Zygi Kamasa who went on to be CEO of Lionsgate, decided to make it themselves. The low budget film was picked up at Cannes and put into completion against multi million dollar movies like The English Patient and Anna Karenina at Festivals from Cabourg to Verona.

Stuart has been nominated for awards from Canada to Bollywood and eventually won Best Director in the USA for his penned and directed ICON movie Freight which also won him a Film Making Excellence award in Mexico.

Stuart who started as a radio broadcaster with the BBC has also specialised in action and worked for all the major studios, HBO, BBC and ITV and hundreds of movies and programs. He is often found at festivals and doing lectures. He is represented by Champions UK.

Laura Aikman – muse, additional material, editing

Actress Laura is Stuart's daughter and harshest critic, she wrote some additional material, did extensive character work that only an actor can do. Laura has an extensive list of credits on IMDB from from both sides of the Atlantic.

The funniest out-take from Lee Mack's Not Going Out is of him and Laura at the bar in the club in the episode where she arrives claiming to be his daughter. Laura's credits range from theatre to film. In television her list of credits is phenomenal for her age, from the critically acclaimed ITV show Liar to plays and films to shows like Waterloo Road and Casualty. Her comedy credits go on and on having worked with Christopher O'Dowd, Ade Edmondson, and Lee Francis as well as Lee Mack and her now long time conspirator Russell Tovey.

She also voices many animations and has regular shows she voices on CBBC including Shane the Chef and Space Chickens.

Laura also plays many characters in video games.

SYNOPSIS – CRUISE SHIP HEIST

When retired Commander Kieron Philips finds a passenger sitting dead in a seat as everyone disembarks the plane, he calls the flight attendant and makes no fuss. He thinks nothing of it. He survived Ireland, Iraq and covert missions but now misses an unexpected bullet when a woman he spent just a few flirty moments with at baggage collection is arrested at customs in South America with millions of dollars.

Within minutes he's sharing a taxi to a cruise ship with two other women and between them all, they're about to reshape his life.

Within hours they're at sea, and he's embroiled in a saga of which he has no knowledge. His cabin is searched by a stowaway gunman, who is intercepted and arrested by Senior Officer Hunter Witowski, head of security. He suspects Philips knows more than he reveals.

Philips starts to wonder if his being on this cruise, at this time, was an accident, or whether someone saw his military skills and put him in the right place at the right time. Is he here to do a job? What job? He can't trust anyone on the ship, and no crazy amount of money is worth either his life or the life of his show-dancer daughter whom he travelled this far to visit. Except she is not his daughter and she arranged the trip.